keep·er

Sydney Keane Series: The Beginning

LARYL DIXON

This book is dedicated to my son.

With all my love.

Acknowledgements

Thank you to God, my Father, for His unconditional love and so much more.

Thank you to my son, my greatest and most precious blessing from Him.

Thank you to my life partner, my true love.

Thank you to my mother, my rock and my biggest fan.

Thank you to my best friend, my constant ally.

Thank you to all who have shared their stories with me. Thank you for visiting that place that we keep hidden, accessible only to ourselves, in order to share and heal. I respect you, I honor you, and I admire your courage. Hold fast to your hearts. Hold fast to your spirits. Each one of you is a beautiful light.

"See that ye despise not one of these little ones; for I say unto you, that in heaven their angels do always behold the face of my Father who is in heaven."

- American Standard Version (1901)

PREFACE

This is her life, one that she never saw coming. She should have, of course. After all, her life had been one of constant movement and confusion, and at the same time, filled with a great amount of love. This sounded like an anomaly and she supposed it was.

And yes, there had been "things." Things that had happened to her that were not her doing. She felt that one day she might be given something in return...some great gift for all the wrongs that had happened in her life. Surely things would be better as she got older...as she aged. Surely all the wrongs would be made right and she would live happily ever after. God would surely see to that.

INTRODUCTION

Sydney was a delightful child and everyone loved her so much. She was born on Mother's Day, and was indeed a gift. Sydney was an only child, and the first grandchild and great-grandchild on her mother's side. She was the second grandchild and great-grandchild on her father's side, but because she was the first grand*daughter* and great-grand*daughter*, that made all the difference in the world. She was the first girl and their favorite.

Sydney's mother, Maeve, was a beautiful woman. She was tall and slender with long, flowing raven hair and emerald green eyes. She was drop dead gorgeous and would have been a gift to Hollywood. It was a dream of hers to be famous one day, but her father wouldn't allow her to leave the confines of East Texas. Sydney's father, Forrest, was a very handsome man with thick, auburn hair neatly combed back and piercing blue eyes. He was clean-shaven and always smelled delicious, as if he had taken all the best of the outdoors and wallowed in it. Forrest was a hard-working man, and he loved the outdoors. Much to Maeve's dismay, his idea of married life was "the man rules the roost," no matter what.

Sydney's beauty was a perfect combination of her parents. Her hair was auburn brown with honey-golden streaks framing her angelic face. Her flowing curls fell to her waist and her eyes were as green as a lush East Texas meadow.

Sydney's earliest childhood memories were in her home in Merriweather, Texas. Merriweather was a small East Texas town with a name that denoted happiness, the easy life, and good things. It was also a place where secrets were kept hidden away. Sydney's childhood home in Merriweather was a white wood-frame house with high ceilings and a bear-claw bathtub. The air conditioner, when they finally got one, was a window unit. The heat needed for winter came from a big heater grate in the floor as well as gas heaters strategically placed. This was not a big, grand house, but it was beautiful. It had a glassed-in porch and a large backyard with a swing-set right in the middle: a gift from her Memaw, her mother's mother. There were five memories in this house. Only five, but that seemed like quite a lot considering she would have only been three and four years old at the time.

Sydney's five memories in this house were happy, sad, and indifferent. For some reason, talking about them made them all seem sad in their own way. Her first memory was when she was told to be sure not to step on the heater grate, but while running and carrying on, that is exactly what she did. Her Papa, her mother's father, scooped her up and kissed her feet at the dining table until they stopped hurting. Her second memory was when she wanted to stay up later one night. Maeve was busy trying to put Sydney to bed, but Forrest said it was fine if his little girl stayed up, as long as she popped the blackheads on his back. She did, and it bought her the next ten minutes she thought she so desperately wanted. Sydney's third memory was a very tender moment between her and her mother, and the only one that Sydney could recall from this young age. Sydney was getting a bath in the big, bear-claw bathtub and her mother was washing the "dirt necklace" from around her neck. Sydney remembered her mother's soft strokes and smiles and knew that she was taken care of and loved by her mother. Her fourth memory was when Forrest had brought her a baby duck. Sydney loved the duck and took very good care of it, if only for those few days. One afternoon while swinging out back, Maeve opened the screen door and the duck came down the back stoop. It could no longer walk, but rather rolled. With a whisk of his hand, Forrest took the duck to the side of the house, pulled a long piece of sugar cane out from under it, and beat the duck until it was dead, putting it out of its misery, he said. Never mind that Sydney witnessed the whole thing. That would only make her stronger. The fifth memory was when Sydney's mother left her father. Sydney's PawPaw stood at the back screen door, tears streaming down his face, wishing that his son would have been a better husband and father, but it was all too late for that.

Chapter 1

1967

"**S**ydney, come eat! It's time for Thanksgiving dinner!" Memaw called to Sydney.

Memaw was a beautiful woman and a strong woman, in every sense of the word. The waves in her strawberry blonde hair brushed the nape of her neck and her golden eyes were the color of amber. But it wasn't wise for an unsuspecting admirer to let her beauty distract from the fact that she was a determined woman who took care of business, and there was no question about that. She was ahead of her time in that regard.

"I'm coming, Memaw!" Sydney called back.

Sydney was four years old and the apple of everyone's eye. She was still the only child on her mother's side of the family thus far, so holidays were always a treat: not just for Sydney, but for all the grown-ups who needed the love and hugs of a child. Sydney had an abundance of both and served them up like a piece of warm pie.

Oh, the table was filled: filled with food and filled with family. There could never be a happier or closer family. Memaw had placed a reel-to-reel audio tape recorder in the living room to record the festivities for future enjoyment. All was well and life was good. There were memories in this house as well, and this was one Thanksgiving that would be brought to life years later by listening to that old reel-to-reel. It remained a solid, and much appreciated, reminder that there truly were good times, that they were a close-knit family, and that they supported and loved one another.

Sydney and her mother lived with Memaw and Papa now, along with Sydney's Aunt Olivia, her great-uncle Edmund, her great-uncle Denton and her great-grandmother, Mama Scurlock. Memaw loved her family beyond measure and she would do anything for them; hence, offering room and board to her mother as well as her two younger brothers, who would work their way through college. After Memaw's daddy died, her eldest brother, Jack, and his wife, Evelyn, had moved to Georgia with a family of their own, so Memaw jumped in to tend to the rest of the family and she did it with love.

Over time, Maeve found that this home setup offered her a great deal of flexibility and she would tend to take advantage of that. Maeve was only eighteen when she had Sydney, so having a bit of freedom at twenty-two was a welcome change. Maeve knew that everyone loved little Sydney, and she would surely be taken care of. So, off Maeve would go in search of Mr. Right and had quite a good time of it on her way. Maeve loved her little girl very much, but it became clear that Sydney was falling further and further to the bottom of her mother's priority list and naturally, it was Memaw's responsibility to fix that as well.

Edmund and his wife, Helouise, couldn't have children, so they offered to take Sydney in. Denton and his wife, Iris, couldn't have children either, so they offered to take Sydney in. But it was Olivia, Maeve's younger sister, newly married to Berk Maddox, a fine young man, who got the prize awarded to her. After all, Olivia loved Sydney as if she were her own, and she had spent so much time with her from the day she was born. This also allowed Memaw the control she would need if and when it was time to return Sydney to Maeve. It would be much easier to control her daughter than either Edmond or Denton, she thought. Olivia would have to give Sydney up, if and when that day came, but neither Edmond nor Denton would have been so easy to convince.

By the time Sydney was in kindergarten, Memaw had bought a motel in Lancing, Texas, right on the Texas/Louisiana border. Sydney spent half of her kindergarten year there with her Memaw, and the other half of her kindergarten year in Houston with her Aunt Olivia and Uncle Berk. Sydney was like Olivia and Berk's firstborn because she was already living with them when their true firstborn, Victoria, arrived. "Big sister" Sydney was, and she would take that duty very responsibly. Then, for whatever reason, Sydney was shuttled back to Lancing to attend first grade. She attended a private school and learned to speak Spanish. She was so proud of how quickly she was able to learn Spanish and she showed off regularly the fact that she could count all the way up to two hundred. Sydney was smart and even at her young age, she knew it. When Memaw wasn't training her on the switchboard, or showing her how to make change for motel guests who bought items at the front desk, Sydney had lots of time to herself and that allowed her the time, and quiet, to use her imagination. She would draw, and write poetry and short stories. She would listen to the array of Memaw's albums and sing along. Sydney was very good at keeping herself busy and never minded her time as the only child.

In second grade, Sydney went back to live with her Aunt Olivia and Uncle Berk. They lived in a three-bedroom house now and just a few blocks up, at the end of the cul-de-sac, was the brand-new elementary school. Sydney lived in a house in a new neighborhood and there were other children to play with. It was different, but it was nice. What a life and picture-perfect. At least, it all appeared that way.

Sydney's Memaw had since divorced her Papa. It was a long time coming. Papa was a beautiful, suave, and debonair man, and that is where Maeve had gotten her stunning looks. His raven hair and emerald green eyes were certainly a showstopper, but his love for booze and women had worn through its final thread with Memaw. After their divorce, Memaw met a younger man named Doyle Baker. Doyle was a handsome man and had been a guest at the motel in Lancing. He played the banjo and that brought her Memaw pleasure, seeing that she was born and raised in the beautiful piney woods of East Texas. It was truly music to her ears. There was also a dose of excitement from this younger man, something that Memaw hadn't been accustomed to in quite a while. And then there was the sexual intimacy from this younger man, which her body had craved for so long. She loved him and the excitement he brought to her.

Doyle had a secret, however. Doyle liked little girls, and his attention was set on Sydney. He liked taking Sydney to run errands when she would come to visit her Memaw over weekends. Sydney didn't want to go run errands with Doyle, but she was brought up to never disrespect nor disobey her elders. She was a "yes girl." Make that a "yes ma'am, yes sir," girl.

Off they would go in his El Camino, and Doyle would have Sydney sit in his lap so that she could drive. Sydney may have been young, but she wasn't stupid. She knew this wasn't about running errands or Doyle teaching her to drive. Once her hands were on the steering wheel and the car was in motion, she would never remove her hands from it and she knew Doyle counted on that. She would never risk having a wreck. Of course, this meant she couldn't remove his hands from her privates either. This was his plan regularly. He touched her and pressed himself deep against her all the while acting as if he were her driving instructor and navigated her every move. She would never forget the smell of his cologne that masked the musky cigarette stench, nor his breath on the back of her neck.

Once home, all was well and no one knew the better. Sydney tried a new trick when going on future outings and would tell Doyle not to "help her" drive. She was sure this would work. She would ask him to please keep his hands to his sides and not touch her because she didn't need the help. She knew how to keep the car on the road. That didn't work, of course. Doyle wanted to keep her firmly placed in his lap and his hands firmly placed on her.

⚔

Visits to Memaw's were not often, but they were too much, nonetheless. Sydney loved her Memaw, but she couldn't bear the sight of Doyle Baker. Doyle had become increasingly obsessed with Sydney, and he wanted her. She was eight years old now.

How could this be happening to Sydney? She knew she was not to blame. She knew that he was a terrible man. Was she weak? Why wouldn't she tell someone? Was she afraid? When Sydney got older, she couldn't remember what had taken her so long to speak up, but she remembered all too clearly when the final straw was broken.

It was a hot summer evening. Sydney, Victoria, and Doyle were in the bed, watching television. Memaw had put the children in bed with him while she attended to the hotel laundry. It was like Memaw to be sensitive to her maids and their needs, so she would let the maids go home at a decent hour so that they could be with their families. Ironically, it took Memaw away from her own, and she had unknowingly laid her granddaughters in the bed with a monster.

Doyle pulled the covers back, pulled his boxers down and exposed his penis to Sydney. Sydney was in the middle, and Victoria was sleeping like a baby to her left. She dared not wake her. Doyle told Sydney to kneel on the floor in front of him and she obeyed him. Why, she didn't know. But she did what he told her to do, and therefore she felt she had to do. He put his flesh in her face and toward her mouth. It was only seconds, but the taste of him and the heat from his body made her want to vomit. She ran to the restroom and washed her mouth out with soap. Sydney heard something behind her. She looked in the mirror above the sink and saw his reflection. The devil himself, hands on each side of the doorway, laughing at her. That was the last time Sydney would ever see him.

Chapter 2

Two years passed in Sydney's life and so much had happened. Doyle Baker had fallen off a bar stool from a heart attack shortly after her Memaw kicked him out for what he had done. That would be one less asshole Sydney would have to deal with.

One day while visiting Memaw, and while Maeve happened to be visiting too, Sydney decided she wanted to go live with her mother, to her and her mother's surprise. Maeve had never approached anyone about getting Sydney back. Maybe she thought it was too late. Sydney was ten, after all. But that day, Sydney just made the decision on her own, and Maeve knew she had been given the gift of her daughter once again. This time, she would hold on to her blessing.

Sydney's abrupt decision to move to her mother's created a wake of despair that she didn't learn until her adult years. Her Aunt Olivia, Uncle Berk, and her "sister," Victoria, who was only five at the time, grieved as if there were a death in the family. By the time Sydney had made the decision to go live with her mother, Aunt Olivia and Uncle Berk had been blessed with a second daughter, Jacqueline, who was only three when Sydney left, and too young for it to affect her the same way it had Victoria.

This was just one more reason the love/hate relationship between Maeve and Olivia, which they had shared for years, would continue, and it was the biggest one by far. Olivia, too, was very beautiful, but for whatever reason she felt she never quite measured up to her older sister. Olivia was jealous of

Maeve from the time she was old enough to feel the emotion. Now, here they were and the prize was taken away from Olivia and given back to whom it belonged, like it or not.

Maeve was married to her fourth husband by the time Sydney went to live with her. His name was Berton Caldwell and he was a professional gambler. Talk about exciting times in Dallas, Texas. She and her mother only lived there from the time Sydney was ten until she was thirteen, but it was long enough to see her mother be physically abused by this man. It wasn't a frequent occasion when Berton would blacken Maeve's eye or bust her lip, but even once was far too much.

Is it possible to love someone who is good to you, and yet hurts someone you love? As a child, Sydney loved Berton because he had never once put his hands on her. Not even when her mother, during a poker party at their home, very spontaneously decided to hop on a midnight plane to Las Vegas with her friends, leaving Sydney with him for a few days. Berton had never touched, nor scolded, Sydney, and he made sure she had everything she needed. Sydney supposed if her mother was okay to stay with Berton, she would be okay with staying too.

Finally, when Sydney was thirteen, Maeve had enough. It was when Berton gave Maeve gonorrhea and she had to have a hysterectomy because of it. The latter likely wouldn't have had to happen, but rather than Berton admit what he'd done, he got himself fixed up with antibiotics and then watched Maeve lay in the bed ill, not knowing the truth of what was wrong with her. The nice doctor got to share that news with Maeve and that was the end.

Maeve quickly reunited with her high school sweetheart, Holden Hightower. She had been engaged to Holden before marrying Sydney's father, Forrest. Sydney was never sure what made her mother choose Forrest over Holden, but she was glad that she did or Sydney, in all her glory, wouldn't have been born.

Holden was a sweet and loving man with a wife and two children at the time he and Maeve rekindled their relationship. Holden was in an unhappy marriage and Maeve had always been the love of his life. Maeve loved Holden very much; always had. And she also never had any thoughts of being alone, so another family unit was born.

The three moved to Windmere, Texas and into a new town house. Windmere was just outside of Houston and closer to the Gulf Coast, and a beautiful town in which to settle for those who loved the ocean. This was where Holden had set up home prior to his marriage to his first wife and he had been there ever since. His soon-to-be ex-wife, Virginia, and his two children, Kimberly and Chad, would remain in Windmere, and so began the every-other-weekend visits when Sydney, Kimberly, and Chad would become a threesome, whether they liked it or not. Sydney was accustomed to change and going with the flow; Kimberly and Chad, not so much. They would learn to accept Sydney somewhat, and they would come to understand that she didn't steal their daddy, but it would take time and a great deal of it.

Maybe this would be it. Maybe no more moving around and life would be settled. This was the man her mother was originally engaged to and loved all those years ago, so surely this was what she would want for the rest of her life.

Chapter 3

Sydney had been a good girl all of her life. She had remained the "yes girl." She didn't disobey, she didn't have a smart mouth, she was loving and kind, and she rolled with every change that was ever dealt her.

And then came adolescence. Why is it that some girls go completely crazy at fifteen? It seems that this is the age, or at least the age range, when hormones are raging, bad decisions are sometimes made, and consequences are forever felt. And with adolescence comes high school. What a world of its own and one that left much to be desired, as far as Sydney was concerned. There were the jocks, the cheerleaders, and the drill teamers, more commonly known as "Bonnie Bratton's Bitches," and so eloquently named after their head instructor. There were the band geeks, the druggies, also known as "the heads," and then just the other misfits that no one really seemed to care much about.

Sydney was popular. She walked in as a fresh-faced freshman with a sweet shyness and a beautiful smile. She definitely got the boys' attention and the girls were happy to invite her to their table for lunch. She made friends quickly. She found herself being accepted by the not-so-popular girls. Then, soon after, by the popular drill teamers, and then the girls who were "bad," but good at it. These girls were rich and lived a little on the edge, something that Sydney had never been exposed to, but seemed preconditioned for. Alcohol and experimenting with drugs soon followed. The drugs were good. Those downers: they were like heaven on earth. Pop one of those with a beer chaser and she was free from any and all bad feelings, those she was conscious of and the ones hidden deep inside.

Sydney met a good boy. Laird Alberich was his name. He was on the football team and an all-American sweetheart. They quickly became involved and two weeks later, the two lost their virginity to each other, and in Sydney's parents' bed, no less. Sydney had a party that night while her parents were out of town, and while others were losing their virginity in her house too, Sydney figured it would be better that hers was lost in her parents' bed rather than someone else disrespecting their space like that. Silly girl.

Life was good with Laird and they were crazy about each other. Once they had lost their virginity, she and Laird did what any teenagers did every time they saw each other. They made love, had sex, or whatever you call it at fifteen years old. They also weren't careful. Sydney had read about teenage pregnancy, and it had been mentioned in her Sex Education class, but that only happened to other people, or so they thought. She had only missed her period by two weeks when she realized that what only happened to other people had come knocking on her door. Sydney took money from her mother's purse and bought an over-the-counter pregnancy test. This was the old kind. No peeing on a stick. This was much more complicated. You had to pee in a test tube first thing in the morning, drop some red drops in it and wait two hours. If the mirror underneath the test tube showed a red ring on the bottom, congratulations, you were pregnant.

⅄

Congratulations, Sydney!

Sydney felt an instant maturity knowing that a baby was inside of her, and at the same time she knew she had done something really, really stupid. And now what?

While talking about her surprise news with a friend over the phone, Holden overheard her conversation and told Maeve.

It was a funny thing about Maeve. If Sydney smarted off, if she was late getting home, or if Maeve just wasn't in a good mood, all hell could break loose. However, if Sydney came up pregnant, she could count on her mother. Maeve was great in a crisis and this was just another.

Maeve asked Sydney if she wanted to keep the child, but Sydney needed guidance and wasn't sure of what to do. When Sydney got older, she didn't recall what her answer was to her mother that day, but suffice it to say, everything was fixed and never talked about again. Laird knew about the pregnancy and followed Sydney's lead as easily as she had followed her mother's.

Sydney became so increasingly addicted to the numbness the downers provided her, that her behavior became erratic and she began to lie to, and cheat on, Laird with other boys in school, and some were his friends. It was too, too bad, and 'twas the end of a beautiful thing.

Sydney then began doing other drugs: cocaine, blotter acid, yellow mollies, black mollies, pharmaceutical 714 Quaaludes, you name it. One thing Sydney was very proud of was the fact that she had never shot up. There would never be a needle in her arm. But there was just that one time that she came close, in wanting to, at least. One of her later boyfriends almost had her talked into it, just by his description of the feeling. Thank God they were on the phone and she wasn't actually with him. She might have been in that dark place just enough to actually think trying it was okay.

Things had clearly gone from bad to worse with Sydney's drug use, so much so that she was even shunned by the very friends who got her started on the happy pills in the first place. Rich bitches and drill teamers had no desire to be friends with someone they deemed to be the "druggie" or "school slut." Shame on them. Sydney knew that judging her was simply a distraction from their own indiscretions.

How did Miss Fresh-faced Freshman Beauty find her way to the bottom of the toilet with the rest of the "heads"? She had, in fact, come from a good family. Sure, bad things had happened, but don't bad things happen to everyone at some point in their lives? Sure they do. "So, fuck them," she thought. "Fuck them all."

CHAPTER 4

Three years is such a short period of time. Why then, do the three years from fifteen through seventeen feel like forever? "It must be the decisions that we make during that time," Sydney thought. When you have lived your life literally on the edge, knowing without question that God has held you tightly in His hand while you so stupidly meandered through, and at times even sped through life, it is understandable that you would have aged more than those three years.

From the time Sydney and Laird were finished, she had managed to make her way through other young men. She had been kicked out of her high school the end of her junior year. It seemed that drug use, skipping school, and forging parents' and teachers' signatures was not looked too kindly upon, so Sydney would be attending her senior year at the scary school her mother never wanted her to have to attend. "Life sucked," Sydney thought, but she had created this situation and she knew it. She hadn't ever felt consequences quite like this, but welcome to the real world, Sydney. Welcome indeed.

Sydney didn't want friends at her new school. She didn't need them. She had her handful of friends from her old school. It didn't take long, however, for Sydney to fall in with the wrong crowd. The druggies must have a *D* on their foreheads that only other druggies can see. It all happened quite fast. Sydney began hanging out with them and doing drugs with them. The fun and games would be short-lived, however.

Maeve had told Sydney over and over and over not to hang out with the wrong crowd. "Sydney, don't you see what you're doing to yourself?" "Sydney, these people are not your friends." "Sydney, if you get caught doing what you're doing, do you really think these people will be there for you?" "These people only look out for themselves, Sydney." "Sydney, I love you, and you have to stop this. Stop this, Sydney!"

Sydney heard her mother, but she didn't listen. She should have listened to the voice of reason, the voice of experience, but she did not.

But then, Sydney had an epiphany of sorts. At least, Sydney called it an epiphany. It actually came as a "come to Jesus" meeting between Sydney and her mother.

Maeve had a gut feeling, a mother's intuition that Sydney was at the dealer's house. Maeve drove there, went to the door, and all it took was the door being cracked open by the dealer's mom when Maeve pushed the door open and walked inside. She told the dealer's mother she couldn't believe she would allow such horrible, incomprehensible behavior in her home, especially considering she had already lost one son to an overdose. Then, just as if a map were laid out before her, Maeve found her daughter. Sydney was hiding in a dark closet in the dealer's bedroom, totally wasted, and the only thing to be seen in that dark closet was the end of Sydney's lit cigarette shaking back and forth. The door flung open and no more fun and games: Maeve yanked her from the closet in one fell swoop, Maeve's fist slammed into her head, Sydney's body fell on the bed like a limp doll, and her friends screamed and begged Maeve not to kill her.

As strange as it sounds, that was the third significant time that Sydney truly knew how much her mother really, really, really loved her. Oh, Sydney knew that Maeve loved her, but there were specific times that stood out. This time was the action verb sense of the word. This was the straight to the heart and desperation sense of the word.

It was the washing of the "dirt beads" off Sydney's neck, which was the first time Sydney could remember the feeling of her mother's love. The second time was when Sydney had run headlong into a glass window in Dallas and her mother had to be sedated at the emergency room while she waited for Sydney to have surgery. It's strange how love, and the show of it, comes in such different forms...how tender the first moment was in comparison to the worry of the second, and then the anger and desperation of the third.

Maeve refused to watch Sydney kill herself with drugs and she wasn't going to put up with the bullshit any more. It was about time. And just in time, for that matter. Sydney never spoke to her "head" friends again. Never. It was as if they had never known one another. All were so terrified after the night Maeve had gone to the dealer's house, eye contact between Sydney and any member of the group was never made when they passed in the halls on Monday, and never would be again.

Sydney focused on her studies for the first time in a very long time, and she took an elective class working in the library the latter part of her senior year. That was certainly a "nerdy" enough job to keep her out of trouble, and usually the smart and studious were the only ones who frequented the rows of library books. Sydney worked the checkout counter, which was a funny play on words to her, considering this is how she met the boy who would introduce her to her future husband. This boy's name was Kyle. He had asked Sydney for her number and she waited for his call. He did call, but they never went out. They just talked on the phone after school and Sydney thought he was cute. Kyle's best friend, Bear, had been admiring Sydney from afar and managed to talk Kyle into giving him Sydney's number. Kyle did, and this would set in motion a chapter of Sydney's life that would be nothing like she would have ever imagined.

CHAPTER 5

Sydney ran at top speed to answer the phone. "Hello."

"Hello. Sydney?"

"Yes, this is Sydney."

"Hey, Sydney. This is Bear. I got your number from Kyle. I hope you don't mind me calling."

"Of course not. How are you?" she asked, somewhat nervously. She had seen Bear before at school and he was a handsome one. Sydney hadn't talked to a "nice boy" in so long that she barely knew how to act. And to actually be talking to someone her parents would approve of? That, in and of itself, was a miracle.

"I'm fine," he said. "I was wondering if you would like to go out sometime."

"Sure." Sydney hoped it would be sooner rather than later. She needed to meet nice people, and she wanted her weekends to be busy again.

"How about this weekend?" Bear asked.

"Thank you, God!" she thought.

"This weekend sounds super." Sydney tried not to sound over the moon, but she was. They discussed the time when he'd pick her up, and everything was set. Sydney would be attending a party at Bear's house.

Sydney walked in and met Bear's stepdad, Vernon Phillips. He was a short man, as wide as he was tall, bald, and smelled of cigarettes. He wasted no time in showing interest in Sydney and letting her know all about his military background, along with how fortunate Bear's mother, Clara, was to have landed him.

"Well, Bear. You didn't tell me that your new gal was such a pretty little thing," Vernon said. "Come over here, darlin', and sit down." He motioned to his lap.

"Are you serious?" Sydney thought. Sydney sat on his knee and the conversation began.

"Bear is my stepson, but I've practically raised him. His daddy left his momma when Bear was only one and his sister, Abigail, wasn't but three. Son of a bitch just left his family." Vernon took a drag from his cigarette.

"That is terrible," Sydney said, wondering why she was being told family secrets upon her first meeting. She found out quickly as Vernon continued on with how he saved the day. More pats on the back for this old fart.

"Yep, just up and left," he continued. "Clara was best friends with my oldest daughter and that's how I met her. Once I gave her a little of ol' Vernon Phillips, she followed me with those two kids in tote and here we are today."

Sydney wasn't impressed. She had a knack for picking up on the idiosyncrasies of people very quickly, usually upon first meeting. It didn't take a rocket scientist to know that Vernon Phillips was all about Vernon Phillips and that Bear had likely suffered to some degree at the hands of this narcissistic old bastard.

⚔

What is it about that house of cards, the house that is built so carefully, one card by one? It looks to be a nice house, but then one wrong move, and it all comes tumbling down. Apparently Vernon had that house. By all accounts, all was well. Everyone had their place and no one dared to rock that house of cards. Vernon was, after all, the military man, and everyone did as they were told, including Sydney. When Sydney began dating Bear, his sister, Abigail, had already moved out and was married to Bruce, also a military man. She had wasted no time in getting out of the house and married, with child, by the time she was twenty. When Sydney would visit Bear's house, it was typically just her, Bear, Vernon, and Clara in attendance.

Clara was a nice lady. She didn't appear to be an overly passive woman, but she was. Vernon had his young girls who would sit on his lap while he played grab-ass, and Clara would glide through the house, acting as though everything was better than fine. One young girl in particular had a crush on Bear and had been frequenting their home. She was a neighbor girl, so stopping by was easy and if she had to put up with Vernon, so be it. At least she got to see Bear and it was apparent that she knew how to handle the hands of an older man, and Vernon was just another. Watching Vernon's inappropriate behavior with this young girl was sickening. She couldn't have been more than fourteen and this made Sydney feel all the more helpless and ashamed for watching it. Why wasn't anyone saying something?

Eventually, this girl got the message that Bear and Sydney were an item and she stopped coming around so much. Thank God. If nothing else, it would keep Vernon's hands off her.

⚔

Sydney was grounded from her car her entire senior year. That revelation came to Maeve the night she dragged Sydney out of the closet, determined that she would stop the drugs and graduate from high school. Sydney running the roads certainly wouldn't help the cause.

That's where Vernon came in. Sydney wanted to spend time with Bear after school each day, and Maeve, being very impressed with Sydney's recent choice of a boyfriend, was fine with it. So, Vernon gladly offered to pick Sydney up from school every day, and she would go back to Bear's house to wait for him to get out of football practice.

It was sick, really. Vernon would take Sydney to the Baskin Robbins, as if she were five years old, and she would get a scoop of Rocky Road ice cream every time. Then they would head back to Bear's house and the familiar rumbling of a lustful man would rear its ugly head.

"Do you know how beautiful you are? Look at you," Vernon would say, as he pressed his lips tight to Sydney's. Those words meant nothing to her, and certainly not coming from him. It felt odd kissing him. How could she? But Sydney knew how to detach herself from the realities of this world when she was in an uncomfortable situation. She wasn't crazy. She was a survivor, and quite frankly, she didn't know what else to do. She would close her eyes, kiss this man, and know that in just a few hours all would be over and Bear would be home.

Vernon took Sydney around to run errands, too. It brought back memories of Doyle Baker. Sydney was too big to sit in Vernon's lap and get first-hand driving lessons like Doyle Baker had provided, but Vernon certainly took her to various places to show her off to his friends. Funny thing was Sydney could tell all of these men thought Vernon was full of shit and she could tell by the look on their faces that they pitied her. Nonetheless, the charade continued.

One day after school, Sydney laid down to take a nap at Bear's house. She was tired from a late night with Bear the night before and she wanted just a moment to sleep. She laid on the small loveseat in the seating area and prayed that Vernon would leave her alone. Bear would be home very soon and maybe that would be enough of a deterrent for Vernon. Besides, Sydney had shared with Bear very small details about his stepfather. She would never have told him that she allowed some of the things he had done to her. She was sure Bear wouldn't understand. But she did give him enough information so that he would be aware. And Bear knew his stepfather. This wasn't his first rodeo, so he could likely figure out the rest of the details if he just put his mind to it. Sydney hoped Bear would step in and save her. Sydney was wrong.

Vernon came to her, knelt down next to her and kissed her. "I want to make you feel good, Sydney. If I ever had a chance to really be alone with you, I could make you feel better than you ever have in your life." Vernon groaned. Sydney didn't speak, she didn't move, but she let him have his way with her. He kissed her mouth hard and pulled up her shirt and sucked her breast. She felt nothing.

There was a knock on the door and then a face in the window. My God, it was Jose, one of Bear's friends. He would not leave. He kept knocking. Sydney was never so happy to see someone, but she was also mortified at what he had likely seen. Jose kept knocking and knocking. Vernon got up and marched to the door. He was angry.

"What do you want?! Why are you knocking?!" Vernon yelled.

"I'm just here because Bear asked me to come." Jose was calm, but he was firm and not backing down from Vernon.

Vernon liked to play badass, but he was in his late sixties, he'd had open-heart surgery, and he smoked. It was a lost cause and Vernon knew it. "Come in," he snorted, and Jose walked in.

Vernon left the room and Sydney and Jose began to whisper about what had happened. She felt mortified knowing what Jose had seen through the window, but she also felt somewhat at ease talking about it with Jose. Sydney was just seventeen and Vernon had a reputation for taking advantage of the pubescent girls. Everyone knew it.

Why then did Sydney feel so dirty? At some point, she knew she had to take responsibility for herself. She had to be able to say "no." No more "yes girl." It had to be okay to say, "No." Sydney had told herself, "It doesn't matter how old the person is who is hurting you and it doesn't matter if they threaten you. Your body is your own, as is your very life. Your body is a gift from God and it is never okay for someone to take your spirit, nor your innocence." Was it too late for Sydney? She hoped not.

With everything that had happened to Sydney, including the poor decisions she had made on her own, she had felt close to God her entire life. Her Memaw, Aunt Olivia, and Uncle Berk had seen to it that she attended church every Sunday. She was baptized at nine years of age and still had the same Bible that Mrs. Butcher had given her that very day, tears in the pages and all. Sydney prayed and even cried out for God to be with her in her darkest moments. She did have desperate moments and cried herself to sleep some nights. She knew God was with her. She knew that He had watched over and taken care of her before. Sydney didn't understand why some of these things had happened to her. And while she did blame herself at times, she knew she didn't bear full responsibility. She knew where most of the blame needed to lie and she did her best to make sure it stayed there.

Chapter 6

Bear picked Sydney up for a special Saturday night. She was ready. It had been some time since just the two of them had done something together, and for it to be a special occasion made her all the more excited. She liked Bear; she liked him a lot. He was a good one. What made her like him even more was that he was what she needed. Here was this great guy who played football and drank milk on a Saturday night over beer any day. It may have felt too good to be true, but she was going with it. They pulled up into Bear's driveway. What was this? Their special night would be here, of all places?

"I have a surprise for you," Bear said, stumbling over his words.

As they passed through the front door, Sydney noticed that the living room was dimly lit and Vernon and Clara had their designated seats. Bear led Sydney to the ottoman and sat her down. She felt uncomfortable and it didn't help that Vernon and Clara had the strangest smiles pasted on their faces.

"I have something to ask you." Bear knelt to one knee, his mother passed him a ring, and he asked Sydney to marry him.

Sydney was completely taken aback. She was being asked to wed, here and now? Sydney looked at Clara and at Vernon. They explained that this had been Clara's engagement ring from Bear's biological father and they wanted Bear and Sydney to have it.

Sydney looked at Bear. "Yes."

Sydney thought of the line, "The future's so bright, I gotta wear shades." That was exactly what Sydney thought. Oh, it wasn't a perfect setup. Her soon-to-be father-in-law was a creep, her soon-to-be mother-in-law was weak, but Bear was what she needed. Sydney kept telling herself that. There wasn't one bad thing about Bear. She had lucked out. She had managed to bring herself out of a bad, dark place and into the light. Yes, Sydney Elesabeth Ewing was about to become Mrs. Bjorn "Bear" Jude Keane and she loved the sound of it.

Graduation day had arrived and hallelujah! Sydney's parents felt it no less than a miracle that she had actually made it. Sydney had to take a full load of classes her senior year at school and she also had to take correspondence courses just to graduate, thanks to all the fun she had through her junior year. But she did it! She'd done it by the skin of her teeth, yes, but she had succeeded, thank God. Sydney's parents invited family and friends that totaled seventeen to attend the ceremony and none missed it. This was a party, a celebration. Sydney was on her way to being a fine, healthy, and respectable young adult. Her Memaw had wanted so much for Sydney to attend college, Oral Roberts University, to be exact. But if getting married kept Sydney safe, so be it. Graduation went off without a hitch. Class of '81. Pictures were taken, there was lots of good food, and the champagne flowed.

The next morning, Sydney and Bear headed to the beach. It was such a fun time with loads of friends and loads of sun; too much sun, to be exact. After a day full of sun and surf, Bear and Sydney headed to Bear's house before taking Sydney home because Vernon wanted to see them. Sydney was as red from the sun as a cherry tomato. There would be nothing touching her skin except the bathing suit she was wearing. Sydney stepped out of the car in her bikini as Vernon and Clara made their way to the car. She could tell by the look on Vernon's face that this was nowhere she wanted to be. Vernon made his way directly toward her with Clara on his heels.

"Please don't touch me, Vernon," Sydney rushed to say. "I am so burned and it hurts just to touch my skin." She was used to coming up with good excuses so as not to be touched, but it hadn't worked in the past. Maybe it would work this time.

Vernon was on a mission and either never heard a word she said or didn't care. He walked to Sydney, put his hands on her waist, and kissed her lips. She felt his tongue touch her lips, making them wet. Clara and Bear stood, looking on with smiles that spelled either denial or stupidity. Either way, Sydney couldn't take it anymore.

"It was good seeing the two of you." Sydney wiped her lips. "I really need to get home. Mother is cooking a big dinner."

"That's fine, dear. It was wonderful seeing you. Take care and make sure to put lotion on that burn. You'll peel," Clara said.

"My God, this woman lives in a dream," Sydney thought, barely able to compose herself.

"Yes, be sure to lotion yourself," Vernon said with a wink and a smirk that sickened Sydney.

Sydney climbed back into Bear's truck, shut the door and held in her tears so hard that her throat ached. It was done. She couldn't take one more touch, one more comment, one more look from that sick son of a bitch. Another ride with Bear in silence.

Bear dropped Sydney off in her driveway. She kissed his cheek and jetted from the truck. Bear didn't ask why. He knew why, but he wasn't opening Pandora's Box.

⅄

Sydney walked into her house, and her mother and one of her mother's closest friends were sitting at the kitchen bar.

"Look who's here, Sydney! Georgia came by to say hello. We haven't seen each other in ages."

Maeve used to go out and have more fun than the law should allow, but ever since Sydney decided to be a bad girl in high school, her mother stopped going out so that she could do her best to keep a rein on Sydney. It was nice that she was venturing back out and friends were coming around more, now that little Sydney had met Mr. Right.

"Hello, Georgia. It's been a long time," Sydney said with a hug. Sydney walked around the kitchen bar to fix a plate of food and her mother started in about how burned Sydney was and how she needed to do this, that and the other.

"Sydney, what have I told you about not putting sunscreen on, sweetheart? When are you ever going to listen?" Maeve asked.

Her mother was just being a mother, but no matter. Sydney didn't want to hear a word out of anyone's mouth. She knew to never mouth off to her mother and she certainly would never have done it in front of any of her mother's friends, but she opened her mouth and out it came.

"I do listen to you, Mother! I do everything you say, so stop making a big damn deal about my sunburn!"

Maeve's mouth flew open, Georgia was frozen, and Sydney couldn't believe it herself. It wasn't the worst thing she could have said to her mother, but this verbal disrespect was definitely not allowed.

"What is the matter with you? Why would you talk to me that way?" Maeve retorted. "I was just asking you something because I'm worried about you."

Her mother's reaction was definitely nicer because Georgia was there, and that was good. It felt good to Sydney. She needed to be able to lose her temper and Maeve to stop for just a moment to try to understand. Sydney couldn't take the pressure or the secrets any longer and she needed her mother.

"He won't leave me alone! He won't stop touching me!"

"What?" Maeve asked. There was just a moment of pause and Sydney and her mother locked eyes. "Who, Sydney?" her mother asked, but the tone of her voice and the shock of her face showed panic. Sydney was sure her mother was thinking, "Not again."

Sydney had been told to never tell her mother about Doyle Baker because she would likely kill him and she would go to jail for the rest of her life. Sydney never doubted that because her mother had shoved the bottom of a broken glass in Doyle's face on one occasion when he had hit her Memaw. Sydney never spoke a word to her mother of what Doyle had done, but after Doyle died, her Aunt Olivia had called her mother and told her what he had done to Sydney. Sydney couldn't have been more than twelve when Maeve mentioned it to Sydney, and only so that Sydney would know that she was aware, but it was never discussed again.

"Sydney, I asked you who!" Maeve yelled. She stood from her bar stool, desperation in her eyes.

"Vernon Phillips," Sydney replied, now without hesitation, but then couldn't believe she had actually let his name pass through her lips.

Maeve went into a fury. With Georgia still there, no time like the present, Maeve picked up the phone and called the Phillips's residence. Clara answered.

"Clara, I need to speak with you about your husband," Maeve said, her voice shaking.

"Yes?" Clara replied reluctantly. It seemed her house of cards was about to tumble down.

"He has been putting his hands on my daughter, and I want you to know one thing, Clara. If he ever puts his hands on my daughter again, ever, I will come to your house and I will take care of Vernon Phillips myself. Do you understand me?"

Sydney couldn't hear anything Clara said and was glad of it. Bottom line, the message was given, loud and clear.

⅄

Bear called Sydney later that evening. "Sydney, I heard about the phone call from your mother."

"Yes, Bear. I couldn't take it anymore. I've tried to tell you what your father has been doing to me, but you wouldn't listen. When he can put his hands on me and kiss me on the mouth right in front of you and your mother, and no one does or says anything, something is very wrong. It's fucked up. I can't do it. I won't do this anymore." Sydney began sobbing.

"I understand. I understand, Sydney, and I'm sorry. Listen..." Bear paused and took a deep breath. "My parents want me to come get the ring, but I still love you and we're still going to get married, Sydney. We're still going to get married."

This was all so surreal. How could Bear sound so calm? Could they still marry, really? How could they with everything that had been done? Sydney didn't ponder long and she didn't worry. Bear said it and she believed him.

CHAPTER 7

The wedding plans began and everyone in Sydney's family jumped in to assist. Sydney was as young and free as the wind. At only eighteen, she was happy to be out of school, happy to be with Bear, and happy to start a new life with him. She looked forward to being a wife and a mother. She wanted children very much and knew she would make a wonderful mother and protector. Sydney had been through a lot. But she had come out of the storm and into the calm and she had managed to keep her soul.

⋏

Then the call came. "Sydney?"

"Yes, who is speaking?" Sydney asked, realizing who it was at the last minute.

"This is Clara. Vernon and I would like to speak with you and Bear this evening. Could you please come over? Please?"

Sydney got sick to her stomach. What could they possibly want? She had felt so free. Free from all of the filth and in an instant, it came flooding back.

"I already spoke with Bear, and he said he is willing to sit down and talk, the four of us," she said quickly, before Sydney could answer.

"That is fine then. Is Bear there? Can I speak with him or what time will he be picking me up?"

"Yes, he is here, and he will be picking you up at seven o'clock. Here's Bear, dear."

"Hey." Bear sounded embarrassed and Sydney thought he should grow a pair.

"Hey," she said back. That was all she said. Sydney wanted him to talk. She needed him to say something and not cow down. She waited.

"Well, my parents want to talk to us tonight. I told them okay. I think they want to apologize for everything."

This all seemed so strange, but Sydney needed to do the right thing, or what she thought was the right thing. If they were extending the olive branch, she needed to take it.

Bear picked her up promptly at seven o'clock that evening. They didn't talk on the way to his parents' house. There really wasn't anything to say that would make this situation better. They walked in and it was like a complete reenactment of the proposal. Dim lighting, Clara and Vernon in the exact same seats, and Bear walked Sydney over to the ottoman.

"Sydney, Vernon and I want you to take this ring back. We love you and we're happy that you are marrying Bear. We don't want there to be ill feelings."

Sydney looked at Clara and she could tell by looking into this woman's eyes that she truly did live in a dream. Sydney was also sure that this ridiculous scenario was as much Vernon's doing as it was Clara's. Of course, he had ulterior motives. He would much rather have Sydney in his life somehow, some way, than none at all and Sydney knew that. Sydney looked at Bear and his eyes were begging her to say "okay" just as much as he wanted her to say "yes" the evening he asked her to marry him.

"Okay," Sydney said.

They all hugged, reunited, and went on about their lives as if nothing had ever happened. Interesting how no one ever referenced Vernon or what he had done. There had never been as much as an apology. This was one more wrong that would never be discussed again, so Sydney filed it away in alphabetical order with all the other shit, right under *V* for Vernon.

Chapter 8

Aunt Olivia gave Sydney her wedding dress that she had worn when she married Uncle Berk. Maeve hadn't married Forrest in a traditional or formal wedding, so there was no wedding dress to pass down. Having Aunt Olivia's dress was wonderful. This was so special to Sydney, as well as to her Aunt Olivia, and Sydney would rather have something sentimental than something new any day. They had the dress altered, bought a veil and shoes, and Sydney was set. Aunt Olivia and Uncle Berk also offered to host the rehearsal dinner at their home and Memaw would foot the bill. It was a beautiful dinner party and Sydney couldn't have been more proud.

It was Sydney's wedding day and Maeve looked beautiful, absolutely radiant. She was so happy that Sydney was happy, and she was also floating on a cloud at the fact that she had seen her daughter through the difficult times, making sure she came out not just alive, but on top. She had met a wonderful young man, a respectable young man. This day represented the new life ahead for Sydney: a new life with Bear. Maeve couldn't have been a happier or more proud mother.

On this day that is typically filled with hope and promise, Sydney felt like a princess on autopilot. She was a mere eighteen years old. She hadn't put a lot of thought in the wedding: the planning of it, nothing. She just knew she wanted it. She would show up, say her vows, and start fresh. Sydney was ready to start fresh.

Holden was ready to walk Sydney down the aisle, but not without the standard daddy/daughter pre-walk conversation.

"Sweetheart, we can turn around and walk right out this door if you're havin' any second thoughts," Holden said.

If she hadn't already made up her mind, she might have processed this moment better, but Sydney just smiled and reassured him that she was ready.

Ready? Sydney's hands were shaking so badly that her bouquet sounded like a pair of maracas. She walked down the aisle and everyone smiled and cried, the typical show of emotion from the wedding guests. Sydney couldn't smile. She was frozen, except for her hands shaking, and she could do nothing to stop them. She was happy to hand the bouquet over to her maid of honor, Patrice.

Patrice and Sydney had been friends since they were ten years old. Sydney had met Patrice in Dallas when she had moved there to live with her mother. Even though she and Patrice lived in different cities now, they had remained friends and that was a comfort to Sydney. The minister gave his speech, Sydney and Bear said their vows, sealed it with a kiss and they were off as husband and wife. The world was their oyster, she thought.

⚓

Francis Blevins, her Memaw's new boyfriend and a very rich attorney in Bayside, Texas, gave Sydney and Bear their honeymoon for their wedding gift. They would stay one night in Lake Charles, Louisiana and then head on to New Orleans, Louisiana. Sydney and Bear arrived in Lake Charles on their wedding night, and wedded bliss had made a quick exit. What was wrong with her? Why wasn't she excited and happy to be here?

"Well, here we are!" Bear said with excitement in his voice. "Let's get this stuff unloaded and get settled in."

Sydney felt crazy. She couldn't make heads or tails of her emotions and she began to cry.

"What is the matter, Sydney?" he asked. "Have I done something?"

She could hear the concern in his voice. "No, Bear. It's not you. I don't know what's wrong with me. I don't even know what to say. I just, I just…"

Bear put his arms around her and did the best he could to make Sydney feel safe and secure. They kissed and he held her, but their marriage would not be consummated that night.

⟡

Thank God for a new day. The sun shone brightly and the drive to New Orleans was beautiful. Sydney had never been to Bourbon Street, but she had heard all about it. Bear had never been either, so this was a new adventure for the two of them. Sydney felt grown now, and it was sinking in that she was really married and that this was her life. This was their life together.

Francis had reserved them a suite at the Fairmont Hotel, walking distance from the French Quarter and Bourbon Street. Sydney didn't know what to think as the bellman rolled their luggage to the end of the hall with the double doors. When those doors flung open, she thought she was in a dream. Sydney had always been exposed to nice things. She knew her etiquette and always considered herself upper-middle class, whether it was the truth or not. But she had never seen a room so beautiful. It was breathtaking, and if there was any question that the honeymoon was in full swing now, it was quickly answered. This was it.

Sydney and Bear had a grand ol' time in New Orleans. Sydney was still shell-shocked that she was actually married, and she was afraid of the independence she now felt. She didn't understand why, when she had craved her independence for so long, but it brought to mind the old saying, "Be careful what you wish for." Every day was a new "settling in" time for Sydney, and she did her best to embrace it.

Chapter 9

Prior to getting married, Sydney and Bear had discussed moving to Merriweather to start their life and family together. Sydney had been born there and she had a great deal of family there. Mama Scurlock had long moved back to the farm, the original homestead that Memaw and all of her siblings had grown up on, and Uncle Denton and Aunt Iris lived one house over on the original homestead. Also, Sydney's father, Forrest, and his side of the family, all still lived in Merriweather. Although Forrest didn't have much to do with Sydney while she was growing up, she would still visit from time to time during her childhood, thanks to Maeve promoting that family togetherness. Sydney would stay with Forrest's parents, Granny and PawPaw Ewing, and she would stay with her Aunt Jolene, Forrest's sister, and her husband, Aubrey. They had three children, Rebecca, Kathryn, and Aubrey, Jr. Forrest also had a brother, Bernard, and he and his wife, Pearle, had two children, Hayden and Lindy. Hayden was always what they called a "sissy" and they blamed it all on Pearle for keeping her son close to her. She didn't want him to turn out like his daddy, feeling as if he had to drink beer or hunt deer to be a man. Lindy, on the other hand, was all tomboy and a daddy's girl, and she wasn't scared of anything.

These visits to Merriweather during her childhood, and spending time with family, were some of Sydney's sweetest memories. Sydney always loved being in the country. She loved the sound of the trees, the wind in her face, the smell of grass and flowers. She ran amuck in all of it during her visits.

Sydney loved to run and play at the farm, exploring things. She loved watching the soap operas with Mama Scurlock. She loved to swing from the rope swing her Granny and PawPaw Ewing had in their backyard. It hung from the tallest branch and had a board with two notches cut out on the sides, which served as the seat. Forrest would push Sydney so high in the swing that her feet could almost touch the leaves of the adjacent tree, and the rope would get a slack in it. It was scary and all too fun at the same time. She loved helping her Nanaw and Pepaw Hightower in the garden and at bedtime, telling scary stories with Kimberly and Chad in the back room that was so dark you could barely see your hand in front of your face. These times could never be replaced and Sydney knew that. These times were still engrained in Sydney's mind and she felt Merriweather would be the perfect place to raise a family, out in the wild outdoors, under the big blue sky. Bear had agreed.

Sydney wasted no time in moving. She never wanted their first apartment to be in Windmere. No way. She knew how that would go. Friends would stop by, parties would ensue, her life would feel as if nothing had changed, and that was not an option. Besides, this was her new beginning, her new start. Sydney's Uncle Denton got Bear a job at the sawmill, so she and Bear found an apartment quickly, packed up and moved to Merriweather.

⋏

This was the life. She and Bear had rented a beautiful apartment in King's Ridge. This was the most exclusive subdivision in Merriweather, and home to the country club and mansions. Her Memaw bought Sydney and Bear their first set of living room and dining room furniture and it was perfect. Their apartment was also right across the street from the junior college, which made it very easy for Sydney to attend.

Sydney was very interested in computers and signed up as a computer programming major. She really applied herself and managed to be a straight A student and she made honor roll. Sydney was all too pleased with herself, but not nearly as much as her family was. They were over the moon. Sydney was actually on the road to obtaining her associates degree. Who would have thought it? She was becoming the fine young woman she had wanted to be and steadily moving in the right direction.

⚓

Sydney knew from the moment she was married that she wanted to have a baby. She wanted that more than anything. She took birth control pills the first two months of her marriage, maybe because it seemed like the thing to do. They were young, after all, and Bear was the sole provider. No matter. Sydney stopped taking them. She knew what she wanted, so she wasn't going to continue to prevent it.

The first month Sydney didn't take her pills, she didn't have her period. She knew about mother's intuition now. She knew she was pregnant even though she was only days late. She took the over-the-counter pregnancy tests, three of them, and while one said she was pregnant, two said she wasn't. It didn't matter; she knew.

Sydney and Bear went to Windmere to visit their parents. While there, Sydney made an appointment with Dr. Gantz, her family doctor.

Dr. Gantz was the doctor who had put Sydney on birth control pills after she got pregnant by Laird. Maeve had explained to him that while she didn't condone Sydney being sexually active at fifteen, she was a realist and wanted to be sure nothing unexpected would happen. It had been too late for that, but Dr. Gantz never knew.

Sydney was excited about her appointment with Dr. Gantz. She had come a long way from her dark days in high school and wanted him to see that she had. She arrived early.

"No," Dr. Gantz said. "Your urine came back negative and your uterus is too tight for you to be pregnant."

Even that didn't matter. Sydney knew there was a baby inside her. Dr. Gantz told her the only way to know for certain would be by a blood test, but she would certainly be wasting her sixteen dollars. That didn't matter either. She paid the sixteen dollars and waited for the call.

The phone rang and Sydney answered quickly. She had been sitting on the telephone all day.

"Hello!" she said with excited expectation in her voice.

"Sydney, this is Dr. Gantz."

"Yes?" She paused. "Please, God, let this be 'yes,'" she thought.

"I can't believe it. I honestly can't believe it, but congratulations, young lady. You're going to be a mother," he said.

This was the best day of Sydney's life. She mattered. There was someone counting on her. There was someone who needed her, all of her, and depended on her. This was not to say that Sydney ever thought she didn't matter, necessarily. But this was different. This was a part of her. This was her baby.

Chapter 10

Everyone was so excited, all family members and all friends. Well, there was one friend who may have been riding the fence. Ruby. Ruby was Sydney's best friend and had been since high school, and she had been one of Sydney's bridesmaids. Ruby was mature and seemed older than her years. She was the first of Sydney's friends who had a job in high school. Ruby worked at Weiner's and quickly moved to manager status. She also had a car and took care of all of her goofball friends who weren't as mature as she was; hence her nickname, "Aunt Roo." This was what her nieces and nephews called her and it stuck with the numb-heads she tended to in school, including Sydney.

"Sydney, do you know what you're doing? Are you really ready for this? Are you ready for this responsibility?" Ruby asked her. Once again, the voice of maturity and reason.

"Of course! What do you mean?" Sydney answered back.

"I just mean you and Bear just got married and this is so soon. You've only been married four months and you're already pregnant. Have you even figured out how to take care of yourself yet?"

"I'm perfectly capable of taking care of myself, Ruby." Sydney felt defensive, even though she knew Ruby had a point. "And yes, I've wanted to be pregnant from day one," Sydney added.

"God, everything is just happening so fast, Sydney," Ruby said.

Maybe Ruby was afraid she was losing her friend forever. Maybe she felt the marriage had taken Sydney from her and a baby would take Sydney even farther away.

"You might as well get on this bandwagon, Aunt Roo. There is a baby on the way, and you've got a shower to plan before too long," Sydney said with a smile. Sydney understood that Ruby needed the reassurance that life was changing, but not their friendship, not ever.

Ruby gave her a nod and a hug, confident that nothing would ever take away from the sisterhood they shared.

⅄

Sydney's pregnancy was a dream come true. She savored every moment of it. She took good care of herself. She stopped drinking completely, she stopped smoking cigarettes, and she ate healthy and well. She felt like a million bucks. Sydney knew she was having a boy. She wouldn't be disappointed if she had a girl, but she just knew in her heart of hearts that she was having a boy. She knew it just as well as she had known she was pregnant in the first place.

There were no ultrasounds done in Merriweather at that time. Her OB/GYN, nor the hospital, had the equipment. Expectant mothers would have to drive to Houston for that. Sydney even asked her doctor if he would perform an amniocentesis, but he said the risk was greater than the justification for doing it.

Sydney knew she was being worrisome—paranoid almost—and she knew why. This child was the most perfect thing that had ever happened for Sydney and she was petrified of losing it. She just wanted to know that her baby, her precious child, was okay. So she would pray and then pray some more.

One night while Bear was working the evening shift, Sydney lay in their bed, praying. She was seven months pregnant and she could feel this precious life moving inside of her. She prayed that God would give her a healthy baby. That He would watch over him and keep him safe. Sydney began to sob and she thanked God for her blessing. She thanked Him for giving her this precious life to care for here on this earth, and she wanted to commit this precious life back to God. She told God that she would care for this baby with everything she had, and she would always know that this child belonged to Him, and He would be his Father. She meant it and felt it with every fiber of her being. Nothing could take away the pact she had made with God.

⋏

Sydney was two weeks past her due date and she was scheduled to be induced in two days on July 21st, her mother's birthday. Maeve had come to stay two weeks prior to Sydney's due date in the event Sydney went into early labor. Here Sydney was, two weeks late instead, and her mother had been there a full month. It had been nice to have her there and the anticipation of this new baby kept the mood light and easy between mother and daughter. Bear had even taken a week's vacation in anticipation of Sydney going into labor. The first night that Bear started back to work, he was on the graveyard shift and naturally, that was exactly when Sydney went into labor.

Sydney woke up at three forty-four the morning of the 20th of July. She was in labor and woke her mother.

"Mother. Mother," Sydney said, rousing Maeve from her slumber. "I'm in labor."

With a flash, Maeve was on her feet. Sydney shaved her legs and then had her mother wash her hair at the sink, washing and rinsing between contractions. They called Bear at work and the foreman made a sign with his arms of a mother cradling a child to let Bear know that his wife was having their baby. Bear rushed home and off they went to the hospital. Sydney and Bear had taken Lamaze classes, so they were both prepared and excited. By the time they arrived at the hospital, Sydney's contractions were just over one minute apart. By all accounts, she should have popped this baby right out, but after hours of labor it was clear that wasn't the plan.

Sydney huffed and puffed, and she stayed focused on her childhood teddy bear, which she had chosen as her focal point for her breathing in Lamaze class. The nurses, as well as her doctor, couldn't believe that she wanted nothing for pain. Sydney had been in hard labor since she arrived and she handled it like no one her age they had ever seen. How could this nineteen-year-old girl handle that kind of pain?

Sydney wanted to feel every bit of it. She wanted to experience the birth of her child in all its miraculous beauty, pain and all. Eleven hours from when her contractions started, Sydney was told by her doctor that her pelvis was too small for the baby to come down. Her blood pressure had skyrocketed and they would have to perform a C-section. That was fine with Sydney—whatever they needed to do to put her precious gift in her arms.

Sydney was exhausted and dozed during her surgery. They had given her a saddle block to deaden her from the waist down. Sydney was in and out, but it was the sound of the suction that made her rouse. It was loud and it alarmed her.

The anesthesiologist could see the panic in her eyes. "Don't worry, sweetie." He placed his hand on her forehead. "All is well. They are just clearing the airways. You have a beautiful baby boy."

⅄

Elijah Clement Keane was his name. Sydney loved the name. It sounded solid and strong. The English meaning for Elijah was "the Lord is my God." The name "Clement" was for her Memaw. Memaw's given name was Estella Clementine Scurlock. Memaw knew that if anyone had a girl in the family, they would likely not name her Estella or Clementine, so she had requested that any boy be named Clement in her honor. Aunt Olivia never obliged with her two youngest, who were boys, so Sydney felt it was the very least she could do. Her Memaw had meant more to her than anyone could know, and it added to the beauty of Elijah's full name. Clement meant "merciful, gentle."

Yes, Elijah Clement Keane: a beautiful name that represented love, kindness, and strength.

CHAPTER 11

Bear had been so excited and overwhelmed with emotion when Elijah was born. When the doctor told him that he had a beautiful baby boy, he broke down and cried like a baby boy himself. All of Sydney's family had been waiting with Bear and saw him have this flood of emotion. They all spoke of how beautiful it was. It wasn't often they would see a man cry, and to see him break down at the news of his newborn son was something to behold.

Something changed, though. Sydney wasn't sure of the exact day, but she had a good idea. Prior to Elijah's birth, Sydney and Bear were never too tired for love. Even throughout her pregnancy, up until her delivery, they made love regularly. Then the ball dropped. The baby came. Had they sunk into that place that Sydney had heard about? Marriage happens and children arrive, and then the love and lust go out the window? Sydney had not sunk there, but Bear had. For whatever reason, he stopped wanting her. Had it been because she had this child? Did he not see her as someone he wanted any longer? Was he burdened by the responsibility of having a family? Sydney didn't know, but it hurt her. She loved Bear and very much so.

Interestingly enough, Sydney had thought she loved Bear when they married, but it wasn't until she was three months pregnant that something came over her. She didn't know what it was exactly, but credited God. Sydney truly felt as though she had fallen in love with Bear. What then, had she felt before? The need to save herself from this wretched world she'd come to know? The need for normalcy in her life, and she had mistaken it for love? Maybe, but regardless, she loved him now and needed to fix what was broken in their marriage.

⚔

It was Valentine's Day, so she decided to venture to the wild side. Sydney was always modest growing up and she was modest as a young woman as well. But this was the day for lovers and she wanted to plan something special. She got a wild idea from a magazine and shaved her pubic hair into a heart. She rounded the top corners, and shaved a dip in the middle. With her legs together, it looked exactly like a heart. Bear would love it. She was stepping outside of her comfort zone.

"Hey, baby," she said, as seductively as she could.

"Yeah, what's up?" Bear threw his keys on the counter and rubbed his head.

She dropped her robe and stood naked in front of him. He looked her over and didn't say a word.

"See? Can't you see what I did?" Sydney asked, somewhat embarrassed by his lack of interest.

"No. What did you do, Sydney?" He was irritable and impatient.

"Look." She pointed to the heart. She felt stupid and more naked than ever.

"Aaaahhh," he said. "I see now."

She could tell that he was doing his best to backtrack. He, at the very least, cared enough not to embarrass her that badly. He went to her, held her, and they made love. It was the first time in three and a half months.

⚔

Married life, mommy life, and college life all moved forward. The clock ticked away and Sydney realized more and more that while mommy life and college life were progressing in a wonderful fashion, married life was anything but wonderful.

They were no longer in their beautiful apartment in King's Ridge. They wanted Elijah to have a yard and a dog, so they rented a small, white frame house with a chain-link fence that surrounded the yard's perimeter. It was nothing fancy, but it was home: just not the home Sydney had envisioned the day they rented it.

Sydney dreaded this day. She needed to talk to Bear and ask him why he didn't want her any more. She had just turned twenty. Sydney not only needed to know why he didn't want her, but she needed someone to hold her, whoever it was.

"Bear, we need to talk," Sydney said, as gently as possible, knowing it wouldn't matter anyway.

"What now, Sydney?" His disinterest made Sydney want to back away. But she didn't.

"Why don't you want me anymore? Do you not love me? Do you not find me attractive? What's the problem?" Sydney didn't care if she'd put him on the spot or if she sounded desperate. She was and he needed to know it.

"No, you're fine. Everything's fine." Bear leaned back on the sofa and rubbed his face. He opened his eyes and fixed them on the ceiling.

God, she hated the way he talked to her: so dismissive and condescending. "No, everything is not fine. It's not fine at all." Sydney stood over him. "We're young and at the risk of sounding ridiculous, I have needs. I can't take this anymore. I'm lonely."

He just looked at her, looked right through her. Did he feel anything at all? She doubted it.

"I'll tell you what, Bear. You think about this, and think long and hard. I can't keep doing this. We haven't had sex in months. Nothing. What am I supposed to do?" She hesitated, but then said it anyway. "I'll do something. I will. I won't be neglected."

Bear stood and walked out the front door.

CHAPTER 12

Sydney's first cousin, Lindy, was a hoot and a half. The two of them had gotten to be good friends since Sydney had moved to Merriweather, and the two of them and Elijah hit the roads often. Sydney loved the long drives on the dirt roads and she loved visiting Lindy's friends and her family on her momma's side.

Lindy was seeing a man named Corbin Mott. He was a ruggedly handsome man with a penchant for good whiskey and strong women, in that order.

"Come on, girl," Lindy said. "Get in and let's go see Corbin and Luke."

"Who is Luke?" Sydney had never heard the name in all this time.

"Luke Aldridge. He's a friend of Corbin's and they work together sometimes."

"Okay, Corbin and Luke Aldridge, here we come." Sydney hoisted Elijah on her hip, climbed in, and down the road the three went.

They pulled up onto a huge piece of property with a small white frame house at the front of it. They continued on toward the back of the property and there was a separate piece of land that was gated and fenced in. A singlewide trailer sat smack dab in the middle of it and horses ran free around it.

"Where are we?" Sydney asked, peering through her sunglasses as if she were in a foreign country.

"We're here, silly," Lindy said. "That house is Luke's parents' house," she continued, pointing at the white frame house, "and that one over there is where Luke lives."

"So he lives in a trailer behind his parents' place?" Sydney asked with a hint of sarcasm. She no more had said it then she felt badly for having done so. Sydney didn't have a snooty bone in her body and some of the best times she ever had were in her Aunt Jolene's house that wasn't as big as a matchbox.

"Yep, that's it and there's the boys," Lindy said with a grin, not taking her eyes off her man.

Lindy and Sydney pulled up as Luke was trying to rustle a pony into a separate fenced area.

"My Lord have mercy," Sydney thought, as she blocked the glare from the sun. He reminded her of the Marlboro Man. No, better. He was tall and he had jet-black hair. It was parted down the middle and flowed to his shoulders. He had a thick black mustache and crystal blue eyes, and those Wranglers and Ropers were looking mighty nice on him. He was the epitome of a cowboy and a damned good-looking one at that.

"Luke, this is my cousin, Sydney, and her little boy, Elijah," Lindy said with a twinkle in her eye. Lindy knew of Sydney's and Bear's problems, and although she didn't agree with infidelity, she wanted Sydney to be happy.

"Hey there, Sydney. How ya doin'? That's a cute little boy you got there."

"Get yourself together, Sydney!" she thought.

"Thank you very much. He's my little pumpkin." She reached out her hand to shake his, something he clearly wasn't accustomed to a woman doing. "It's nice to meet you," Sydney said, and she felt a little spark, the one that you feel when there's a connection with someone, imagined or otherwise.

She and Lindy sat on the edge of the fence line while Elijah ran and romped nearby. Corbin and Luke continued on with their cowboy ways while Sydney and Lindy sat in admiration.

"So, he seems nice," Sydney said with a lilt in her voice that almost made it sound like a question.

"Yeah, he's a good guy. He'll be a good catch for someone," Lindy said. "His wife is Marlene, as in Marlene of Marlene's Boutique in town. They're separated and getting a divorce."

"Really? How long have they been separated?" Sydney asked.

"Oh, it's been quite a while. I think neither wanted the hassle of filing and getting the attorney and figured it's just easier this way, separating and all. Regardless, they're not together and haven't been for a long time."

Just what Sydney was hoping to hear. She wondered for a moment why Bear wasn't really entering into the picture. The only picture she had of Bear at this moment was brief and it was when he walked out the door without a care of what her needs were. Sydney had wanted to fix her relationship with Bear, and had tried to get through to him up until that day that he walked out the door. Now, she didn't really care. Just like she told him…she wouldn't be neglected.

Lindy, Sydney, and Elijah frequented Luke Aldridge's property over the next couple of weeks. Nothing ever happened between Luke and Sydney, but it was pretty clear that the door was open. Someone just needed to walk through it. One day after visiting, Lindy took Elijah back to the truck and Sydney and Luke were alone in the wide-open space, sun on their faces. He went to her and stood close to her. He cradled her face in his hands and leaned down to kiss her. It felt awkward to Sydney: awkward, exciting, and somewhat surreal. She had been a devoted wife until recently and now she was crossing over. Everything was in slow motion. He leaned in; she closed her eyes, and she let it happen. She wanted it, after all. At least she thought she did.

Oh, the joys of small town life: gossip, gossip, and more gossip.

Sydney never participated in the local gossip and she had her handful of friends she kept close. First and foremost, she had Ruby back in Houston. Ruby came one weekend every single month without fail—her best friend forever. She also had her cousin, Lindy, and they were very close. Sydney also had a couple of friends her age who she had met in college in Merriweather:

Richelle Gomez and Theresa Pritchett. Richelle had a husband, Reynaldo, and both were military, so they had moved around internationally. It just so happened Reynaldo was stationed in Merriweather for the time being to handle Marine recruiting. These two were nothing like the locals and didn't know anyone to gossip about if they wanted to. Theresa, her other college friend, came from a very privileged upbringing in a small town up the road and she never participated in the local gossip mill either.

Two who did participate in the local gossip were Sydney's Granny Ewing and Aunt Jolene. Those two would talk about anyone and everyone in Merriweather, including family members. Their words could cut like a knife, but they would clean it up just as easy as you please by adding "God love her" or "bless her heart" to the end of every sentence.

So why in the world would Sydney think she would be sheltered from their words?

"Well, there she is, a runnin' the roads again, God love her," Granny would say to PawPaw.

That damn kitchen window. It was like a moving picture show. Granny always knew who was coming and going, where and when, and she would call Aunt Jolene every time she saw Sydney's car pass.

"Let me know if Sydney shows up at your place," Granny would say. "If she doesn't, she's headed to that Luke Aldridge's again. I'll tell you what right now. That Bear is a good boy. He works hard to take care of his family and look at her. Just look at her. She should be ashamed of herself. Doesn't she know the whole town's a talkin', bless her heart?"

Aunt Jolene would agree with Granny regarding Sydney, as did everyone else on her daddy's side of the family. Sydney was officially a tramp in their eyes, but Sydney didn't give a rat's ass. They didn't know what was really going on in her marriage. They never took the time to ask, nor care, and Sydney was getting what she needed.

Sydney pulled up at Luke's trailer and couldn't get out of the car. A horse had walked up to her car door, as if to greet her, and she couldn't get him to budge. This was the first time it really hit her that Luke lived right in the middle of the horse pasture, shit piles and all. The horses ran free all right, but she hadn't seen one come right up to the house. Sydney thought it was rather comical. How did she wind up here, of all places? Luke came out and shooed the horse away. She couldn't help but chuckle at how different this was compared to where she'd come from, as she unloaded Elijah from the car. Luke took Elijah from Sydney and hoisted him in the air; Elijah laughed hysterically. Luke was good with Elijah and that was important to Sydney, right along with how much he cared for her. Could she see herself living here? No. But she was happy for now. Yes, people could talk all they wanted.

⋏

Bear had been on his five days off, the normal break right after working the graveyard shift and before he started days. Sydney played the good wife and catered to his every need just to keep the peace. Today was Bear's first day back to work on the day shift and Sydney was glad of it. The phony bullshit was getting to her and the less she had to look at Bear and feel his disgust, the better.

Sydney got up early, dressed herself and Elijah, and started breakfast.

"Where are you going now, Sydney?" Bear asked.

"Nowhere. Why?" Sydney answered, with calmness in her voice that surprised even her.

Sydney had been thinking about herself so much lately, she hadn't really given Bear a thought except to know what his work schedule was for the week so that she could plan when she and Luke would see each other. She went on about what she was doing and it didn't occur to her that Bear would actually start to pay attention. He hadn't paid attention in so long. Why would he start now?

"Well, people are talkin', Sydney. I had a guy at work ask me what I thought of my wife runnin' around, fuckin' someone else." Bear had complete disdain in his voice and contempt in his eyes. Funny. Sydney knew it was because his pride and ego were hurt. Certainly not because he was hurt by her disloyalty. He didn't love her anymore.

"Well, that's a hell of a note, Bear. Some friend that is, telling you your wife is fucking someone else and you listen to that shit? Well, good for you." Sydney was nervous, but kept on. "God forbid you knock the hell out of him for saying such a thing. How dare you let someone talk about me like that?" She stared at him and held her ground, as if she meant every word she said.

"I'm just telling you what the man said, Sydney. He said it was with some Luke Aldridge character. You know anyone named Luke Aldridge?"

Sydney thought fast, but she was slipping and Bear could likely see it. "Yeah, I know a Luke Aldridge. He's friends with Corbin Mott, and I met him through Lindy." Sydney shuffled the dishes around in the sink and tried to get rid of her nervous energy. "So," she continued, "I go to someone's house with Lindy and all of the sudden we're fucking now. That's just great, Bear, just great. So now you give a shit?"

Sydney hoped that he would have, but he didn't. He grabbed his lunch box and walked out the door.

Sydney threw some things in a bag and loaded Elijah in the car. She knew she had eight hours before Bear would be home and she made good use of her time. Sydney was smart enough to know, however, that this lie was bubbling to the surface. Her short-lived fantasy was about to come to a screeching halt.

⚔

Sydney heard a car coming up Luke's drive. After what Bear had said earlier, any car coming up Luke's drive would make her nervous. Thank the Lord, it was just Lindy.

"Hey, girl," Lindy said with a seriousness that Sydney wasn't accustomed to hearing from her.

"Hey. What's up?" Sydney asked, not sure she wanted to know.

"Does Bear own a crossbow?" Lindy asked.

"Yea, he made one for hunting. He just finished it a few weeks ago. Why?" Sydney asked.

"Uh, huh." Lindy stared at Sydney. "Well, word has it that Bear's been drivin' around, lookin' for you. Supposedly he knows about you and Luke and has taken a day off from work here and there to see what you're up to."

There was a pause, but Sydney was still processing what Lindy was saying.

"Bottom line, Sydney, you'd better be careful or decide what you're goin' to do once and for all. He's drivin' around with that damn crossbow and his rifle, and it ain't huntin' season, sweetheart."

Sydney's mind was spinning. It sounded serious, yes, but it also sounded so twisted. Would Bear ever really have those thoughts? Infidelity was a bad thing, but he didn't care about her in the first place. Why would he care now, and enough to actually harm her? Sydney knew in a perfect world she should break it off with Luke right then and there and head home. But she knew what awaited her there. Nothing. She wasn't ready to give up Luke, but she knew she'd best be heading home if Bear was on the road. It would be best if she were there when he showed back up. Sydney picked up her sleeping baby, loaded him in his car seat, and headed back to the last place she wanted to be.

⅄

"Well, well. Glad you decided to grace me with your presence." Bear's tone reeked of sarcasm.

"What do you mean?" Sydney asked, doing her best not to make eye contact. "You know what? Before we get into this, Bear, let me go lay Elijah down. He's sleeping and I'd like to keep it that way if this is what we're about to get into."

Sydney took Elijah to his room and did her best to think of what she would say next. She was nervous and couldn't stop thinking about what Lindy had said.

"Now, what were you saying?" she asked as she walked back into the room.

"I'm just sayin' thank you for gracin' me with your presence. You been gracin' anyone else today?" Bear stared at her and although she wished she still had Elijah in her arms so she could run right back to where she came from, she stood motionless. He had a look about him that seemed crazy. She'd never seen him like this.

Sydney found it oddly interesting that as long as she talked to him about what her needs were, he never cared. But when she acted on what her needs were, he did. Did he really love her and just realized it, or was it all about him? She didn't know, but she didn't care. It was too little, too late.

"Bear, let's stop this and let's talk. I've tried to talk to you for so long and tell you how I've been feeling, but you never listened to me." Sydney walked to him and was gentle in her steps and her delivery in what she had to say. "I have loved you and you know that. We had a wonderful marriage and then something changed and it wasn't me. Ever since we brought Elijah home, you've had nothing to do with me. I don't understand."

Bear didn't speak, but just looked at Sydney. He never diverted his eyes from hers, and she felt that she was finally getting through to him. His guard was coming down.

She continued. "I've always been here for you to talk to and you know I want to understand. Is it me? Do you not find me attractive anymore? Is there someone else?" She didn't believe there was or he wouldn't be behaving the way he had been, but she thought she would ask and put that ball back in his court.

"No, Sydney. There is no one else." He sat down and put his face in his hands.

Sydney wasn't sure if he was crying, but she stood there and waited. He raised his head and looked out into the open room, not saying a word. She could tell he had been crying, but she stayed still and waited for him to speak.

"You know, I have a lot on my mind. That's all. I'm sorry if I haven't been the husband that I should have been, but I love you and I love Elijah."

"It's okay. It's okay." Sydney made her way to him. She sat down next to him and put her arms around him. He let her and they sat there for some time.

Sydney fixed them a nice dinner and they talked, really talked, for the first time in a long time. Sydney was honest about her feelings and Bear was too. They loved each other, but both needed something more. Sydney wasn't ready to totally throw in the towel on her marriage, but she wasn't ready to throw in the towel on Luke Aldridge either. She came clean about having seen Luke, but she kept secret how often. She dipped her toe in the water, but she wasn't about to jump headlong in the deep end.

Bear was disappointed in Sydney, but took some of the responsibility. He knew it was partly his doing. Sydney had talked over the past several months until she was blue, and he owed it to her to listen. He finally was.

It seemed so strange that she and Bear were able to amicably agree to separate. This wasn't a decision of divorce, but rather a decision to take a break from each other. They needed time apart to figure out what would be best for them and for Elijah. Bear would stay with his friend and co-worker, Chuck, and his wife, Lorraine. Sydney and Elijah would stay in the house.

The three of them had a wonderful, relaxing evening. It was more like Sydney and Bear were friends as opposed to spouses, but it was nice. There was no tension and watching Bear with Elijah made Sydney happy. He may not have been a good husband, but he was a wonderful father.

CHAPTER 13

Maeve called bright and early the very next morning. God, her timing was always perfect, whether Sydney liked it or not.

"Good mornin', darlin'," Maeve said.

"Good mornin', Momma. What's goin' on? It's early, huh?" Sydney rubbed her eyes as they adjusted to the clear beam of sunlight that had made its way through the curtains. Sydney rolled over to look at the clock. "Six thirty on a Saturday morning?!" Sydney couldn't believe it. She'd had a late night talking with Bear and she was running on about four hours of sleep.

"Oh, yeah. It's early, but I thought I would call and let you know that Georgia and I are headed that way."

"Oh really?" Sydney said as she shot out of bed. "Um, what for? I mean, I'm happy you're coming, but is everything okay?"

"Everything is fine. I just want to see my baby girl and that precious grandson of mine. Is that a crime?" Maeve said.

Sydney knew her mother, and she knew there was much more to this than met the eye. "No, Momma, that is not a crime." Sydney smiled. Even though she knew there was more to this, Sydney would still be glad to see her mother.

Three hours later, Maeve and Georgia pulled into the driveway, kicking up gravel when they stopped. They hadn't wasted any time in getting there. Both were in rare form and in a great mood.

"You come here to me, you beautiful thing, you," Georgia said, walking toward Sydney with her arms outstretched. "It's been a month of Sundays since I've seen you, young lady! Are you eating? I think I felt some ribs right about there," and she goosed Sydney with both hands.

Yes, it was good that they were there. Sydney didn't realize how much she had missed her mother, even though it had only been a couple of months since she'd visited her parents in Windmere, and she always loved that crazy Georgia. She was something else.

"Hey, darlin'," her mother said, and gave Sydney a kiss and a good momma hug. Sydney was only five three and her mother was six three in her heels. When Sydney got a hug from her mother, her face was buried right in Maeve's bosom, and today it felt especially good. It made her feel safe, and whatever her mother was doing there, really, Sydney was still glad she had come.

After Maeve and Georgia stole every ounce of sugar from under Elijah's neck, the three sat down for the visit.

"So, Sydney. Tell me about this Luke Aldridge," Maeve said, not holding back and with conviction in her voice.

"Ooooh. So that's what this is all about. You didn't come for just a visit. You came to meddle," Sydney said, half joking. Apparently, word had already made it from good ol' Merriweather, Texas all the way to Windmere.

"Now, Sydney. Don't you talk to me like that. I'm your mother and I have a right to be concerned about my daughter and my grandson," Maeve shot back.

Georgia, sitting next to Maeve, gave Sydney a tilt of her head and pursed her lips to say she fully agreed.

So did Sydney. Maeve was right. And she was likely disappointed that Sydney had not confided in her. But it was private, and Sydney was a little embarrassed. How could she really justify infidelity to her mother, even though she felt she had every reason in the world to have done it?

"I'm sorry, Mother. I really am," Sydney started.

Maeve eased herself back on the sofa and waited for Sydney to continue. She was happy that she had easily won this round with Sydney, and she was ready for the story: good, bad, and ugly.

Sydney told Maeve and Georgia how she had met Luke just a few months earlier. She also told them why she so easily slipped into a relationship with him. Maeve and Georgia didn't say a word while Sydney talked of her relationship with Bear, or lack thereof. But by their expressions, and being that they themselves were two passionate women, Sydney could tell that they understood bad decisions being made based on unfortunate circumstances.

Sydney sat forward in the dining room chair and looked at her mother. "And there's something else," Sydney said. "Bear and I have decided to separate."

"When? When did this happen, Sydney?!" Maeve was floored by the fact that her daughter had kept this from her.

"Just last night, Mother. Don't get all upset. It was just last night," Sydney replied, trying to calm the situation. "My word, I've only had four hours of sleep. It literally just happened. I was going to tell you today."

"Oh, sweetie. Come here." And Maeve sat forward on the sofa, arms outstretched to Sydney.

Sydney walked over and sat on her mother's lap and let her hold her as if she was a child, and for a moment she felt like one.

"Well, I don't know about you, Georgia, but I'd like to meet him," Maeve said.

Sydney was stunned.

"Oh, sure." Georgia shifted herself on the sofa. "I'm always up for meetin' a handsome man."

"Are you two crazy? You want to meet Luke?!" Sydney asked, not believing that the mood changed in a matter of an instant.

"Well, yes, Sydney. Of course, I want to meet this man who has found a way into my daughter's heart. If he's that special, I want to meet him." Maeve was serious. She was sorry about Sydney and Bear's separation, but she also wanted to lay eyes on the man who all this fuss was made over.

Sydney called Luke. "Hey, are you busy?"

"Ah, I was just out there tryin' to rustle up those damn horses. That one stallion keeps gettin' out of the fence and on to the McAllen's property. Gotta be their mare that he's interested in and I've got to get that fence line fixed today." He sounded like such a man's man, such a cowboy, and Sydney loved it. She'd never dated anyone quite like him.

"Well, I have a proposition for you," she said.

"Sounds interesting. And what might that be?" Luke said, and by the tone of his voice, Sydney knew what he was thinking.

"Sorry to disappoint, sweetheart, but it's not that. My mother is in town and would like to meet you."

"Your mother?"

"God, Luke. I'm sorry. This has been a whirlwind. Bear and I agreed to separate last night and my mother came to town pretty unexpectedly this morning."

Sydney waited for his reaction and was shocked when he said, "Okay. Where and what time?" Did he really care about her enough to go through the whole "meet the family" thing, or was he just being polite? Regardless, it was set and they would meet at seven o'clock that night at the Lone Star.

⋏

Sydney, Maeve, and Georgia arrived at the Lone Star at six thirty. It worked out well, as Sydney was in dire need of a stiff drink because of this meeting of sorts, and she had a little bit of time before Luke arrived.

Seven o'clock. He was right on time, of course, and he was a jaw-dropper when he walked through the door. Sydney had never been able to go anywhere with him in public; not that she hadn't seen him cleaned up, but seeing him cleaned up and at his home was different than seeing him cleaned up and making his way to their table. All eyes were on him, including her mother's and Georgia's. Sydney knew that even they were taken with his good looks.

"Luke, this is my mother, Maeve. Mother, this is Luke." Sydney watched her mother's expression. It was obvious Maeve was shocked by how handsome he really was, and it wasn't often that Sydney saw her mother somewhat speechless.

"Hello there, Maeve. Very nice to meet you." Luke took Maeve's hand.

"Very nice meeting you as well, Luke. This is my dear friend, Georgia." Maeve's words dripped with Southern charm.

Sydney almost laughed out loud at the sight of Georgia. If Georgia could have taken her shirt and pants off right then and there, she would have. The look in her eyes said "take me now," and even Luke had a knowing grin as he took her hand.

"Very nice to meet you, Georgia," Luke said, and pulled up the chair next to Sydney.

Cocktails began and Luke was gentleman enough to ask both Maeve and Georgia to dance. Maeve passed her dance ticket to Georgia so that she would have a moment alone with Sydney.

"He's very nice," Maeve said.

"Yes, and handsome, don't you think, Mother?" Sydney asked with a grin, putting her mother on the spot.

Maeve looked out on the dance floor. "Yes, and very handsome." She looked back at Sydney and they both laughed. It was a girl moment, and her mother knew exactly why Sydney would have been attracted to Luke.

The evening ended after a wonderful time, and Maeve and Georgia went on to the car to give Sydney a moment to tell Luke goodnight.

"Thank you so much, Luke. I know this was likely awkward, but my mother wanted to meet you and I figured if you were up to it—"

Before she could finish her sentence, Luke took her in his arms and kissed her. "No worries, sweet one. I was glad to do it and had a great time. Your mother is a very nice lady and that Georgia—"

Sydney interrupted him with a kiss, and wished she could take him and the kiss elsewhere. "I'd better get going. My chariot awaits." She smiled. "I'll talk to you tomorrow," she said, with a final hug and a wave goodnight.

⅄

The three ladies chatted about Luke, and the evening, all the way back to Sydney's place, just as Sydney had expected. Sydney paid the babysitter and checked on Elijah. He was sleeping soundly. He always looked so precious when he was sleeping. He always looked so precious, period. Sydney had a flash of when she and Elijah were in the hospital after Elijah was born and the nurses would come to Sydney's room to meet the mother of the gorgeous baby in the nursery. No doubt, they, too, could see the preciousness of this angel. Sydney kissed his head and walked back into the living room where Maeve and Georgia were flipping through channels on the television.

"Okay, ladies. That was a ball, but I'm headed to bed." Sydney hoped it would be that easy to make her exit.

"Just a minute, Sydney. Can't we visit for just a few minutes?" Maeve asked.

"Momma, it's one thirty in the morning and Elijah will be up in just a few hours. I'd like to take advantage of that and get some sleep. Can't this please wait until tomorrow morning?"

Those four hours of sleep from the night before had long run their course with Sydney. She was exhausted, physically and mentally.

"That's fine, but I'd like you to go to bed thinking about something and we can finish discussing it tomorrow," Maeve said.

"Oh, no. This is it. Lower the boom already," Sydney thought. "Go ahead, Mother," Sydney said, obviously irritated.

"I've been thinking, and I want you to come home with me for just a little while," Maeve said. Sydney tried to speak and her mother continued, "Let me finish. I would like for you and Elijah to come home and stay with Holden and me for a while. I think it will be good for you. You can clear your head and decide what you want to do. If you choose to divorce Bear and be with Luke, so be it. You may decide you want to work things out with Bear. But I've found that when you can physically remove yourself from a situation, it helps to see things more clearly."

Sydney was too tired to even process all of this, but she wasn't one bit surprised that this was her mother's agenda all along.

"That's fine, Momma. That's fine. We'll talk in the morning. Sweet dreams and I love y'all," and off to bed Sydney went.

"Good night, sweetheart," her mother and Georgia said in unison.

Sydney would not sleep, and she knew her mother and Georgia wouldn't either.

"Good morning!" Sydney said in her best "bright-eyed and bushy-tailed" manner.

Her mother and Georgia raised their heads from the sofa bed and it was obvious their eyes hadn't been closed long.

"Say good morning to your Meme and Aunt Georgia, Elijah."

Sydney got a kick out of watching her mother and Georgia doing their best to act as if they had gotten a good night's sleep. She knew they had likely been conspiring all night on how best to address the situation this morning.

"Good morning, sunshine," Georgia said.

Maeve pulled the covers over her head and with a grumble and sarcasm said, "I think I'm gonna puke. All this morning chipperness."

"Oh, Mother. Come on and get up. Let's make some breakfast and visit before you and Georgia head out."

That got her mother's attention. Sydney was skirting the issue at hand. Without a word, Maeve got up out of bed, got her Elijah's morning sugar, and started breakfast for everyone.

"So, Sydney," her mother started.

"Here it comes," Sydney thought and was ready. Not for an argument, but for what her mother's idea was. Normally, Sydney would have been much more defensive, but at this point, she had enough sense to know she didn't have the answers and maybe her mother was right. Maybe she did need time. Her conversation with Bear had confused her; she still wanted Luke, but not for a husband; and although she didn't want to leave, a break might be best.

"Yes, Mother," Sydney said, ready to discuss her options.

"Now, I want you to listen and not interrupt. Okay?" Her mother knew Sydney, and she was ready for her defensiveness, although it wasn't going to happen this time.

"Okay," Sydney said, surprising her mother.

"You and Elijah come home with me. Holden would love it. You wouldn't have to stay more than a week or two, but I think that would be long enough for you to clear your head. You need to be able to make a sound decision. This is, after all, your future and Elijah's future."

Sydney knew her mother was right. And even if Maeve did have her own agenda, Sydney could use the break, and going home for an extended stay sounded perfect.

"Okay," Sydney said.

"Okay what?" blurted Maeve, as she whirled around with egg flying off the spatula. She had never anticipated Sydney agreeing with her so easily.

"Okay. We're coming," Sydney answered. "I think you're right, and a week or two at yours and Holden's would be nice. I do need the break and Elijah would have a ball, I know."

Maeve grinned from ear to ear, looking more like the Cheshire Cat than Sydney's mother. "Well, that's it then. Go ahead and get the car loaded with yours and Elijah's things while I finish breakfast and clean up, and then we'll hit the road."

"What's the rush?" Sydney asked. "I still need to talk to Bear, and I'd like to talk to Luke about it as well. Elijah and I can come up this afternoon."

Maeve sat down next to Sydney and put her hand on Sydney's leg. "Sweetheart, there is no need to postpone this and there is no need for you to bring your car. Let's all ride together and I'll bring you home when you're ready to come back. While you're there, you can use my car for whatever you want." Maeve had a serious look and was not breaking eye contact with Sydney.

Sydney didn't want to ruin the moment, that feeling of "everything is going to be fine," so she agreed. But as always, she knew her mother like the back of her hand. She knew that Maeve wanted to control this situation, as she did everything else. And she knew more than anything that Maeve didn't want her to have her own car in the same stomping grounds she had escaped after high school. Maeve didn't want Sydney to be tempted by another life and leave Elijah, as she had left Sydney all those years before.

Sydney understood her mother's concern. Maeve giving up Sydney for those few years was something she'd never forgiven herself for, even after all this time. She was petrified Sydney would make the same mistake. Sydney went along with the idea to ease her mother's concern, but she knew herself better than that. She would never do to her child what had been done to her. She loved him too much.

Sydney called Bear at work and told him of her plans for her and Elijah to head to Windmere. This would be a little break from Merriweather and a nice visit with her family. When she and Bear had spoken two nights before, it was perfect. Why would they argue now? Why mess that up? He didn't. He hurriedly agreed. Besides, he would like to sleep in his house, in his bed, and he needed the break as much as she did.

She then called Luke. He was very understanding, and was easy to agree as well. Was it because he truly was that unselfish and understanding, or did he need the break just as much? He was the "other man," and while he never acted as if it bothered him to be seeing a married woman, he could have been feeling pressures Sydney was too selfish to notice.

Sydney packed her mother's car with her and Elijah's things and they hit the road. The three ladies laughed and cut up the whole way. It felt as though a hundred pounds had been lifted from Sydney's shoulders, and for the first time in a long time, she was excited about what the future held.

CHAPTER 14

The excitement of being back home in Windmere for her "emotional retreat" wore off the first week. It was life as usual and it made the realities of Sydney's life sink in that much more. A full week and Sydney was no closer to clearing her head than when she walked in the door.

Maeve and Holden worked all day and Sydney would have dinner fixed when they got home. She would have taken Elijah to the park—something, anything—but she had no car. She was stuck and it wasn't just physically, but emotionally. She was supposed to figure out what she wanted by looking at four walls every day? It made her angry with herself and furious with her mother. She would not be manipulated like this again.

⁜

"Mother, can I use the car, please?" She felt as though she were sixteen again and there was nothing pleasant about that.

"Where are you going?" Maeve asked.

"Does it matter?" Sydney thought. "Ruby invited me to go dancing at that new club on Shaefer. I'd like to go if you can watch Elijah for me. I won't be too late." Sydney held her breath, hoping she would get the pass to go and blow some of the energy that was about to boil over.

"What is 'not too late,' Sydney?" Maeve asked, and wasn't doing a good job at all controlling her tone.

"Mother, can I go or not?" Sydney was angry and it was in her voice. "Remember, I'm not a child. I'm grown, I have a son, and if I want to stay out until the club closes, so what."

Maeve knew that Sydney had a point, so she decided she would save her aces for later, when she needed them more. "That's fine, Sydney. Just be careful and…you know."

Sydney did know. No drugs and no cavorting around with the scum that she used to run around with. Yes, Sydney knew, and she knew she would never go there again. Maybe it hadn't been long enough for her mother to feel secure in that, but Sydney knew. Never again.

⚓

Sydney got home right on time and eased up the stairs as quietly as she could.

"Sydney?" her mother called out in a loud whisper.

"Yes, ma'am?" Sydney answered.

"Come here. Did you have a good time?" Maeve had a better tone to her voice compared to the one Sydney had left hours earlier.

Sydney tiptoed into Maeve and Holden's bedroom. Elijah was sandwiched between them, sound asleep, with his arm thrown over the back of Holden's neck. It was precious. Sydney walked over to the bed and lay across the foot of it. She could tell her mother hadn't shut one eye and wouldn't until she knew Sydney was home safely.

"Yes, actually. I had a great time," Sydney said. "Ruby was a blast as always, and it was so great to see her. We ran into some high school friends and, don't worry, it's not anyone you would know and no one I used to run around with."

Maeve gave a visible sigh of relief.

Sydney continued. "One guy I saw, who I haven't seen since I was a junior, was Nate Tattinger. He and Laird were good friends in high school and played football together."

That was all Maeve needed to hear. If he was a friend of Laird Alberich's, he was a friend of Maeve's. Maeve had always loved Laird and thought he was a fine young man, even though he had gotten Sydney pregnant. As always, Maeve understood the bigger issues in life and she had chalked Laird and Sydney up to teenage puppy love and an unfortunate circumstance in the end.

"Well, that sounds like fun. I'm glad that you and Ruby had such a good time." Maeve nestled down into her pillow and turned off her lamp. "Come give me a hug. I love you, Sydney."

"I love you too, Momma." She hugged and kissed her goodnight.

⅄

Sydney was on her third week at her parents' house and she'd never been more acquainted with MTV. She didn't like that her mother was clearly getting her way, but she also wasn't ready to go back to Merriweather. She wasn't happy anywhere. She didn't want to be in Windmere and she didn't want to be in Merriweather, so where the hell did she want to be?

Sydney knew it was Bear's five days off on his shift change, so she called him. For the first time since being in Windmere, she felt as though she might miss him.

"Hey. How are you?" she said.

"Well, hello stranger," Bear said.

It was good to hear his voice. He sounded good, and happy to hear from Sydney as well.

"How is everything? How's my boy?" he said.

"Oh, Elijah is great. He's busy as a bee and into everything, of course. You want to talk to him?"

Before Bear could answer, Sydney had summoned Elijah. "Elijah, come talk to Daddy. Come here, Daddy's on the phone."

Elijah hadn't started to walk until he was fourteen months old and when he did, he did it on his toes. It was the cutest thing Sydney had ever seen, and at almost two years old, he was still on them. Elijah ran on his tippy-toes over to the phone.

"Daddy. Daddy." Elijah squealed with laughter when he heard his daddy's voice.

"How's my big man? Whatchu been doin', boy?"

Elijah squealed some more and off he ran.

"Well, he's off and running," Sydney said. She had her ear to the phone when Bear had been talking to Elijah. No matter what she felt or didn't feel for Bear, it made her heart feel good to know that Elijah had a daddy who loved him, no matter what. "So, it's your five days off, right?" Sydney asked.

"Yes, it is and I was thinkin' of comin' to Windmere. I'd love to see you and Elijah, if that's okay with you, and I need to see my folks."

Sydney was excited. Maybe she was lonely more than anything else, but she did miss him and it would not only be good for Elijah, but likely good for her. "That sounds perfect. When will you be here?" She tried not to sound overly excited, even though she felt it.

"I'll head on in tonight, visit with the folks, and how about if I come over to your parents' place in the mornin'? Maybe you and Elijah and I can go do somethin'."

"That sounds perfect. Call me in the morning when you have a definite time and we'll be ready."

⚓

Bear walked into Sydney's parents' house and he looked rested and happy. He was relaxed and at ease with her. Bear was definitely happy, no doubt about it. But something was different about him this day. Sydney was stunned at his appearance, but she didn't allude to that at all.

"Well, you look great." She smiled, and knew he would pick up on the insinuation that single life wasn't treating him so badly.

He grinned and paid her the same compliment, but she knew it wasn't true.

Elijah ran to his daddy, arms flailing the entire way.

"There's my man! How are you, buddy?" Bear picked Elijah up and kissed him. Bear took a moment to look long and hard at Elijah. Then, they sat down on the floor and Bear played with Elijah for a while.

There was definitely something different about Bear. The most obvious thing was that he was dressed differently. Not that it was that big of a deal. People change, their tastes change and that was okay. But this was different and outside of the normal scope of things, in Sydney's mind anyway. He didn't seem like the same person she had left in Merriweather, and she noticed it more and more during their visit. He was tanned and dressed in tight jeans, a bright green tank top, and he had a blue bandana tied around his neck.

Sydney was accustomed to being around gay men. Her cousin, Hayden, was gay and "out," and Maeve had several gay male friends. Sydney's immediate thought was that Bear looked gay, but she knew it couldn't be that. Bear was out of the loop enough to think that he was dressed "cool," not "gay." This wasn't cool to Sydney. Whatever it was, it was strange and what Sydney expected out of this visit, she didn't get.

They ended their visit that afternoon and Sydney was more unclear about going home than she had been. The Bear she was considering going home to was vastly different from the Bear she'd seen this day. This Bear was someone she felt she didn't really know.

⚔

Sydney was coming up on her seventh week in Windmere. My God, how did all of this happen? How could something that felt so right and good have her feeling so bogged down and unhappy? There was nothing and no one that interested Sydney, and she wondered what she was still doing there. So much had happened in just these few weeks, and it really drove home the fact that she was to never live in this town again. Sydney mulled over each incident and each was another point on the scorecard of her needing to go home.

One incident was when Phoebe had come over to see Sydney and Elijah. Phoebe had been one of Sydney's bridesmaids and they had gone to high school together. Phoebe was a cheerleader at the school that Sydney got kicked out of, but they were best friends for a time and did drugs together back in the day. Phoebe was thin and gaunt now. She had always been beautiful and she got a job for a high-powered stylist in Dallas right out of high school. She was the administrative assistant to the fashion expert, and worked her way up to an executive position. This thin, gaunt look of Phoebe's wasn't her trying to emulate the filthy rich who graced the pages of

Town and Country. No, she was on cocaine and Sydney knew it. Phoebe was so into it, she couldn't even look Sydney in the eye. That was the one and only visit Sydney and Phoebe had. It was clear their lives were drastically different and Sydney prayed that Phoebe would find her way back before she fell too deep.

Then there was Nate Tattinger. "What the fuck, Nate Tattinger?" Sydney thought, every time his sorry ass entered her mind. When she first arrived back in Windmere, she would go dancing with Nate and they would have fun, there was no doubt about that. Sydney had kissed Nate a few times, but that was all she had done and she really didn't even want to do that. After a few weekend nights of hitting the dance floor with Nate, Sydney was at Nate's apartment and they were watching television. They sat side by side on the sofa. Out of nowhere, Nate eased his body on top of Sydney and began to kiss her. He shifted his body and Sydney was underneath him. Nate wasn't a tall guy, but he was built like the trunk of a tree. He was stout and strong and would be like hitting a wall, should you run full speed into him. He took Sydney's hands into his left hand and held them over her head. She couldn't move and she couldn't believe it because she was strong, and knew it. He then began tickling her with his right hand, but Sydney could tell by the crazy, disconnected look in his eyes that tickling her wasn't what was foremost on his mind. The more Sydney moved, the more Nate pressed against her. She stopped squirming and just looked at him. She couldn't have been more than two to three inches from his face. "What are you doing, Nate?" Sydney asked calmly, knowing there was nothing left to do. He stopped, gave a nervous, bizarre chuckle, and raised himself off Sydney. She knew exactly what he was doing and she knew that she was fortunate that he had snapped back into reality. He never called her after that night and Sydney was thankful for that. Regardless, Sydney would never have seen him again. She knew that he knew he was guilty as charged for what he had intended.

Then, there was the night that Georgia's three sons wanted Sydney to go out with them to listen to live music. Sydney had asked her mother to watch Elijah that evening, but she wouldn't do it. Maeve felt that Sydney had been going out too much… "Too much," meaning every Saturday night. It was total bullshit to Sydney. She didn't go out too much. She and Elijah were stuck in that house every day with no car and all she wanted was her Saturday nights to decompress. Well, this was one time that Sydney was glad her mom declined to baby-sit Elijah. The phone rang a little after three o'clock that next morning. That was never a good sign. Sydney was roused from her sleep. "Oh no!" Sydney heard her mother yell. Sydney ran into her parents' room. Maeve and Holden were sitting upright in the bed and her mother began shaking her head back and forth with a dreadful look on her face. Sydney stood still and didn't move until her mother hung up the phone. "It's the boys, Georgia's boys," her mother said. "Brett lost control of the car. They hit a pole and Royce was ejected from the car." Her mother took a deep breath and started to cry. "They've rushed him to the emergency room, but as it looks now, he's paralyzed from the chest down."

"Please, no!" Sydney thought. She couldn't believe it. She was friends with all three of them, but closer to Brett. "What about Brett and Marcus? Are they okay?" Sydney asked.

"Brett was driving and thrown from the car too, but he's okay. He was able to get up and get to Royce. Royce was still conscious in the road, but couldn't move. Marcus was very banged up and wedged between the passenger seat and the dashboard. Royce was in the back seat." Maeve curled into a ball, sobbing.

Sydney stood, stunned. She felt for her friends and couldn't believe this was happening. But she also thought about how she could have been in that car. Where would she have been sitting? Would she have been in the front seat with Brett? Would she have been in the back seat? She couldn't stand to think about it. It was too much to even imagine, but the reality of it would resonate.

Yes, it was time to go home and Sydney felt it more and more. There was nothing for her in Windmere but the ticking of the clock and the realization that she hadn't progressed one iota.

⅄

Sydney hadn't heard from Bear in a little over a week. He had been good about calling to check on Elijah, but his calls became more and more infrequent. That was a pretty clear indication that he was busy with other things, or someone else.

Sydney had given her life, and Elijah's, a lot of thought and she knew their current way of living could not continue. She needed to pick herself up by her bootstraps and get on with it. She called Bear. She wasn't really sure what she would say, but her fingers dialed the phone as if they had made up their own minds.

"Hello?" Bear sounded as if he was expecting a phone call, but it wasn't Sydney's.

"Bear? This is Sydney," she said.

"Oh, yeah, hey." His words ran together and it sounded as if someone had let the air out of his sail, and it was apparently Sydney.

"Are you busy?" Sydney tried to act as though she hadn't noticed the disappointment in his voice.

"Well, I was waiting for a phone call. I'm going to be heading out shortly. Is everything okay?" Bear asked, but he was disinterested and Sydney could tell.

"Everything is fine. I just wanted to talk to you. Whose call are you waiting for and where are you going?" Sydney didn't care that she was being nosy. She didn't have much time and she felt it, and after all, they were still married.

"I met someone," he said.

Instantly, whether accurate or not, it felt as though the boat she thought she had securely docked was slipping away.

"You met someone?" Sydney didn't care how she sounded. She was shocked.

"Yeah, actually. I did." Sydney could tell Bear was somewhat uncomfortable saying it, but he also had an ease and arrogance to his voice. She knew why. It was because of what she had done.

Sydney didn't waste any time. She had been thinking long and hard about what she should do. Not necessarily what she wanted to do, but what she should do. She truly felt that it was her responsibility as Elijah's mother to give her marriage another shot. If all worked out, they were all the better for it. If it did not, at least she could say she tried.

"Bear, please don't think I'm saying this just because you're telling me you met someone. Please. I have been thinking about this for quite a while, and a lot lately."

She paused and hated how she was putting her feelings and vulnerability out there for him to see, and possibly take advantage of.

"I think we owe it to Elijah to give our marriage another shot. There is a lot of water under the bridge and I know that. But if we both commit to trying, and really try, we can maybe make this work."

There was a deafening silence that seemed to last forever.

"You mean to tell me that you have now decided that you want to come home and make this work? Is that what you're saying, Sydney? Is that what you're saying?" Bear sounded frustrated more than anything, but Sydney could hear the mix of emotion in his voice: part anger, relief, angst, and love. He sounded confused and Sydney knew it was a mess.

"Yes, Bear. That's what I'm saying. The timing may be off, considering you're waiting to hear from your new girlfriend, but yes, that is what I am saying."

Sydney was pissed. She knew what she had done was wrong, but it was his fault in the first place and she kept telling herself that. He was an ass to her before, and she needed to keep that in her mind's eye. He was lucky she would even want to give it another try.

"But one thing, Bear. We're not coming home if you are going to continue to see this woman or anyone else, for that matter. If we come home, it's the real deal. This isn't a trial run. We need to work on us and be a family again. You have my commitment as long as I have yours."

"What day are you planning on coming home?" he asked, without another word.

"I'll see you Saturday." Sydney hung up the phone.

There was no romantic interlude that had precluded this reunion: just a plan and a commitment.

Chapter 15

Maeve delivered Sydney and Elijah back to Merriweather that Saturday morning. Sydney had thought she would have missed it more than she did, but when they pulled into the driveway, she felt more sad about her situation than happy to be home. She would be okay, though. Sydney was a strong one. Besides, she had made a commitment to Bear, for Elijah and for herself, and she was sticking to it and giving one hundred ten percent.

Sydney got out of her mother's car and unloaded Elijah from the back seat. Her mother was getting their things out of the trunk when Bear walked out onto the porch. Sydney noticed that something was missing.

"Where is my car, Bear?" Sydney wondered if he was having something done to it. Maybe he was getting it cleaned up for her.

"I sold it. I couldn't keep on with the notes. No one was driving it and I didn't know if you were even coming back," Bear answered, and he was nervous in even saying it. He was smart enough to know that Sydney would be livid.

"You did what?!" Sydney yelled, and she didn't care how it sounded. She wasn't back home to be treated like shit again. She was planting her feet firmly in the ground. She wouldn't be a doormat and she wouldn't be treated like the weak wives of Bear's friends.

"Where is my fucking car?! Who did you sell it to?" she demanded to know.

"I sold it to Chuck and Lorraine." Bear stood motionless, knowing that Sydney was about to have a meltdown.

Sydney handed Elijah to her mother and asked that they go in the house. She knew her mother was likely shitting her pants as well because had Sydney taken her car to Windmere, this little situation would have never happened.

"Great. You sold it to Chuck and Lorraine. I'm sure they fucking loved that." Sydney glared at Bear and wished she were anywhere but right back where she was.

"So, where's the money, Bear? Once you paid the car off, where's the rest of the money? Because you sure didn't send me jack shit in Windmere."

He dropped his head and felt as worthless as he should have. "I sold it for the payoff, Sydney. They wanted a new car and I needed to get out from under it."

Sydney couldn't believe it.

"So, that self-righteous bitch is driving around in my car and probably getting her rocks off every time she starts the engine." Sydney knew that Lorraine wasn't her biggest fan. Sydney had always been stronger than any of Bear's friends' wives, and while they would get together occasionally, Sydney felt as though she had to fake the fact that they actually had anything in common.

"So, now what?" Sydney continued. "I had no car in Windmere, thanks to the bright idea of my mother, and I come home and have no car."

Then it occurred to Sydney. How could he have sold it? Her name was on the title.

"Wait a minute. Wait just a damn minute. How did you sell it? My name was on the title. How did you manage that one?" Sydney waited, but didn't have a clue what his answer could be.

"I forged your signature." Bear put his hands in his pockets and looked away, as if something was going to drop from the sky to save him.

Sydney acted as though she never heard those words. What could she do, after all? Nothing short of pressing charges on her husband for forgery, and that wasn't an option at this point. She walked past him on the porch and stopped long enough to say, "You get me a car. I don't know how you're going to do it, Bear, but figure it out because I'm not sitting in this house all day, every day, waiting for my man to come home, with an apron tied around my ass. I'm not doing it!"

She walked in the house and shot a look at her mother. No words needed to be spoken. Maeve knew and felt responsible. Maeve also knew that it was likely in everyone's best interest that she hightail it right back to Windmere.

"Darlin', I'm sorry," Maeve said.

"That's fine, Momma. It's just fine." Sydney did everything she could not to say more.

"Okay. Well…I love you," Maeve said. There really wasn't much else to say. What was done was done. "I'll call and check on you and Elijah just as soon as I get back home."

Sydney hugged and kissed her mother, and Maeve walked past Bear without a word.

So, here she was. Welcome home, Sydney. Home, sweet home.

⬩

Bear pulled up in a car that was approximately the length of the block. Sydney wanted to laugh, but it was too pathetic to waste the energy. He had sold her brand-new Mazda 626 for the payoff, and pulled back up in a tank that was no less than ten years old.

Sydney wasn't a car snob and a means of transportation was a means of transportation. It was certainly better than walking. However, Bear wasn't getting away with this. He sold her new car and expected Sydney to settle for this?

"What is that?" Sydney asked, with disgust in her voice.

Bear stepped out of the car. Sydney could tell by the look on his face that he knew it was nothing to be proud of. He didn't leap out with excitement about her "new" ride. He crawled out, knowing full well what she would say, but he was apparently willing to take that chance.

"Bear. What is that?" Sydney repeated.

"It's a car, Sydney. What the hell does it look like?" Bear shot back defensively.

"It looks like a fricking tank. That's what it looks like. It's as long as this block, Bear."

Both stood looking at each other, but Bear didn't speak.

"I don't know what you're going to do with it, unless you plan on driving it yourself," Sydney continued. "If that's the case, I'm more than happy taking your truck. But for the record, I'm not setting foot in that car."

Bear looked at Sydney and she could tell he was angry. Really angry.

"What the hell? I get you a car and you won't drive it?" he asked.

"That's right. You should have never forged my signature and sold my car to your friends for the payoff. And now you expect me to drive a car that you won't even drive. Will you, Bear? Will you take the car and give me your truck?"

He was pissed and he knew Sydney was right. He had messed up by forging her signature, if nothing else.

"Fine. I'll take the son of a bitch back to Hubert's. Thank God he's your kin, or I may not be able to get the money back."

Sydney didn't know he had bought it from Hubert and quite frankly, she didn't care. He needed to take it back to wherever it had come from.

⚔

The phone rang the next morning and it was Sydney's Memaw.

Sydney was so happy to hear her Memaw's voice. Memaw had always been the "constant" in Sydney's life. No matter where Sydney lived or with whom, no matter what whirled around her, her Memaw had loved Sydney from the day she was born and was always, always there for her. Sydney and her Memaw had a special bond. Sydney was like a cross between a daughter and a granddaughter to Memaw, likely because she had lived with her, and it made their relationship that much more special. And Memaw had often told the story of when they brought Sydney home from the hospital. She said that she was in an unhappy time in her life. Papa was sleeping around with Lillian Boudreaux, Memaw's best friend, and it was a very difficult time for Memaw, of course. The one thing that Memaw looked forward to during that time was the birth of Sydney. Memaw told Sydney that the day they brought her home from the hospital, Sydney's hand had touched Memaw's face and Memaw knew right then and there that everything would be all right. And it was.

"Memaw! What are you doing? I'm so glad you called!" Sydney said. She wanted to cry. If anything could make her feel like all was right with the world, it was her Memaw. She never sugarcoated anything. She was direct, smart, and a problem-solver.

"I spoke with your mother yesterday and she told me about Bear and what he did with your car," Memaw said. "What a little son of a bitch." Yes, that was her Memaw, saying it like it was. "I'm getting you a dependable car, Sydney. I'm not going to worry about my granddaughter and great-grandson not having a dependable means of transportation." Not giving Sydney a moment to say a word, she continued, "Now, here's what we're going to do. I'll keep the car in my name. That way, shit-ass can't sell it out from under you. I'll give you time to get back on your feet, and in three months you can start the payments directly to me. Once the car is paid for, I'll sign it right over to your name. How does that sound?"

"Memaw, I don't even know what to say," Sydney said.

"Oh. And one more thing and I want you to listen, Sydney. I'm having it insured and you are the only one on the policy. I'm not putting Bear on the policy at all. He is to never drive your car."

That was Memaw personified. She had a deal for Sydney, but it was by her rules and that was just the way it was.

"Yes, Memaw. I understand."

Bear had been an ass and Memaw was just letting him know that he didn't win this round.

Memaw came to Merriweather, as she did regularly, to stay at the farm and to see her mother, Mama Scurlock, and the rest of the family. Memaw didn't take Sydney with her to buy Sydney's new car during her visit because she knew Sydney all too well. Sydney would likely want something sporty like the car she had previously. So, Memaw went on her own and pulled up to Sydney's house in the new car that she felt would be best for Sydney and Elijah: a beige

Buick Regal with a brown top. No, this wasn't a car that Sydney would have picked for herself, but she was as happy as a clam in the sunshine to have it.

"Memaw! Look at it!" Sydney was excited and wanted Memaw to know how much she appreciated her.

"You like it?" Memaw asked, with a smile that showed she was proud of what she had done for her granddaughter.

"I love it!" Sydney said, giving Memaw a hug and kiss as she ran to the car and climbed in. Sydney sat in it, looking over everything and knowing how blessed she was. She was loved beyond measure and she knew it.

Bear pulled up behind the new car. Memaw looked at him with little to no expression. He might as well have been an expected piece of dog shit on her Farragamos. He got out of his truck and walked over with a grin on his face. Sydney was glad to see a smile and not a pissy attitude, but she knew he was smiling not because Sydney had a car, but because he didn't have to buy it.

"Whoa. This is beautiful," Bear said, hugging Memaw.

"I'm glad you like it, Bear," Memaw replied, as politely as she could.

Sydney knew what her Memaw was also thinking... "Too bad you'll never get to drive it, you shit."

CHAPTER 16

Sydney and Elijah had been home in Merriweather for one full week when Sydney decided to register for another semester at the junior college. She had taken off a few months from her classes and she had three months before she needed to start making payments on her new car, so this was a perfect time to squeeze in some more school credits. Besides, it would keep her focused on what she had committed to, and that was making her marriage work. She didn't really give Luke Aldridge a thought. She knew they were long over because she never received the first call from him when she and Elijah were in Windmere. Funny thing was that she really didn't worry about it. They were over before they even got started, and she knew that now.

Sydney wondered who all knew she was back at home. She hadn't contacted her dad, Forrest, or any other member of his side of the family. They had, after all, talked about her like a dog before she left, so why contact them now? Did they really deserve her? Sydney felt she had begged for their unconditional love her whole life and she didn't want to do it any longer.

She did have Maeve's side of the family, however. Every single one of them, and they did love Sydney unconditionally. Maeve's side of the family was so close to the point of being unique and that extended out to distant relatives. They had a family reunion every year right there in Merriweather, and they were about to celebrate their fiftieth reunion in just a couple of years. Sydney was proud of her heritage and how her ancestors had kept the family connection alive, and she loved the reunions. She loved her family. She knew if nothing else, she had their love and their support.

Sydney and Bear seemed to be merely coexisting, but Sydney stayed focused on settling in and she was ready to get her life back into the swing of things, to include married life. She registered for her classes at Merriweather Community College and registered Elijah in Love's Door Day Care. It felt good to feel productive, as though she was accomplishing something. Sydney enjoyed her classes; Elijah loved Love's Door and everyone there loved him.

It was no wonder. Elijah was such a beautiful child, inside and out. There was barely a moment that he didn't have a smile on his face, and was laughing. He was a happy child and his inner light shone brightly. He was well-mannered and Sydney taught him to respect adults, just as she had been taught, saying "thank you" and "yes ma'am and no ma'am, yes sir and no sir." He was perfection and she loved him more than her own life.

Sydney tried to stay focused on her classes, but things at home were strained, to say the least. She was still glad that she had come home, however. Marriage was never said to be easy and she was actually proud of herself for hanging in there. Bear was still Bear and had no interest in Sydney, but she kept her word and that included keeping her pants on and staying faithful to her husband. At least she was doing what she thought was right.

One day after classes, Sydney picked Elijah up early at the day care. He wasn't in his room and it scared Sydney. His teacher saw Sydney frantically looking through the kids in the class and said, "Oh, Miss Sydney. Elijah is in Miss Gabby's room. She sneaks in here and gets that precious angel every day."

Sydney smiled and took a deep breath of relief as she headed down the hall to Miss Gabby's class. Sydney didn't know who Miss Gabby was, but thought it sweet that someone had taken such a liking to Elijah.

Sydney rounded the corner and recognized Gabby immediately. She was her distant cousin. She knew Gabby from the family reunions. Gabrielle was her given name and she had a voice like a songbird. Sydney loved listening to her sing at the family gatherings every year. Sydney had always suspected that Gabby was gay. She just had that quality about her, the tomboy she was. But Sydney was never quite sure.

"Well, hello there!" Sydney said. "You may not recognize me, but you and I see each other at the reunions. I'm your cousin. Well, somewhere down the line." They both laughed.

Their family reunions were so huge they literally had it at a hotel in Merriweather so that anyone who didn't live locally could get a room and stay the weekend. The reunions always lasted a full weekend. Most of the family would arrive Friday night and those who wanted to party could party together in their rooms. And Sydney's mother and Gabby's oldest brother, Harold, were the party. They would have a ball in Maeve's room and looked forward to every year when they could do it again. Maeve's room was definitely the place to be for the more party-oriented family members, so she made sure to always get the suite. Saturdays were when the rest of the family would arrive and the day was filled with swimming and so much fun for the kids and the adults. Saturday nights, family would gather and sing and reminisce. That was where Sydney would see Gabby and listen to her sing. Sunday was the day that everyone had the big family reunion meal and would head home that afternoon.

"Yes, somewhere down the line," Gabby said. "Of course, I remember you. Let's figure this out," she continued. Sydney and Gabby talked about how they were related and realized they were actually fourth cousins, once removed, but Sydney just called it fifth cousins. Regardless, it was plenty far up the family tree.

It was nice visiting with Gabby. She had a wonderful personality and this was the first time that Sydney had actually ever spoken with her.

"I hear you're in love with my little boy," Sydney said with a smile.

"Oh my gosh, I love this baby!" Gabby scooped Elijah up and gave him a squeeze and a kiss on the cheek. "I had no idea he belonged to you. I just knew he was the sweetest thing I'd ever seen, so I'd sneak him in here with me during the day. I hope you don't mind."

Sydney was glad that if someone was getting attached to her Elijah, they were yet another family member. "Of course not," Sydney said. "I'm glad he's in here with you. How old are these kiddos in your class?" Sydney asked.

"They're all three years old," Gabby answered.

"Well, Elijah is two, so as long as the other kids treat him well, which I'm sure you see to that, and he's learning things, I'm great with him being in your class."

"Great," Gabby said and they gave each other a hug.

Sydney left with Elijah, but she couldn't stop thinking about Gabby. Sydney had never given Gabby a thought unless they were at the reunion. That wasn't the case today. Gabby was a beautiful young woman. She was one year younger than Sydney, which made her twenty years old. Gabby had dark brown hair to her shoulders, parted down the middle and feathered on the sides. She had a full mouth and eyelashes so thick and long that it looked as if she had glued falsies to her lids. Sydney wasn't sure what this feeling was that she had about or toward Gabby, but there was definitely something exciting about her.

Memaw called Sydney a week before the reunion. Memaw was in charge of coordinating the entire event and was great at delegating to those she needed for assistance. "Sydney, I need you and Gabby to help with something," Memaw said.

Sydney had told Memaw about Gabby slipping Elijah into her class daily, not aware that he was her family member, and Memaw had gotten the biggest kick out of it. If there was anything in this world that made Memaw happy, it was family connecting.

"Okay, what do you need?" Sydney asked.

"I need you and Gabby to sit at the front of the hospitality room at the hotel on Saturday and make out name tags for everyone as they arrive and register. Now, you'll need to be on time, Sydney. Don't be late."

This was one of Memaw's pet peeves and the biggest of all. It drove her crazy if anyone was even five minutes late, which just added to the fact that Memaw was a perfectionist.

"I'll be on time and I'll pass the message on to Gabby. Not to worry," Sydney assured her.

"Okay then. I mean it, Sydney. You and Gabby be at the hotel Saturday morning to help me with this. Ten o'clock will be fine."

"Okay, Memaw. I'll see you Friday night also, right?"

"That's right, but we're talking about Saturday morning right now, Sydney." Memaw was a businesswoman, an entrepreneur, and she didn't have time for babble. She wanted to be clear as a bell when getting her point across and she hit her mark every time.

"Okay. I love you," Sydney said and the two hung up.

"Okay, girls," Memaw said, as she set Sydney and Gabby up at the table. "Here are the name tags, the pens you need, and here is a list for everyone to sign as they come in. I need that so we know exactly how many are here. It helps when planning for next year."

"No problem. We've got it, Memaw." Sydney gave her Memaw a wink.

"Yes, Aunt Estella. We've got it," Gabby chimed in. Gabby and Memaw were second cousins, but Gabby called her "Aunt Estella" because Memaw was first cousins with Gabby's daddy, Harlan, and the same age as he. Gabby also had a healthy respect for Memaw, as did everyone in the family.

Memaw knew Gabby was a spitfire and liked that about her. She gave a smile back to Gabby. "Don't try to butter me up, Gabby Oates. You two stay focused and behave yourselves. I'll have Elijah with me," and off she went with Elijah on her hip to handle the rest of the details.

Gabby and Sydney handled their duties that day and managed to visit intermittently. Being family meant the ice had already been broken and now it was just a matter of getting to know each other better. They were comfortable with each other and knew that they had both acquired a new friend in the other.

Sydney's semester was over and it was time to start making the car notes to Memaw. She was also tired of living in the house she and Bear had been cohabiting in. She needed something new. Brand-new apartments had been built in King's Ridge. They were gorgeous and very contemporary. Sydney was ready to move and she felt like somewhere nice, bright, and airy was just what the doctor ordered. Sydney approached Bear about it, and he cared whether they moved or not about as much as he did about anything else she presented to him. Nothing really mattered to Bear.

Sydney got a job as a receptionist at a small law firm in downtown Merriweather. She made four dollars per hour and although it wasn't a lot of money, it was over minimum wage, it supplemented their income, and allowed her the ability to live where she wanted. They gave notice at their small, white framed house and headed up town.

⏶

"Look, Bear! Isn't it beautiful?!" Sydney was so excited and nothing, not even Bear, was going to bring her down. To Sydney's surprise, he was actually somewhat excited himself. Maybe he needed something new, too, and this would be a welcomed change.

"Wow. This is beautiful. I see what you mean now," Bear said.

Sydney had tried to get him to go with her to look at the apartment before they moved in, but he knew that if Sydney wanted to move badly enough, that's exactly what would happen, so it didn't really matter whether he was all the way on board or not.

"Yeah, this is really, really nice," Bear continued, as he made his way through the hallway and on to the bedrooms on each end.

"Look at this." Sydney opened the French doors in the dining room. They led to the patio that also had a door coming from the master bedroom. It was hard not to be excited about how beautiful it was, how new it was. They would be the first to live in this unit and it felt like a fresh start, again.

Bear walked to Sydney and hugged her. "You did good, babe." He was clearly pleased and that made Sydney happy too.

Chapter 17

L ife moved along and the excitement of the new apartment ended shortly after Sydney and Bear had moved in. Right along with their furniture, the heavy baggage called their marriage was moved in, and it made the new apartment just another place for the two to cohabit. Nonetheless, Sydney continued her commitment to her husband and their marriage.

Sydney and Gabby had become closer. They spent a great deal of time together, and Sydney and Elijah had started to attend church with Gabby every Sunday.

Sydney loved church. She always had growing up, and she also loved the fact that she always left church feeling good, really good. Sydney was spiritual and she had a strong faith in God. She continued to pray daily and even when she didn't go to church regularly, she felt that closeness to God. Even when she didn't make all the best decisions, she felt that closeness to God. Sydney knew He would never leave her. But going to church felt good to Sydney, and she felt as if she was doing her part in being a better Christian.

Gabby seemed nervous this particular Sunday. She seemed antsy and it wasn't like her.

"What's wrong, Gabby? Is everything okay? You seem a little preoccupied or something today." Sydney felt close enough to Gabby to address it and hoped she would be honest. Not much bothered Gabby, so it would be interesting to see what she had on her mind. "Did someone do something? Did something happen at church?" Sydney asked.

"No, no," Gabby answered. "Nothing happened at church. There's just something that I've been keeping from you. We've gotten close and I just feel like I need to talk about it and honestly, I want to talk about it." Gabby lowered her head and started to cry.

"Gabby, what's wrong? Tell me." Sydney knew that whatever it was, it wasn't anything she couldn't handle hearing.

"I just don't want you to hate me." Gabby looked up at Sydney, her eyes filled with tears.

"Gabby, I could never hate you. You know that. Please. Tell me."

"I had an affair with a woman, Sydney." Gabby lowered her head again and continued to cry. "I'm so ashamed. Her name was Tina and we worked together at Joe Bragg's body shop." Gabby wiped her nose and raised her head, curious now to see Sydney's reaction.

Sydney stared at Gabby, but looked at her with an understanding and without judgment. Sydney gently put her hand on Gabby's, and Gabby continued.

"She was married. I fell in love with her, and she was married. It just happened. It just happened." Gabby was sobbing now.

Sydney grabbed some tissue and handed it to Gabby. "Gabby, listen to me. Don't do this to yourself. You were in love with Tina and it happened. Was it unfortunate that she was married? Yes, of course it was, and for all the obvious reasons. But you loved her and clearly she felt deeply for you or she wouldn't have had the affair."

Sydney didn't bother telling Gabby that she knew all too well about having an affair and all the fallout that occurs because of it.

Sydney continued, "But feeling guilty after all this time doesn't do anyone any good. Is Tina still married to her husband?"

"Yes," Gabby answered. It was clear to Sydney that this was a touchy point with Gabby.

"Okay then. Tina has moved on with her life and you need to do the same. Honestly, Gabby, you need to let it go, either way."

"Did you even hear everything I just said, Sydney? It wasn't just that Tina was married. I slept with another woman." Gabby hadn't hoped for a negative reaction from Sydney, but she was shocked nonetheless that she hadn't gotten one.

"Yes, Gabby. I heard you, and so what. Did you think that would bother me?"

"I just didn't want you to hate me." Gabby looked longingly at Sydney.

"I would never hate you, and certainly not for that. It's okay. It's all okay."

Sydney hugged Gabby and Gabby hugged her back, not wanting to let go. It was as if she were a little girl who had finally gotten the forgiveness or approval that she so desperately needed. Yes, Gabby got what she wanted: Sydney's approval.

⚔

Gabby, Sydney, and Elijah continued to be the fabulous threesome. Gabby adored Elijah and he felt the same about her.

Sydney and Bear continued going through the motions of marriage, except for the main one that distinguished them as husband and wife. Even so, everything was copacetic. Bear had been working a great deal of shift work and he had another five days off coming up. He had an idea of taking Elijah on a camping trip over the weekend and Sydney thought that was a great idea: a father and son trip. Elijah was excited about going camping with his daddy. He had just turned three years old, so he was old enough to really enjoy himself. Elijah would also have other kids to play with because a couple of Bear's buddies at work were also going and taking their sons.

⚔

Sydney helped Bear load the truck with all the camping gear. She was glad that Bear and Elijah were getting some father and son time, but she wished she were going with them. Gabby had already arrived that morning and she waited inside for Sydney to say her goodbyes.

"Okay, guys. You all set?" Sydney asked.

"Yes, Mommy," Bear said. "Elijah, tell Mommy we're all set."

"We're all set, Mommy!" Elijah clapped his hands in excitement.

Sydney leaned in the window and kissed Elijah goodbye. "You be safe and take care of your daddy, okay?" She kissed Elijah again and smiled at Bear.

She made her way around to Bear's window. "You take care of my boy, Daddy. You hear me?" Sydney said with mock authority in her voice, and she winked at Elijah.

"I'll take care of your boy," Bear said, and reached over to tussle Elijah's hair.

"You've got yours and Elijah's tent, sleeping bags, lantern, the Old Smokey…" she started.

"Sydney, take your fanny back in the house. We've got everything we need and we'll be fine. We'll be home day after tomorrow. Say bye to Mommy, Elijah."

"Bye, Mommy," Elijah said and waved goodbye.

Sydney cried when she got back into the apartment. This was the first time that Bear had taken Elijah for a whole weekend and Sydney wasn't with them. She cried just as hard the time Bear's parents kept Elijah for a weekend in Windmere. She didn't like being without her little boy. She felt as though a piece of her was gone when he wasn't with her.

"Now, now. Come on, Mommy," Gabby said, half understanding and half teasing. "They're only going to be gone for two days. They'll be home day after tomorrow and you know Elijah will have a ball."

"I know. I really do know it." Sydney dabbed her eyes. "It's just hard. I'm not used to it and I don't like it when Elijah's not around."

Sydney knew she was like most mothers who miss their children when they're not with them, but it was even more than that. Maybe it was because of her own childhood. Sydney always wanted Elijah to know that she loved him more than anything in this world and she would never want to be without him.

"Okay, I'm drying it up." Sydney threw her head back and sniffed hard. "What do you say we go for some Mexican food and margaritas?" she asked Gabby.

"I thought you'd never ask," Gabby said, and off they went to fill the empty space of time.

Sydney and Gabby stayed at the restaurant for hours, sitting outside, sipping margaritas and talking about everything. Sydney shared with

Gabby all of the things she had done in her adolescence…the good, the bad, and the ugly. She told Gabby about her pregnancy all those years earlier and how she thought of it at times. She told her about Doyle Baker, about Vernon Phillips, and about the boys in school who she gave herself to. Maybe it was the tequila or maybe just the need to talk; likely both. Sydney needed to feel cleansed at times, and this time the tequila was only helping her cause. She talked about her biological father and how he never really had much to do with her and how she hadn't always lived with her mother. She then followed it up with how much she was always loved. It always sounded so strange, even to her, but it was the truth. Bad things happen to everyone, Sydney never ceased to tell herself. She was still fortunate, even with all the baggage. She still had Elijah, her mother, Holden, her Memaw, her Papa, her Aunt Olivia and Uncle Berk, and all the others who truly loved her.

The two walked back to Gabby's car. Sydney took the keys. Sydney had done most of the talking at the restaurant, leaving Gabby with not much to do but listen and drink.

"I'm driving," Sydney said.

"I can drive. I'm perfectly fine," Gabby retorted, and hiccupped right on cue.

They laughed hard and climbed in the car. When they got back to Sydney's apartment, she asked Gabby to stay the night. Sydney didn't like staying by herself anyway and Gabby had no business driving. Gabby agreed and they plopped down on the sofa together. Sydney had shared so much, but now it was Gabby's turn.

"Sydney, I really appreciate you sharing so much with me tonight. I know it couldn't have been easy to talk about all of that and it means a lot to me that you would trust me that much." Gabby was serious and seemed more sober than she had been before.

"Of course, I trust you," Sydney said and continued, "Why wouldn't I? You're my friend, you're my family, and I love you."

Sydney was comfortable being open like that. Her family was that way and she had been brought up that way.

Gabby stared at Sydney and didn't say a word. She had already gotten to know Sydney well enough to know that Sydney meant "I love you" in the most honest and pure of ways.

Sydney did love her, genuinely, and Gabby felt the same about Sydney. But Gabby also felt as though she was falling in love with Sydney. Sydney had taken Gabby into her life, shared her life and immediate family with her, and Gabby saw hope in Sydney. Gabby wanted to tell Sydney how she felt, but she knew that if she tried to tell her this night, Sydney wouldn't hear what she was saying. Not really. She would blame the alcohol. Gabby felt she had only one opportunity to share these feelings with Sydney, so she would bide her time.

When Gabby did not respond, Sydney continued, "You know I love you, right?"

"Yes, I know you love me. I love you too," Gabby replied and hugged Sydney.

Sydney could tell the mood had changed and although she wanted to continue visiting, the bed seemed to be a good alternative.

"Well, I say we get a good night's sleep and do something fun tomorrow. What do you say?" Sydney asked.

Gabby knew the best thing to do was to go to sleep as well, and they would start fresh tomorrow. "That sounds good to me." She gave Sydney a knowing smile.

Sydney gave her a quilt and Elijah's pillow and tucked her in. Sydney was a good caretaker and Gabby embraced it.

A

"Rise and shine, sleeping beauty!" Sydney said as she bounced into the living room. Sydney was already showered and dressed for the day.

Sydney was one of the few people who enjoyed being a night owl and could still wake up with the roosters and be in a good mood.

Gabby eased the quilt from her face. "You have got to be kidding me!" she grunted and yanked the quilt over her head.

"Am I the only person in the world that wakes up in a good mood?" Sydney asked. "Come on, girlfriend. Fanny up and let's get goin'."

Gabby made her way to the bathroom and never asked what was on the agenda. She was with Sydney and it didn't matter. She knew it would be a good day.

The two hopped in Sydney's Buick and hit the roads.

"Where are we off to, fair lady?" Gabby was excited about the answer.

"I thought we would take a drive to Grand Springs and have a picnic," Sydney said.

Gabby looked in the backseat, not sure what she was looking for, and saw a basket of goodies with a cooler.

"Well, well. Aren't you the domestic goddess? And full of surprises to boot," Gabby said, and she was pleased with where this was headed.

They pulled onto the grounds of Grand Springs. It was absolutely beautiful. The day was warm already, but the humidity was low, and the trees made a canopy that offered them shade. Sydney loved this area. Every year, during the reunion weekend, Sydney would accompany some of her family in from Georgia to Grand Springs. The Georgia bunch would come in for the Oates family reunion, but they also had a Stearn family reunion to attend while they were in town, and that was always held at Grand Springs. It made no matter that Sydney accompanied them. She knew everyone at this reunion as well and was related to some of them by marriage. Sydney liked to joke that the family tree in Merriweather didn't fork too much. Being here reminded her of those wonderful times.

Sydney unloaded the picnic basket and cooler, and found a spot by the edge of the water. She liked this spot in particular. A creek ran across a portion of the road and moss had formed in its path. When Sydney was younger, she and her cousins would run down the road and slide on the wet moss to reach the other side. Those were memories she treasured, and such an innocent time.

"What a glorious day." Sydney leaned her head back, closed her eyes, and took in the fresh air. The breeze was cool and the movement of leaves gave way to flashes of sunshine on her face. She savored every moment. These times didn't come often: they were fleeting, really. Sydney felt her heart and soul were full and she relished in the blessings of this earth that God had provided.

Gabby watched Sydney. She had never met anyone quite like her. Sydney had an innocence about her even though she had so much to tell. So many things had happened in her life, but it was as though Sydney held on to every piece of good that she could.

Sydney realized she had entered her own world for a moment and spun around to see Gabby staring at her.

"What?" she asked Gabby, smiling and picking up the blanket. No words needed to be spoken. They both laughed and spread the blanket out on the ground.

"This is absolutely beautiful, Sydney," Gabby said, as she bit into a fresh peach. "Thank you for sharing, yet again."

"And I'm happy to do so. Have you never been here?" Sydney asked.

"No. I never have. I've heard of it, of course, but never had an opportunity or inclination to come. I wish I would have." Gabby looked around and took it all in. It was like heaven on earth and they couldn't have wished for a more perfect day.

"So…" Sydney started, with a tone that hinted to something other than idle conversation.

"So, what?" Gabby asked, curious as to where the conversation was going.

"So, I bent your ear completely off last night talking about all of my things. Surely you've got some things of your own to share," Sydney answered.

Gabby did. She had a lot of them, but she didn't share her secrets often. She really never did. They were too ugly. They were even uglier than Sydney's, in Gabby's opinion. Dare she ever say a word? She wanted to open up. It might feel good to open up to someone: to someone who did love her, someone who would believe her, and possibly protect her from the animals of this world.

"Come on, Gabby," Sydney said. "I can tell you're thinking about something. Spit it out."

The way that Sydney blurted it out sounded insensitive to Gabby at first, but Gabby knew it wasn't intended. Sydney had no idea what Gabby was about to say. Sydney likely thought Gabby might have done drugs before, or maybe she had been promiscuous in high school, or maybe she had gotten pregnant. If only that were the case.

Gabby went on to tell Sydney her own story. It was a horrible, ugly story. It was a nightmare, actually. She told a story of sexual abuse at the hands of her father and her uncle and her older brother, Hubert. Her father and uncle had made sure to put their hands on her any time they felt the urge. Her mother did what Sydney found reprehensible, and stuck her head in the sand. Hubert actually had intercourse with Gabby. He had sexually abused Gabby from the time she was five years old, but the intercourse with Gabby would start after he was married and had moved away from home.

When they were younger and Hubert still lived at home, he not only sexually abused Gabby by fondling her, but he managed to completely se-duce Gabby, both physically and emotionally. In their own private world, Gabby would believe that Hubert loved her and she worshipped him. She was thirteen the first time she had intercourse with her brother, and it would continue for the next year until he stopped. He left her feeling abandoned and unloved.

Sydney was stunned to learn the secrets Gabby had shared with her. It was hard to comprehend such abuse, and that it happened right under her mother's nose and she did nothing. To say Sydney's mind was spinning was an understatement.

Sydney drove them back to Sydney's apartment. They talked on the way, but it was quiet mostly. What was there to say? Sydney was processing every-thing Gabby had said and she wanted nothing more than to beat the fucking asses off of her piece of shit family...the family that was Sydney's also. How could they? How could this woman be victimized so horribly by every man in her immediate family except for one? Not her oldest brother, Harold. Did her father, uncle, and Hubert ever talk about it? Did each one of them know that they were all violating Gabby? Were they their own sick group? Or did each think they had their own little secret and Gabby was keeping their secrets too? It made Sydney ill.

They walked into the apartment. Sydney unloaded the picnic basket and cooler, and poured a glass of wine.

"Would you like one?" she asked Gabby.

"And make it a double," Gabby answered.

They looked at each other and Sydney took their glasses to the coffee table. They sat on the floor and sipped their wine for a moment. Sydney was still processing everything and Gabby waited for Sydney to say something… anything.

"Gabby, I honestly don't know what to say. I feel like I want to do something and I haven't a clue of what to do."

"Sydney, there is nothing you can do."

Sydney thought about that for a moment, but Gabby was right. There was nothing she could do. This had been a long-kept, ugly, dirty secret, and if Gabby had her choice, she likely wouldn't want the demons brought to light now anyway. Gabby was a strong woman herself. At least she felt like she was.

The two finished the bottle of wine and moved to the sofa. Gabby leaned into Sydney and Sydney held her close. Gabby seemed like a hurt child. It was apparent that revisiting all of that pain had affected Gabby, and she was drained. Sydney wanted to take care of Gabby and to protect her. She wanted to help her get past all of what had happened to her. They fell asleep, embraced and secure with each other.

▲

Sydney wasn't expecting Bear and Elijah to be home early, but she was ready and chomping at the bit for them to walk through the door. She made sure to get up early, made the apartment tidy and orderly, and she'd already put a roast in the oven. Sydney let Gabby sleep in. Even if Gabby was not totally asleep, at least she was resting and that was as good as anything.

Gabby could smell Sydney's cologne as she passed. She could hear Sydney humming as she busied herself throughout the apartment. Gabby wished for Sydney to come to her, but Sydney did not. Sydney was anticipating her husband and son being home. Gabby did not want to leave. She felt safe there. She felt safe with Sydney. The sunshine filled up the room and the aroma of the food made Gabby feel as if she was "home." Not her home, but the home she craved: the home with Sydney.

"Gabby? Gabby?" Sydney touched Gabby's shoulder.

Gabby rolled on her back as if she'd just woken from her slumber.

"Hey, sweetie," Sydney said. "Time to rise and shine. I'm not sure when Bear and Elijah will be home. I thought you might like to clean up before they get here."

"Good idea," Gabby said.

Gabby didn't really give a shit about cleaning up for Bear. She thought he was a worthless piece of shit for how he treated Sydney, how he neglected her. Gabby would never do that. She did, however, want to clean up for Elijah. She loved that little boy. Gabby headed to the bathroom and Sydney hollered to her, "And I'd love for you to stay for dinner."

The door flung open. Bear walked in, lugging all of the camping gear, and Elijah was hot on his heels.

"Hey, baby!" Sydney ran to Elijah. She picked Elijah up and whirled him around and then started to help Bear get things unloaded from his arms.

She kissed Elijah's face. He seemed a little detached. "How's momma's boy doin'? Did you have fun?" Sydney asked him.

"Uh, huh," Elijah said.

"Uh, huh?" Sydney asked. "Well, that doesn't sound like a little boy who had fun camping. Did you have fun with Daddy or not, booger?"

"Yes, ma'am," Elijah said.

"Good then." Sydney kissed Elijah again and put him down.

Elijah immediately ran to Gabby and she took him out on the patio. Gabby and Elijah had become even closer. Now that he was three years old, Gabby was officially his class teacher. No more sneaking him from the room down the hall.

"And hello to you, Daddy," Sydney said to Bear.

Sydney stood to his side and she put her arms around him. He didn't look at her.

"Hello." He continued to unpack the bags and put the items on the table.

This was nothing new to Sydney. It didn't even embarrass her any more. He was an ass and she knew it just as well as he did.

She let go of him and walked into the kitchen. "I have a roast on. It should be done within the hour."

Bear walked to their bedroom. "Sounds good. I'm going to shower and I'll be back in a few."

Sydney walked out onto the patio with Gabby and Elijah.

"Well, I see Mr. Personality is home," Gabby said.

Sydney laughed. It also didn't embarrass her that everyone else thought he was an ass too. Anyone who could see the way he really treated her knew all too well.

"Yes, Mr. Personality. That would be my husband."

She got tired of calling Bear her husband. It didn't feel as if he was and it sounded foreign to Sydney when she said it. She and Gabby stayed on the patio with Elijah, and Bear never made it back into the living room. Sydney peeked through their bedroom window from the patio and saw Bear splayed across their bed with a towel draped across his midsection. He was sound asleep. Sydney was glad that she had asked Gabby to stay.

Chapter 18

The next day, Bear started back on the graveyard shift. He would be home all day until he headed out at eleven o'clock that night. Sydney thought she, Bear, and Elijah could get out of the house and do something that day. It was yet another beautiful one and she wanted to take advantage of it. Besides, she hadn't seen Elijah in two whole days and he was ready for some fun too.

"Elijah, go tell Daddy that we want to go to the zoo," Sydney said.

"Daddy, Daddy! Mommy said we're going to the zoo! Come on, Daddy!" Elijah yelled as he ran top speed down the hall to their bedroom.

"Yeah, yeah. Tell your mommy that the two of you can go without me. You two go have fun, okay, buddy?"

Bear had said it all loud enough for Sydney to hear. She walked to their bedroom and Elijah just stood there looking at Bear, hoping that his daddy would change his mind, it seemed.

Sydney was over it. Yet again, she was fucking over it. How much could a person really be expected to take?

"Come on, Elijah. You and Mommy are going to the zoo."

And that they did, and had a wonderful day together. Sydney packed in as much fun as possible, and postponed going home for as long as possible.

Ā

There was a knock on the door that night immediately after Bear had left for work. It startled Sydney; someone knocking at the door that late scared her. But it was so sudden after Bear had left, Sydney quickly assumed he had forgotten something. She looked through the peephole to be sure it was Bear, but it was Gabby. Sydney unlocked the door and opened it.

Before Sydney could say a word, Gabby spoke. "Sydney, I am so sorry for coming over this late and without calling. I didn't want to call because I didn't want to wake Elijah, and I didn't want to come over until after Bear left." Gabby started to cry and walked past Sydney to the sofa.

"What is the matter, Gabby? What happened?" Sydney's mind immediately went to Gabby's family and all the horrible things that had happened to her.

"Nothing has happened, Sydney. I just need to talk to you."

Sydney sat next to Gabby on the sofa. She sat right next to her, leg to leg. "What is it? Tell me." Sydney put her arm around Gabby.

"I love you, Sydney," Gabby said. "I mean, I really love you. I'm in love with you." Gabby didn't give Sydney time to respond. "Don't hate me," she continued. "Don't think I'm trying to break you and Bear up." Gabby continued to cry.

Sydney hugged Gabby, but Sydney was smart. She didn't necessarily doubt Gabby's feelings for her, as they had become very close, but she still felt that Gabby was trying to manipulate her emotions somehow. The crying and the waiting outside for Bear to leave so that she could profess her love for Sydney—it seemed a bit dramatic to her. Sydney didn't, however, let it bother her enough to not take it in and accept it. She did accept it. It was out in the open now and Gabby knew it would give Sydney food for thought.

Every day, Sydney thought about Gabby. She thought about what it would be like to make love with her. Sydney had thought about women before, even in high school, but she never dreamed she would be in a position to act on it. The only time a female had made an advance toward Sydney was her freshman year. Sydney had just started high school in Windmere, and Tara Steadman was instantly her friend. They had classes together and became close quickly. Sydney had invited Tara to spend the night. They went swimming that night and had snuck into the Riunite wine Sydney's parents kept in the pool house refrigerator. They drank it and felt free. They had shed their swimsuits and went skinny-dipping. The moon was full and illuminated the pool. Sydney was in the shallow end and Tara was in the deep end. Tara was holding on to the end of the diving board and she would pull herself out of the water and then lower herself back in. She did this over and over. Sydney was young. So was Tara. But Tara was sexy. She didn't have the awkward body of a fourteen-year-old. She was more adult in her figure and in her mannerisms. As she rose up and then lowered herself into the water, Sydney couldn't take her eyes off her nude body. Tara then asked Sydney, "Sydney, have you ever thought about being with another girl?"

"No," Sydney said. That was all she could say. "No." She would have never admitted to that. She would never have admitted that she would sneak into Holden's nightstand and go through his *Playboy* magazines. She would never have admitted that her favorite *Playboy* was filled with pictures of lesbians. Some were beautiful women and Sydney could tell they were professional models. They had makeup on and their lipstick was smeared around their mouths where they had kissed each other. But there were other pictures of women just as beautiful and completely natural. They were "real" women and they had sent in their photos for the layout. Some had no makeup, some were more masculine, some were more feminine…they were just women. It looked so natural to Sydney, but she would never have admitted that either. That was the last time Tara would ever spend the night. Her question scared the shit out of Sydney and Tara likely knew it as they drifted apart.

What would it be like to be with Gabby, with any woman for that matter? Sydney felt alive for the first time in a long time.

Gabby and Sydney continued to spend time together over the next few months, but they never made love, nor did they ever kiss. They didn't even speak of what Gabby had said, but they knew it was there. It was the elephant in the room and it seemed to be growing every day. It may not have been so much love as it was desire, but at a point, it was certainly easy to confuse the two. It was not easy, however, to keep either in the shadows.

CHAPTER 19

Sydney's Papa had come to Merriweather to spend some time with Sydney and Elijah. It had been a long time since Sydney had seen her Papa, although she did talk to him on the phone frequently. Bear was on the graveyard shift again and Sydney was glad that her Papa was there to stay the night. Sydney loved her Papa. He was a recovering alcoholic and he had made some very bad decisions earlier in his life, but who hadn't? She loved him so much. Sydney could remember her Papa putting her to bed when they all lived together in his and Memaw's house. She could remember jumping up and down on the bed as she pointed to a fly that Papa was trying to swat and he couldn't follow the speed of it as fast as Sydney could. "There it is, Papa! There it is!" Sydney would say, pointing her finger in this and that direction. He would just laugh and remember that feeling of youthfulness that he had long since passed.

Papa also always wanted to be the first person to call Sydney on her birthday, so he would call her at five thirty that morning every single year. He beat everyone every time and got the biggest kick out of it. "Happy birthday, darlin'," Papa would say. Sydney loved it and would have been disappointed had he not been first to call on her special day.

"Hello, darlin'," Papa said, as he strolled up the sidewalk looking every bit like a movie star. He had been called a womanizer by many and maybe that was true. But Papa was a gorgeous man and could he help it if every woman with a pulse wanted him? No. And unfortunately, his self-control found itself in the red.

"Hello, Papa." Sydney walked to him and couldn't wait for her kisses and hug.

Papa had a ritual. He would kiss exactly three quick pecks on the lips, consecutively, and then hug. Sydney never knew why he did it that way, but he had as long as she or her Memaw, or her mother and Aunt Olivia, for that matter, could remember. He was something else.

"I'm so glad you're here!" Sydney took his overnight case. "Come in, come in," she said. "Elijah," Sydney called out. "Elijah, Papa is here."

Elijah ran around the corner and slid sideways in his socks. Papa laughed and hoisted Elijah up.

"Look at you! You are growing like a weed!" Papa looked at Sydney. "I believe this boy gets better looking every day, just like his momma."

"Oh, Papa." Sydney never lacked for admiration from her Memaw or her Papa, that was for sure. He sat down and bounced Elijah on his knee, for as long as Elijah would allow it, while he and Sydney chatted about this and that.

"Where's Bear?" Papa asked.

"He's actually working a double tonight," Sydney answered, but she knew Papa was really only asking to be polite. "I'm afraid you won't be seeing too much of Bear, Papa," she continued. "He was scheduled for the evening shift, but picked up the graveyard shift also, so that he could get the overtime. We need it and he was also helping a friend out. He'll be home by eight in the morning, though, and you can get a glimpse of him before he heads off to bed."

Papa didn't comment and Sydney started to get dinner together. Papa had been a fan of Bear's in the beginning, right along with everyone else who thought he was the grandest thing Sydney could have ever come across. But after Bear and Sydney's separation, things changed and so did some of her family's feelings toward Bear, and that included Papa's.

"Do you mind if Gabby joins us for dinner, Papa?" Sydney asked, knowing it wouldn't make any difference at all. "The more the merrier" was Papa's way of thinking.

"No, darlin'. Why would I mind? I haven't seen Gabby in, well, I don't know how long. It'll be nice to see that pretty thing." Papa put his Kleenex box on the coffee table, lit a cigarette and leaned back on the sofa. He had stopped drinking years before, but this was one vice he wouldn't be giving up.

"Okay, well, I'm glad you're fine with her coming because she should be here just any time." Sydney gave a wink to her Papa.

He got a kick out of his Sydney. She had him wrapped around her little finger and always had.

Elijah ran to answer the knock at the door.

"Elijah, ask who it is. Remember?" Sydney reminded him.

"Who is it?" Elijah asked, with his sweet voice. Sydney loved this age so very much. She ran to peek out the peephole before Elijah could open the door and saw that it was Gabby.

"It's the big, bad tickle monster, that's who," Gabby grumbled in her deepest voice through the door.

Elijah took off down the hall, laughing and screaming, sure that as soon as his mother opened the door, Gabby would come running to him for tickle time. He was right.

"Hey there, Cookie," Gabby said, making her way back in the room with Elijah.

Cookie was Papa's nickname, which had been taken from his last name, Cook. Antony Garrett Cook he was, and his name served him well: a beautiful, distinguished name for a beautiful, distinguished man.

"And what do you have there, Miss Gabby? Is that a sack of potatoes you have on your back?" Papa hugged Gabby and wrapped his arms around Elijah at the same time.

They all laughed and visited, and Sydney loved the sound of it. She knew that Gabby's constant presence at her home may have started being a thorn in Bear's craw, but she didn't care. It was depressing when he was home and lonely when he wasn't. Sydney had gradually stopped caring about his feelings, with regard to those types of things, and she didn't care to turn the ship around.

Something felt different this night. There was a buzz in the air between her and Gabby—an electricity—and there was no denying it. There was a major attraction, and one that was now all-consuming. It was that elephant in the room that had continued to grow, and it filled up the room now. Would Papa notice? Sydney did her best to move through the evening hiding her feelings, but they were beginning to have more control of her than she had of them.

Elijah was down for bed and soundly sleeping. Sydney had fixed her Papa a place on the sofa. She kissed him goodnight and turned off the television. It had already been decided earlier in the evening that Gabby would spend the night as well. Sydney went to her bedroom and it felt as if every nerve in her body was exposed. It was a feeling she had never experienced. She knew what she wanted to happen and wondered if it would happen this night.

Gabby climbed into Sydney's bed on Bear's side. Sydney crawled in on her side and laid on her back. Her head had barely rested on her pillow when Gabby rolled on top of her and kissed her. Sydney had always wondered what she would do and how she would feel if they ever kissed. It was beautiful and natural, and at the same time it was absolute heated, raw emotion and want. Sydney felt as if she were in pure abandon in one instant, and in the next she couldn't believe this was actually happening. Gabby sat up and strad-dled Sydney's legs. She pulled her nightgown over her head and then pulled Sydney up to her and raised Sydney's nightgown. Sydney lifted her arms and let Gabby disrobe her. Not a word was spoken. Gabby gently lowered Sydney back down to her pillow and laid her naked body on top of Sydney's. The feel-ing of this woman on her—their breasts touching, their stomachs touching, the softness of Gabby's skin, and the softness of her lips—it felt as though Gabby had moved right through her. Sydney felt as if she were "home."

⚔

Sydney heard a noise. She rose up and realized that Gabby was not in the bed with her. Sydney heard the noise again and walked toward her bathroom when she heard Gabby crying in Bear's closet. Sydney turned on the light. Gabby was squatted down in a fetal position with one of Bear's rifles in her hand.

"Gabby!" Sydney exclaimed in a loud whisper. "What are you doing?"

Gabby said nothing.

"Answer me! What are you doing?"

Gabby began to sob and cry hysterically. "I'm sorry. I'm sorry. I can't believe I've done this. I never intended this to happen." Gabby gasped for air, trying to get her words together.

Sydney stood motionless and couldn't speak.

"I would never want to break you and Bear up. I never would and now I've done this again. I'm just sorry, Sydney. I'm so sorry."

Sydney squatted down next to Gabby and took the gun from her hands. She put the gun in the far corner of the closet and gently raised Gabby to her feet. Sydney knew that if Gabby was this fragile, or possibly insane, there was nothing to do but remain calm and make sure that Gabby felt reassured.

"Gabby, come here. Just come lay down with me," Sydney said gently, as she led Gabby back to the bed. "Sssshhhh, ssshhhh," Sydney kept saying.

Sydney was scared and confused. This night had come as no surprise. It was what they had both wanted. And now, after something that Sydney felt was beautiful and real, Gabby decided that the guilt was terrible enough to get a gun and consider doing something? It made no sense to Sydney.

Gabby finally calmed down, but continued to cry on Sydney's shoulder as Sydney held her.

"Gabby, tell me what is going on. Why in God's name would you do such a thing?" Sydney was so confused, it was beyond belief. She had stepped into a new world and was willing to enter it with Gabby. How could Gabby do this, after everything?

"I just...I just...I never meant to hurt you. I never meant to hurt yours and Bear's relationship."

Sydney's head was spinning and in that instant, anger filled her up. Was Gabby so delusional that she actually believed what she was saying, or was she the master manipulator toying with Sydney's feelings?

"Gabby, I love you. I wanted to be with you. No one made me do anything. I wanted to be with you. Do you understand me?" Sydney said.

Gabby continued to sob.

"Do you understand me?" Sydney repeated, and she could feel her emotions flailing.

"Yes, yes. I understand you," Gabby answered.

Gabby, her head on Sydney's shoulder and her hand on Sydney's breast, shifted her face toward Sydney's. She kissed Sydney softly on her mouth. "And I love you," Gabby said.

They were falling. They were falling into the abyss that would become their relationship.

Chapter 20

Fall had come and gone and had brought with it the beautiful trees filled with golden and ruby leaves, as well as the start of the holiday season, all of which Sydney loved so very much. The holiday season was Sydney's favorite time of year. She loved every single part of it and especially the family gatherings and the delicious country cooking.

Now, Old Man Winter was showing his face just in time for Christmas. The trees' bare arms reached to the heavens, and the beautiful blanket of leaves lay below them. Sydney thought it just as beautiful, and she loved the crispness of the air, and the feelings that the holidays evoked.

This was the first time that Sydney and Gabby would be apart in months and it was especially difficult for Gabby because it was the holiday season.

Sydney, Bear, and Elijah were spending the holidays in Windmere with both families and Sydney had been looking forward to it. Her marriage was still on a full downward spiral, but it had been doing that for so long, it was like old hat to Sydney.

The phone rang at Bear's parents' house. "I'll get it. I know it's probably Mother calling to see when we're headed out." Sydney ran for the phone.

"Hello," Sydney said, assuming she'd hear her mother's voice. She assumed wrong.

"Sydney. This is Gabby. I miss you. I miss you so much." Gabby's voice cracked. "I can't believe we're not going to be together for the holidays, that I won't get to spend them with you and Elijah."

Sydney did her best to appear normal. She understood that Gabby was upset, but she didn't like that Gabby had called her at Bear's parents' house. She should have known better.

"Hey, Momma. I knew it was you. We're about to be heading out in just a few," Sydney said, pretending to talk to her mother and being sure to speak loud enough for the present company to hear. Sydney then whispered, "I miss you too, Gabby, but I've got to go. We'll be home in a few days and we'll celebrate Christmas then." Without a moment allowed for Gabby to speak, Sydney raised her voice again, pretending to talk to her mother. "Okay. I love you too. See you shortly." She hung up the phone.

Sydney kept thinking about Gabby calling, and she hoped she wouldn't call again. Sydney did miss Gabby, but she also knew that she wasn't feeling the same loneliness that Gabby was clearly feeling. Sydney was surrounded by family and her focus was on them, Elijah, and somehow even Bear. Something about the holiday cheer allowed for a smoke screen to envelope Sydney's marriage and home life. Everything would appear to be fine, if even for these few days, but Sydney was treading on very shaky ground and she knew it. Her current situation couldn't remain the same forever and it was just a matter of time.

CHAPTER 21

The holidays had come and gone, and spring had arrived. Sydney and Gabby were still lovers, and Sydney and Bear were divided. And yet, Sydney wasn't about to take the responsibility for her marriage crumbling, even though she was having an affair with Gabby. She had been clear with Bear before she went back to him—"You have my commitment as long as I have yours"—and those words had stayed with Sydney all of this time. The fact was that she had never had his commitment nor his love. He certainly didn't deserve hers, she would tell herself, and any guilt she would feel, she tossed out with the garbage.

Sydney and Gabby had taken a weekend trip to Windmere with Elijah. They stayed at Sydney's parents' house, and Sydney and Gabby had gone dancing with Sydney's cousin, Hayden, that Saturday night. Hayden had taken them to a gay bar in Houston, the first that either had ever been to, and they had an experience like none other. Sydney danced and danced and danced for hours, even when Gabby and Hayden couldn't take any more. Sydney felt such freedom and it was wonderful.

After a full weekend, they pulled back into Sydney's apartments at eight thirty that Sunday night. Bear wasn't expecting them until a little later, but they had gotten an earlier start than anticipated. As Sydney turned the corner to her apartment building, she saw Bear standing outside with a woman. They were standing close, and were talking. Sydney slowed down and coasted on in, trying to get a good look at who it could be. It was Theresa Pritchett, her friend from college. It wouldn't have mattered what either of them said. Sydney was no fool and the look in their eyes told the whole story. Sydney parked her car and she, Gabby, and Elijah got out. Gabby grabbed her bag and Elijah, and made a quick path to the apartment.

"Well, hello there, Theresa. How are you?" Sydney acted as though there was not a problem in the world with the bitch being there.

"Oh, hey, Sydney." Theresa was so nervous, her voice shook. "I had, uh, just come by to see you, and Bear was nice enough to invite me in. Um, I guess I'll talk to you later." She made a beeline to her car.

"Fuck you," Sydney thought. She wasn't stupid. And she wasn't angry because Bear might be doing the same thing she was. She was angry because her marriage had been a farce and it took this mess to end it, once and for all.

Sydney didn't say a word to Theresa, not even a response to her idiotic, "I guess I'll talk to you later" comment. That would never happen, as far as Sydney was concerned. She and Bear walked back to the apartment without a word between them. It was as if they both knew what was about to happen. It was time.

Gabby had already taken Elijah into his bedroom to play when Sydney and Bear walked into their living room. Sydney sat on the sofa and Bear on the loveseat. She just looked at him and she tried to see the man she had married those few years ago. Bear did his best to look at Sydney, but couldn't. He dropped his head and stared into his lap.

"Do you want a divorce, Bear?" Sydney asked. No reason to beat around the bush. They had done that long enough.

He looked at her. "Yes." He broke down, sobbing.

It was odd to Sydney. She knew that Bear may have been sad on some level, but more than that, he seemed relieved. Sydney did not cry and she did not console him. She said, "Okay. Then let's get one." It was that simple.

⅄

By this time, Sydney worked for a CPA firm as an administrative assistant, but she still had her connections to very good attorneys, having worked in the legal field for that time. She called her favorite attorney contact, Randolph

Calhoun, and made an appointment for herself and Bear. Sydney and Bear had decided to make their divorce as amicable as possible, for Elijah and for them. There was no argument about infidelity, who got what, none of that. They had made that decision and they were sticking to it.

"Hello there, Sydney," Randolph said as they entered his office. "Hi there," Randolph said to Bear as he shook his hand. "You folks have a seat."

Sydney and Bear sat in two side by side chairs directly across from Randolph's desk.

Randolph sat down, leaned his chair back and put his hands behind his head. "Well, I gotta tell ya. This is a new one. Two people getting a divorce and there's no fussin' or fightin'. You just agree on everything, huh?" He smiled.

"Yes, actually, we do." Sydney felt put on the spot, but continued with her explanation, warranted or not. "We want what's best for Elijah and regarding any materialistic things, we don't have much anyway. Bear is keeping his truck and I'm keeping my car. My grandmother had bought us the living room and dining room furniture when we married, and the master bedroom furniture was already mine when we married. Elijah's furniture is actually hand-me-downs from my Aunt Olivia and is very sentimental to me."

"Yeah," Bear chimed in, "I just got me an efficiency that's already furnished and there's just no need to fuss over livin' room or dinin' room furniture."

"Uh, huh." Randolph kept his same position and eyeballed Sydney and Bear. Something was making him uncomfortable.

Randolph rose forward in his chair, put his glasses on, and leaned over his pad, pen in hand. "Alrighty then. So, Sydney, you're filing for this divorce, correct?" Randolph asked.

"No, we're both filing for divorce," Sydney said. "We are in agreement and we're both filing."

Randolph peeked over his glasses at Sydney. "No, I don't think you understand. Someone has to file for this divorce and it can't be the both of you. There's a petitioner and a respondent." He waited as Sydney and Bear mulled that over without speaking.

"Well, I guess that Bear is filing then," Sydney said.

Bear threw a sharp look her way, which she ignored.

"Why are you having Bear file?" Randolph asked, with a confused look he didn't try to hide.

"Because it will forever be on the court documents who filed for this divorce and I don't ever want my son to think his mother didn't try at this marriage, that I wanted this divorce. This wasn't my doing, as far as I'm concerned." Sydney was making a statement.

She had conviction in her voice and Bear never took his eyes off her. Sydney felt somewhat hypocritical placing the blame on Bear, but she quickly talked herself out of it. The fact was, had Bear ever loved her like he should have, had he ever cared even an ounce about her feelings, she would have never had an affair with Luke Aldridge in the first place, and she certainly wouldn't have been involved with Gabby now. She had loved Bear with everything she had, and he pissed all over it. Yes, he was most definitely to blame.

"Now, Sydney, you need to realize that if you have Bear file for this divorce and anything should happen where the two of you no longer agree, I will be obligated to be Bear's attorney and you will have to find another one." Randolph made sure that he conveyed the seriousness of what he was saying.

"I understand that, but everything will be fine. We're not arguing about anything. We're totally in agreement, aren't we, Bear?" asked Sydney, and barely gave Bear a glance before she continued. "I just don't want my son to think that I left his father without doing all I could, and if it shows that I filed, that is how it looks. I'm not so prideful that I really care if to everyone else it looks like Bear left me." Sydney had made up her mind.

Randolph went over exactly what he had previously said again, and it was apparent to Sydney that he desperately wanted her to change her mind. He didn't want to have to represent Bear should something change. He didn't want to, and it couldn't be more obvious to Sydney without him coming right out and saying it. Sydney wasn't sure why Randolph was being so adamant. She was just ready to get this done.

Randolph finally realized he was fighting a losing battle with Sydney and agreed to continue with Bear as the petitioner.

⚔

Sydney walked into the apartment and threw her purse on the table as she plopped down on the sofa. It was a beautiful day and light flooded her living room. Just what she needed: a reminder that there was light at the end of this tunnel and all was going to be fine. She felt such peace. Elijah was in daycare with Gabby, and Sydney was alone. She normally didn't like being alone, but this particular moment felt good. There wasn't a sound to be heard except the hum of the ceiling fan. "Peace," she thought.

⚔

Gabby had moved into Sydney's apartment the same day that Bear moved out. They were living their life as "roommates," and saying they were family certainly threw everyone off. The two of them never really thought of that particular point, unless they were preparing name tags at the family reunion, but it was a good card to play so that the town wouldn't talk. Besides, that wouldn't look too good. A woman having an affair with another woman behind her husband's back? That would be enough to get Sydney tarred and feathered in Merriweather, Texas, and she certainly didn't need to draw attention to anything while the divorce was moving forward.

Bear was being the attentive dad, which Sydney appreciated. He made sure to make time for Elijah: took him camping, let him spend the day at his apartment, and even came to Sydney's apartment complex to watch Elijah swim at the clubhouse pool. It was a little awkward at times, when Bear would have Elijah deliver a handpicked flower to a cute thing by the pool. Some people didn't realize that Bear and Sydney were even separated, so it looked as though Bear was flaunting his infidelity. Sydney wondered at times if she deserved that, but she didn't dwell on it long.

One evening, Sydney had decided to rearrange the furniture in the apartment. A change was in order. Sydney thought it would not only be a nice change, but a nice surprise for Gabby.

Gabby was visiting her parents and just Sydney and Elijah were at home. As Sydney was pushing the loveseat from one side of the room to the other, Elijah jumped from the sofa to the loveseat and back. He finally jumped headlong onto the loveseat and Sydney gave him the "tickle monster" routine. She loved him so much and it was nice for it to be just the two of them. It didn't happen often. Sydney tickled Elijah and leaned down to kiss him. Elijah stuck his tongue out just as soon as Sydney's mouth reached his.

Knowing a child's undeniable innocence, Sydney yelled out, "Oh, French kiss! French kiss!" She laughed and bent down to kiss Elijah again and he stuck his tongue out again.

Sydney quickly rose up. "Elijah, Mommy was playing when she said 'French kiss,' but you're not to stick your tongue out like that when someone kisses you. Okay?"

Elijah looked embarrassed, very much so.

"Sweetheart, come here to Mommy. Don't be embarrassed. It's okay." She wrapped him in her arms.

Something wasn't settling with Sydney. It was as if something was just presented to her, and she didn't know what.

"Who showed you that?" she asked, the words falling from her mouth.

"Daddy," Elijah said.

Her world stopped.

⅄

Maybe it was because of Sydney's past. No, it was definitely because of Sydney's past. It's not that nothing surprised Sydney, because things did, but nothing ever really knocked her on her ass. She was a realist and the older she became, and the more she knew of the dirtiness the world held around her, she began to somewhat expect dirty things to seep in. But she would have never, ever expected this. Something took hold of her and it was something stronger and more powerful than she could have mustered on her own.

"Daddy showed you that?" Sydney kept calm, eerily calm. She didn't want to embarrass or upset Elijah any further, and she didn't want him to stop talking. "Where did Daddy show you that?" she continued.

"At camping." Elijah didn't look at her, but played with his fingers.

"Oh, when you go camping with Daddy?" Sydney said. "What else do you do at camping?"

"Play," Elijah said.

"Well, that's good. That's good, sweetie." Sydney continued to do her best to stay calm. Her stomach was a knot, but she knew she couldn't wait. She had to continue. "What else did Daddy show you, sweetie?" My God. She wanted to know, but could she really bear to hear it?

Elijah went on to tell his mother about the other immoral and wicked acts his father had done to him.

The innocence of a child. The innocence of her baby boy. He had not a clue of the magnitude of what he had said. But Sydney did and she would not be stopped in making this wrong, this ultimate act of betrayal, right. She would not crumble, nor be moved. She would raise herself straight upright and she would prepare for the biggest battle of their lives.

CHAPTER 22

Sydney laid her precious boy down to sleep. Elijah was unaware of what he actually said, of what it all actually meant, or that his father was an evil monster. He had no idea, and Sydney wanted to keep it that way. She would never want Elijah's spirit to be compromised as hers had been. She would protect him. She thought she had up to this point. She'd be damned if she didn't now.

Gabby returned home, and Sydney told Gabby the horrific details of what Elijah had told her. Gabby was horrified by what she heard, but had the same "we're going to get him" approach as Sydney. They were both survivors, after all.

Sydney thought, and she was being very methodical in her process. She had to keep it together. She had to be strong. She remembered that a child psychologist, Deb Whitmire, subleased an office from her CPA firm. It was already well into the evening. She would call her first thing in the morning.

Sydney picked up the phone and called her Memaw. "Memaw. This is Sydney." Oddly enough, her voice was solid and strong.

"Yes, sweetheart. How are you? What a nice surprise," Memaw said.

"Do you have a second? I need to talk to you."

"Of course. Let me turn this TV down." Sydney could hear her Memaw settle in for whatever was on Sydney's mind. "Okay, what is it?" Memaw said, and only thought she was ready for what Sydney was about to say.

She told her Memaw everything Elijah had told her in excruciating detail. Her Memaw was stunned, but Sydney realized very quickly where she had gotten her strength. Her grandmother had quite the same reaction as Sydney. She was mortified by what she'd heard, but she had a resolve that could not be moved. Sydney told her Memaw of her plan to call Deb Whitmire first thing the next morning and she would call her immediately afterwards.

Memaw would be waiting for Sydney's call and she would pray. She, too, knew of sexual abuse. These things were not spoken of when she was a child, but they happened. Her paternal grandfather would come to visit and he would find his place of slumber in the bed with his grandchildren. He put his hands on Memaw one time too many times, and she told Mama that she never wanted to sleep in the same bed as her grandfather again. Mama looked her in the eyes and told her not to worry, she would never have to sleep in the same bed with him again. Nothing was ever spoken, but Mama kept her only daughter away from wandering hands and protected her. Now, Memaw's granddaughter was about to do the same for her son.

The next morning was a Wednesday; Sydney called the CPA firm she had previously worked for, and asked for Deb Whitmire's office. Deb was no longer there, but thankfully Sydney found out that she had moved to her own location in Merriweather and was now the director of psychological and mental health issues in the entire East Texas region. Sydney called her and shared with her what Elijah had told her the previous evening. Deb wanted to see Elijah as soon as possible and scheduled a meeting with him for that Friday. Deb told Sydney that on their first visit, she would initially have Sydney come into the meeting with her and Elijah. It would be imperative that he felt safe and comfortable. Deb would then visit with Elijah alone. If, based on what Deb and Elijah discussed, this moved forward, she would have Elijah and Sydney back for a second visit. At this second visit, she would have dolls for Elijah. There would be a Mommy doll, a Daddy doll, and an Elijah doll. There would be others as well. During this meeting, she would have Elijah act out whatever may have occurred using these dolls. This would be videotaped in the event the case ever went to trial. She also made clear to Sydney, that if this did happen to Elijah, even if Sydney did not want to press charges against Bear, Deb would still be giving the case to the DA's office and they would go after Bear. She wanted to stress that with Sydney. Apparently, too many women dropped the charges when dealing with "their man," even though they had hurt the most sacred gift, their children, or someone else's.

"Stand by your man," Sydney thought, as Deb went through the details. The thought of a woman siding with a sick pervert was incomprehensible to Sydney. Sydney knew that if Elijah said it, it had happened, and she was moving forward like a steamroller not to be stopped.

⚓

On Thursday, Sydney called Bear and asked him to come over. She told him that she needed to speak with him about Elijah. Bear obliged, no questions asked. It may not have been the smartest thing for Sydney to do, but she was not letting one more day go by without looking this sick, perverted, son of a bitch in the eye and letting him know that she knew. She knew. He came to the door and Sydney felt as if she were going to be sick. Elijah was in his room and Sydney had not let him know that his daddy was coming.

"So, what's goin' on, Syd?" Bear almost had a spring in his step.

Who was he? He never called her "Syd." Did he have a split personality? Was he completely psychotic, or was he the most calculated liar and master manipulator she'd ever met? Likely all of the above and to top it all off, he was a pedophile and she was married to him.

"I have to talk to you about something." Sydney walked back to her bedroom. Bear followed her and sat passively on the foot of her bed. Sydney told Bear everything Elijah had said. Bear looked wild-eyed, as if he wanted to bolt out of there, but he didn't move.

"Where is Elijah?" he asked.

"He's in his room. Why?" Sydney realized what a stupid question that was after she'd asked it.

"Elijah!" Bear yelled out to Elijah.

"Don't you dare yell at him! Don't you dare say one unkind word to him, Bear! And don't you dare make him feel afraid about what he said!" Sydney knew she would just as soon kill him if he tried to hurt Elijah now.

Elijah came into the room. "Hi, Daddy!" Elijah said, but didn't go to Bear as he typically would have.

"Hey, big guy! Come give Daddy a hug." Bear tried his best to look and seem comfortable in his own skin.

Elijah went to Bear and hugged him, but it was clear that it was because he was told to, not because he wanted to.

"Elijah, Mommy told me that someone did something to you, some bad things. Who did that, Elijah? Who did that to you?"

Not a second passed, but the anticipation of what Elijah would say was overpowering.

"You did, Daddy."

"Out of the mouths of babes." Sydney had heard this saying a million times and she finally understood its full and powerful meaning. Elijah was not intimidated and even at three years old, could not be moved.

"Elijah, Daddy didn't do that," Bear said firmly, and acted as though he couldn't have been more disgusted. No doubt he was, by his own actions.

"Yes, you did," Elijah said, with a truth and conviction that only an innocent child could have.

Sydney jumped in so that Bear couldn't say another word. "Elijah, why don't you go back to your room, sweetheart? Mommy and Daddy are going to talk some more. I'll come in there in just a few minutes." Sydney watched her angel turn on his heels and run down the hall, as if he had not a care in the world. If only that were the case.

"So." Sydney didn't say another word. Just "so."

She looked at Bear with a contempt that was so thick he could barely continue looking at her. He didn't want to, but he had no choice. What was he to do? Turn his head? Look away? That would be a dead giveaway. Sydney wasn't a fool. She knew exactly why he wouldn't divert his attention from her. He was the most skilled liar she had ever met, and she had met many. He was also the sickest. Bear sat, speechless.

"Are you fucking deaf, Bear? Are you fucking deaf? I said 'so'! Don't you have anything to say? Anything?!"

He never took his eyes off her and talked calmly and logically, as if he were on her team. "I don't know, Sydney. I don't know what to tell you. Maybe it was someone at his school. It had to be. Maybe one of his teachers."

"Someone at his school? Someone at his school? No, Bear. It wasn't anyone at his school. First, Elijah would never say that you did something that you didn't do. That is first and foremost. Second, before you start trying to blame some man at the school, let me just fill you in. There are no male teachers at the school. Every one of them is a woman. Every single one."

Bear continued to make eye contact with Sydney. "Maybe it is a janitor or something."

Sydney was going to be sick. She knew. She had known, but watching him calmly and methodically grasp for straws, as they all came falling to the ground, made her physically ill. "I can't talk to you anymore. Come on. I'm walking you to the door. You have to leave. I want you to leave now." Sydney walked past Bear and headed to the door.

He followed her to the door and left without a word. Hindsight being twenty-twenty, he could have done anything to her and taken Elijah. She was a fool to have put her back to him after confronting him about such a horrific crime against his own son. She knew that the instant he left and it wouldn't happen again.

Chapter 23

The next morning, Sydney and Elijah went to Deb Whitmire's office. It was a pleasant surprise to see that her new office was actually an old house in the historic district of Merriweather. It was a large white frame, two-story house with a deep wrap-around porch, which was painted gray. The shutters were painted black and there was a porch swing and wicker furniture adorning various areas of the front porch. The grassy area next to the house served as a parking lot, but because of the detached garage right next to it, it looked more as though family and friends had come to pay a visit, rather than damaged people coming to deal with their demons.

Sydney took Elijah in and the receptionist gave her the paperwork to fill out. Sydney couldn't believe it. As she entered the day's date on the paperwork, she realized it was the date she was married: five years to the day. Jesus, God. And here they were. She heard someone coming down the stairs, but she didn't look up out of respect for whatever hurt soul may be trying to make their way back out the door they had come through without being noticed. It wasn't a hurt soul. It was Deb.

"Hello there. Sydney, right?" Deb walked over to Sydney and she wasn't as Sydney had expected. She was a tall, capable looking woman. She had a very strong look about her. Not a masculine look, but a strong look: physically and in every other way. And yet she exuded a warmth and openness right along with that strength, so it was easy to instantly feel safe with her.

"Yes. It's very nice to meet you." Sydney took Deb's hand.

"And you must be Elijah." Deb squatted down to his size to make eye contact.

Elijah smiled at her and nodded his head. "Yes, ma'am."

"Well, let's go upstairs. I have a fun room for you, Elijah. I have lots of games, toys, crayons and coloring books. You can play while we visit. How is that?"

Elijah looked at Sydney as if to ask if it was okay.

"Go ahead, sweetie. Mommy's right behind you."

Elijah ran up the stairs ahead of Deb and Sydney. As the two rounded the stairwell, Elijah was already on the floor in the room Deb had prepared for him. He was comfortable and wasn't paying Deb, nor Sydney, any mind.

"Sydney," Deb whispered, "because Elijah is so comfortable right now, would you mind if I start my session with him now?"

Sydney wanted to be with Elijah. She wanted to hold him tight and not let go. And she wanted to be there for the first part of the session, but she understood where Deb was coming from. "If Elijah is okay with that, I understand and it's fine," Sydney said.

"Elijah, are you okay with Mommy waiting right out here?" Deb asked.

He looked up from the toys and at Sydney, awaiting approval if it was okay.

"Mommy will be right out here, sweetie. I'm right here. Ms. Deb just has a couple of questions for you and then we're all done. Okay?"

"Okay."

"All right then. You come right over here and sit," Deb said to Sydney. "That way you're right outside the door in case Elijah decides he wants you to come in." It was a small desk with a small chair positioned against the wall right outside of the room where Elijah and Deb would be. "We won't be long," Deb continued. "Likely about twenty to thirty minutes, if that. I just need to hear what Elijah has to say about what happened. Obviously we'll need to ease into that, but once we begin the discussion, it should go fairly quickly based on what you've told me. He is an open little boy when discussing what happened to him, and that is very good."

Sydney sat in the little chair at the little desk and she felt like a little girl waiting her turn. How could this be happening? She didn't let herself dwell on the "how's" and the "why's." It was happening and she knew she had to stay focused. She had to stay strong.

Sydney looked at her watch when she heard the door open. It had been a little over thirty minutes.

Before Sydney could say a word, Deb smiled at Elijah. "Elijah, why don't you run downstairs? There is a nice lady at the front desk named Miss Kym. Tell her that Deb said you need a watermelon pop."

"Yum! Go on, sweetie, and Mommy will be down in just a second." Sydney did her best to act normal, whatever that was.

"Yeah!" Elijah hightailed it downstairs for a pop, and to wait for Sydney.

"It happened." Deb looked Sydney hard in the eyes to be sure she not only made her point, but that Sydney understood the magnitude and severity of the situation.

"It did?" Sydney couldn't believe those words were the only ones that would come out of her mouth. She knew it had happened. She knew it. Elijah said it. But to hear this child psychologist who had just spent time with her son, say in two words what had encompassed months, if not years, of Elijah's abuse…it sent Sydney reeling.

"Yes, Sydney, it did. It definitely did."

There was a pause as Sydney tried to gather herself, not having a clue of what to say.

"Now, what are you going to do?" Deb kept her voice firm and deliberate.

"What do you mean, 'what am I going to do'?" Sydney asked. "I'm going after him. That's what I'm going to do. He's not getting away with this. He's not getting away with what he's done." Sydney may have felt better had she been able to shed a tear, but she couldn't. She was firm in her own resolve.

Deb put her arm around Sydney's shoulder. "Well, you'd better hold on to your seat, Sydney, because you're about to be in for one hell of a ride."

▲

Sydney took Elijah home and she thought. She thought long and hard. She wondered how she and Elijah wound up here in this place. Elijah was the best part of her. She wondered how Bear could have so monstrously hurt and victimized the best part of him. How does a parent do that to a child? How does a human being do that to a child?

Sydney took some alone time this particular night and reflected. She had a way of looking at her life in pieces, like chapters in a book or scenes in a movie. She didn't clump it all together and feel sorry for herself. Had she thought of it all as one big picture, it would certainly make it worse. So, she thought of it piece by piece and it made her life story.

Yes, her father never paid her any mind, none that he showed anyway. But that was likely because of the way he was reared by his parents, her Granny and PawPaw. They loved their children, but Sydney remembered her mother telling her that Forrest had once said he never remembered his mother hugging him in his life until he went off and joined the military. It was only then that she hugged him goodbye.

And yes, Sydney's mother did leave for those few years. But Maeve was going through a selfish time, which ultimately turned into bad times all the way around because of it. Bad things had happened to Maeve during that time, partly due to the company she kept and choices she made, but also due to circumstances far outside her control. It was clear that the best place Sydney could have been during that time was with her Memaw and her Aunt Olivia and Uncle Berk. They had taught her about faith in God and they had given her stability. Everything wasn't always perfect, but it was far better than most had it, no doubt. And through it all, Sydney loved her mother so very, very much and was glad that she had come out of it all, out of all the dark places and back into the light, and with the family that loved her so.

Doyle Baker. It was also no one's fault that Doyle Baker had turned out to be such a perverted bastard. How could Memaw have ever known what he was capable of?

Then, there were Sydney's bad choices, which she had made on her own, but she chalked that up to puberty and being foolish.

Vernon Phillips. Everyone knew he was an ol' bastard, but Sydney was seventeen at the time and she took some of that responsibility whether she deserved it or not. He was a fuck head, but she was smart enough that she should have spoken up sooner. Sydney was, however, also knowledgeable enough to know why she hadn't. She was trapped in that place that many abused children are: that place where whatever age you are, when put in another abusive situation, it feels as though the clock is spinning backward in time and you're right back in the same place where you started. Only the faces change.

Now there was Bear. Sydney didn't know what to make of it all. Did she attract these people? Was there something about her that was a magnet for pedophiles? How in God's name could she have married one? How?

These pieces made up Sydney's life story. But this particular piece was now a chapter in Elijah's life story too.

Sydney was about to write another chapter. One that had never been written in her life story, but it would be written in Elijah's.

▴

The following Monday, Sydney contacted another attorney to represent her in her divorce, now that Randolph Calhoun was no longer an option. Her name was Maureen Rogers and she was known to be quite the pit bull in Merriweather. There wasn't a man in town involved in a divorce who would want to look across the table at that woman. Maureen was a badass and she knew it. She had relocated to Merriweather from Houston, for what reason nobody really knew, but she definitely showed the men that there was a new sheriff in town and she wasn't putting up with women being treated like second-class citizens.

At their first meeting, Sydney told Maureen everything: every single thing except the part where she was having a relationship with a woman. No doubt, Maureen knew it anyway. Surely she knew of the accusations Bear had been making about Sydney and Gabby around town, but she likely didn't give a shit about that. Everything paled in comparison to what he had done.

Maureen explained that all she would be handling was the divorce, clean and simple. She further explained that the district attorney's office would be handling the case against Bear and pursuing the criminal charges against him. That took a little sinking in for Sydney to get it, but when she did, she was comforted that the big dogs were on her side and they didn't take a liking to pedophiles. Maureen then went on to say that Bear had already retained an attorney from Houston to represent him. He was preparing for the inevitable.

It was at that moment that Sydney decided to keep the surname of Keane. This was Elijah's last name. No, she would not be going back to her maiden name in an effort to disconnect from Bear. She would keep the last name given to her son. They were in this together. Always.

Maureen gave Sydney the names of the district attorney and the assistant district attorney, and let her know she would likely be receiving a call from them soon.

Sydney was ready.

⋏

Sydney did receive a call the very next day, but it was from a very nice lady from the Merriweather Police Department. She called to set a time for Sydney to meet with the lead detective on the case. Her meeting was set for the following morning, nine o'clock sharp. Immediately after that call, Sydney received the call from the assistant DA, Arthur Neumann, letting Sydney know he was aware of her scheduled meeting with the detective and based on information received from that meeting, the case would proceed accordingly. Sydney looked forward to her morning meeting and as far as she was concerned, there was only one way to proceed: to go after Bear, full throttle.

Chapter 24

"Ms. Keane?"

Sydney heard her name and turned around to see a big burly man with shoulders as wide as any professional football player. In just saying her name, she could hear his strong East Texas accent. He was in his early thirties, had reddish-brown hair, a gentle face and warm eyes. The gentle giant, Sydney supposed.

"Yes, I'm Sydney. It's very nice to meet you." She stood to take his hand.

"It's nice to meet you too, Ms. Keane. I just wish it could be under better circumstances."

There was a moment of silence that Sydney wanted to fill, but she didn't know what to say.

"My name is Heath Bridges. I'll be the lead detective on the case involving your son, Elijah."

All of the sudden, the room got cold and everything continued to sink in. And Sydney was continuing to sink into the realization of it all. She had never had any dealings with a detective in her life and now they were moving forward into a criminal case against Bear, a man she had once trusted. She had to keep reminding herself that she was strong and that she could do this. She could do this for Elijah.

"Well, Detective Bridges," Sydney started and paused. "I hope you understand that I will do whatever it takes to protect my son. You tell me what you need for me to do and I'm there."

"Thank you for being so cooperative, Ms. Keane. The first thing I need you to do is write down everything you can remember that Elijah has told you from the beginning until now. Don't leave anything out. What may seem like something small to you may actually be a key piece of evidence against Bear. Do you understand? Just think really hard about everything and write it down. Keep a daily journal of anything else that may seem significant. We're building a case and you're a key person in this, obviously."

"I'll do that and you do me a favor. Call me Sydney. Ms. Keane makes me sound old. Deal?" she said with a smile.

"You gotta deal, Sydney." He grinned back at her.

Sydney went home and immediately took out her pad and pen. She wrote down everything she could remember from the first night Elijah had told her about Bear. Sydney was good at remembering details and she made sure to include every one, no matter how difficult. Detective Bridges had told her that she should hear from someone in his office over the next day or two, so to have everything ready when they contacted her. She would have it ready. All of it.

⅄

"Hey there," Gabby said softly, as she came behind Sydney and put her arms around her. "Supper smells good. What are we having?"

"Smothered pork chops. I'm making some mashed potatoes and green beans too. Hungry?" Sydney took in this fleeting moment of normalcy.

"Yes, I'm hungry, but why don't we sit and take a minute together," Gabby said, taking the spoon from Sydney's hand. She led Sydney to the floor by the coffee table and went back into the kitchen to pour herself and Sydney a glass of wine.

"Now then." Gabby walked over to Sydney and sat next to her.

"Where is Elijah?" Sydney asked.

"I've bathed him and he's watching *Fraggle Rock* until dinner is ready," Gabby said, proud of herself that she had covered all bases.

"Ah, I see. Well, this is nice." Sydney leaned into Gabby. The potatoes and green beans could wait just a few minutes and a glass of wine was a much appreciated thing.

A knock on the door startled both Sydney and Gabby. Who would be coming over this time of evening? It was six thirty already and they weren't expecting anyone. Sydney looked through the peephole at two gentlemen dressed in suits.

"Who is it?" she asked.

"Yes, ma'am, we're from the Merriweather Police Department and Heath Bridges asked that we pick up some notes from you, ma'am."

"Shit!" Sydney whispered and looked at Gabby. "Gabby, grab the wine off the coffee table and put it on the bar, please."

Sydney wiped her face and smoothed her hair back as if she had been doing something wrong, but knew she hadn't. She opened the door and asked the two gentlemen in. They waited in the foyer while Sydney retrieved the folder of notes she had just completed earlier.

"Here you go, gentlemen. Detective Bridges told me it would be a day or two. Did he change his mind or something?" Sydney didn't care that she may have put them on the spot.

"Oh yeah, Ms. Keane. Sometimes they do change their minds and this is a case they really want to stay right on top of. The sooner they get your information, the better."

She looked at them, knowing damn good and well that they were full of shit, but wasn't sure what their motive was. "Well, there you go then. That is everything I could think of and if I think of anything else, I'll call Detective Bridges."

Elijah rounded the corner, curious of whose voices he heard. He walked to Sydney and leaned in close to her.

"Say hello, Elijah. These are…" She stopped, realizing she hadn't even asked their names.

"Hey there, little guy. My name is Officer Skinner." He made eye contact with Sydney when saying his name.

"And I'm Officer Brickland," chimed in the other gentleman.

"Can you shake their hands, Elijah?" Sydney asked and Elijah reached out to shake each.

"Well, ma'am, we'll let you get back to your evening," Officer Skinner said, opening the door. "Sure smells good in here. You ladies have a good night. Oh, and nice to meet ya, Elijah," and they both gave a smile as they headed out the door.

Sydney knew something significant had just happened, but she wasn't sure what it was. She would be finding out first thing the next morning.

⚓

Sydney woke early the next morning and was as impatient as ever for the clock to read eight o'clock. The moment it did, she called Heath Bridges.

"Yes, I need to speak with Detective Bridges, please. This is Sydney Keane," Sydney told his secretary, and her voice was that of determination. Sydney would drive to his office if she had to, and it was likely that his secretary had read that loud and clear.

It was no more than a minute before Heath Bridges picked up the phone. "This is Detective Bridges," he said, as if he didn't know who was calling or why.

"Detective Bridges, this is Sydney Keane. I'm just a little confused about something." She paused for just a moment and he didn't say a word, so she continued. "You had told me to get all of my notes regarding Elijah together and you would pick them up in a day or two. Next thing I know, I have two total strangers from the police department knocking on my door at six thirty yesterday evening—no phone call, no nothing. Please tell me what that was about. Please." Sydney was irritated by it because she didn't like being played, but she made sure to sound as nice and polite as she could.

Detective Bridges let out a deep breath that Sydney was sure he didn't intend for her to hear. "Sydney." He paused. "Here's the deal. Before we can move forward with investigating Bear, the district attorney's office wants to be sure that you're a-okay. They want to be sure that you're not the vengeful wife whose husband filed for divorce and she's just ticked off at him for doing it."

Sydney sat, completely stunned, which seemed to be her usual self these days, and knew exactly where this was going and why.

"A lot of times women will get upset and say all kinds of things to get back at their husbands," Heath continued.

Sydney likely should have sat silent, even for just a moment, to make some sort of impact, but she couldn't. She was mad as hell.

"Okay. You're telling me that whole thing was planned. Everyone, but me, knew that someone was coming to my home last night completely un-expected. They would be checking *me* out to be sure *I'm* 'a-okay,' as you put it. That's just lovely. I'm not the one who did anything wrong, Detective Bridges. I'm trying to protect my son."

Then there was silence because even though this was the standard proce-dure, Heath Bridges knew Bear Keane was a bad egg and they were wasting precious time.

"I understand, Sydney. I do," he said, knowing good and well he didn't. He'd have to be in her shoes to do that. "Just know that they may pop in ran-domly throughout this process. They may, they may not, but it is a possibility."

"I'll keep that in mind just so I'll be dressed and ready when they get to my door. But I'm telling you, all they'll find in my home is a mother who loves her son. They'll find dinner cooking like they did last night, maybe a glass of wine poured after a long day, and that's about it. But have them come on. Just have them come on." She hung up the phone and cried.

Gabby had gotten up early and gone to work. She left Sydney sleeping with Elijah. Sydney had gotten up in the middle of the night and gone to check on him and stayed. Light filled Elijah's room that morning and when Sydney woke, it reminded her that there was light—there was still good in this world. She lay next to Elijah and stroked his hair while he slept. She kissed his eyelids and remembered the pact she'd made with God. He would be Elijah's Father. He would watch over him and entrust this precious gift to Sydney here on this earth. She would protect him. She would never forget that. God was going to lead them to exactly where they needed to be.

⅄

Just an hour after Sydney had hung up with Heath Bridges, he called back and asked if she'd like to go to lunch to discuss any additional details. That was fine with her. Whatever they needed to do to keep the ball rolling, but asking her to lunch did seem a little strange to Sydney. However, this was a man and maybe chatting with her over lunch suited him better than hunching over his desk with pad and pen in hand. She took Elijah to Love's Door and waited for Detective Bridges to arrive at her apartment. He arrived at twelve o'clock on the nose.

"How do you feel about a drive to Hadley?" he asked, when Sydney opened the door.

"Hadley for lunch? Hmmmm…that's fine. A change of scenery would be good," Sydney said.

Sydney locked up and walked to his pickup truck. No doubt, if you were to count all of the trucks in the Merriweather and Hadley area, you would run out of numbers before you ran out of trucks. She hoisted herself in and they hit Highway 59 North for the thirty-minute drive.

On the way, Detective Bridges made small talk. It was easy conversation that flowed so easily even Sydney got lost in it. She always felt on guard, somewhat, but she felt comfortable with Heath Bridges, for whatever reason, even though he had hidden something from her before.

"You know, Sydney, people are kind of wondering about what the situation really is. I mean, your husband files for divorce, you accuse him of molesting your son, and he accuses you of having an affair with that Gabby woman you live with…" He paused a moment. "I mean it really just seems rather convoluted."

Even though he had just lilted right through the comment as if he were talking about the weather, Sydney felt as if he were making some sort of accusation toward her.

"Well, you know what, Detective Bridges," Sydney began.

"Call me Heath. Please," he interrupted.

"Okay. Well, you know what, Heath. I don't really care what people think because I know the truth. Bear and I both wanted that divorce. The only reason that I didn't file for the divorce is because down the road, if my son ever had questions on who threw in the towel, I wanted him to know it wasn't me. I'm not above making mistakes, but I tried hard to make my marriage work. It makes me sick to even say that. Make my marriage work? God help me. Make my marriage work with a pedophile."

She had to stop for a second to let the words she just said actually process in her own mind.

Sydney continued, "They're looking at a piece of paper showing that Bear filed, but just ask Randolph Calhoun. He'll tell you real quick that we both wanted the divorce."

It didn't matter how kind Heath had been before. Sydney was getting angry now just thinking about it all.

Heath didn't say a word.

"Yeah, Randolph will tell you. Ask him. He practically begged me to file so that he could represent me if anything came back to bite me in the rear. He had no idea it would be this, but I'm convinced he knew something would."

Sydney didn't even reference Gabby, but Gabby was a non-issue with regard to the case at hand, and Heath Bridges either didn't notice she hadn't mentioned Gabby or he didn't care. They needed to focus on the important things and that did not include whether or not Sydney and Gabby were lovers.

They both sat quiet for a few minutes. It was good. It made Sydney feel like Heath was at the very least thinking about what she had said.

"You know what," he started, "I will talk to Randolph. You're right. That is exactly why the questions came up as to whether or not you made up this story to get back at him. Bear, I mean."

"Let's get something straight," Sydney said. "No matter how much I hate Bear, I love my son more and I would never, never in my life tell such a horrible lie to get back at Bear. I have nothing to get back at him for. Nothing."

Heath wanted to reach out his hand to her, just to touch her and let her know that he truly was on her side, but he couldn't. He had already started the ball rolling for his next surprise and there wasn't any turning back now.

"I have an idea, Sydney. The best way to just nip this in the bud is to take a lie detector test. How do you feel about that?" he asked, and held his breath.

"Lie detector test? Sure. I'll take a lie detector test. When?" Sydney asked, not having a clue that she was already on her way.

"Well, we can do it now, if you want. We can knock it out before we even go to lunch," Heath said, as if he had just come up with this grand idea.

"Okay. Let's do it," Sydney said, still having no idea she'd been set up.

Sydney entered the freezing room. It was dimly lit and there was a glass window that she couldn't see through. Heath assured her that he would be waiting right outside and to just relax. Everything would be fine, he said. The gentleman conducting her test was a man somewhere in his fifties with gray hair and a bald spot in the middle. He looked rather plain, Sydney thought, but who wouldn't seem plain sitting in a dimly lit room all day asking questions. He didn't introduce himself. He wasn't there to make friends, but he did tell her how the procedure would take place. He explained how he would hook this contraption to her, he would ask her some random questions regarding her name and such, and then they would move on to the questions regarding Elijah. That was fine with Sydney. She was a little nervous because this was new to her, but she wasn't scared. He began and they moved through all of the questions one by one. "Your name is Sydney Keane?" he asked. "Yes," Sydney replied. "You live at 717 King's Ridge Drive?" he asked. "Yes," Sydney replied. "Your birth date is May 12, 1963?" he asked. "Yes," Sydney replied. Then the real questions began. Sydney didn't allow herself to get upset by the vulgarity of them. The vulgarity wasn't a bad joke they were trying to play on her. The vulgarity of it was the fact of it. She answered all of the questions one by one by one.

Once Sydney had answered all of the questions, the gentleman escorted her out of the room. Heath still stood in his chosen place on the other side of the window that Sydney wasn't able to see through. Heath could see through his side, all right. He had watched Sydney answer every single question.

"I told you to relax, Sydney, not fall asleep." Heath laughed out loud, as if he himself was relieved. She had passed the test. Now he had all he needed to leave Sydney alone and move on to the bastard he'd been wanting to get his hands on all along. "You ready for that bite to eat, young lady?" He placed his arm behind Sydney to lead her out the door.

They drove back to Merriweather and parked it at Darla's Drive-In. Darla's had been a Merriweather landmark, still in the exact same place and still using carhops, since Sydney's mother and father were running the roads. Sydney ordered her standard large Frito pie with onions and a large root beer with lots of ice. Heath ordered his lumberjack meal and they waited on Lorraine the carhop to return with their food.

"Heath. I don't want to step on any toes or embarrass you or anything, but I need to say something." And boy did she ever. "I may not understand the ins and outs of detective work and it may take me a minute to catch on to what is going on, but my momma didn't raise a fool. You knew from the get-go that we weren't going to Hadley for lunch. You never planned to take me to lunch. Your whole plan was to take me for the lie detector test and you lied to me. *You* lied to *me* about taking me to take a lie detector test. Ironic, huh? How do you expect me to be honest with you when you have yet to be honest with me? Please. That man had all those questions about Elijah ready and waiting—waiting for me."

Heath just sat there and stared at Sydney. What was he to say? He had been a damn liar. It was his job to make sure he investigated every part of the equation, and if that meant lying to get it done, then so be it. He was required to investigate Sydney first and if everything checked out, cross her off the list, and then move on. Moving on meant building the case against Bear, the son of a bitch, and Heath was looking forward to doing just that.

"You're right and I'm sorry. Just trust me when I tell you there is a method behind the madness. All of that is behind us now, and I'm moving forward in building the case against Bear. Clearly you're telling the truth, Sydney, and I know that and have proof of it. And don't forget, we have Deb Whitmire's statement too. Now, I need to talk to Elijah—" Before he could finish his sentence, he could see Sydney bristle. "Don't worry, Sydney. We don't discuss bad things with Elijah. We open the door and allow him to talk about what he wants to talk about. If he is comfortable and talks, great. If not, we don't push it."

"Okay," she said. "I do want to be there, though."

"You can be there, but not in the room. We prefer that because we don't want Elijah to feel like he can't say something because you're there, or that he should say something in particular because you're there. It will just be easy and open and you can be right in the next room watching and listening to everything."

"That sounds fine then," Sydney said, as Lorraine rolled up with their food.

CHAPTER 25

The following day was Elijah's second appointment with Deb Whitmire. This would be the day Elijah would meet with Deb and "the dolls." This would be the day Elijah would be videotaped, showing in graphic detail what his father had done to him. When they arrived, Deb took Sydney and Elijah to her office where she had met with Elijah previously. She showed Sydney and Elijah the video recorder and explained to Elijah that she would be taping a movie while they talked. She also showed Elijah the dolls. Just watching Elijah, at the tender age of three, Sydney couldn't help but think how amazingly resilient children are. How smart they are and how they have a deep understanding that most adults could learn from or should tap back into. Deb made Elijah comfortable on the floor with the dolls and walked Sydney back out to the little table with the little chair right outside the door. Sydney waited, not so patiently, as Deb went through everything with Elijah, and when it was over, Deb had everything she needed. There was just one more thing, the final thing she needed from Sydney. She needed Sydney to return to take a psychological test just to wrap up her section of the case file. They knew Sydney was being honest, and they had all the evidence in the world they needed against Bear, certainly with the videotape of Elijah and the dolls, but this would be the final piece of evidence they needed on Sydney.

"Hold on to your seat, Sydney. One hell of a ride, Sydney," she thought over and over. Sydney thought it every time she felt that she and Elijah were being victimized in order to finally be able to punish the guilty.

Sydney returned and took the test. She was done with her part now. But only with the part that solidified who she was in this nightmare. She was the mother and she was doing everything in her power to protect her son.

⅄

Sydney had already picked up Elijah from Love's Door and there was no opportunity to discuss things with Gabby at that time, so Gabby came home from work, anxious to find out how things had gone at Deb's office.

"How was it?" she said immediately when she walked through the door. "Are you okay?" She plopped her purse on the sofa. She just stood and watched Sydney, hands on her hips, ready for whatever the news was.

"Everything went fine, Gabby. I just had to take a psychological test and I'm sure we'll have the feedback soon. I wish I understood more about it, though." Sydney had a puzzled look on her face. "I mean, it's hard to know what to say. You have to answer all of the questions honestly, obviously, but some are so random, you can't be sure what they're reading into them."

She and Gabby moved to the kitchen and she poured them a glass of wine.

"For instance," Sydney continued, "one question may be, 'When you see something dead on the road, do you look at it or away from it?' What the hell is that? I mean, if I look at it, does that mean I like seeing bad things, and if I look away from it, does that mean I try not to see bad things? That I'm in denial? It's all so damn confusing."

She took a swig of her wine and Gabby put her arm around her.

"You know what, Sydney, you can't worry about it. Be honest and let them do the rest. It's scary, I know, but you can't overthink this."

"I know. I know, but it's hard. Here is Elijah, precious Elijah. To say he's been hurt by his father is an understatement. I tell the proper people and I'm the one they investigate. They come here whenever they feel like it, I take a lie detector test and they weren't even up front about that, and then, even after passing the lie detector test, I am asked to take a psychological test. I understand to a degree, but they need to investigate Bear. Heath said they were moving forward with that, but I'm just ready for them to get the fuck on with it, like now."

"So, what is the next step? Where do things stand now that your testing is done?" Gabby asked.

"Well, they have Deb's report on Elijah, the videotape of Elijah, my lie detector test, now they should have my psychological test soon..." Sydney paused. "I guess that's it. Heath Bridges said that he needs to see Elijah now, so I'm assuming that is the next thing."

"What?! Why do they need to see Elijah?!" Gabby exclaimed. "Didn't they get what they need from Deb? Do they not trust that? God, this pisses me off!"

"Look, Gabby. It's another step that they need to take in moving forward with the case against Bear. I don't like that they have to meet with Elijah either, but they do. Heath said that when he speaks with Elijah, I'll be right in the next room watching and listening, and we go from there. If they need their own report, then so be it. I'm just ready to get this done so that they can once and for all get moving on Bear."

⚘

Sydney woke early the next morning, hoping and praying she would hear from Heath Bridges. If she hadn't by noon, she would be calling him.

The phone rang. Sydney was practically sitting on it and answered at half-ring.

"Hello." Sydney had her fingers crossed that it was Heath.

"Sydney, this is Heath Bridges. I didn't wake you, did I?"

Sydney gave a little laugh and looked to the ceiling, thanking God it was him. "No, you didn't wake me. I was actually just sitting here hoping you would call early."

"Well, are you free today? Could you bring Elijah in this afternoon to visit with me?" Heath asked.

"Absolutely!" Sydney said. The sooner the better, she thought. "What time?"

"Let's say about two o'clock. How's that?" Heath asked, knowing she would have made it at whatever time he suggested. Sydney was ready to move forward and Heath knew it without question.

"We'll be there."

⅄

Sydney dressed Elijah and took him to McDonald's for lunch. She wanted to discuss with him what was about to happen the best way she could. Sydney didn't want Elijah to be afraid or intimidated, although that would have been a first for Elijah. He loved everyone and everyone loved him.

"Elijah, you and Mommy are going to see a friend of mine. His name is Heath Bridges and he is a very nice man." Sydney spoke calmly and directly, making sure Elijah paid attention. "Elijah, did you hear Mommy?"

"Yes, ma'am." He kept playing with his Happy Meal toy.

"Can you look at Mommy for just a minute?"

Elijah looked up with his innocent, precious eyes. He looked right at her and she knew how much he loved her and trusted her to protect him. It brought to mind the unthinkable, again, but she kept her emotions in check.

"Anyway, we're going to see a friend of Mommy's. His name is Heath Bridges and he is a very nice man." Sydney continued, lowering her voice like the Jolly Green Giant. "He's a big man and he just might hoist you over his shoulder and tickle, tickle, tickle you…" And she tickled Elijah.

Elijah laughed hard. "No, no, no, Mommy!" he yelled.

"Yes, yes, yes, Elijah!" and she did just that. Over her shoulder he went, and she bounced with him out to the car.

⅄

They pulled up at the police station at 1:50 p.m. on the nose.

"Come on, sweet pea. Let's get on in here. Mr. Heath is expecting us at two and that's just ten minutes away. Hurry, hurry." Sydney unbuckled his car seat. She straightened his clothes and did a quick brush of his hair. "Okay, here we go," Sydney said.

Elijah was ready to meet "Mommy's friend," and "Mommy" was just trying to keep it together. She hadn't been in the room when Elijah talked to Deb, but she would be seeing and hearing everything now. She knew it would be different listening to Elijah talk to someone else other than her about these things, borderlining on unbearable.

"Yes, we're here to see Heath Bridges, please." Before his secretary could comment, Heath came through the door. He didn't even look at Sydney, but immediately started bonding with Elijah.

"Hey there, Elijah. How are you? Your mommy has told me a lot about you." Heath was good with kids. Sydney could see that. His smile and his eyes were warm.

"Elijah, can you tell Mr. Heath 'hello'?" Sydney said, and Heath looked at her with the same warmth he had given Elijah.

"Hello, Mr. Heath," Elijah said, and wrapped his arm around his security blanket, Sydney's leg.

"Hey, why don't you and Mommy come in here in my office and let me show you some things I have in here? I think you might like some of this stuff, Elijah." Heath looked at Sydney and nodded, indicating that this was the plan for the moment.

Sydney and Elijah followed him, but it wasn't his office. It was a room where he and Elijah would visit. This wasn't Heath's first go-around with this type of thing, apparently. He had toy cars on the desk and an airplane attached to a string hanging right above the middle of the desk. Clearly, he had just tacked it in the ceiling, but he had everything covered to make Elijah as comfortable as he possibly could. Heath motioned for them to sit down. Sydney took the seat next to Heath and put Elijah in her lap.

"So, tell me what you and Mommy did today?" Heath asked Elijah.

Sydney answered, "Well, Elijah and Mommy went to McDonald's before we came here, didn't we, Elijah?"

"You did?" Heath chimed in, acting as if it were the most desired destination on earth.

"Yes, sir," Elijah answered.

"Well, that's great, Elijah. I love McDonald's. Did you get the Happy Meal with the prize in it?"

Elijah looked at Sydney in mini panic mode. He didn't have his toy with him.

"Whoops! We must have left that in the car. You want Mommy to run and get it real quick?" Sydney asked. Elijah nodded his head.

Heath looked at her as if this was their perfect opportunity to make the transition so that she could leave the room. Sydney got a knot in her stomach. She didn't want to leave Elijah and she didn't want to mislead Elijah. She thought she was ready for this, but she wasn't. It didn't matter. It still had to be done and some other time wouldn't be any easier.

"Okay, Mommy is going to the car and I'll be back in a few minutes. Can you stay here with Mr. Heath?" In that moment, Heath picked Elijah up, stood him on the desk in front of him and showed him the airplane that hung from the ceiling. Elijah didn't even answer Sydney. He was interested in the airplane now, so she quickly made her exit.

"Ms. Keane. You and I have not formally met. I'm Mary Bothwell, Detective Bridges's secretary. Follow me, please."

Mary had caught Sydney immediately when she had come out of the room. She took Sydney to an adjoining room where Sydney could see and hear everything going on between Heath and Elijah.

"Ms. Keane, this is Assistant District Attorney Arthur Neumann. Mr. Neumann, Ms. Keane. Ms. Keane is Elijah's mother."

Sydney reached for Mr. Neumann's hand and they shook. "Very nice to finally meet you, Mr. Neumann," Sydney stated.

"Likewise, Ms. Keane."

"Okay then. I'll leave you two." Mary walked to the door.

"Oh. Nice to meet you as well, Mary. Thank you so much," Sydney said and the two ladies smiled. There wasn't much to smile about, but it was somewhat comforting to know they were now all on the same page and had the same goal.

Sydney sat next to Arthur Neumann and neither said a word. They just watched Elijah and Heath.

"So, what do you think of my cars and my plane, Elijah? You like 'em?" Heath asked.

"Yes, sir." Elijah said, never taking his eyes off the plane. He was still standing on the desk, right in front of Heath, and he was moving the airplane back and forth.

Heath had his giant hands wrapped around Elijah's ankles so he couldn't fall. Watching Elijah with Heath, this man investigating Elijah's father for what he had done, was so sad. Why did it have to be this way? No doubt, Heath Bridges was thinking the exact same thing.

"Elijah, can you sit down here with me and we'll play with these cars for a minute while we wait for your mommy? She'll have my hide if you fall off this table."

Elijah smiled at him and sat down on the table facing Heath, with his feet dangling on his lap.

"Can we talk a minute, Elijah?"

"Yes, sir," Elijah said.

"Well, we need to talk about Daddy. Okay? But you need to talk loud enough for that thing to hear it." Heath pointed to a microphone where Sydney and Arthur could hear, but also where Elijah would be recorded, again.

Sydney felt as though she was going to crawl out of her skin, but she sat stone still.

"Yes, sir," Elijah said.

"Okay. Are you going to talk to me about Daddy?" Heath asked again, making sure Elijah understood where this was going.

"Yes, sir," Elijah repeated.

"I know you've already talked about it, but we need to talk about it again. Okay? What did your daddy do to you?"

And the nightmare continued. Talk of sexual abuse that belabored every vile detail imaginable. Yes, Sydney had heard it all before from Elijah, but she was hearing it again, and so were these two men. There were no words to describe how she felt. She felt as if she wanted to take Elijah and run, as if she wanted to kill Bear, as if she wanted to knock the hell out of

Heath Bridges for making Elijah relive it all. The necessary evil, that was all there was to it.

Sydney found out more that day. She found out that this didn't just happen when Elijah went camping with Bear. She had suspected as much, but had no idea that it was happening every time Bear kept Elijah at his apartment.

After the interview, Sydney ran to the car and retrieved Elijah's Happy Meal prize. She ran back to the room where Heath and Elijah were and handed Elijah his toy.

"Did you and Mr. Heath have a nice visit?" Sydney asked. God, her words sounded grossly absurd, and she knew it, but what else could she say?

"Yes, ma'am." Elijah reached for her.

"Well, Mr. Heath, I guess we'll get out of your hair. Is it okay if I get Mr. Man home or do you need anything else from us?" Sydney picked Elijah up and kissed his cheek. She hoped Heath didn't need anything further and she could take Elijah home and away from there.

"No, you can head on home. Bye, Elijah. It was nice meeting you, and thank you for talking with me. Okay?"

"Okay," Elijah said, and Sydney opened the door.

"Hey," Heath said, as Sydney was leaving. Sydney stopped and turned around, but kept Elijah's head on her shoulder. "Buzz me when you get home."

"Will do." She wasn't sure what he had to say, but she wanted to hear it, every word.

"Hello there, Mary. This is Sydney Keane. Heath Bridges asked that I call him. Is he in?"

"Yes, Ms. Keane. One moment, please."

Sydney held for a good two minutes and wondered if this was just more bad news Heath was about to lay on her.

"Sydney?" Heath sounded as if he'd run a relay race to get to the phone.

"Yes, this is Sydney. Is everything okay? You got what you needed from Elijah, right?" Sydney asked, praying he had.

"Oh, yeah. We got everything we need. That's what I wanted to talk to you about. We are moving forward with Bear. I'll be driving to his place today to question him. Also, the district attorney's office is reviewing the video of Elijah that Deb provided and they will be reviewing the taped conversation I had with him today. No doubt charges are going to be filed." He paused.

Sydney couldn't speak for a moment. She was once again processing what all was about to happen. She'd been on this runaway train for the past few days and she had waited for this moment. Now that it was here, the realization that Bear was about to be arrested, and rightfully so, was sinking in. It all seemed surreal at moments, and all too real at others.

"Sydney, are you there?" Heath asked.

"Yes, I'm here," Sydney replied, but still didn't know what else to say.

"Are you okay?" Heath asked.

"I'm okay. I'm okay. It's all just so sad. It's not sad that Bear will finally pay for what he's done, of course. It's sad that it was done in the first place. I'm sad for Elijah, I'm sad for me, and I'm sad that Bear is such a sick bastard that he could do something so horrible."

Heath sat for a moment as he took in what Sydney had just said. "Yes, it's sad, Sydney, but right now I'm not thinking about how sad it all is. I'm thinking about getting him off the street so he can't hurt Elijah anymore and so he can't do this to any more kids. That's what I'm focused on right now."

Sydney could hear the anger rising up in Heath's voice and she was glad. It had been a long time coming, she felt. "I understand. I do. Believe me, I feel the same way. It's just more than that to me. You understand," Sydney said.

"Yes, I do. Okay, Sydney. Gotta run." As Heath hung up the phone, Sydney could hear him say to some person unknown, "Let's go get that son of a bitch!"

⅄

Sydney would talk to Heath over the next three days. Heath had been by Bear's apartment twice in the first two days, but Bear either wasn't there or never answered the door. Heath left his card and notes on the door each time, but still had not heard from Bear. He had also tried to call Bear, but Bear had his phone disconnected. It pissed Heath off. Bear had his three strikes and now he was out: out of luck and out of time.

Heath issued a warrant for Bear's arrest and Bear was picked up in Hadley and put in jail. He spent one night in the slammer and faced arraignment where bail was set. A whopping ten grand with a premium charge of a thousand dollars, which Bear quickly made. Free again. But he was also ordered to take two lie detector tests; he failed both. Everything was moving forward now and the district attorney's office was making sure of it.

⚤

The day had arrived for Sydney's and Bear's divorce hearing. It was the first time she had seen the bastard in weeks. From the moment Elijah told what Bear had done and Sydney had confronted him, Bear stopped all communication with Sydney and Elijah. That was perfectly fine. It screamed acknowledgment of his guilt. That was obvious.

Sydney walked into the courtroom and there he was. Bear was a sick bastard and he looked uglier than she'd ever seen him. The filth of his insides was making its way to the outside, and he looked like pure evil to her.

This was also the first Sydney had seen Maureen Rogers in weeks. Anything and everything paled in comparison to what Bear had done, so their divorce and the proceedings were like a walk in the park. It was a non-event. From the beginning, she and Bear had agreed on everything and that did not change. She would get everything and primary custody of Elijah. Now, all minds were on the bigger fish to fry and that was Bear.

Sydney looked across the room at Randolph Calhoun, and he looked back at her with such sadness on his face. He was Bear's divorce attorney now, just as he said he would have to be. Randolph had felt that something bad was up the pike, but he could never have imagined this. Sydney gave him a knowing look. He had tried to tell her when she and Bear had met with him. He had tried to tell her with few words. Randolph had wanted nothing to do with Bear if it all came down to it. Now, here he was representing Bear, and he would have just as soon been in a snake pit.

Bear's criminal defense attorney was also in the room and sat on the other side of Bear. He likely felt it best to be there just in case someone started throwing stones at the son of a bitch. The divorce proceedings ended and now, undoubtedly, the "hell of a ride" that Deb had made sure to mention to Sydney was about to begin. It was right around the corner with the preliminary hearing being scheduled just three weeks out.

CHAPTER 26

"**S**ydney, this is Arthur Neumann."

"Hi there, Arthur. Checking on me before the preliminary hearing?" Sydney asked.

"That's what I'm doing. You okay?"

"Yes, I'm fine. I'm ready to get this done."

"Good. I need you here early. I want to go over some things before we get in front of the judge."

"I was planning on getting there early. How early are you talking about?" Sydney asked.

"An hour to an hour and a half."

"No problem. I'll be there."

Sydney finished getting ready and knew she was overthinking everything from how much makeup to put on, to what clothes, jewelry, and shoes she would wear. Whether she deserved it or not, she was about to be under the microscope and she herself would be judged. Sydney opted for black slacks, a conservative, but stylish button-down blouse, sling-back pumps, beautiful earrings from her mother, and a diamond pendant her Memaw had given to her when she was just sixteen. Wearing their jewelry made her feel protected and she needed that because her mother nor her Memaw could be there. They had made an urgent trip to Georgia to help Uncle Jack. Aunt Evelyn had been diagnosed with cancer, and Uncle Jack and all of their children were beside themselves.

Sydney and Gabby decided it best that Gabby stay home with Elijah, so Sydney mustered her courage and went alone, the grown woman that she was. She arrived an hour and a half early and right on time for Arthur Neumann.

"Sydney." Arthur walked briskly toward her with file in hand. "Come. We need to go over a couple of things." He took her to a side hallway free of any passersby.

"What is it, Arthur? Is everything okay? Did something happen? You seem—"

"Everything is okay, Sydney. We don't have a great deal of time, as I need to speak with others prior to the hearing as well, so I need you to just listen."

Sydney didn't say a word. She just looked at him and he knew he'd made her feel like a moving piece in this game of catch.

"I'm sorry, Sydney," Arthur quickly said.

"It's okay. Tension is running high. But I'm listening and I trust you."

"Thank you, Sydney." Arthur touched Sydney's arm. "Here is what I need you to do." He took a deep breath. "Bear's attorney is going to ask you questions and will try to rattle you. Don't let him."

"I won't. I'm getting up there and I'm telling the truth. He can't rattle me."

"I understand, Sydney, but he is going to play hardball as much as he can get away with in this prelim hearing. Remember, we're making our case so that we can take this on to trial. He doesn't want that."

"Okay. I'll keep in mind what you've said and I'll be okay. I promise."

"Just know that you can't let him make you overly emotional or then he's in. You want to stay calm and just answer the questions. No matter what he does to rattle you and move things in a different direction, just answer the questions and stay on point."

"Okay."

"Now, I will be asking you specific questions also, and they will pertain to your conversation with Elijah. There will be some specific questions, so be prepared for that. I need you to be strong."

"I will. I'm ready."

∧

Arthur couldn't have been more accurate in his description of how the proceedings would transpire. He stayed right on point and asked the key questions regarding what Bear had done to Elijah.

Sydney did just as she was instructed and assured him that she would do. She remained calm and on point.

Then, cross-examination by Bear's attorney; again, very accurately described by Arthur. Bear's attorney did everything he could to rattle Sydney, but to no avail. His final question for Sydney was what had prompted her to ask Elijah additional questions when he had made the initial comment about what Bear had done to him. Sydney told him of her own sexual abuse, keeping it brief, and how having that happen in her past made her understand the questions that would need to be asked. She told him that she faced it headlong and would not turn away from it. She didn't turn away from it with regard to herself, and she certainly wouldn't with regard to her son.

That promptly nipped any additional questions he may have had right in the bud.

Sydney felt confident and proud for how she had handled herself in court. She looked forward to hearing Arthur's feedback.

"We got him. We're going to trial, Sydney," Arthur said, with a bittersweet smile. It was always good to win, but a case such as this was never a happy one.

"That is so wonderful, Arthur. Thank you." Sydney felt a sense of relief for the time being. "How did I do on the stand?"

"You did great, Sydney. You definitely kept it together; so much so that the judge made a statement that there was a coolness to you. He didn't really see a lot of emotion."

"Please tell me you're kidding." Sydney felt as if she had the wind knocked out of her.

"Don't worry. We're going to trial and that's all that matters."

"Don't worry? I'm upset, Arthur. I'm instructed not to be rattled or too emotional. Quite frankly, I have sense enough to know that and that's not my personality anyway. And yet, if I'm strong and controlled, and I refuse to be rattled, I'm cool and unemotional?"

Sydney let out a sarcastic grunt and shook her head.

"Sydney—" Arthur started.

"Maybe I should have worn my housedress and looked like a beaten-down bride. Maybe the judge would have liked me better that way, good ol' boy that he likely is. And then what? Bear's attorney gets the best of me? No way."

Sydney turned on her heels and waved her hand in the air. "Thank you again, Arthur," and the door closed behind her.

⚔

Days passed. Weeks passed. Sydney was in the middle of this tornado, but seemed to be an outsider at the same time. The district attorney's office moved fast and furious in making their case against Bear and they had all they needed from Sydney and Elijah. Heath Bridges had continued his investigation of Bear, which led to even more information from a time before Bear and Sydney had met. Heath shared those details with Sydney, ones that she could have never possibly imagined. It seemed that Bear and Kyle had been lovers in high school. Not that they were a couple, so to speak, but they shared their sexcapades with a rich insurance man in Windmere. Somehow, some way, details that Sydney never got from Heath, Bear and Kyle had come in contact with this man and they would not only perform sexual favors on him, but they would also perform sexual favors with each other for his pleasure. All for money. Even in the midst of all the chaos and insanity that Sydney already knew to be true, this seemed foreign. Unbelievable. She asked Heath where he got his information and he would not divulge it. She never asked again. It didn't matter. None of it did anymore. One thing was for certain: Bear was going to pay for what he'd done to Elijah. Sydney already didn't know this man she'd once been married to. She never did. So the fact that he had another secret—the fact that he was involved in a sexual triangle in high school with his best friend and some pervert insurance guy—really didn't hold her attention. It was one more piece in the puzzle of Bear Keane. One more brick in the wall that would one day come tumbling down.

CHAPTER 27

"**O**kay, this is it," Sydney said. "Say 'bye, bye, house.'"

"Bye, bye, house," Elijah and Gabby said in unison.

The lease on the apartment had run out. Just as well. They would have moved sooner had it not been for a hefty fee to break the lease. What was once thought to have been Sydney's dream home was actually a place that held ugly things. It was time to go.

"Okay, sweet one. Come on." Sydney took Elijah's hand. "Are you excited about staying at the farm for a while? Memaw is waiting for us and she has a big dinner cooked."

"Thank God. I'm starved." Gabby grabbed Elijah's other hand.

Sydney and Gabby took three big steps and swung Elijah's feet in the air and lowered him back down. They did this all the way to the car, Elijah laughing with pure abandon. It made them laugh too and if even for just a moment, it was just the three of them, safe and whole.

They drove to the farm, which was on the outskirts of Merriweather and past the sawmill. The sawmill smelled like a barnyard floor, but as everyone who lived in Merriweather said: "Smells like money to me." Bear still held his job there. The same job her Uncle Denton had gotten him when they married. As if Sydney didn't have to think about his sorry ass enough, she got to think of it every single time she drove to her family's homestead. Regardless, it was wonderful that Memaw had offered the farm to them as a place of refuge. There was no doubt about that. The farm had always been a source of comfort to Sydney. She remembered the times that she had stayed with her Mama Scurlock. These were precious memories to Sydney. When she was a young girl, Sydney would sleep with her Mama. The bed was pushed into a corner so that Sydney was right under the window next to the wall and Mama was on the outer side of the bed. Every night, Sydney could hear wolves howl just outside the window, and every night Mama would comfort her by telling her that nothing could harm them and everything would be all right. "Ironic," Sydney thought. Too bad Mama couldn't keep Sydney and Elijah safe from this big, bad wolf.

Aunt Iris and Uncle Denton had always lived in the original house right next door. Sydney could remember as a child them coming over every morning for breakfast. Mama would be up early and would have a feast prepared when they walked through the door. Was there anything as truly comforting as being a child and waking up in your great-grandmother's bed, listening to her shuffling in the kitchen, and the smell of bacon, eggs, and coffee filling the air? The answer was no. There was nothing more comforting, and Sydney wished she could feel one single ounce of that peace now.

Sydney pulled up the drive and the dogs came running, following the car on both sides and barking the entire way. "We have arrived!" Sydney announced, and pulled up by the door to unload.

Elijah worked double time getting out of his car seat and Gabby worked double time assisting in his endeavor. Sydney stepped out of the car and looked toward the house, even more happy to be there than she had anticipated. There, perched on the front porch, were Memaw, Uncle Denton, and Aunt Iris, cocktails in hand.

"As they say, it's five o'clock somewhere," Memaw hollered, and they all broke out in laughter.

Yes, this felt good. Even if fleeting, even if temporary.

Sydney and Gabby joined in on "happy hour" and had a cocktail before dinner. They all visited while Elijah fed the cows pears, which had fallen from the tree by the fence line. The subject of Bear never came up. There was plenty of time for that. This night they would visit, love, and laugh, and deal with the realities tomorrow.

⁂

Sydney rolled over and caught a flash of sunlight through the blinds. She could smell bacon, eggs, and coffee. Was she dreaming? If she was, she didn't want to wake up. God, let her stay right here, right here in this place between heaven and earth. She felt a fleeting moment of safety, just like she had with her Mama Scurlock.

"Elijah, time to eat!" Memaw called down to Elijah, who had gone downstairs to try his hand at playing the organ. "Come on now. It's getting cold."

"Yes, ma'am!" he called out, and the patter of his little feet barreled up the stairs.

"All right. Time to rise and shine." Sydney threw the covers back and went to put her feet on the floor.

"Not just yet," Gabby retorted. She threw her arm around Sydney's waist and pulled her right back down into bed.

"Stop it!" Sydney scolded her in a loud whisper.

"What?" Gabby knowingly shot back, and goosed Sydney in her side.

Sydney shot out of bed like a bullet and quickly rounded the corner into the bathroom. No one knew of Sydney and Gabby's relationship. Oh, they assumed something; maybe they wondered. But they likely chased that thought off as soon as it reared its head. Instead, everyone was just glad that Sydney had her cousin, distant or not, as a support system. Sydney's family was all too happy that these two were best friends and that Gabby watched over Sydney and Elijah when they weren't around to do it themselves. Little did they know that Gabby needed Sydney as much as Sydney needed Gabby. They were two of a kind, these two. Damaged, yet determined.

Sydney and Gabby took their disheveled, first look of the morning, selves to the dining table. "Yum. Everything smells good, Memaw," Sydney said, breathing in the fragrant air.

Memaw gave a laugh. "Well, I hope you like it. My idea of breakfast has gotten to be Toaster Strudel and sausage biscuits, but I wanted to cook you something special your first morning out here."

"And I appreciate that." Sydney gave her Memaw a wink and a smile. "We all appreciate that, don't we, guys?" Sydney asked Elijah and Gabby. No words came. Just happy faces already dusted with flour from the biscuits and jelly making its way down their hands.

"All right then. Looks like we have some happy campers." Memaw made her way around the kitchen bar to the table, coffee in hand.

"Sydney, I've been thinking," Memaw started, and took a sip of her coffee.

"Oh, Lord," Sydney thought. "Here it goes." When Sydney's mother and Memaw prefaced a sentence with "I've been thinking," you just never knew what may be around the corner.

Memaw pulled out a chair and sat down at the table across from Sydney, ignoring that Gabby was even present. This was between Memaw and Sydney. "I've been thinking that you should move to Bayside when all of this is over." Sydney looked at her Memaw, wide-eyed, and tried not to choke on the piece of bacon she'd just put in her mouth. Memaw continued, but talked slowly and deliberate so that Sydney would take in what she was saying. "You know you don't want to stay here in Merriweather. Not after all of this. If you move to Bayside, I will pay for you to finish college and you can work for me, managing my town houses. You won't have to pay any rent because part of the pay for managing the town houses is me providing your town house free of charge."

It hadn't been long after Memaw met Francis Blevins that she sold her motel in Lancing and moved to Bayside to be with him and continue her real estate career. She had purchased land in Galveston County and she had also purchased thirty town houses in Bayside.

Gabby sat, speechless. She was smart enough to know that she needn't speak a word. Memaw would have certainly thought this was no concern of Gabby's, and Sydney would surely make her decision on what she felt was best for Elijah. Gabby didn't think her opinion didn't matter. She knew it didn't. No problem. She would go with Sydney and Elijah wherever they went: Bayside or Timbuktu.

Sydney gave a chuckle. "Wow, Memaw. That's a lot to absorb. College, working for you; looks like you've got it all figured out, huh? Can I take some time to think about all of this, please?" Sydney rubbed her forehead as if to rub the answer into it. All of this sounded like a sweet deal, but Sydney needed to mull this over.

Memaw started again. "You know me, Sydney. I don't like worrying about you and Elijah, and I don't like a bunch of shit that doesn't make sense. You three are welcome to stay here at the farm as long as you want. You know that. I'll only be here every fourth weekend, unless you need me sooner. I'm sure your mother will be coming up too. But the truth be told, you and I both know you don't want to stay here forever. You don't and you won't. Your education is top priority if you want to be able to support you and Elijah, and I'm offering to foot the bill and give you a job. Take advantage of that, Sydney."

Sydney couldn't deny that her Memaw was right. It was a deal of a lifetime and she'd be a fool not to grab it by the tail and ride. Sydney, Elijah, and Gabby could stay at the farm until the trial was over and then move on to Bayside to start fresh. That sounded like a perfect idea. Sydney looked at Gabby. Gabby looked at Sydney, understanding full well that this was too good to pass up. It was clear on Gabby's face. Sydney had her support.

"Okay, Memaw. Deal."

CHAPTER 28

It had been a week since Sydney had heard from Heath Bridges or Arthur Neumann. She wanted to stay right on top of things to the nth degree. Sydney knew from recent conversations with both gentlemen that they were headlong in preparation for the upcoming trial. And although she knew that, she also knew that one week without a word was quite long enough. She would call.

"Yes. Mr. Neumann, please. This is Sydney Keane."

"One moment, Ms. Keane," his secretary said. "I believe he's just coming out of a meeting. Let me see if I can get him for you."

Arthur answered the phone quickly, knowing himself that a week had been quite long enough. "Hey there, Sydney. I know why you're calling. Curious if we've got the trial date set, right?"

"Well, yes, actually. I have no idea where things stand and I need an update. I'm just ready, Arthur. You understand." Sydney sounded a bit irritated and rightfully so.

"I understand, Sydney." Arthur tried to sound apologetic. "Believe it or not, I was actually going to call you today. It looks like we'll be going to trial in October and I'm working on getting the actual date finalized."

"October? That's not too far away. That's great news." Sydney felt a surge of relief. It didn't last long.

"We need to discuss some things about the trial, Sydney. We are moving full speed ahead on this, as you know, but I need to make you aware of some things and I'm not sure if Heath or anyone else has discussed these things with you."

This didn't sound good to Sydney. "What things?" Things couldn't get any worse, could they?

"Well, like Elijah testifying. In preparing for trial, I need to know if that's an option with you. How do you feel about that?" For the first time Sydney heard no real emotion in Arthur's voice. Maybe he had to check that at the door when dealing with the scum of the earth who hurt children.

"He's four, Mr. Neumann," Sydney answered, and pictured her baby on the stand, repeating again what had been done to him. "He's four years old," she said again. "I thought that the videotape was his testimony."

"The videotape is evidence, Sydney, and I completely understand you not wanting Elijah to take the stand." Arthur sounded like himself again and he sounded relieved. "If you don't want that, we won't even go down that road and I'll handle this another way. That was my question."

Sydney took a deep breath and let it out. "Okay then. If there is another way, let's do that. I don't think I could handle Bear's attorney asking Elijah anything. I mean, my God. Asking a four year old questions, and trying to do what? Trip Elijah up just so he can protect that son of a bitch who's paying his salary? What a job." The thought of it infuriated her.

"Don't worry," Arthur said. "I will file a motion so that we can record the testimony of Elijah and play it in court for the jury. Will Elijah have to tell us what happened again? Yes. But it will be the last time and I don't believe there will be any issue with this due to Elijah's age. No, Elijah won't have to be in court at all."

"Thank God. Okay. Can I ask you another question?" Sydney asked.

"Absolutely, Sydney," Arthur said.

"What is going to happen? What do you think will happen at this trial? There's no chance that Bear can get off, is there? Please tell me he can't get Elijah again." Sydney fought to hold back her tears.

"I'll tell you what, Sydney. I'm going to do everything in my power to see to it that never happens," Arthur said, with conviction. "I can't imagine that things won't turn out exactly like they should. We have Elijah's taped conversation with Heath Bridges, we have the videotape of Elijah that Deb Whitmire provided, we will have his taped testimony, and we have you. This seems like a slam dunk to me, but we have to make sure all of our *t*'s are crossed and our *i*'s dotted. We don't want any surprises."

Sydney let out a sarcastic chuckle. "Huh. No surprises. Pardon my French, but that's a kick in the ass." They both sat silent for a moment. "I know you need to go, but real quick..." Sydney started.

"Go ahead." Arthur made sure to give her this time. Sydney needed to work these things out and fully understand the process.

"If Bear is convicted, how long will he get? What is the process?" Sydney had wondered, but there was no room for wondering any more. She needed to know.

"Well, Bear will likely get at least five years of prison time and then when he's out, he'll have a probation period that would likely be about three to five years. Somewhere along those lines. Of course, that's just an estimate. We'll have to see what the judge decides." Arthur could tell by the silence that Sydney didn't like his answer. "Sydney, you there?"

"Yeah, I'm here." Sydney worked the numbers in her head. "So, there's no guarantee, huh?"

"No, Sydney. There's no guarantee. What are you thinking?" Arthur was genuinely curious. He knew Sydney was young, but no pushover. She was smart and had taken this bull by the horns when many women would turn their heads.

"What am I thinking? I'm thinking that there's no rehabilitation in prison. I'm thinking that they'll make a girl out of Bear for what he's done. They hate people like him in prison and he'll surely come out worse than when he went in. I'm thinking that he'll behave himself in prison and do whatever he has to do to get an early release. Rest assured, he won't be in prison for more than two to three years if the original sentence is five. I'm thinking that he'll be on probation for three to five years and then he'll have full visitation of Elijah. That's right, isn't it? Once he completes everything, he'll have full visitation again. Isn't that right?!" Sydney had worked this all out in her mind and spewed it on the phone with Arthur.

"Yes, Sydney. That is right. If he completes his prison term and completes his probation with no additional offenses or problems, yes, he will have full visitation again." Arthur knew Sydney didn't like how it sounded, and he didn't like how it sounded either.

Sydney felt as if a bolt of lightning went right through her. "Well, based on my calculations, that would make Elijah about ten or eleven years old and I can tell you, Bear having full visitation will be over my dead body." Sydney hung up the phone.

Sydney was used to digging down deep for what she needed to survive and when it came to Elijah, there was no place too deep. She was strong and she was powerful and she felt it. She had a voice in this and she was going to make people listen.

⋏

Sydney was waiting in the reception area when Arthur walked into his office that next morning. "Mr. Neumann, you have a visi—" his secretary started.

"Yes, I see that." Arthur smiled at Sydney.

"Follow me, Sydney," Arthur said, never missing a step on his way to his office. Sydney jumped to her feet and followed along. Arthur continued, "I have to make this somewhat quick, as I have a trial in an hour."

"I'll make this quick, don't worry," Sydney said. "I don't want Bear to go to jail," Sydney blurted out, and Arthur stood, stunned.

He shook his head and looked at her. "Excuse me? You don't want Bear to pay for what he's done? It's not up to you now, Sydney. This is in the district attorney's hands and we are prosecuting Bear. At this point, you have no say."

"Listen to me." Sydney struggled to hold back her anger at the suggestion she would ever want Bear cut loose. "Of course I want him to pay. How dare you even say that to me," she shot back at Arthur. "But I also want to protect my son. Some bullshit five-year stint; two or three years in prison, two or three years on probation… Give me a fricking break. That doesn't protect my son and it doesn't protect other children either. It takes Bear off the street for the time he's in prison. And while he's in prison, he'll know every day what it feels like to be violated because that's what they do to child molesters. He won't be rehabilitated. He won't and you know it."

Arthur motioned for Sydney to sit down. He needed to hear what she had to say and he wanted to give her that. Whatever it took to make this wrong right.

Sydney sat on the edge of the chair and continued. "What are the other choices? There has to be another choice. I want to keep him away from Elijah above anything, and I want him to get help or he'll never stop hurting children. What can we do?"

For a moment, Sydney felt helpless and she didn't like it. She felt she was at the total mercy of Arthur Neumann. He needed a good answer and this wouldn't and couldn't wait.

Arthur looked at Sydney across his desk. He knew what she was saying was right. He folded his hands, leaned forward and looked at her dead-on. "We can go for a maximum probation period of ten years. I can let the judge know that these are your wishes and I can state the reason you have come to this decision. We can also request that Bear is ordered to attend group therapy for sex offenders, and we can request supervised visitation with Elijah throughout the term of his probation period." He kept his eyes on Sydney. It was apparent that although this wasn't the perfect answer, it was better than the previous plan of attack.

"Let me get this straight," Sydney said. "I can request that Bear have ten years probation. That would make Elijah fourteen and he could legally decide whether he wanted to be with his father or not, and trust me, I would handle that when that time comes. Until then, Bear could not see Elijah unless I am there."

"That is correct. You or anyone who you choose to be there in your absence," Arthur answered.

"Oh no. It will be me and only me when Bear is around. Period. And we can also have it ordered that Bear attend the therapy sessions," Sydney said, in a questioning tone.

"This is correct, Sydney." Arthur kept looking at her. "But understand: the judge has the ultimate say. I can request this, but the judge will do as he or she sees fit."

"So, you will tell the judge this is what my preference is, and of course, this is contingent on Bear being found guilty, which he will be. Right?" Sydney wanted to be absolutely clear.

"That is right. That's what we're going for—a guilty verdict—and we'll go from there. I have all the confidence in the world that we'll get it, so don't worry about that." Arthur looked at his watch and looked at Sydney.

"I know. I'm getting out of here." Sydney stood from her chair. "Thank you for speaking with me, Mr. Neumann. I do appreciate it." She shook his hand and walked ahead of him back into the reception area.

"I'm off to court," Arthur said to his secretary, and he passed Sydney as he headed to the front office door. He stopped and looked back at her. She looked strong and yet fragile standing still in the middle of the room. "Sydney, I'll call you in the next few days. Don't worry. Everything is going to be fine." The door closed behind him.

This new plan didn't feel good, but it felt better than the previous alternative. As far as Sydney could tell, she was doing the right thing for everyone.

Chapter 29

Sydney drove to Love's Door and surprised Elijah and Gabby. "Mommy!" Elijah ran to Sydney. She needed that so much. After her conversation with Arthur Neumann, all Sydney wanted to do was hold Elijah and tell him everything was going to be okay. Almost as much, Sydney needed Gabby to hold her and tell her that everything was going to be okay.

"Hey, Mommy." Gabby gave Sydney a hug. "Everything okay? How did things go with Mr. Neumann?"

"Everything went fine. He totally understood where I was coming from and gave me some alternatives. Well, an alternative, basically. I'm not sure there are lots of choices here, but this one seems to be the best for everyone. You getting out of here right at six today?" Sydney asked.

"God willing and the creek don't rise." Gabby looked back at the messy room and the kids playing hard.

Sydney smiled at Gabby and picked Elijah up. "Okay. Tell Aunt Gabby we'll see her at home at six thirty," Sydney said to Elijah.

"Bye, Aunt Gabby! See you at six thirty!" Elijah and Gabby blew kisses.

"Hurry home," Sydney looked back and mouthed, as she and Elijah headed out the door. "Off we go for Happy Meals!" Sydney said, and Elijah squealed with excitement. If only life were back to being that simple: Happy Meals and smiles. Sydney had to keep reminding herself that they never were that simple. They never were.

Arthur called on the second morning after their meeting. "Sydney? This is Arthur Neumann. Is now a good time?"

Any time was a good time for Sydney. She hated not having information. Patience was not one of her virtues, so phone calls at any hour were welcome when dealing with this. "Absolutely. What's going on?" Sydney asked, ready for whatever he would throw at her.

"Well, let me tell you what's been going on. Bear's attorney has filed a motion to suppress the videotape of Elijah." Arthur braced himself.

"Whoa, whoa, whoa!" Sydney shouted. "Suppress the videotape of Elijah? That is the key evidence other than Elijah's conversation with Heath Bridges, isn't it? Can his attorney do that?!" Sydney felt as if the air was knocked out of her gut.

"Actually, he can," Arthur said.

"On what grounds?" Sydney eased into the chair by the dining table. Her knees felt weak and she was sure she was working on a stomach ulcer.

"Number one, he cited that because Elijah is on the videotape and not actually testifying on direct examination, it denies Bear his constitutional right to confront his accuser," Arthur began.

"Oh my God!" Sydney yelled.

"Number two," Arthur continued, "because Elijah was not sworn prior to the videotape being conducted by Deb Whitmire, Bear's attorney, Mr.…ummm…Espinoza cited in the motion that sworn testimony is a prerequisite to a valid adjudication and references Landry vs. State, 504 SW2d 580."

Sydney sat still, in shock. She couldn't believe the lengths that someone would go to in order to defend someone like Bear Keane. He was a pedophile. And all of this was to protect Elijah, to keep him safe from Bear. Sydney wondered if Mr. Espinoza would defend a man his own son had accused of molestation. Of course, he wouldn't. Sydney hoped he didn't sleep at night and was sure he didn't.

"And last, but not least, number three." Arthur paused.

"Go on," Sydney said.

"The defendant asserts that many of the questions posed in the tape by Deb were leading questions, which suggested the answer desired. It also states that Elijah had been interviewed by Deb four days prior to the video-taped conference conducted by her."

"That's because we had to have an initial meeting, for God's sake! Deb had to meet with me, and she had to meet with Elijah to decide if this would even move forward! You don't just bring a child in, swear them in and start videotaping! Are these people idiots?!" Sydney couldn't believe what she was hearing. She was doing her best to understand how things could so quickly do a one eighty and how it was all so unfair. She sat quiet now.

The silence was deafening, but Arthur gave Sydney time. She didn't know whether to run, hide, scream, cry, throw something, or pack her bags and leave with Elijah to somewhere unknown.

"So, what does this mean?" she started. "I mean, I understand that there is a likelihood of the videotape not being used, but now what? What does all of this mean?"

"It means we move forward with what we have. Don't pay any attention to what the motion says, Sydney." Arthur tried to calm the sea of despair that he knew was churning inside her.

"Don't pay any attention to it?" Sydney asked, and shot out a half laugh at how ridiculous that sounded. "Why did you call me about it if I don't need to pay attention to it?"

"Sydney, I had to call you to keep you abreast of what is going on. But I'm telling you, regardless of what was entered in the motion, the only reason that Bear and his attorney want this tape suppressed is because they know that we have Bear up against the wall. Think, Sydney. That's all this is about. If that videotape of Elijah comes in front of a jury, we would be hard-pressed to get the outcome you want. Folks don't like men who molest children, and watching Elijah talk about what his own father did to him… Well, the jury will find Bear guilty, no doubt. While we can tell the judge what sentence you prefer, it is ultimately up to him, and I can say with certainty he would send him to prison. Do you understand, Sydney?"

Arthur understood all too well. He saw this type of dance between his office and defense attorneys every day.

Sydney was angry. She was very angry, but she did understand.

"Yes, I understand, and it pisses me off," Sydney said. "First we want all the evidence we can get our hands on to nail Bear's nuts to the wall, and now we have to squash the videotape. The videotape, of all things, that tells the story in detail. My God."

"Look, Sydney. Bear originally pled not guilty. In the Defendant's Motion to Elect Punishment, Bear's attorney stated that they elect the punishment in this cause to be assessed by the jury. Now his attorney has seen the videotape. The videotape would hang Bear and his attorney knows it, so now there's no way they want this to go before a jury. They are just grasping for straws. Trust me, Sydney, the walls are closing in. We've got him. There's no doubt about that, with or without the videotape. And remember, we want a particular outcome in this." Arthur waited for Sydney to respond.

"Okay. Okay. What now? Is there going to be a trial? What happens? Just tell me that." Sydney just wanted an answer. She wanted something that made sense and she was ready for all of this nightmare to be over.

"Yes, Sydney. There is going to be a trial. Now, Bear may plead out and honestly, in order to get the result you want, we may need to put something on the table. Look, I can't say enough that the writing is on the wall. We've got him. It's just a matter of what direction we take this. You know how you want this to turn out in order to protect Elijah; therefore, that's what I'm focusing on while still making sure Bear receives punishment. It may not be to the degree of what he deserves, but it will be punishment nonetheless, and you and Elijah can get on with your lives."

His words resonated with Sydney, and at the same time, there was an emptiness to them.

"Try not to worry, Sydney. Trust me. I'm handling things and will be keeping you posted as soon as I hear anything and dates are set." Arthur waited for a response from Sydney that didn't come. "Sydney? You there?"

"Yes, I'm here. I was just thinking. That sounds fine. Just let me know as you know, and I'll stay in touch too."

On that note, Sydney hung up. She was emotionally and mentally drained, but she wasn't about to let anyone get the best of her. Not Bear, not his attorney, not anyone.

⅄

The phone rang early that Sunday morning and Elijah ran to answer it. "Hello!" he said, excited to have reached the phone before Sydney.

"Well, hello my angel dump!" Maeve said. Sydney's mother had her sweet terms of endearment that everyone loved. Dump was short for dumplin' and a list of additional loving terms also filled the "Maeve dictionary." "How's my big boy doin'?" she asked.

"Hi, Meme!" Elijah said, excited to hear from his grandmother.

Sydney rounded the corner. "Tell Meme you love her and hand Mommy the phone."

"I love you, Meme! Here's Mommy." Elijah handed the phone to Sydney and bolted back into his room where Gabby waited with a pile of Legos that could surely build an entire city.

"I love you too, darlin'!" Sydney heard her mother say as she got the phone.

"Elijah, Meme said she loves you too!" Sydney hollered.

Elijah knew he was loved and it warmed Sydney's heart to know that. She loved how safe he felt now and kept the faith that God would see to it he always did.

"Hey, Momma. What a nice surprise. What's goin' on?" Sydney asked, glad her mother had called.

"Well, I hadn't talked to my baby girl in a few days and thought I'd check in. Any new news?"

Sydney didn't like talking about the case. It was all-consuming and any minute of so-called peace was a welcome one. She did understand, however, that everyone wanted to stay abreast of what was going on, and needed to. She pulled up her patience and filled her mother in on everything she and Arthur had discussed the Thursday before.

"I'll tell you what. That son of a bitch." Maeve was never at a loss for words and never, ever held back with the expletives when required. "He is the vilest son of a bitch I've ever known. I'll tell you, Sydney. I've been thinking so much about all of this, of course, and it occurred to me..." Maeve paused and Sydney could tell in her mother's voice she was shaken by all of this.

"What, Mother? Are you okay?" Sydney asked.

"Yes, I'm okay. I just was saying, it occurred to me that no one, and I mean no one, has ever been able to get something over on me. Not ever. I'm a pretty smart ol' broad and I know people. I can tell about people. If Bear Keane can fool me, he can fool anyone."

Sydney didn't like how that sounded, although she knew it was true. Hell, she was married to the bastard and he'd fooled her, and she considered herself every bit as smart and intuitive about people as her mother.

"Don't say that, Momma. I know what you mean and I feel the same way. But we have to have faith that he won't fool anyone else. Number one, there's so much evidence that no one in their right mind would be fooled by Bear. Just try not to worry. Please."

"I know, darlin'. I do, and I certainly don't want to upset you. I'm saying big prayers for you and Elijah and that this whole mess has the final resolve that it should. I love you, darlin'," Maeve said, trying to hold back her own emotion.

"I love you too, Momma." The two hung up.

"This whole mess," Sydney thought. A mess it was, indeed, and still the understatement of the universe.

Arthur called Sydney that following Wednesday, September 17, 1986. Things were well on their way to a final outcome, but Arthur needed to run something by Sydney.

"Hey there, Sydney. I've got a question for you." He was doing his best to sound upbeat; things with Sydney could go either way once he told her what his idea was.

"Sure. Is everything okay?" Sydney asked. At this point she was ready for most anything.

"Oh, yeah. Everything is fine, but I need to run something by you and I'd like to know your thoughts."

"I'm ready," Sydney said, and she was.

"Okay," Arthur began. "Since Bear and his attorney want to squash the videotape and you want Bear to get probation, I can offer a deal to Bear and his attorney. In exchange for Bear's plea of guilty, we could reduce the charge from Aggravated Sexual Assault to Indecency With A Child. We would accept Bear's plea of guilty without recommendation as to punishment, but the probation department would be ordered to do a pre-sentence investigation and they would recommend a sentence."

Arthur sat silent, as did Sydney. All she heard was they would lessen the charge if Bear pled guilty.

"Sydney, can I explain?" Arthur asked, quickly filling the void of silence.

"Please do," she said and waited.

"We know Bear's guilty. Bear and his attorney know the writing is on the wall. We know it was Aggravated Sexual Assault, as do they, but offering Bear a lesser charge will almost ensure one hundred percent that he will take the deal and the probation department will offer him the maximum amount of time. I can just about guarantee that. Besides, I've already run this by a guy in the probation department. They're aware of the charges, the evidence, and I'll tell ya, these folks don't tolerate child abusers, in any sense of the word."

"So, basically, this will work it where Bear gets exactly what I'm hoping for: maximum probation with supervised visitation and mandatory counseling."

"That is exactly right. Remember, if this just goes before the judge, we can tell him all day long what you want, but at the end of the day, it is his decision and what he feels is best may not reflect your wishes."

"Okay. Go ahead and do it. I mean, if you feel sure this will go the way we want it to, go ahead."

"Sounds good. I'll get the letter out today. You take care and I'll be back in touch."

Arthur hung up and Sydney was glad that this was finally coming to a close. She could feel it. This hell, or this portion of it anyway, would soon be over. It was an odd feeling, however. Sydney had made sure to protect herself on the inside. She had made sure to be strong. She had put on her armor that couldn't be penetrated. She was ready for trial; she was ready for war. And now it could all go away with a simple plea, with a simple, "Yes, I did it," from Bear. All of these months of hurt and worry and desperation and it could all just go away with one word: "Guilty." Sydney may be getting her way with regard to Bear's punishment, but Bear didn't know that. He was still just looking out for himself. Some things would never change and that was certainly one of them.

CHAPTER 30

"**W**e are going out to dinner!" Sydney shouted out from the upstairs window. Gabby had just gotten home from work, and she and Elijah were rough-housing outside with the dogs and stopped long enough to holler back. "Yeah, Mom! Where are we going?" Gabby asked.

"Yeah, Mommy! Where are we going?" Elijah called out, following suit.

"It's a surprise. Come and get cleaned up," Sydney said.

She was ready for a night out. This certainly wasn't a celebration, but just knowing that things were coming to an end gave Sydney that slight feeling. It was somewhat of a celebration. Bear would pay, one way or the other; Elijah would be protected, and Sydney would see to it. The law would see to it. It sounded like something wrapped in a nice bow compared to what all they'd been through. Yes, a margarita was in order.

Elijah and Gabby bounded up the stairs, Gabby goosing Elijah the whole way. Watching Elijah and Gabby having fun and loving each other made Sydney feel good inside. If she allowed herself, she could actually think of them as a real family. It felt like one. It felt like all was right with the world when the three of them were together. But how quickly the realities of the world and society rushed in to remind her that they were a different kind of family: the kind you kept to yourself.

"Okay, pootie rootie! You come here to me!" Sydney grabbed Elijah the moment he hit the top of the stairs.

"Mommy!" Elijah yelled, laughing hard.

"Oh, yes, mister. Off with the clothes and let's get you cleaned up. In the tub we go!"

Sydney stood Elijah in the bathroom and helped him to undress while Gabby stood in the doorway. Sydney looked up at Gabby with a smile. Gabby smiled back knowingly. She understood all too well that they needed a night away from the farm. They needed a night to relax and to take in some different scenery, the three of them together, even for just a bit.

Sydney helped Elijah into the bathtub. "How was your day?" Sydney asked Gabby.

"It was good. How 'bout yours?" Gabby had a feeling things had gone somewhat well; hence, the spontaneous dinner plans.

"It was okay." Sydney nodded her head and glanced back at Gabby. "I talked to Arthur Neumann today." Sydney looked back at Elijah, bathing him.

"Oh? And how did that go?" Gabby knew it likely wasn't anything too terrible based on Sydney's mood, but she was accustomed to the answer going either way, so she prepared herself.

"It was a good conversation. Well, I guess I'll call it good. 'Good' if you take 'good' in context with the situation," Sydney said.

"I hear you," Gabby said.

"Will you help Elijah get dressed while I freshen up and we'll head on out? We can talk about this over Mexican food and a large margarita."

Sydney passed Elijah over to Gabby and hugged them both. "Group hug!" Sydney called out, and the three laughed and hugged even tighter. It felt so good, Sydney didn't want to let go. These times, even fleeting ones, were so special. Every single one of them. Sydney was accustomed to enjoying these types of moments. She knew all too well how fleeting they really could be.

⅄

Sydney pulled into the restaurant and the parking lot was packed. It was Friday, after all, and Sydney wasn't the only person with a margarita on her mind.

"Wow," Sydney said, working her way through the cars. "Let me drop you and Elijah off at the door and y'all go in and get on the wait list for a table."

She pulled to the door and let Gabby and Elijah out.

"Hurry, Mommy," Elijah said.

"I'm right behind you, big man," Sydney said and blew Elijah a kiss.

She worked her way through the parking lot and around to the back of the building. Sydney didn't like the back of the building. Something didn't feel safe to her, but she parked and walked back through the parking lot, trailing behind a large group of laughing "happy hour" girls. She was glad that she had dropped Gabby and Elijah off at the door. She was ready for happy hour herself and wasn't in the mood to wait.

Sydney felt something. The kind of feeling when you know you're not alone. Or the kind of feeling when you know someone is staring at you, watching you. That sixth sense that makes the hairs rise on the back of your neck. Sydney definitely had that feeling.

A truck idled slowly through the parking lot behind Sydney. The engine was loud. It sounded like a typical jacked-up truck in East Texas. It could have been anyone, so she told herself not to get ahead of herself worrying. She was glad that she was trailing behind the party crowd, but it was clear she wasn't with them. Sydney felt safer than had she been totally alone, but she wished more than anything she was in the restaurant with Gabby and Elijah. She heard the engine gun and stop, gun and stop, gun and stop. "Who is this fucking idiot?" she thought. Without losing her stride, she turned to see a big bosomed woman with frizzy dark hair driving, and Bear in the passenger seat. The woman gunned the truck again and again, starting and stopping until she caught up to Sydney. When she reached Sydney, she slowed the truck back down to a slow idle and stayed side by side with her. Sydney didn't dare look at either of them. Once at the front of the restaurant, the truck stopped and Sydney rushed to the front door. Now feeling somewhat safe, Sydney couldn't help but glance back. Bear smiled and tipped his cap as if to say hello and the two pulled out of the parking lot as if nothing had happened.

"Over here!" Gabby hollered and waved through the crowd. Elijah was sitting on the edge of the bar with Gabby standing in front of him. "My God," Gabby said. "What is wrong? You look like you've seen a ghost."

Right then, the hostess yelled out "Oates" and the three followed her to the table. Thank God, because Sydney's knees were about to give way. She knew that Bear had played things perfectly once again. She knew he was sending a message. She knew the type of manipulation, control and mind games that Bear was capable of. But how do you tell an attorney or a judge, "He was with a girl and she gunned the truck and when they got up to me... well, he tipped his hat." "Yeah, right!" Sydney thought. The whole thing sounded ridiculous, but she knew. Oh yes, she knew.

"So tell me what happened." Gabby leaned across the table and stared at Sydney straight on. Gabby could tell it wasn't good. It wasn't good at all.

"Tell you what," Sydney said, looking at Gabby and then at Elijah already occupied with the crayons and pad, "let's talk about that when we get back to the farm." She looked back at Gabby and gave her a look as if to say "please."

"Okay. That's fine," Gabby said, but it was clear she was worried and concerned as to what could have happened from point A to point B in a matter of minutes.

Sydney put it all on the back burner and enjoyed her meal. She mainly enjoyed the margarita she had been looking forward to and knew the recent development of the evening had prompted her to order a second. Gabby could tell she'd be driving back to the farm and let Sydney decompress with her friend, Jose Cuervo.

They pulled into the farm and even with the dogs barking up the drive, Elijah was out like a light. Sydney got out and eased Elijah out of his car seat. His arms went around her neck, his head on her shoulder and it brought tears to her eyes instantly. There was nothing more pure than that. No better gift, no better blessing, no better anything. He was her angel. Her emotions bubbled to the surface. Gabby could see it.

"Here, Sydney. Let me take him upstairs and put him to bed. Come on, honey. Hand him to me." Gabby took Elijah from Sydney's arms.

As Gabby took Elijah inside, Sydney crouched by the car and cried. At the farm, there wasn't a sound at night, except maybe the crickets, so she cried silently, but hard.

Gabby came out to the car and raised Sydney up, taking her inside. This was somewhat new to Gabby. Sydney was always so strong. It wasn't that Gabby had never seen Sydney cry, but it was a rarity. And to see her this worn down and vulnerable certainly was.

"Come here, Sydney." Gabby led her to the sofa.

"Where is Elijah?" Sydney whispered, still sobbing.

"He's in bed and sound asleep. Come here."

Gabby sat on the sofa and leaned her body back on the pillows and armrest. Sydney sat next to Gabby and laid her head on Gabby's chest. She cried and she cried and she cried, Gabby rubbing her hair and her back all the while. Gabby didn't bother asking what had happened earlier at the restaurant. All she wanted was for Sydney to feel better.

Sydney woke up just as the sun peeked through the blinds. It was early and her head hurt. She remembered everything. She remembered crying and had no recollection of when she stopped and when she finally went to sleep. She knew she likely didn't stop until she fell asleep. She raised her head and looked at Gabby sleeping soundly, still holding Sydney. Sydney rose up and kissed Gabby's forehead, covering her with a quilt on the sofa.

It felt strange to have let go emotionally the way she did. Sydney wasn't used to that. No matter. She wouldn't dwell on it. Clearly, she needed a good cry and she got one. She went into the bathroom, gave herself a long look in the mirror and got ready for another day.

Another day came for Sydney. And another and another and another.

Arthur Neumann stayed in contact with Sydney, and only as much as necessary. Sydney wanted more. She wanted full disclosure at all times.

Unfortunately, that wasn't in Arthur's plan, so she left him to do his job in getting the bad guy: Bear Keane.

Sydney did her job and allowed nothing to cloud her mind as Bear's day of reckoning approached. Nothing would…nothing could. She had heard the saying many times: *can't see the forest for the trees.* That old saying didn't pertain to Sydney. She never thought it had before, and she knew it didn't now. She was crystal-clear. She saw everything. She saw the forest and the trees, and they were ugly.

She was ready. Ready for her day…ready for Elijah's day. And it was just around the corner.

Chapter 31

This was the day, October 30th, 1986. Sydney was rock solid in her mind, her emotions, and her demeanor. She had prayed nonstop for this day to come and that all would be just as it should be. God was watching over them, just as she always knew.

"All rise. Hear ye, hear ye. The court for the District of Merriweather County is in session. The Honorable John Whitaker presiding. All having business before this honorable court draw near, give attention, and you shall be heard. You may be seated."

Judge Whitaker entered the courtroom. He was a huge man, standing well over six feet tall and looked more like a graying Paul Bunyan than a judge. He looked like the type of man who had a tender spot only for those he loved, and the rest would be wise not to poke the giant.

He sat with documents in hand, cleared his throat, and peered over the top of his glasses at Arthur Neumann. "Regarding Case Number 31626, the State of Texas vs. Bjorn Jude Keane, I understand there is a plea agreement between the State and Mr. Keane."

Arthur Neumann stood. "Yes, Your Honor. In the said offense of Indecency With A Child, the State has offered Mr. Bjorn Jude Keane a plea agreement whereby in exchange for his plea of nolo contendere, he will be given ten years probation, the maximum probation period allowed, as well as mandatory group counseling for sex offenders, and mandatory supervised visitation with Elijah Clement Keane, both of which will be for the duration of said maximum probation period of ten years."

Judge Whitaker shifted his attention to Bear and his attorney. They stood.

"Mr. Keane, do you fully understand the terms of this plea agreement? Do you fully understand that for your plea of nolo contendere, you are waiving your right to a trial by jury, you will be held to the full extent of said terms, which include ten years probation, mandatory group counseling for sex offenders, as well as supervised visitation with your son, Elijah Clement Keane?"

"Yes, Your Honor. I understand," Bear replied, lacking the sound of respect that would have been wise to show the judge.

"Your Honor," Bear's attorney quickly stated, "the plea agreement also states that if all terms of the probationary period are met, the charges against Mr. Keane will be dismissed and he will not be required to register as a sex offender. Although those terms are in writing, I would also like to confirm those verbally with the State and in your presence as well."

"Mr. Neumann?" Judge Whitaker inquired.

And before Sydney could utter a word…

"Yes, that is correct, Your Honor." The words shot from Arthur's mouth like broken glass.

Sydney was unaware of the final terms of the agreement. She reached out and placed her hand on Arthur's arm, but too late. It was all done now.

"Therefore, I accept the defendant's plea of nolo contendere. Mr. Bjorn Jude Keane," Judge Whitaker said, leaning over the bench, "I want to be very clear on something." The judge's eyes narrowed down with a look of an animal about to pounce on his prey. "In all my years on this bench, I have seen some pretty terrible things, but I can tell you I have never had the misfortune of coming into contact with a man quite as vile as you, sir. You were given the duty of being a father to your son and instead you took that duty and not only threw it out the window, but mocked it in order to satisfy your own sick urges. If it were up to me, you'd be under the prison."

Bear stared at the judge like a sheep waiting for the lion to attack. He couldn't run; he couldn't move.

"You can say 'thank you' to that little lady right there, Mr. Keane." Judge Whitaker pointed with his arm and finger straight as an arrow at Sydney. "I can assure you, she is the only reason you're not going to prison. Don't you breathe wrong or I'll be seeing you again and you won't be this lucky, Mr. Keane." The gavel came down and it was done.

With that, Judge Whitaker rose. "All rise," the bailiff called out and Judge Whitaker exited the courtroom.

The air stood still and hung in the courtroom. Sydney felt as though she were in her own world. It was all surreal. She heard nothing but the sound of her own breath. She looked about the courtroom as though she were watching a movie. Bear shook his attorney's hand. His mother and stepfather hugged him. Bear, nor Vernon or Clara, or his attorney for that matter, even looked at Sydney. They all kept their heads turned from her until they were out of the courtroom.

"Darlin', are you okay? Sydney, are you okay? Sydney?!" Maeve called out and shook Sydney's shoulders. Her mother's face and voice faded in as if the picture had come into focus and the volume had been turned up. "Sydney?"

Sydney focused on her mother and snapped to. "Yes, yes. I'm okay," Sydney said, and her mother hugged her close. Gabby came from behind Sydney and enveloped her along with Maeve.

"Memaw," Sydney said, as her grandmother came to her with a smile so gentle, she almost looked angelic. Memaw took Sydney's face firm in her hands and said, "Come on, Sydney. We need to get you packed. I've got the town house ready for you three. No time like the present."

Memaw gave Sydney a quick kiss on the cheek and they were out the door with Maeve and Gabby in tow.

The four of them pulled up at the farm and the back screen door flew open. "Mommy!" Elijah yelled, as he ran out on the porch. All Sydney needed was to see that precious face. The violent storm of all of this and then, his precious face. It made everything all right and Sydney knew it would be. It had to be. There was nowhere to go but up from right here.

Chapter 32

Memaw had already moved all of Sydney's furniture to Bayside and had it in storage, ready for the move-in. The town house had been newly painted, wallpapered, and fresh carpet put in. A fresh, new town house for a fresh, new start. The moving truck was there, ready for the furniture to be unloaded when Sydney, Gabby, and Elijah pulled in.

"Look, Elijah." Sydney took in the scenery. "This is our new house."

Gabby reached over and put her hand on Sydney's leg and gave it a squeeze. Sydney looked at Gabby with a smile, but Gabby was taking in the scenery just as intently as Sydney had been. All of this was likely very scary for Gabby. She had never lived outside of Merriweather, and as much harm as Gabby's family had done to her and as unfortunate as it may be, her family and Merriweather were familiar territory. This was certainly not.

"You okay?" Sydney asked Gabby, taking her hand.

Gabby looked back at Sydney, doing her best to not show her sheer fear. It was all sinking in now. "Oh, yeah. I'm fine, just fine." She turned her head back toward the window.

⋏

The three moved in and everything moved forward just as planned. Sydney worked for Memaw and Francis. Francis didn't practice law much anymore, but he did have his personal investments, as did Memaw, so there was still much work to be done. Sydney split her time working in their shared office and managing Memaw's town houses onsite. She registered Elijah in a wonderful preschool. It just so happened that it was called Love's Door, just like his preschool in Merriweather. It was housed within the Methodist church in Bayside. This did give Sydney some comfort and Elijah was excited that he would still go to Love's Door. It may have been different, but the name brought him familiarity and Sydney welcomed the easy transition for him.

Gabby got a job at the Sailors' Club and Bar in Bayside and made friends there. Sydney frequented the establishment on weekends and so began their new group of friends. Sydney and Gabby lived openly to their friends, who were both straight and gay, but still kept their relationship an unspoken fact to their families. Sydney knew it was truly the worst-kept family secret, but no matter. As Maeve had always said about those who speculate about things not their business: "If you don't say it, then it's not so. Let them think what they want to think." Little did Maeve know that Sydney would use this same advice with regard to her relationship with Gabby and what her family may think of it. Let them think what they wanted to think. She had more important things to worry about.

Over the next four years, Elijah would start grade school and thrive. He was such a happy boy and knew how much he was loved by everyone. He reminded Sydney of herself when she was his age. She never lacked for love and attention from her family, and Elijah was no different. Sydney and Gabby both continued with their jobs, and also registered at the Bayside Community College. Sydney was ready to get on with her education. Thankfully, there was not a word from Bear Keane. He had supervised visitation rights with Elijah, but never once exercised those rights. Sydney took note of it, but never wished for anything any different. The farther away he stayed, the better. And thank God, Elijah never once asked about his father. Not once. Sydney took note of that as well and knew that she would keep watch over her little boy. At any time he seemed troubled or wanted to talk about things, Sydney would handle it immediately. But the words of what had happened would never leave her mouth to her precious son. If he did not come to her to discuss it, there was no reason to. Life would continue on as it was, just as long as possible.

Chapter 33

"**All good things** must come to an end." What a shitty statement Sydney always thought that was. "Why must all good things come to an end?" she wondered. Yes, it was a shitty statement and Sydney stood by her opinion, but there was some truth to it. She had experienced it quite enough.

By the very grace of God, something just hit her this day, completely out of the blue. Something brought Bear to mind, as it had before, but this was different. She couldn't shake it. She had a feeling and she knew from past experiences to go with her gut.

Sydney picked up the phone and called the Adult Probation Department in Merriweather.

"Yes, my name is Sydney Keane, and I would like to speak with someone about my ex-husband, Bear Keane." Sydney felt a knot rise up in her stomach.

"Okay, Ms. Keane. Can you tell me what this is regarding, specifically?" the operator asked.

Sydney wanted to tell her that it was regarding her piece of shit, pedophile ex-husband, specifically. But she took a deep breath, kept herself in check and replied, "Yes, again, this is with regard to my ex-husband. He was placed on probation for molesting our son, and I am checking in to see how things are going with regard to his probation."

Sydney paused for just a second, but it was long enough for the operator to respond, had she been able to speak. Her pause didn't surprise Sydney.

Sydney never spoke to anyone about the incident that they weren't completely taken aback by the monster who had molested his biological son.

Sydney continued, "He has supervised visitation, but has never exercised that right, so I am basically checking in to see if there is anything I need to know. It's been four years and honestly, I wish I would have called before now."

"Ms. Keane, can you hold one moment? Let me get someone for you. Don't hang up. I'll be right back," the operator replied.

"No problem. I'll hold. Thank you so much."

Sydney was nervous and wondered why in the hell she had waited so long to do this. She felt afraid. Maybe that's why she had waited. Maybe four years of pretending like life could actually continue normally had served its purpose and now it was time to face the realities of it all, again. She knew Bear was on probation, but were there intricacies, other details, within these four years of probation that Sydney didn't know about?

"Ms. Keane!" a lady said, as if she had run a track race.

"Yes, this is she," Sydney said, not sure if this was the operator again or not.

"Ms. Keane, this is Sharyn Eaves. I was Bear's first probation officer when he received his sentence."

Ms. Eaves sounded fairly young and also very strong. That made sense to Sydney. She couldn't imagine a pushover being able to do this woman's job. Sydney liked that.

"Ms. Eaves, thank you so much for taking the time to speak with me. Honestly, I can't believe I haven't called before now, but Bear just hit my brain and I thought I'd call and check to see how things are going. How is he doing in group therapy and all of that?"

"Well, I gotta tell ya, Ms. Keane—" Sharyn started.

"Please, call me Sydney," Sydney interrupted.

"Okay, and you call me Sharyn. Anyway, this is interesting that you've called. I just got a letter across my desk yesterday stating that Bear has requested a hearing to get off probation early."

"What?! Can he do that?!" Sydney's voice boomed.

"Oh, yes. He can do that," Sharyn said, "but that doesn't mean that he gets off. This is just a hearing and I can assure you, we're going to do everything we can to fight it."

Sydney tried to get her thoughts together. "Oh my God," Sydney said. "Why hasn't anyone called me about this?"

"Honestly, Sydney, we're not required to contact you, but also, as I had mentioned, this just came across my desk yesterday. I'm just glad you called," Sharyn said.

"You and me both." Sydney tried to sound as nice as possible. She was taken aback at that fact that they were not required to contact her. That was one tidbit she was never told. There had to be so much more that she didn't know.

"You said that you're doing all you can to fight it. Is this for any reason in particular or just so he completes the ten years he was originally ordered?" Sydney asked.

"Yes, we have reason." Sharyn proceeded to go right down the line of all the things Bear had done, or better yet, had not done.

Sharyn went over dates and conditions of his probation in which he was in violation, and it all started literally the day after his trial four years ago. On October 30th, 1986, Bear was granted ten years deferred adjudication probation. He received a copy of the judgment and the conditions of probation were discussed and explained to him. He was instructed to attend the sex offender group counseling conducted the following morning, October 31st, at seven thirty, and he failed to attend. A violation report was filed that very day with a cost imposed of five hundred and ninety dollars: five hundred in fines and ninety in court costs. Even so, that wasn't the only time he didn't attend. There were numerous months that he didn't attend. In addition to that, he was periodically in violation for not paying his probation fees and there were times he wouldn't report to his probation officer at all. Violation reports were consistently filed, but each time, Bear received what Sydney considered a slap on the wrist, an additional fine, and the monthly amount of the fine was just added to what the son of a bitch already hadn't paid in full.

Sydney was stunned and the two sat silent for a few seconds.

"When I walked out of those courthouse doors on October 30th, I had just heard the judge tell Bear that if he even breathed wrong, he would be put in jail. How could this happen? How can he get away with all of these violations and nothing happen to him? How can that be?" Sydney asked.

"Sydney, I understand. I do, and I wish I had the answer. But I can tell you this. We're going to do everything we can to be sure that Bear doesn't get off." Sharyn said it with conviction, but what was Sydney left to think now? Everyone had spoken with conviction about the case, and certainly the judge had. Did it all go out the window once the gavel came down?

"Can I attend the hearing?" Whatever the answer was, she would be there, no matter what.

"Absolutely, you can be there. I think that would be great," Sharyn said.

"Okay, when is the hearing?" Sydney asked and at that, Sharyn gave her all of the information.

The original hearing was scheduled for October 2nd, but was moved to November 7th. Sydney would be there. She asked Sharyn to please keep her attendance under wraps. Sharyn assured her that they would.

Maeve had spent the night with Memaw the night before and picked Sydney and Gabby up the following morning of November 7th. She wouldn't hear of not going to the hearing with Sydney, and Sydney was glad of it. The more, the merrier and Sydney wanted the support of her mother there. And one thing was for sure: if anyone tried to mess with Sydney, Maeve would rear up like a mother bear and that would be that. Sydney was strong, but there was comfort in knowing that her mother was with her.

The drive was a fast one. It would seem that the anticipation of it all would make the drive to Merriweather longer, but it flew by. It flew by just as fast as all the things that whirled in Sydney's head. The three chatted some on the way there, but all in all it was a quiet ride, each submerged in their own thoughts about when and if this would ever end.

When they arrived, Sydney jumped out of the car and headed toward the door.

"Sydney," Maeve called out, still seated in the car and doing her best to grab her purse and other belongings. "Wait a minute!"

"Mother, please. Just hurry," Sydney shot back. This day was certainly important to Maeve too, but Sydney needed to get inside and get inside now.

Gabby waited for Maeve. By the time the two reached the steps to the courthouse, Sydney had already walked inside and stopped right in front of the closing door behind her.

Maeve opened the door. "Sydney, you need to move on in, please," Maeve said, slightly irritated.

Sydney took a step forward and Maeve and Gabby stepped in behind her. Sydney quickly grabbed her mother's arm and pulled her to the right of the entrance; Gabby followed.

There he was. There was Bear, nice and clean-cut, dressed in his Sunday's best. He looked every bit of what a "white bread" boy would look like and he hid his evil well. Next to him was a striking woman. She was his and Sydney's age. She was slightly taller than Bear, slender in build, and she had a very attractive face. She actually smiled at Sydney, once catching her eye, and before Sydney knew what she had done, she smiled back.

As she looked past Bear, there was another group of people Sydney did not recognize. Maybe they were here on another case. Just then, a short, petite woman looked over at Sydney. She smiled and walked over to Sydney.

"Sydney?" she asked, just as she passed Bear.

"Yes, I'm Sydney," Sydney answered, still unable to focus her thoughts.

The woman smiled wide and stuck her arm out straight, hand open. "Hello, I'm Sharyn Eaves."

"Oh, hello, Sharyn! It's a pleasure meeting you." Sydney smiled and took her hand.

Sharyn had a firm handshake, as did Sydney. Strong women, and they both recognized and appreciated that in each other.

"This is my mother, Maeve, and this is my cousin, Gabby." Sydney introduced everyone with their appropriate title. Everyone shook and did the usual, polite formalities.

Sydney looked back past Bear at the group where Sharyn had just come from, but couldn't help notice that Bear and the woman were staring at her. Bear had a look of disbelief that Sharyn and Sydney actually knew each other. Sydney got satisfaction out of that. Looked like he wasn't the only one with surprises.

"So," Sydney looked at Sharyn and then back to the group, "who are those people you were with? I hope you don't mind me asking."

"Oh, no, no. Not at all. Those are the other probation officers who Bear has had over the past four years, along with other employees in our office who are simply here to fight this as well."

Sydney looked at her, not quite understanding.

Sharyn pointed at a tall, lanky man with dark hair and a meek sort of way about him. "That is Theo Benek. He is the chief probation officer in our office. Don't let his looks fool you."

Sharyn had apparently read Sydney's mind.

"Then, there," Sharyn pointed to a lady who was the same size and build as Sharyn, but a full-on pistol, best as Sydney could tell, "that is Kat Starr. Kat is Bear's current probation officer. Again, all the rest of the folks are employees of the department and are just here as support for us since they know Bear's story and none of us want to see him get off."

"Wow," Sydney said. It wasn't anything profound or articulate, but it was all she could come up with. She stared at the group and thought how wonderful it was that someone, an entire group, as a matter of fact, was not fooled by Bear Keane. They were trained to deal with the lowest of the low at times, and thank God they knew who they were dealing with now.

Sydney kept her eyes on Kat Starr. Could she be gay? Sydney didn't think every woman she saw was gay. But there was something about Kat Starr, and Sydney was usually spot-on when sizing someone up. It was apparent that she was a ball-busting machine and Sydney loved the fact that this little package of dynamite was Bear's very own probation officer. Before Sydney knew what she had done, she chuckled out loud.

"What is it?" Sharyn asked.

"Oh, nothing. I'm just happy that there are people who see him for exactly who he is," Sydney answered. It was true.

"Well, we certainly do. Bear won't participate in group counseling even when he does show up. To this day, he won't admit what he did. He sits in class and smirks. He laughs when others are sharing their stories. To be honest, Sydney, he likely hurts the group by being there. He pretty much does more harm than good and he doesn't want any help for himself." Sharyn diverted her attention to Bear and with a look of disgust, shook her head.

Bear shot a smile over. Sydney knew that smile. Then he took his woman's hand and made his way over to Sydney. Sydney didn't budge, nor did Sharyn. The only movement Sharyn made was to shift her weight from one foot to the next to make sure everyone knew she was firmly planted.

"Hello there, Sydney." Bear smiled.

"Hello," Sydney answered back. She was on autopilot and didn't know why. Why was she even acknowledging him?

"I want you to meet my fiancée, Annette." His grin was so bright, he could have been on a toothpaste commercial.

Sydney put her manners on, the ones the women in her family had taught her. No need to make a scene, not now.

"Hi there, Annette." Sydney extended her hand. "It's very nice to meet you."

"It's very nice to meet you too, Sydney." Annette took Sydney's hand.

Hers was not a firm handshake, but it wasn't jelly either. Annette had a warm smile and as weird as it seemed, Sydney could tell that she could actually like Annette. They could likely be fast friends had it not been for these circumstances.

"Well, I'll let you ladies get back to it." With that, Bear turned, placed his arm around Annette's waist, and they took their places again.

"Hm!" Maeve shot out. "Get back to it, my ass."

"Mother," Sydney said, looking back at Maeve and Gabby, having forgotten for a moment they were right behind her.

"That little son of a bitch knew not to look at me," Maeve said. "I'd have told him to kiss my ass if he tried to introduce me to his fiancée. His fiancée?! For God's sake! I hope like hell she doesn't have any kids!"

That was the truest statement her mother could have said, and all four ladies looked at one another, knowing it. Not a word was said between them, but it was unanimous: let's hope like hell she doesn't.

"I'd better get over here with the group," Sharyn said.

"Oh, yes. Of course," Sydney said. "What do we need to do?"

"You just stay here where you are. We may or may not need you to come in. It just depends on which way this looks like it's going to turn. I'll be right back."

And with that, Sharyn shuffled hurriedly over to the group and they filed inside the courtroom. A blonde-haired woman, average in build and appearance, walked up to Bear and Annette, and the three filed in behind the rest.

"What is going on?" Maeve asked, irritated that they may have driven all that way for nothing. "Are we not going in there also?"

"Mother, let's just stay right here. Let's do what Sharyn said and if we need to go in, she'll come and get us," Sydney said, but felt somewhat the same way as her mother.

Gabby was doing her best to stay as far out of this as possible. When Sydney had her mind made up about something, there was no changing it. And Gabby certainly didn't want to get in the way of anything Maeve said. So, she grabbed a seat on the bench and stared out into the open space.

Maeve walked out the door and dug in her purse. Sydney knew her mother was likely stepping out for a much-needed cigarette. Sydney walked over to Gabby.

"You okay?" Sydney asked her.

"Yeah, I'm fine," Gabby answered back, not so convincingly.

"What's wrong, Gabby?" Sydney asked again, hoping to get an easy answer this time.

"Nothing. Really. I'm fine." Gabby leaned her back against the wall.

Sydney could already tell this was another one of those times when Gabby wanted her attention, but today was not the day.

"Okay then." Sydney walked over to the door of the courtroom, not allowing herself to be pulled in by whatever Gabby may or may not need, as selfish as it seemed. Today her focus was on this, period.

Sydney heard the gavel clank the wood and stepped back from the door. Sharyn Eaves had made sure to be the first out. She took Sydney's arm and they walked to the bench where Gabby sat.

"He didn't get off," Sharyn said.

"Thank God!" Sydney gasped with relief.

"Yeah, with all of us there, there was really no way. At least, that's what we hope for. And let's face it, Bear has created such a situation for himself by not obeying the conditions of his probation, the judge would be crazy to let him off early." Sharyn's voice was a little shaky and she still had a flow of energy coming from her. She had gotten herself mentally ready for the hearing and that adrenaline wasn't subsiding easily.

"Did it help that we were here? Did the judge even know we were here?" Sydney asked, curious as to the difference it actually made.

"Yes, it always helps that you are here. It's not to say that we won't ever have you in there. But if there's no need, then why even put yourself in the position to be around him?"

Sydney halfway agreed with that. But she had already been around him that particular day and she wasn't afraid of Bear anymore. Not in the least. She had grown a lot in four years, and she was turning into more and more of a woman: her own woman.

"Look, Sharyn," Sydney said, feeling strength in her words, "I want to be here every single time. He's got six years to go, so I'm sure this isn't our one and only go-around with this. I will stay in touch with you, but please, please, stay in touch with me as well."

Sydney made sure to look Sharyn straight on and she gently put her hand on Sharyn's arm. Sydney spoke slow and deliberate. "He will never get off early if I have anything to say about it. I want to always be here and I am more than happy to enter that courtroom any time. It doesn't bother me in the least. Okay?"

Sharyn looked back at Sydney. She nodded her head and gave a smile. "Okay."

Sydney reached down, took Gabby by the arm and they walked outside where Maeve stood, tall and proud right outside the door. Upstanding citizens or convicts, there wasn't a soul entering that courtroom who didn't stare at the beauty puffing her cigarette in a Mae West fashion.

"Are we done?" Maeve asked, somewhat surprised to see Sydney and Gabby.

"Yes, we're done. He didn't get off probation, thank God. They didn't need us in the hearing this time, but there could be a next time." Sydney made sure her mother knew this drive wasn't for naught.

"And I'll be right here the next time, too." Maeve dropped her cigarette and squashed it with her Ferragamo heel. "We ought to see how many more we can get up here next time," she continued. "That little son of a bitch needs to know that he doesn't stand a snowball's chance in hell if we have anything to do with it."

The three ladies hopped back into Maeve's Cadillac and down the road they went. Sydney felt good and empowered. So did her mother. They had done what needed to be done, even if it did just mean being a physical presence. Sydney looked back at Gabby, and she was already dozing off for the ride home. "Just as well," Sydney thought.

CHAPTER 34

As independent as Gabby seemed at times, she wasn't. She had a strong person-ality, but "independent" she was not. Whatever plans Sydney had for her-self, Gabby would follow suit. When registering for her spring college cours-es, Sydney had decided to change her major to communications in hopes to be the next Joan Lunden on *Good Morning America*. Gabby decided she wanted her communications degree as well, but in radio rather than television. They signed up for the same courses as often as their required coursework allowed. Rather than motivating each other, they did just the opposite. It all became quite too much for Sydney. Working in her Memaw's office, managing her Memaw's town houses, cooking dinner every night and helping Elijah with his homework in the evenings only to start her own studies late at night… Something had to give. Elijah came first, and she had to work in order to make a living, so her education made the bottom of the priority list. Nothing was going as planned. Absolutely nothing.

Elijah was eight years old when Sydney had enough and decided they would move from Bayside to Houston. As Sydney and Gabby's secret life bubbled to the surface, Memaw became more and more controlling and hard on Sydney. Sydney's relationship with Gabby was the unspoken disgrace that Memaw could not deal with. The wonderful relationship Sydney and her Memaw always had was disappearing and it was driving Sydney to the brink. Sydney took responsibility for some of the failings, but not all of them. She just wanted to live her life.

Even with all of this, Sydney knew where a great deal of her unhappiness was coming from, but she was stuck. She had brought Gabby with her. They had planned a life together and at the time, the future looked as bright as the sun. How had it all come crashing down? Sydney realized "it" didn't come crashing down. Gabby came crashing down. Maybe it was finally being on her own, away from her abusive family. Maybe it caused Gabby to truly reflect on what had happened to her as a child and she didn't know how to process or handle it. Maybe it was Gabby watching Sydney do everything she could to protect Elijah, and then realizing there was no one ever there to protect her. Maybe that started everything.

But then Sydney would reflect back to the first night she and Gabby made love. She would remember Gabby in Bear's closet with the rifle in her hand, crying uncontrollably. If there were ever a sign, that was surely one. Gabby had been a tortured soul and had these somewhat hidden issues for all of her life, Sydney supposed. Certainly, since her abuse started as a young child, they couldn't stay hidden forever. Nothing ever does. Sydney always had compassion for Gabby, but she could no longer be everything that Gabby needed her to be. Their relationship had become a mess, to say the very least. Because of Gabby's abuse as a child and her inability to deal with it, so started the train rolling down the tracks, full speed ahead, no final destination. Everything was out of control and Gabby certainly was. She would have outbursts like no one Sydney had ever seen. The worst incident was when Gabby took two of her own great-grandmother's pitchers and basins, held them high above her head, and slammed them to the floor one by one; pieces flew through the air like pieces of Gabby's pain, sharp as a knife. How could Sydney leave her? Would she herself ever be free of Gabby's pain that she had so long carried? These were somewhat selfish questions, but Sydney wanted and needed to know.

CHAPTER 35

It was the summer of 1990 and the family of three—along with Daisy, their little mutt of a dog—would be moving to Houston. They would take one quick pit stop, however. Sydney couldn't handle the thought of moving from Memaw's town houses straight to her mother and Holden's home. She and Gabby had no money saved whatsoever and although Sydney needed out of Bayside, she was still dependent on her family. What a shit-hole mess she had found herself in.

The pit stop? That would be the farm. There wasn't a better place to clear the mind, heart, and soul. Sydney, Gabby, Elijah, and Daisy-dog moved back to the farm just for the summer. Gabby went back to her old job at Bragg's Body Shop, and Sydney opened the phone book and made calls to look for a job. She found a job in one day: Lampton Ford in Hadley. They needed a receptionist and Sydney was working within the week. Thankfully, Aunt Iris kept Elijah every day, so Sydney and Gabby were able to save their pennies for the move to Houston. Three months of saving should help in having them in an apartment of their own and independent in no time.

At the end of the summer, they all moved to Sydney's mother's house: Sydney, Gabby, Elijah, and Daisy. Throw in Maeve, Holden, and their two poodles and you definitely had a house full. Everyone was on their best behavior. Sydney and Gabby quickly found jobs. Gabby worked at the Briar Oaks Country Club as a server, and Sydney found a job that she loved at the St. Martin Hotel on Post Oak. She worked as a secretary in the catering department. Both Sydney and Gabby had made sure to get jobs in Houston. They wanted to move out on their own quickly and they wanted their jobs and new home to be in close proximity. Sydney registered Elijah in the elementary school in Windmere and hated that she would soon be moving him again. What Sydney had hoped would be a maximum three-month stay at her mother's home turned into a six-month stay. As one might anticipate, things turned sour those last few months. Gabby and Sydney were fighting, Sydney and Maeve were fighting, and Sydney felt the effects of acute stress. Sydney had never had an anxiety attack before, but was now having them daily; twice daily, as a matter of fact. Sydney had an attack every morning in the car on the way to work and every evening in the car on the way home. Once again, something had to give and it wasn't going to be her sanity.

It was interesting. Sydney could think back on her life, every facet of it, and feel as if she'd come so far. She truly thanked God for being with her, for guiding her and helping her get past the hurt, abuse, and anything else that would hold her back in life. My God, she had made mistakes, but she still knew who she was. And yet, here she was. She was twenty-seven and although she had come far in many ways, she knew without question there was so much more out there for her. She just needed to find it. And when she did, she needed to recognize it and hold on to it for dear life.

Moving out of her mother's house was not without its battle scars. Maeve had long suspected Sydney's relationship with Gabby, but nothing was ever discussed. When Sydney told Maeve that she and Gabby would be moving out together, Maeve had a meltdown. Over the course of the six months, Maeve had hoped that the problems Sydney and Gabby were having would finally have their day in court and the two would split for good. That didn't happen, much to Maeve's dismay. It was an ugly scene between Sydney and Maeve, but it was for the best. Sydney needed to be on her own, and Gabby would be moving in with her.

Sydney did a great deal of research on the best schools in Houston and decided on San Felipe Elementary for Elijah. She and Gabby found a condominium right off Westheimer on a quiet little street that you would never dream was in such a busy area of the city. Sydney loved their new condo. It was quaint and cool. Bricks laid the way through a courtyard mindfully manicured with plants contained in raised brick beds; fountains trickled soft running water throughout. It was peaceful and serene and just what the doctor ordered. Once at the doorway of their building, it felt as if you were entering a sprawling, grand home. Not so, but grand in Sydney's mind nonetheless. Enter, and there were four doors: two on the lower floor, one to the left and one to the right, and two upstairs, positioned the same. Sydney's and Gabby's new home was the door to the left, bottom floor. A tall iron fence jetted off the front of the condo and made its way all the way down from the living room, past Elijah's room and ended on the corner, taking in Sydney and Gabby's room. It was lovely, and Sydney felt safe and comfortable.

There was nothing about her new home Sydney would change. The carpet throughout was slightly darker than champagne and the back wall in the dining room, which opened to the living room, was covered in mirrored glass, and the floors in the kitchen were black and white checked. Sydney would have never thought of picking that type of floor in the kitchen, which made it all the more appealing. It was different. She was different. This was her life, living as an independent woman for the first time, and it felt good.

Elijah attended the YMCA's after-school program and made many new friends. He loved his newfound "place." That place where children begin to find themselves and embrace a sense of independence. There was an independence, a sort of rebirth. Sydney felt it, as did Gabby, and it would get them through the next two years.

CHAPTER 36

Over the course of the next two years, Bear would try to get off early probation twice more. It became an annual ritual with him. Thanks to Sydney's relationship with Sharyn Eaves, which grew into an odd sort of long-distance friendship, Sydney was always abreast of what was going on with Bear. A month didn't pass that Sydney didn't call Sharyn, and Sharyn always made sure to inform Sydney of the latest status on Bear Keane. It was always more of the same. Nothing changed.

During these two years, Bear and Annette were married and now had a son they named Cody. Annette would accompany Bear to both hearings. Each time they all met at the courthouse, it felt strangely monotonous even though they had only met there a total of three times. It was an annual reunion of sorts.

These two particular times that Bear had his hearings, he didn't so much as look in Sydney's direction. But Annette would make it a point to approach Sydney, say hello and be cordial. Strangely enough, Bear never stopped her from doing so. And as odd as it seemed, it was as if Annette understood why Sydney was there. She didn't appear to be angry at all that she had to be in court every year to defend her husband for a heinous crime in hopes that he got off probation early. She seemed somewhat indifferent about the situation and that made Sydney feel uneasy. There was surely more to the picture than met the eye, but rather than overanalyze, Sydney would simply keep her line drawn clearly in the sand.

It was becoming apparent that Bear was not going to get off probation early. Not any time soon, anyway. As much as he wished for it each year, he did the bare minimum that was required and he showed no signs of wanting any type of help or rehabilitation.

Then, at the second hearing, the judge did something that could have never been predicted. He removed Bear from group sex offender counseling. The judge's words verbatim were, "Mr. Keane, you may not want help for the horrible things you've done, but these other men do. I am removing you from sex offender counseling. You are a disruption and hindrance to the group. If you don't want help, that is your choice, but I will not allow you to hinder these other men in their progress."

Sharyn Eaves made her way to Sydney at a much slower pace than she had at the first two hearings. She shared the news that Bear, once again, was not let off probation early.

"There is something else. What is it?" Sydney asked.

Sharyn told Sydney exactly what the judge had said. The timing couldn't have been more perfect. Just as Sharyn had finished her sentence and Sydney's jaw dropped, Bear walked by, holding Annette's hand, and shot Sydney his best "fuck you" smile.

"Are you fucking kidding me?" Sydney asked, looking back at Sharyn. Sydney was angry and she didn't care. She didn't care that Bear heard her, nor did she care that her language was foul for the first time with Sharyn Eaves.

"No, I'm not kidding you," Sharyn answered. That was all. There was nothing left to say.

"That's just fucking lovely. He may not have gotten off probation early, but he still got what he wanted. He never wanted to do group counseling and now he doesn't have to. How can that be? That was the whole reason I didn't want him to go to prison. Well, one of the reasons anyway. I just wanted him to get help, so he wouldn't do this again. Why?"

Sydney just stared at Sharyn, hoping she would say something that would make sense of all of this.

"I don't know, Sydney." Sharyn looked as though someone had knocked the wind out of her and she knew that Sydney had a point. "I really don't know," she continued. "The truth is that Bear is hurting the group. He truly is. Does he need extensive therapy and counseling? You better believe it. But if he is going to act like a jackass at every group therapy session, that is unacceptable. He certainly doesn't need to hinder those who are trying to be better."

"So, you approve of this?" Sydney looked at Sharyn with a look of betrayal.

"I won't say that I approve of it completely, but I understand to a degree," Sharyn answered.

"Smart and safe answer," Sydney thought.

Sydney opened her mouth to speak and shut it quickly.

"What, Sydney? What were you about to say?" Sharyn asked her, not sure she wanted to know.

"I was about to say," Sydney started, and then paused to choose her words carefully. She didn't want to fly off the handle and have something be misconstrued. "I was about to say," she continued, "that while I appreciate everyone working on mine and Elijah's behalf, I don't understand Bear being given leniency. I wanted him to get ten years of probation and I appreciate the judge seeing to that. But I also wanted him to have mandatory counseling. That wasn't as punishment for Bear, but to help him. It was to help him so that he could become a better person and so that he wouldn't hurt any other children. I don't have all the answers if he was affecting other members of the group, but Bear should not have been allowed to work the system until he got what he wanted. Quite frankly, because he was in violation of his probation requirements, he should have been thrown in jail."

There wasn't anything left to say. Sharyn gave Sydney a look, an understanding smile and hugged her. This day didn't end like the other two hearings. This one was different and Sydney felt it. It felt like an open hole. There was a void. Sydney hugged Sharyn back, feeling confident that Sharyn understood, but knowing she could offer no answer.

Sydney walked out the door and toward where her mother and Gabby had assembled for a cigarette. Sydney took Gabby's cigarette from her hand and took a long drag. She watched as Bear and Annette walked to their car.

It was a beautiful day. The sky was crystal blue and there was a nice breeze in the air. Bear and Annette walked hand in hand. Everything seemed picture-perfect to any outsider.

It was at that exact moment that Sydney had another epiphany and it hit her like a ton of bricks. She knew without question that Annette would call her one day. One day, Annette would definitely be calling her.

Chapter 37

Six months had passed and Sydney knew she had approximately five more before it was time to contact Sharyn Eaves again. If Bear stuck to his annual routine, and Sydney knew that he likely would, Bear would attempt early probation once again. Although somewhat temporary, and she knew it, Sydney embraced the normalcy she had created until the clock struck that dreaded hour once again.

Sydney had tucked Elijah into bed, poured herself a glass of wine and laid back on the sofa. The day had been long. Gabby would be home in a couple of hours and Sydney was savoring her time alone. Peace. It was a rare commodity, so she clicked off the television and eased into the cushions with her wine and magazine.

The phone rang.

"Of course." Sydney raised herself up from the deep impression on the sofa she'd already made, disappointed that her alone time was so abruptly interrupted.

She picked up the phone from the kitchen bar. "Hello."

"Sydney?" a strange voice asked.

"Yes?" Sydney answered back. Her mind worked double time to figure out who was calling. The woman's voice sounded somewhat familiar.

"This is Annette, Sydney. Do you have a minute?"

Sydney stepped backward and leaned against the refrigerator. She stayed there and steadied herself.

"Of course," Sydney said, as if they were friends. This was, after all, the call she knew she would be getting. She knew it like she knew stars filled the sky, and yet, when it happened, she couldn't quite absorb it. "What is going on?" Sydney asked, knowing she had just opened the door wide for whatever was coming.

"I think Bear is doing things to Cody," Annette said.

Sydney kept her back to the refrigerator and her knees gave way to a seated position. "My God," she thought. Of all the things that could happen, and that Sydney had expected, and here they were. Sydney stared at the black and white checkered floor as Annette started, detail by detail.

"Sydney, are you there?" Annette asked.

"Yes, I'm here, Annette." Sydney had to take a breath and get her thoughts gathered from the splintered kaleidoscope they'd just fallen into. "I'm here. Tell me. What has happened?"

"I don't know what to think, Sydney. I don't know what to think," Annette answered. She sounded scared, confused, and as if she didn't really know who to turn to. Sydney could feel her desperation through the phone.

"Let's start at the beginning, Annette. Take a deep breath and let's just start from the beginning. What is making you think that Bear is doing something to Cody?"

Sydney wanted to know the answer and at the same time, it sickened her. Cody was a baby. He was only eighteen months old. If Bear started his perversions this early with Cody, he surely had with Elijah.

"I…I know this may sound crazy, but it's when he changes Cody's diaper. He always wants to change Cody. Most men seem to mind that, but not Bear. Does that sound crazy?" Annette sounded more desperate. Talking about this wasn't giving her any sense of relief or validation, but making her more upset.

"No, that doesn't sound crazy, Annette. It doesn't." Sydney stopped for Annette to continue.

"I just…I just don't know. When I change Cody, he says 'Daddy, pee-pee. Daddy pee-pee.' But when I try to ask Cody what that means, he can't tell me. He doesn't understand." Annette sounded so incredibly desperate. She sounded wildly confused, as if she were dropped in the middle of a maze and told to find her way out.

"Annette, all I know to tell you is that if you feel that Bear is doing something to Cody, you have to take Cody and get out of the house. Do you understand me?" Sydney felt almost as desperate as Annette sounded. If she could drive to Merriweather and take Annette and Cody out of the house herself, she would.

How could these two women, in an instant, have this bond? Sydney wondered. Love for their children.

"How can I? How can I? Bear won't let me leave, Sydney. He won't."

"Listen to me, Annette! Bear can't stop you!" Sydney reeled in her emotions. She needed patience, but she also needed Annette to understand. "This is not a game, Annette. This is your son. If you're not there to protect him, then who is?"

Annette sat in silence.

"Now, listen to me. If you feel inside of your soul, your heart, that Bear is abusing Cody, then he very likely is. It doesn't matter what makes sense or doesn't make sense, if he'll let you leave or not. If you feel that this is happening, you have to get out. Do you understand me?" Sydney waited.

Annette stayed silent.

"Are you there, Annette?"

"Yes, I'm here," Annette answered. Her voice sounded calm, but as though she was crying.

"Go to Heath Bridges, the detective, or to Arthur Neumann, the assistant DA. Tell them what you think is happening. They will tell you what to do. You can also call Deb Whitmire, the child psychologist. Annette, they helped me. They will help you."

Sydney wanted to help Annette herself, but she couldn't get that involved. She didn't need for people to say she got all of it started with Annette. No, this had to be Annette's battle, but Sydney would certainly be there for her.

"I will. I will do that." Annette sounded determined, yet fragile.

Chapter 38

Sydney, Gabby, Elijah, and their little dog, Daisy, continued living in domesticity, but it would be short-lived. The beginning of the end had already begun for Sydney and Gabby some time ago. They were just codependent enough to ignore it. Yes, the end was coming and there was no stopping it. And when the end came, it came not gently, but with a grand finale.

⋏

July 4, 1992

Sydney and Gabby had decided to join the rest of the family at the farm for fun and fireworks. Elijah loved the time with his cousins, and entertaining the adults with firecrackers and sparklers.

Gabby was out of sorts, not quite herself, for the entire trip to the farm. Sydney tried everything to get Gabby to talk to her, but Gabby was tight-lipped, not sharing a thing. When they arrived at the farm, Gabby had barely put down her luggage when she announced that she would be going for a drive. She would like to see her parents. Although completely out of left field, and Sydney not liking the horrible feeling that had instantly hit her gut, Sydney didn't say a word. She wasn't letting anything ruin this day, nor this trip. Gabby was an adult and it was her choice. She left and Sydney did her best to put on her "everything is okay" face, knowing full well that it wasn't.

Time ticked on, hours went by, and there was no Gabby.

Then, a sound. It sounded like an explosion of sorts. A car came crashing through the fence on the far side of the property and the light from the headlights bounced uncontrollably as the car hit potholes in the pasture. It came to an abrupt stop in the middle of the pasture. The horn blared and echoed through the summer air.

Everyone ran to the car, except Memaw, who kept the children at the house. Gabby was slumped over the steering wheel, sobbing uncontrollably. The smell of bourbon filled the car. She was alive, but far from okay.

It was the final straw. There was no turning back now. This was the end of them.

Independence Day had indeed arrived.

Chapter 39

As they say, "There is always sunshine after the rain." Well, at least the sun was rising on the horizon. After Sydney and Gabby's breakup, Gabby did get herself help from a wonderful therapist. She was diagnosed with post-traumatic stress disorder that stemmed from her years of abuse as a child. Just as Gabby was getting cleansed by her new therapist, Sydney was feeling cleansed as well. She knew Gabby was getting better and getting on with her life, and she knew that she and Elijah were getting on with their lives too.

This was the first time in Sydney's life that she was on her own. There was no one telling her what to do, no one expecting anything from her, no one fussing about one thing or the other. She was free and it felt wonderful. She was truly on her own, just her and Elijah. Sydney relished in the simplest of things, like grocery shopping for just her and Elijah, watching her budget and paying her bills on time. She was thirty now and for the first time in her life, she truly felt her independence.

Sydney found a new home for herself and Elijah. She stayed in the same area so that Elijah would remain in the same school and at the YMCA, but they needed a change of scenery. She found a lovely condominium right behind the Baptist church. They had been built in the 60s and something about it reminded Sydney of her Memaw: the style of it, everything.

Sydney loved the Galleria area. She felt so safe there and it brought back wonderful memories. The apartments she and her mother had lived in with

Memaw and Papa when Sydney was a small child were on Westheimer and were still there. The apartments where she lived with her Aunt Olivia and Uncle Berk when they brought Victoria home from the hospital were on Chimney Rock and still there. And the Methodist church where Sydney was baptized when she was nine years old was on San Felipe and still as beautiful as ever. This area definitely felt like home to Sydney. It came second only to the farm.

Sydney had moved on from her job at the St. Martin as well. She was single now and needed to make more money to support herself and Elijah, so she got a job working for twelve oil traders. It was a one-girl office and less than one mile from her new condominium. As chance would have it, it was right down the street from the church where she had been baptized. Maybe that was a sign of good things to come.

Sydney enjoyed working for the guys and she wore many hats. She was the receptionist, she handled all of the accounting, she handled all contract transmissions, she kept the kitchen and supplies stocked; it was a great job and she was good at it. The only thing Sydney didn't tend to was her boss, much to his dismay. He was a womanizer and he had plenty of them. Conrad O'Kenna was his name. He was in his late thirties and very successful, and the trail of women who called for him and filed through the front office door never seemed to let up. There was even a high-priced call girl who serviced the nice gentlemen that Sydney worked for, whether they were married or not, and it all happened in the confines of O'Kenna Fuels and Services, Inc. Sydney just tended to her business and went home every evening.

Sydney had worked for Conrad for just a few months when on her birthday, Conrad surprised her with a gift. It was something she would need to try on, so he offered up his office for her to do so. My, my…it was a black leather halter top with a zipper all the way up the front. Sydney chuckled as she tried it on and wondered if Conrad had a hidden camera somewhere in his office, so she faced the wall while she changed. She knew there were ulterior motives connected with the gift, but she would accept it like a lady and that would be that. Conrad knocked on the door to get a peek at his wares and Sydney modeled it modestly. He was pleased with his choice of gifts for her. It would, however, be the only time Conrad would have the opportunity to see her in her new black leather halter.

There were times that Sydney did go beyond the call of duty and she was happy to do it. For birthdays and special occasions, Sydney cooked a feast at the office for the guys. Some didn't have families and some of their families were out of state. For those, the most company they would typically receive during these special times would be the bottle of Jack Daniels as long as it lasted. It made Sydney feel good to give the guys a home-cooked meal with a woman's touch.

That's what Conrad wanted: a woman's touch, and he wanted Sydney's. His only problem with Sydney was that she didn't fall in line with the others. He never wanted that in the beginning. He just wanted his eye candy at the front desk and nothing more. But he became attracted to Sydney. As time went on and Sydney still showed no interest in Conrad, he paid closer attention and suspected her alternative lifestyle. He didn't approve, but his fantasizing about it made him want her that much more.

It was bonus time. It was mid-December, and Conrad had told Sydney she would be getting the same bonus she had received the Christmas before: twelve hundred dollars. Sydney loved getting her Christmas bonus. It was like a little savings account that she finally had access to at the end of the year for Christmas gifts.

Mid-December came and went and there was no bonus, so Sydney used her paycheck to buy Christmas gifts for Elijah and family. She had to cover Santa's duties for Elijah as well, so there was no time to wait. She would just pay her bills with her Christmas bonus when she received it. Conrad was likely waiting until Christmas Eve to give it to her, she hoped. They were open that day for half a day and it was like him to enjoy watching someone squirm.

Christmas Eve came and everyone was ready for the holiday break. The guys had enjoyed their Christmas meal that Sydney had cooked for them the day before. Everyone seemed to truly appreciate it and that always made Sydney feel good.

Conrad had several visitors that morning, including his accountant. He was the epitome of how you would picture an accountant. Although he was a nice man, he was a very "head down" sort, and he had a nerdiness that couldn't be denied. Upon his arrival, Conrad asked Sydney to go downstairs to check the mail before they closed up shop. She did, taking time to spread holiday cheer with a couple of girls in other offices as she made her way down to the mailbox and back. Everyone was getting ready to leave their offices early for their Christmas Eve festivities.

Sydney came back into her office, dropped the mail on the table, and turned toward her computer. There, on her computer screen, in all her glory, was a young, dark-haired girl, nude, with her legs spread open and having sex with a Coke bottle. The scene lasted approximately fifteen seconds and looped back to the beginning, playing over and over again.

Sydney pushed her chair back, still trying to grasp what was going on. Who had done this to her? Who had put this on her computer? She walked to Conrad's office and knocked on the door.

"Come in." Conrad laughed loudly.

Sydney opened the door. There was Conrad, Dalton—who was Conrad's right-hand person and sidekick—and the accountant. They all laughed hysterically and stared at Sydney. The accountant didn't look like his normal "head down" self now. Nor did he look nerdy. He looked like a twisted-up piece of shit like the rest of them. Sydney couldn't say a word. She walked back to her desk, grabbed her purse and left.

She got into her car and lit a cigarette. She fought back the tears the best that she could. Her hands were shaking and she kept looking back for Conrad to come. He never did.

Sydney drove home, threw open the door, plopped herself on the sofa and cried. She had to get her bearings before she picked Elijah up and that was in an hour. If she'd have been able to pour herself a drink, she would have. That would have to wait.

"Fuck! My fucking bonus!" Sydney yelled out loud. "How could I forget my fucking bonus?!"

Sydney was hysterical now. She needed her money and couldn't wait until after the holidays. Conrad was leaving town until after New Year's. She'd call

Dalton. He was a fucker for being a part of what they put on her computer, but he was the only person to call other than Conrad himself.

"Dalton, this is Sydney," Sydney said. She made herself sick sounding so timid, but she needed her money and as Memaw always said, "You get bees with honey, Sydney, not vinegar."

"Yes, Sydney." Dalton still laughed and made no attempt to hold it in.

"I'm calling about my bonus," Sydney said.

Dalton's laughter stopped instantly and he didn't say a word.

"Dalton, did you hear me?" Sydney asked carefully.

"Yes, I heard you," Dalton answered. By the way his voice sounded, Sydney was sure that he was summoning Conrad.

"Conrad told me I was getting the same bonus that I got last year. I expected it mid-month, but didn't get it, and I haven't gotten it yet. Do you know when he was planning on giving it to me?"

"Sydney, Conrad changed his mind on your bonus. He said there are things that have needed taking care of in the office that weren't, and—"

Dalton would have continued, but Sydney interrupted him.

"Dalton, are you kidding me?! Everything Conrad tells me to do, I do. I take care of everything in that office for all of you. I always go far above what is on my job description, and that is for sure. And I'm good to all of you guys. I've never been called in once regarding an issue. He can't do this to me. I counted on that money based on what he said and now I can't pay my bills."

Sydney waited for some miracle. Maybe Dalton would approve a bonus.

"Sydney, bonuses are not guaranteed. I'm sorry." Dalton hung up the phone.

Sydney was livid. Surely she had been this mad before, but she didn't remember it now.

"You son of a bitch!" she yelled at the top of her lungs and slammed the phone down over and over until the mouthpiece popped off the receiver. She picked up the piece and couldn't help but laugh. Maybe she was delirious. Maybe she was just exhausted. Maybe she was just fucking tired of all the shit that men had doled out to her throughout her life. But then she paused for a moment and thought about the men in her life who had *never* hurt her. Sydney thought about those who loved her, cared for her, and nurtured her and she was indeed blessed to have them as a reminder that there were good men in this world. She grabbed her keys and headed to the Y to pick up Elijah.

⋏

On her way to the Y, Sydney got her thoughts together and took hold of her emotions. This was Christmas Eve, Sydney's favorite holiday, and not Conrad O'Kenna or anyone else would ruin it for her, and certainly not for Elijah. She would get this figured out, one way or the other.

Sydney pulled up in front of the Y. Elijah bounded out the door with his bag of Christmas goodies, grinning from ear to ear. They apparently had a party and his teeth were still green from whatever Christmas treats he had eaten.

"Hey, love bug!" Sydney said, as Elijah got in the car.

He smiled big. "Hey, Mom." He gave her a hug.

"How was your day? You ready for some good food, fun family time, and, drum roll please…presents?!" Sydney goosed Elijah.

Elijah laughed hard and swatted Sydney's hand. "Yes, Mom! Stop!"

Yes, this was what it was all about. Her and Elijah. Sydney pulled slowly out of the Y parking lot, taking in all the Christmas lights and decorations on their way home. "'Tis the season for Christ, love, family, and friends," Sydney thought. She had been looking so forward to this time, so she let all of her worries melt away. She would handle Conrad O'Kenna after the Christmas holidays.

CHAPTER 40

C hristmas Eve was at Maeve and Holden's house. Everyone was there: Memaw, Francis, Papa, Uncle Berk and Aunt Olivia, Victoria, Jacqueline, Stephan and Daniel, and Tara. Stephan and Daniel were Uncle Berk and Aunt Olivia's young sons. They came a few years after Jacqueline was born and both were such blessings to the family. Tara was a wonderful young lady who attended Aunt Olivia and Uncle Berk's church and became their live-in nanny. She was most certainly a part of the family and everyone knew what a blessing she was as well. Kimberly and Chad were there also, Christmas Eve always being Holden's holiday time with his children.

God, Sydney loved these times. Her family was like any other in many ways. They may fuss and everything wasn't always perfect, but what did set them apart was that they loved hard and they were fiercely loyal. Her Memaw had instilled in them that family always came first and that lesson stuck. In spite of anything that had ever happened previously, family did come first and there was love that couldn't be denied.

Memaw and Francis would dance and Papa would inevitably "cut in" with a wink and a pat on the behind for Memaw. It was easy to see how the two had come together all those years ago. Papa lived with Aunt Olivia and Uncle Berk now. He couldn't live on his own any longer since having his heart attack and Aunt Olivia, being so close to her father, was happy to welcome him into her home. Memaw continued to send him money every month. She didn't have to. She had long sold their motel in Lancing, but she was good and she always did what was in her heart to do, what she believed was right. Continuing to assist Papa was another of those things and she was happy to do it.

Sydney visited with Victoria, Jacqueline, and Kimberly. Sydney, Victoria, and Jacqueline were like sisters and always had been, and Sydney and Kimberly were much closer now than they had been as youths. The girls all piled right back up and talked about their latest boyfriends, makeup, hair, clothes and all the other things sisters talk about. Elijah, Stephan, Daniel, and Chad all shook the Christmas gifts under the tree and tried to guess what treasure each box held.

Sydney looked around the room. This was her treasure. This was her gift: her family. She held on to every precious second of this moment.

CHAPTER 41

It was the New Year and Sydney was so very happy to see it arrive. Sydney was in the group of people who saw January 1st as the opportunity for a fresh start to a New Year. Any changes that she needed to make, she set as New Year's resolutions. Yes, she was one of those people. And "new starts" were quite fine with Sydney. They kept her from lingering too long in unhappy situations, or that was her hope.

Sydney's New Year's resolutions for 1993: First and foremost, no more lingering in unhappy or unhealthy situations, and that included relationships. Her second New Year's resolution was that she would no longer seek the attention of someone else if she were unhappy in a relationship. Simply end the relationship and move on. Her third New Year's resolution was to not rush into a relationship in the first place. Sydney had never had time to herself. She knew it would be good to have time to herself, and having that time to herself didn't have to mean being lonely. Having time to herself meant "strength" to Sydney. It meant her and Elijah, and focusing on staying happy, and that was exactly what she did.

CHAPTER 42

October, 1993

The air was crisp and the leaves were just turning their beautiful red, yellow, and amber colors. It was a perfect day for a ball game at Memorial Park. Sydney had been invited to an AIDS benefit softball tournament by Rylee, a girl Sydney had admired from afar in high school. She was a grade ahead of Sydney; she was the coolest girl in high school, and homecoming queen. She was far too cool to hang out with Sydney during that time, but their parents were dear friends and that led to a wonderful friendship the two shared as adults.

Attendees of the AIDS benefits softball tournament were instructed to bring food and clothing to benefit those suffering with AIDS. Sydney was happy to participate and she was happy to involve Elijah in giving to those who were in need. Sydney and Elijah unloaded all of their goods and took their seats on the bleachers with Rylee and others.

And there she was.

It came as a surprise to Sydney that this woman had caught her attention so completely. She was tall, slender built, with very short salt-and-pepper hair. Her features were small and delicate, and she had almond-shaped eyes that emitted a kindness that was comforting to Sydney. She was beautiful in an unconventional way; stunning, really.

A loud crack shot through the air and Sydney saw the beauty's bat meet the ball with full force, sending it straight down the middle of the field, just to the left of second base. Around the bases she sprinted, sliding into home base a millisecond before the ball hit the catcher's mitt.

Home run! Sydney, along with her friends, shot to their feet and cheered. The beauty let out a laugh, high-fiving her teammates.

Sydney looked back at Rylee. "Who is she?" Sydney asked.

"Her name is Skye," Rylee said.

"Of course it is," Sydney thought. "Skye." The ethereal beauty of it seemed quite appropriate.

"Does she have a last name?" Sydney asked.

"North."

Sydney looked back at Rylee and smiled. "Skye North, you say? Seriously?"

"Skye North, I say. Seriously."

Sydney, Elijah, and the rest of the group continued to cheer Skye's team on to victory. After the game was over, Skye sat on the bench next to Elijah, directly in front of Sydney. Skye immediately struck up a conversation with Elijah, not even giving Sydney a glance to ask for any type of approval. There was a part of Sydney that was intrigued by Skye, but she was also a bit surprised at the gall Skye had in making her seat nice and comfortable next to Elijah. Sydney reminded herself that Skye was friends with several of her friends, so she was certainly "good people." Sydney watched while the two visited; Skye asked Elijah his name, about school, if he enjoyed sports, and such. Elijah was totally comfortable with her and was happy to have a newfound buddy at the ballpark.

Skye finally turned to Sydney and introduced herself.

"I take it this fine young man belongs to you?" Skye asked.

"Yes, this fine young man certainly does." Sydney smiled at Elijah.

Skye stood up and walked to the cooler. "Can I get you two something to drink?"

"Sure. That would be great."

Skye walked back over and handed Sydney and Elijah two cold drinks and sat back down. Before Skye could officially introduce herself, Elijah stood up and walked out into the middle of the adjacent field. Sydney could tell he was bored and he was definitely sulking.

"Let me go get Elijah and I'll be right back," Sydney said, setting her drink down.

"Let me," Skye said.

Skye ran to the top of the bleachers and untied two balloons that had been placed at the highest right corner of the bench. She then ran back down the bleachers and out to the middle of the field where Elijah was standing. Sydney could tell by Elijah's body language that he was very happy to have his newfound buddy back, and Skye handed Elijah a balloon. Sydney watched as the two talked and each let go of their balloons. Skye took Elijah's hand and they walked back to the bleachers and took their seats in front of Sydney.

"Well, what were you two doing?" Sydney asked.

"That's our little secret, huh, Elijah?" Skye nudged Elijah with her shoulder.

"Yeah, Mom. That's for us to know and you to find out." Elijah laughed and nudged Skye back.

Skye laughed and winked at Sydney.

There was the spark. It was undeniable. Sydney had felt a lot of things before when meeting someone new, but she had never felt this.

Sydney nervously glanced at her watch and saw the time had snuck up on her. "Well, Skye. It was very nice meeting you, but my fine young man and I must be going." Sydney wished she had more time.

"Mom!" Elijah belted, dragging out the word as much as possible to show his dissatisfaction in her decision.

"Sweetie, I have to take you to Meme and Pepaw's for the night. Remember, I'm meeting Aunt Roo's new boyfriend tonight."

Elijah stared at Sydney, standing his ground while seated next to Skye, and Sydney stood hers in gathering her purse.

"Hey, man. It was very nice to meet you and maybe I'll see you again sometime soon," Skye said to Elijah as she put her hand firmly on his shoulder.

"Okay. That sounds good." Elijah looked at Skye and tried not to appear as disappointed as he was.

"Come on, sweetie." Sydney stood.

The two headed to the car and Sydney made it a point not to look back, even though she surely wanted to.

"She was nice," Sydney said to Elijah.

"Yeah, she's real nice," Elijah said.

"What did you two talk about when she brought you the balloon?"

"She just said that if you make a wish on a balloon and let it go, your wish will come true."

Elijah knew his mom's next question, so with barely a pause he said, "But if you tell your wish, it won't come true, so don't ask me, Mom."

"Oh, well, excuse me, sir." The two laughed, as they raced to the car.

⟨⟩

Sydney dropped Elijah off at her parents' house and went home to freshen up for her dinner with Ruby and new boyfriend that evening. Bob Carrington was his name and Ruby met him on a blind date, out of state, no less. Alice, one of Ruby's dear friends from work, had coaxed the single Ruby to join her in Phoenix for a girls' getaway trip. Alice had three men there ready and waiting to meet Ruby: all handsome, successful, and single. It just so happened, Bob was the first man Ruby met on this "looking for love" trip and she was smitten: hook, line, and sinker. Apparently, so was Bob. Ruby had only been home one week when Bob bought his airline ticket and flew to Houston to see her again.

Sydney couldn't wait to meet her best friend's new love, and Sydney also couldn't get Skye out of her mind. She felt happy and excited every time she thought of her.

When Sydney arrived at the restaurant, Ruby was seated at the table, nervously fixing her napkin in her lap and steadily sipping her margarita. Bob was nowhere to be seen.

"Hey, honey pie! Where's Mr. Right?" Sydney grabbed her chair and motioned to the nearest waiter. "I'll have what she's having, please."

"Oh my God! Thank God you're here!" Ruby hugged her friend as if they hadn't seen each other in ages.

"What's going on? Are you okay?" Sydney leaned back and looked at Ruby. "Ah. I see. I believe you're in love, Ms. Ruby," Sydney said with a smile.

"Ssshhhh! Don't say that! He'll be back any minute. He just ran to the restroom."

"Well, if it makes you feel any better, so am I!" Sydney said, half joking.

"What?!" Ruby blurted out, her eyes wide and wanting to hear all about it.

There was no time for that now. In walked the handsome, successful, Phoenix, Arizona bachelor Ruby had told her all about.

"Hello, Sydney. Ruby has told me all about you." Bob shook her hand.

"Likewise." Sydney nudged Ruby's leg under the table to show her solid seal of approval.

The three visited for hours until it was apparent that Ruby and Bob were ready for their time alone. Sydney was so happy for Ruby. She was happy that Ruby was happy, period. But it made her heart smile all the more to know that Ruby had found true love. It was obvious that she and Bob felt the same way about each other. Sydney wasn't envious of her best friend's happiness. She just hoped one day she would find it too.

Sydney drove home and played out the earlier portion of the day in her head. "Skye," she thought. Yes, Skye was definitely giving Sydney something new and exciting to think about.

⊁

It was Sunday morning and Sydney woke with Daisy nose-to-nose, ready to go outside. She could see the sun bursting through the sheers in her bedroom and that instantly put a smile on her face as she welcomed the day.

"Come on, Daisy-doo." Sydney put on her robe and house slippers, and walked into the courtyard. It was a beautiful fall day and it felt full of possibilities.

Her phone rang. "Come on, come on!" Sydney rounded up Daisy and sprinted to the phone.

"Good morning!" Sydney said, not knowing who was on the other end, but sharing her Sunday morning enthusiasm.

"Well, good morning back to you, Ms. Chipper. What did you put in your Post Toasties this morning?" Rylee asked, sounding a bit sarcastic for it being so early.

"I might should ask what you put in yours, ornery." Sydney said back as she laughed.

"Alright, alright. I am calling you because my phone has been ringing off the wall last night and this morning with a particular someone wanting your phone number. Traci called. Ann called. Then, Traci called back, wanting your number to pass along."

Sydney was a bit taken off guard and didn't say anything as she tried to figure out exactly what Rylee was talking about.

"I'm not giving your number out without your permission, so get a pen and paper, Sydney. Let me give you her number so you can call her and my phone can stop ringing."

"Can you please tell me what you're talking about?" Sydney dug a pen and matchbook out of her bedside table drawer.

"The chick you and Elijah were talking to. Skye. Here is her number."

Sydney's excitement shot right through the ceiling. She felt as happy as a giddy high school girl. She didn't hang up the phone after Rylee gave her the number, but simply pressed the button to get a dial tone and immediately called Skye. This was something Sydney had never, ever done before. She had never made the first call to anyone she had been interested in, ever. But this was different. Skye was different. And this was also a new time in Sydney's life and she was embracing it.

⅄

"Hello," Skye said.

"Skye? This is Sydney." Sydney surprised herself at how completely comfortable she felt.

Skye laughed. "Can you hold a minute, Sydney?"

"Sure." Sydney wasn't sure what was so amusing and suddenly did feel a bit awkward.

"I'm sorry," Skye said, when she got back on the line. "That was Ann, a friend of mine, who just called me back to tell me that Rylee isn't giving out your number. I was on to Plan B of how to get your number when you called. I must say your timing is impeccable."

The two laughed and Sydney instantly felt comfortable again and admired how Skye just put herself out there. She was perfectly happy to let Sydney know her level of interest and that was quite impressive to Sydney.

Skye asked Sydney out for their first date. She wanted their first date to be the three of them: Skye, Sydney, and Elijah. She invited them to the Renaissance Festival for the day and then they would carve Halloween pumpkins at Skye's apartment that evening. It was every bit the perfect day, just as it had sounded, as were many dates thereafter that were calendared in ink.

The three would spend a great deal of time together and the comfortable feeling that Sydney had from the very beginning had become even more so, like putting on your favorite warm coat and feeling cozy and protected. Sydney had fallen in love with Skye. Skye felt the same and the two had expressed their love to each other. And Elijah loved Skye very much, and Skye loved Elijah equally so. The seed to Elijah and Skye's special bond was planted on day one at the ball field without any doing from Sydney and she loved that fact. Sydney kept reminding herself that she knew this was different from the very start. This love they shared not only felt good, but right.

CHAPTER 43

Skye and Sydney shared stories: their past, their mistakes, the fun they'd had, to include the fun they were happy to have survived. And then as always, it went to family, and then to the more deep secrets of oneself.

One evening, Sydney told Skye more about her past and more about her ex-husband—God, how she hated that word—and what he'd done to Elijah. It seemed as though that secret would be a secret that Sydney would keep to herself, she often thought. But surprisingly, she never did. If she felt close to someone and trusted them, she shared her and Elijah's story. It was as though sharing it made her and Elijah stronger. It was their story, after all, and Sydney would never allow a veil of shame or lies hide that fact, and especially from someone she trusted.

Sydney saw the look on Skye's face. The look that someone has when a door has been flung wide open and all they have to do is walk through it. Skye's wheels were turning and Sydney could see it in her eyes.

"What's the matter, Skye? I didn't mean to get too personal. I'm sorry."

"Don't you dare apologize, Sydney. Please. I'm glad that you told me. I'm so sorry for Elijah. I can't imagine what he went through, and that's your child. My God."

"Yes, I know. It is the most inconceivable nightmare. And to think that son of a bitch is still out there…"

Skye stared out into the living room. No focus, just a blank, dead stare.

"What are you thinking, Skye? Tell me."

Skye dropped her head and shook it back and forth as if to say no.

"Tell me. What's the matter?" Sydney put her arm around Skye's shoulder and pulled her slightly closer.

"I lied. I can imagine what Elijah went through. The only difference is that I didn't have anyone to help me...protect me."

"What do you mean?" Sydney knew what Skye meant. Skye was one more broken person in this menagerie of life. "Skye?"

"My dad. He did things to me and my two sisters. Sydney, I don't even remember my younger years as a child," Skye said. "I remember flashes of living different places growing up, but I don't remember a damn thing before I was about twelve. If it weren't for my Gram, my mom's mom, and my Aunt Joan, my mom's sister...I was just very close to the both of them."

There were no words spoken. Sydney didn't know what to say. How can you say, "it's okay," when you know damn good and well that it's not. She pulled Skye even closer to her and kissed her brow. "God bless her," Sydney thought.

"When I got older, my dad would put naked pictures of men in our closets. He would cut out pictures of penises and tape them to the walls. I remember him putting a mirror under the bathroom door one time when I went to shower, and from then on I had to keep a towel pushed under the door and I watched it from the shower to be sure he didn't move it."

"God almighty." Sydney felt that familiar knot in her gut rear its ugly head again.

"He did the same things to my sister, Gwyn, too. My little sister, Brooklynn, would go to get undressed in her room, or just change clothes, and my mom would make her shut the curtains because Daddy would go outside to sneak a peek and Mom knew it. She knew it and she didn't ever say a fucking thing to him: nothing that made any difference, anyway. We were all Daddy's girls, his property, and Mom loved him. She still does."

"Skye—" Sydney started.

"No. I don't need to be coddled. I'm just telling you." Skye paused for a moment. "You know, all I remember is what I just told you. The fact that I can't remember anything before twelve years old tells me a lot. It tells me that I don't want to remember."

Sydney wondered what it was about this common thread. "Is it something we subconsciously recognize in each other, and then we meld together in an effort to fix the broken pieces?" she thought. It would have been easy for her to cry.

"What's the matter, Sydney?"

"Nothing." Sydney wrapped her arms around Skye and laid back on the pallet, holding her tight. "Nothing."

Chapter 44

Skye and Sydney had become inseparable. They were full-on in love and they had a solid partnership with each other, which was also a stable foundation for their family unit. Sydney had finally come out to her family. Maeve wasn't surprised, and said as much, but Sydney really knew that her "coming out" words to her mother were words that many parents don't welcome hearing. Memaw really wasn't surprised either, but confirming her suspicions and saying the words out loud sent her into a tailspin fueled by her generation's mentality. What would their family members say? What would their friends say? It was too much for Memaw to absorb for a time. But Maeve stepped in and reminded her mother that Sydney was the same precious child they had loved from the moment she took her first breath. She had the same sweet and giving heart, she was the same bright young woman, and most importantly, she was still theirs. Memaw understood the fundamental truth of it all and opened her heart to Sydney's happiness and desires for her and Elijah's lives. Memaw wanted them to be happy and they were with Skye.

Memaw got to know Skye and grew to love her immensely, as did the rest of Sydney's family. Skye was a wonderful person with a heart of gold and that was apparent to everyone. Not long after Skye moved into Sydney's apartment, Memaw told Sydney that she wanted to give them a gift. She wanted to give them a down payment if and when they chose to purchase a home together. It was an amazing gesture and one that they accepted just one year later.

Skye's sister, Gwyn, and her family lived in the suburbs of north Houston. She and her husband, Raymond, went on regular camping trips with their three girls and other families in their neighborhood. Elijah was always invited. It gave him the opportunity to get out of the city and enjoy himself, and it also allowed him the opportunity to meet several new friends. When a home in their neighborhood came up for sale, Sydney and Skye jumped on it. It was an easy "in" for this alternative family. Gwyn and Raymond knew many families in the neighborhood, many of whom knew of Skye and that she was gay, and they liked her. But most importantly, Elijah knew several children already, so it would be an easy transition and it was. Memaw stuck to her word and provided the down payment and also, with her real estate license still intact after all of those years, handled the purchase of the home, start to finish. They were in. Sydney and Skye nestled into domesticity as if it was their favorite, comfortable chair, and Elijah thrived in his new school.

The three began spending more and more time with Skye's family, and she and Elijah were accepted as members of the family. There was that one thing, however. That one very big thing that sucked the air out of the room: Skye's father and what he'd done to her and her sisters, and then Skye's mother and her choosing to protect her husband rather than her children. It was unfathomable and yet, Sydney could only compare each gathering to watching a play or a movie. All of the actors had their places. They had their roles; they had their lines. It didn't matter what had happened in real life. This was pretend and everyone would give their best Oscar-winning performance. It made Sydney sick to watch such utter bullshit.

Then, like a bolt of lightning that shot through her very soul, Sydney realized she was just as much a part of this masquerade as anyone else. She wanted to protect Skye from any further hurt, and in doing so, she was just another actor cast in her heartbreaking story.

CHAPTER 45

Time marches on, as the old saying goes, and it certainly did. Sydney, Skye, and Elijah were immersed in normalcy as much as they could possibly be. Oh, there was the very rare occasion that a teenager would yell "dykes" while passing the front of their house, but the three stood strong and did their best not to let feelings or reaction to such ignorance creep into their home.

Sydney had accepted a new position with a downtown law firm and she loved it: Lawson & Geoffreys, LLP. God had laid this treasure right in the palm of her hand at the beginning of the new year. L&G, as they called it, was a highly respected, Texas-based law firm, which had been in business for over fifty years. This job was the perfect gift and perfect start for her new year. Yes, this was the cake *and* the icing, and the cherry on top was the fact that she didn't have to worry about the likes of Conrad O'Kenna any longer. Another fresh start.

Sydney dove right in and took on as much of her department's workload as she possibly could. She worked in the accounting department and loved staying busy. Her get-up-and-go was just the attitude they were looking for and she quickly made friends at her new office. All was moving along so very nicely.

It was another busy day at the office when Sydney's phone rang.

"Yes, ma'am?" Sydney said to Harlene, the firm receptionist, a beautiful black woman with a personality you couldn't help but love.

"Girl, somebody named Bear Keane is callin' for you. You keepin' secrets from me, woman? And here I thought you liked girls." Harlene laughed. "Here you go." The phone call clicked in before Sydney could say a word.

"Hello," Sydney said, still absorbing the fact that the devil was on the other line.

"Hey there, Sydney. It's Bear."

"Bear. What do you need?"

"Well, don't sound so excited, sweet cheeks. I just wanted to let you know that I am about to be off probation, but I'm sure you already knew that. Ain't that right, Columbo? Always keepin' me from doin' what I need to do."

Sydney didn't say a word.

Bear waited just a moment for her to comment and continued, "Anyway, now that I am about to be off probation, I am going to exercise my parental rights and I will be seeing Elijah as often as possible. How's that for ya?"

Sydney whirled her chair around to face the vast space in front of her. "Listen to me, you mother fucker. There will not be one single day in this lifetime that you will be alone with Elijah. Do you understand me?"

"You listen to me, you fucking bitch," Bear seethed and sounded like the evil presence within him. "I'm not scared of you anymore. Your grandmother had money and y'all got that whole fuckin' thing goin' and now here we are. Guess what, bitch? Now, I've got money and I will be seeing my son."

Sydney didn't know what Bear was talking about in referencing her grandmother's money. The State didn't charge a fee for going after pedophiles. Sydney let out a sarcastic chuckle.

"Now see there, you fucking idiot. That's where you made your first mistake. You're not scared of me? Let me be really clear with you, Bear. I'm glad you have money. You better start rolling those fucking pennies right now, and you better get your momma's too, and anyone else's money you can get your hands on because I will never, ever, ever let you out of court. You'll spend your last rotten dime trying to win this battle, you piece of shit. Make that war."

"Fuck you!" he yelled, and hung up.

Sydney had rattled him, and that was a good sign. She had meant every single word she'd said and she hoped he knew that.

She turned her chair back around to face her desk. There was no time. Every second mattered now. He was a worthless, rotten excuse of a human being, but Sydney wouldn't underestimate what he might do. It seemed clear that he was saying all that he said for the benefit of someone else in the room. That certain someone just might be pushing him to fight for his so-called rights. Rights? It was nauseating that he would have any right to anything after what he'd done.

With but a fleeting thought, Sydney rose from her chair and headed out the door. She walked straight to Palmer Lawson's office. Mr. Lawson was the managing partner of the law firm and the kindest man. And it didn't hurt that he was the president of the Houston Bar Association.

Sydney peeked her head into Mr. Lawson's door and tapped lightly. "Mr. Lawson?"

"Why yes, Sydney. How can I help you, young lady?"

"Do you have just a moment, Mr. Lawson? I need some advice, if I may."

"Come right in and shut the door."

Sydney told Mr. Lawson about what Bear had done to Elijah. As the words poured from her mouth, she couldn't believe she was sharing her personal life with this man: her boss, by all accounts. Then, she told him that she was a lesbian. She told him that she was fearful that Bear would use that against her in his quest to see Elijah alone.

"You wait right here, Sydney." And with that, Mr. Lawson picked up the phone and called Carmen Michel, a top-notch and very expensive family law attorney.

"Carmen. Palmer Lawson here. I have a young lady who is an employee of mine, and she has quite a predicament." He went on to tell Ms. Michel the entire situation and by the time they hung up, Sydney had an appointment to meet with her scheduled for the next day.

"I cannot thank you enough, Mr. Lawson. I feel that I owe you an apology as well, but I just didn't know where else to go or what to do, quite frankly."

Sydney felt slightly embarrassed, but also as though a fifty-ton weight was just lifted off her.

"You came to the right place, Sydney, and if you need anything else at all, don't you hesitate."

"Thank you again, so much."

On her way back to her office, Sydney let what had just occurred sink in. When she thought further, she had no explanation for what made her go straight to Mr. Lawson, and with barely a thought, shared her secrets. She realized quickly, however. It was to protect Elijah. And it was God.

⅄

Sydney couldn't wait to get home. Her mind was racing. She wasn't one to sit idle, nor mince words. The ball was rolling, once again, and she wasn't going to be on the receiving end without a fight, once again.

"Oh my God," Sydney said, dropping her purse to the floor as she came in. "Elijah, take your book bag to your room and hop in the shower, sweetie."

"Mom, come on. Can't I wait until after dinner?"

"Normally, yes. But I need you to go ahead and shower now. Then dinner and homework. Okay?"

"Aaahhhh!" Elijah said, exasperated, just home from a big day himself.

"Come here." Sydney pulled her son close to her. "How about a nice, relaxing, no-rush dinner, and then homework? I'll help."

"Okay," Elijah said, with a half, not totally convinced, smile on his face.

"Hi," Skye said, cleaning out the fridge as she stared at Sydney knowing something wasn't quite right.

Sydney looked into the hallway, finger in the air. She wouldn't discuss anything until Elijah was out of earshot. "Ah, water," she said, as she heard Elijah turn on the shower. "You are never going to believe what happened today!"

"Okay," Skye said. "Tell me what happened today." Her head was stuck mid-way into the refrigerator.

"Can you look at me? This is serious, Skye." Sydney fell back onto the chair.

It was interesting about Sydney. Too many times she knew it was a time to cry, a time to let her emotions flow. It would be healthy and it would be good for her. So was getting the fucking bad guy.

"What's going on?" Skye closed the fridge and dropped the sponge in the sink.

"Bear called. He said he's about to get off probation and he's going to see Elijah. I knew this day was coming, but for God's sake, he hasn't asked to see Elijah except for two times in all these years and now here he is? He was obviously just biding his time." Sydney bolted from the chair and paced the living room.

"Sydney, come here." Skye walked toward Sydney with her hand outstretched. "Come here, honey."

Sydney stopped in her tracks. "Don't. Don't patronize me and don't try to calm me."

Skye just looked at her. "I'm not the enemy, Sydney."

Could there ever have been more true words? Skye wasn't her enemy. She had stood by Sydney and Elijah through thick and thin. She knew their story from virtually day one and not only accepted it, but took it on.

"I'm sorry," Sydney said, and went to Skye. "I'm so sorry."

"It's okay. I'm here for you, Sydney. For you and Elijah. You know that."

"Yes, I know that."

The two poured a glass of wine and sat down.

"I talked to Mr. Lawson today and told him everything. I didn't know what else to do. He called a friend of his, a very high-powered family law attorney, and I have an appointment with her tomorrow. Mr. Lawson is wonderful and I've known that, but what he did for me, for us, is just unreal. Until tomorrow…" Sydney rose as she heard Elijah's shower turn off.

CHAPTER 46

Sydney walked into The Law Office of Carmen Michel. It was a boutique firm and a beautiful one.

"Hi there. How can I help you?" asked a beautiful, fresh-faced young lady from behind the receptionist desk.

Sydney couldn't help but think that this young lady couldn't have possibly worked there long or she would certainly have the bewildered look of someone dropped in the middle of family law hell. "Blissful marriage? Kiss it goodbye, sister," Sydney thought. She was cynical and she knew it, and she didn't care.

"Yes, I'm here to see Carmen Michel. My name is Sydney Keane."

"Oh yes, Ms. Keane. She's expecting you." The young lady picked up the phone and spoke softly into the receiver.

Was it just Sydney's imagination or was this young lady already judging her, the lesbian woman trying desperately to maintain custody of her son from the pedophile ex-husband?

"Sydney Keane," the woman said, as she came through the door.

She was beautiful. She was every bit as fresh-faced as the young lady behind the receptionist desk. Her smile was pearly white, her shoulder-length blonde hair looked like something out of a magazine ad, and her face could light up a room. Sydney was quite younger than her, but she didn't feel it.

"Carmen Michel. It's nice to meet you." She reached her hand out to Sydney's.

"Sydney Keane," Sydney said, feeling a bit silly considering the woman had just said her name. "But you already know that." Sydney offered an embarrassed smile.

"Yes, I do." Carmen sent an understanding smile back. "Come on back, Sydney. Let's get down to business." And there was no question that was what was about to happen.

They entered Carmen's large corner office. Floor-to-ceiling windows covered the two adjacent walls. Carmen Michel looked over the city, certainly feeling somewhat in charge, but you wouldn't know it by her unassuming Barbie-doll good looks. No doubt she was a barracuda in the courtroom and no one ever saw it coming.

"Have a seat." She motioned for Sydney to sit in a large straight-backed chair across from her desk.

Sydney sat down and suddenly no longer felt nervous or embarrassed. She was instantly hyperaware that she was there to get down to business. The business of Bear Keane.

"So, tell me, Sydney. Palmer gave me the *Reader's Digest* version over the phone, but I want to hear it from you."

Carmen was leaned back in her big, leather chair, pen in hand, confident and ready for whatever direction this was going.

Sydney reiterated what Mr. Lawson had told Carmen while Sydney was in his office the day before, but she went into searing detail, start to finish. She told of her marriage to Bear, his odd behavior after the birth of Elijah, her infidelity and relationship with Gabby, and how Elijah had told her what his father had done. She told of how Bear had tried a number of times to beat the system and get off on early probation. She told of his second marriage, his other son, and what his ex-wife had suspected, and she told how Bear had been lying and covering his ass all these years. She told how he had called her yesterday to take back what he wanted most: her son. But she also told Carmen what she had said to him, how he would never see the day he got Elijah alone, and how he had screamed "fuck you" and hung up on her.

Carmen leaned over her desk. Rage filled her eyes. "You know what I think, Sydney? I think you scared the son of a bitch."

"You think I scared him? How?" Sydney asked, closing her eyes and shaking her head, hoping the answers would fall on the desk in front of her. She wanted answers. She was ready for a fight, but needed someone with the legal knowledge to tell her what to do. She needed Carmen.

"Listen to me, Sydney. Is this son of a bitch married?"

"I'm really not sure."

"Well, what we do know is that he has another son who he has hurt, he has an ex-wife that he clearly lied to and manipulated, and she's a mess, and it's safe to assume that whoever he's currently seeing is likely in the exact same situation and doesn't even know it. Correct?"

"Yes."

"Don't you see? If all this comes out, his sick lies and the fabricated story he's been telling all these years will sink, and the truth will come to the surface. He doesn't want that, Sydney. That's the last thing he wants."

Carmen looked calm now and sure of her assessment. She leaned back in her attorney chair and eased a satisfied smile on her face.

"Here. It's fifteen hundred dollars." Sydney pulled an envelope from her purse. "It's all I have right now, but I can pay you more and will."

Sydney felt like a child. She felt weak. This wasn't her and it was as foreign as anything she had known. She pushed the envelope across the desk and left it resting in front of Carmen.

Carmen looked at the envelope. "Tell you what, Sydney," Carmen started as she rose back over her desk and pushed the envelope back to Sydney. "You keep your money. I have a feeling you won't be hearing a peep from Bear Keane. That chicken shit never saw you coming with the curve ball you threw him. Great job, by the way." She gave Sydney a wink and another satisfied smile. "Remember, he won't want all of this to come out. He's worked too hard to cover it up. If you hear from him again, you call me and we'll go from there, but I don't think you will."

"So, you don't want—" Sydney started.

"No, I don't want your money. Keep it. Take care of yourself, your son, and your family unit. Again, if you hear from that lowlife scum, I'm a phone call away. Okay?"

"Okay. Thank you, Ms. Michel. I truly can't thank you enough."

⚕

Sydney drove straight to pick Elijah up from school. She hoped that Carmen was right and that Bear would back off, even if just to protect his own ass and horrible secrets. She just wanted him to go away, and to leave Elijah alone.

Sydney had always kept in the back of her mind that she may have to have this conversation with Elijah—the conversation of what his father had done to him—should Elijah ever bring it up or if she saw signs that Elijah was having issues because of it. Elijah had never brought it up and there had never been any signs that would alarm Sydney. Regardless, she knew she had to address it now. If Bear decided to exercise his right to see Elijah alone, Elijah was now thirteen and he could decide whether he did or did not want to spend time with his father, and the judge would take Elijah's wishes into heavy consideration. Sydney had to make sure that Elijah did not want to be alone with Bear. This was a catch twenty-two. Sydney didn't want to ever have to have this talk with Elijah, but she could not let him be alone with the man who had so horribly violated him.

"Hey, sweetheart!" Sydney yelled from the car window. Elijah waved, said goodbye to a little girl, and ran to the car. God, why couldn't life have been easier? Why did this beautiful, innocent boy have to be subjected to so much and why now would he have to be reminded of it? There was no other way.

"Hey, Mom!" Elijah shouted, out of breath, when he opened the door. He had a big smile on his face.

"Hmmm… What's that big smile for?" Sydney asked. "Could it be the little blonde up there by the front door?" Sydney goosed Elijah in his side and laughed.

"Mom! Stop it! That's just my friend, Brittany."

"Mmmm-hmmmm." Sydney gave Elijah a doubting look. "Just your friend, huh?"

"Sheeeeesh." Elijah smiled and dug in his book bag, hoping to change the subject.

Sydney didn't want to spoil the moment. She didn't want to put a dark blanket on a beautiful day and a sweet conversation she was having with her son. She and Elijah should be talking about Brittany, girl crushes, how his day was, and what homework he had for that evening. Instead, she had a pull at her gut that reminded her once again that this monster had yet to be slain.

"So, I heard from your dad yesterday," Sydney said, as matter-of-fact as she could.

"Dad?" Elijah looked at Sydney, puzzled, as though she had surely made an inaccurate statement.

"Yes, your dad. He called me yesterday. He wants to start seeing you, Elijah. How do you feel about that?"

Sydney braced herself. This would be a telltale sign of what, if anything, Elijah remembered.

"Yeah, I'll see him." Elijah paused, and continued. "I've wondered why I couldn't see Dad or why he really never came around more. When does he want to see me?"

That pull in Sydney's gut turned into a full-on grip: a twisting, churning knot.

Sydney needed to tell him, but she was entering into uncharted territory and she would tread lightly, for Elijah's sake.

"Well, Elijah. That's what we need to talk about, sweetie." She paused, just for a moment, knowing it had to be said. "I don't want you to be alone with your dad, Elijah. I can't let you be alone with him, honey."

"Why?" Elijah looked at Sydney for only a moment before he diverted his attention to their opening garage door.

It made Sydney feel as though Elijah knew something. Like when a person asks the question, but they really don't want to know the answer.

"You know what, sweetie. It's complicated. Let's do this. Tomorrow is Saturday. Tonight, let's have movie night, popcorn and all that jazz, and we'll talk about it tomorrow. Is that okay?"

"Sure, Mom." Elijah gave her an understanding look. And again, Sydney had the feeling Elijah knew or felt there was something, and he seemed open to the discussion. It made her feel that much more steadfast in her decision.

⚜

"Hey, Skye!" Elijah called out as he rushed through the door and headed straight to his room.

"Hey back atcha!" Skye called out.

"Mom said its movie night! Popcorn!" He ran to his bedroom, book bag flinging across his bed and clothes dropping to the floor as fast as he could make it to the shower.

"Mom said its movie night, huh?" Skye turned to Sydney and gave her a warm, welcome home hug.

"Now, this is nice." Sydney dropped her briefcase to the floor and returned the favor.

"I've got dinner almost done. I hear popcorn is on the menu too." Skye leaned her head back giving Sydney a content look of love.

No matter that the outside world was whirling around her, Sydney always felt safe with Skye. She loved her and she trusted her.

"Wow, you got home early today. What gives?" Sydney noticed the pots on the stove and the fragrant smell of food filling the house.

"I know you've had a rough couple of days, so I thought I would come home and take care of dinner…give us a nice head start for the weekend."

"And I appreciate it much, and I love you."

Skye leaned back a little farther. "What?" Skye asked, seeing that look.

It wasn't a conscious look that Sydney gave, but it was one where once again the wheels were turning and Skye could see them, full speed ahead.

"What do you mean, 'what'?"

"You know what I mean, Sydney. What? I can see you're thinking something and I have a feeling it's not about dinner, so what is it?"

"It's Elijah. I think he knows, Skye. I think there is something inside him letting him know that something is very wrong regarding his dad."

"What makes you say that?"

"I have been thinking about this situation with Bear, and while I agree with Carmen Michel that Bear will probably just back off, I can't be certain. No matter what, I can't let Elijah be alone with him. Not ever. I think I need to talk to Elijah and let him know why I can't let him be around his dad alone."

"My God, Sydney. What are you going to say?"

"Well, I already started to address it on the way home. I told Elijah that Bear had called me and wants to see him. I guess I wanted to see his reaction. He did show some curiosity on why he didn't spend time with his dad, why he doesn't come around and all that. I told him that I don't want him to be alone with his dad."

"What did he say?"

"He asked me why, but that was right when we were pulling into the garage. I told him we'd have movie night tonight and we'd talk about it tomorrow. There is no good time, Skye, but I surely didn't want to do it tonight."

Skye looked as if she were frozen. She just stared at Sydney.

"What, Skye? Do you not agree that I need to talk to Elijah about what happened?"

"No, I do agree. But I just don't know how you're going to go about doing it."

"I love you and you know that, so please don't be offended, but I feel like I really need to talk to Elijah alone. I don't know how he is going to react and I don't want him to be embarrassed or upset because anyone else is around. I just don't know what to do, but I feel sure that it just needs to be the two of us."

"Agreed. Tell you what. Let me make you and Elijah a picnic lunch. You two get out of here and go to the park. It's going to be a beautiful weekend and I don't think your talk with Elijah needs to happen here."

"I couldn't agree more. I don't want you trying to make yourself scarce, and also, home is our safe haven."

"Okay, honey. Come here." Skye gave Sydney yet another comforting hug.

Tonight would be movie night. Tomorrow and what it held would show itself soon enough.

CHAPTER 47

"**A**ll right, family." Skye leaned her head into the car. "You two be careful and, Elijah…" Tears welled up in Skye's eyes. "I love you, buddy."

"I love you too, Skye." He smiled back at her.

"Okay, here we go." Sydney shut the car door. She mouthed "I love you" through the car window and waved goodbye to Skye.

Skye stood in the driveway for as long as Sydney could see her in the rearview mirror.

It felt as though Sydney was saying goodbye to something, something that she was going to miss terribly. She realized that she was. That was exactly what was about to happen. In order to protect her son, she was about to say goodbye to the only piece of hope Elijah had held on to when it came to his father, and Elijah was about to say goodbye to that as well. This was terrible, but it wasn't her doing. It was Bear's. It was always his doing.

Sydney and Elijah pulled into the park. It was a beautiful day. The sun was shining brightly, the breeze was blowing, and soccer teams were scattering the playing fields around them. Sydney grabbed the picnic basket from the backseat and Elijah grabbed his football. By looking, anyone would have thought this was the picture-perfect day for mom and son. If they only knew.

She laid the tablecloth over the cement picnic table and took out their lunches. Elijah sat down across from her and munched on chips, not looking at Sydney for the first few minutes.

"Elijah, are you okay?" Sydney asked, watching him intently.

He raised his head and smiled at Sydney. "Yeah, Mom. I'm okay."

"Do you still want to talk about this? About your dad?"

"Yes, ma'am," Elijah answered, keeping eye contact with his mom.

"Okay then." Sydney paused. "Elijah, the reason I don't want you to be alone with your dad is because he has done bad things."

"Like what kind of bad things?"

"Well, he has hurt people."

"What people?"

"He has hurt children."

Elijah dropped his head and stared back at his sandwich.

Sydney didn't say a word. She gave him time to think. Maybe he needed to absorb what she had just said. Maybe he already knew.

Elijah looked back in Sydney's eyes. "Did he hurt me?"

"Yes, Elijah. He did." Sydney paused and waited.

Elijah's eyes filled with tears and he shook his head back and forth as if to shake any memories that had flooded in, right back out of his head.

"Do you remember, Elijah?"

He nodded. "Yes, ma'am."

"What do you remember, Elijah?"

"I don't want to say."

Those words pierced Sydney's heart like a knife. She knew that he knew. It was obvious now. He didn't want to say. He couldn't say the words.

"It's okay, sweetie. You don't have to say because I already know."

Elijah stared at Sydney now, as if to ask how. How could she know everything going on in his head right at this moment? It had been for as long as he could remember that he had never discussed these things with his mother.

"Do you remember telling me, Elijah?"

"No, ma'am."

"Well, you did. And I won't go into any details that would make you uncomfortable, but I will tell you this. You told me what your dad had done to you when you were three years old. We went to trial and rather than risk going to prison, your dad pled no contest and got ten years probation. I wanted that to happen so that you would be older, thirteen exactly, and you wouldn't have to be alone with him. But now he is off probation and he wants to exercise his rights to see you alone."

"No, I don't want to see him."

"And that's okay, Elijah. That's okay. You don't have to and no one can make you see him, not even him, if you don't want to." Sydney reached over and took Elijah's hand. "I love you, sweetie."

"I love you too, Mom."

"Hey, listen." Sydney leaned back and opened her sandwich, trying to bring things back to any sense of normalcy. "I know this is big stuff, Elijah. It is, but I want you to know that every single person who was a part of that case and investigation absolutely adored you."

Sydney wanted Elijah to know that he had such a support system, not just in her and in their family, but with people who didn't even know them until the case had come to light—people who fell in love with this little boy.

"Really?" Elijah asked, opening his sandwich.

"Really." Sydney told Elijah about the big, burly Heath Bridges and how Elijah played with the airplanes in his office. She told him about Arthur Neumann and Deb Whitmire.

"I have an idea. Would you like to go see Deb Whitmire again? She is a wonderful lady and she is the one who helped us when you told me what had happened. I know she'd love to see you again."

"Yeah, sure. I would like to see her again."

It was as if even Elijah knew that it would be best for him to see Deb. Any positive support, and any positive reinforcement, would be best for his healing and moving forward, and maybe on some level he felt that too.

This situation was hell, but Sydney felt a peace and she kept a strong hope that this peace would not go away.

"I'll get it set up and we'll go next week. If she's open on Saturday, we'll go then. Deal?"

"Deal."

Sydney and Elijah enjoyed the rest of their afternoon. Their weekend as a family was wonderful and quite normal feeling.

For a moment, the thought crossed Sydney's mind of how odd it was that things were so normal, and certainly after her conversation with Elijah. Sydney realized, however, this was how she had survived and her son was no different than she was. Was any abused child really any different? What happened to Sydney had happened. No one could take that away, as much as she would want it to be. It was a part of her. But what Sydney was steadfast about was the fact that it would not define her. It would not define her as a woman, nor would it define her as a human being. It was tragic, and yet reassuring, that Elijah was following in her footsteps of survival.

On Monday, Sydney called Deb and made Elijah's appointment for that Saturday. Deb was somewhat surprised to hear from Sydney, but pleasantly surprised. It wasn't often that child victims had the support they needed. All too often they did not.

Their week continued to be filled with normalcy. They stuck tight to their daily schedules to help keep that normalcy. Everything could wait until Saturday. They all knew "it" was there. Yes, Saturday would wait.

Chapter 48

"Okay, family," Skye started. "I'm sending you off, but not without all my love. I'm here, I'm thinking about you, and I'm saying giant prayers."

Sydney was proud of Skye. Not a tear. She wasn't sure she could have done the same.

"And we thank you, Skye," Sydney said. "And we love you." With that, Sydney put her arm around Elijah and they stood side by side in front of Skye like little soldiers.

"Yes, we love you, Skye," Elijah said, in his best serious military voice.

"You two! Get out of here!" Skye swatted their backsides as they ran out the door.

Maybe they were all crazy. Maybe playing make-believe wasn't so bad after all. For that moment, everything was as fine as it could be under the circumstances. Two hours from that moment, however, would be Elijah's realization and validation that what he recalled to be true, was.

⚔

"This is it." Sydney said, pulling into the dirt and gravel driveway next to the two-story white framed house.

Sydney stared out of the car window at the house, remembering it much bigger ten years ago. The house was still painted white, top to bottom, but now the shutters were painted white too. The long, deep front porch was still beautiful, with its porch swing and white wicker furniture, and now large hanging ferns ran the length of the front of the house, as did honeysuckle wrapping around the railing. Everything was so pristine and clean. Sydney understood the message they were sending. And any passersby who didn't know any better would think it was a home filled with love, good things, grandma, and freshly baked cookies. Love? Maybe. But good things, grandma, and cookies? Nope.

"Hmmm," Sydney let out before she could catch herself.

"What, Mom?" Elijah glanced outside at what his mother could possibly be scrutinizing.

"Nothing, sweetie. We're here. You okay?"

"Yes, ma'am."

"Let's go. Lock your door." Ironic, she thought. The bad guys had already gotten in.

They walked up the stairs of the porch and through the front door. The glass in the front door was surely the original. It was thin and crystal-clear and rattled when they opened it. All so inviting.

"Yes, ma'am? How can I help you?" the lady behind the front desk asked with a deep East Texas accent.

Before Sydney could say a word, she realized it was Miss Kym, who was already on her feet and rounding her desk.

"Well, my word. Sydney Keane." She enveloped Sydney with the most loving hug Sydney could have imagined. "And you are Elijah," she continued, smiling at him warmly.

"Yes, ma'am," Elijah said, a bit shy.

"Do you mind if I give you one of these too?" She opened her arms wide to Elijah.

"No, ma'am." He laughed as he leaned in for the love hug.

"Well, that just made my day," she said. "Look at you, young man. How very handsome you are."

"Elijah, you may not remember Miss Kym, but she was here the first time we came," Sydney said, still amazed that Miss Kym was actually still there.

"Oh yes. And I am *always* the go-to person for lollipops! May I offer you one, Elijah?" She hoisted the large bucket from under her desk.

"I'm okay, but thank you," Elijah said.

"Okay then, but you know where I am if you change your mind." She gave Elijah a wink and slid the bucket back under the desk.

"God bless Miss Kym," Sydney thought. Who could bear being in this type of position for very long, except for those literally blessed by God to have the ability to withstand it all?

"Well, I know she's ready to see you two," she said with a smile. "Just give me one moment and I'll be right back."

She walked up the stairs and just a moment later came to the landing and motioned for the two of them to come up.

As Sydney and Elijah passed the front desk, Sydney asked Elijah, "Do you remember any of this?"

"No, ma'am," he answered as he took the first step up the stairs. Sydney followed, her hand on his back and wishing she could take it all away.

"Just follow me, Elijah," Miss Kym said. "Deb is looking forward to seeing you again. It's been a long time." She turned and smiled at Elijah with such genuine warmth.

They reached the top of the staircase and Deb met them in the foyer area. "Hello, Sydney. My, my, it's been a long time. Elijah," Deb said, quickly focusing her attention to the precious boy in front of her. "My goodness, young man, look how you've grown."

Everything was surreal. The house seemed smaller, Deb seemed smaller, and everything seemed as if Sydney was looking in a doll house. Everything was miniature in size compared to ten years ago. Maybe it was because Sydney had grown in ways she didn't realize until now.

"Come, come. Follow me." Deb walked to a doorway to the right of the staircase. "Do you remember this room, Elijah?"

"No, ma'am," he answered.

"Come here. I want to show you something. This is where we were the first time I met you and we visited." Deb walked into the room, but Elijah did not. He stood at the doorway.

"Okay. Follow me." Deb came out of the room, and Elijah and Sydney followed her down the hall and into a room, which was very nicely decorated and very inviting. Elijah took the chair in front of Deb, and Sydney sat off to the side. She wanted her presence to be felt as a support to Elijah, but this was his meeting.

Deb didn't mince words. "Elijah, you understand why you and your mom are here?"

"Yes, ma'am."

"And how do you feel about that?"

Elijah shrugged. "I don't know."

"Okay. Well, you wanted to come, right?"

"Yes, ma'am."

"Then I want you to feel comfortable, Elijah. I want you to know that we won't talk about anything today that you don't want to talk about. Okay?"

"Okay."

"But I do want you to know that you and I talked about a lot of things a long time ago. You were three years old. There isn't anything that you will say to me today that I'm not already aware of. Okay?"

"Okay."

"Your mom told me that the two of you talked about your dad."

"Yes, ma'am."

"Do you remember things about your dad and what he did to you?"

"Yes, ma'am."

"Do you want to talk about those things?"

Elijah looked at Sydney. It was clear that he was uncomfortable. He loved his mother and trusted his mother, but he didn't want her to hear what he had to say. Even though she already knew it all, he didn't want her to hear him say it again. This would stay between him and Deb.

Sydney understood Elijah's look. He was dismissing her as gently as possible.

"Sydney, would you mind if Elijah and I have a moment alone?" Deb asked.

"No, not at all." Sydney lifted herself from her seat.

She lied. She wanted more than anything to be in the room and to be a support and comfort to Elijah. Once again, she wanted to hold him tight and not let go. She walked out the door, closing it gently, feeling more dismissed than she ever had. She walked down the hall and took a seat at the small desk outside the door where she, Elijah, and Deb had first been. Sydney realized this was the exact desk where she had sat when Deb met with Elijah for the first time. Everything around her, this house and Deb, may have seemed small for a moment, but it all came rushing back to her now. Nothing was small.

⋏

By the time Elijah came out from his meeting with Deb, Sydney had moved to the front porch and positioned herself in one of the wicker chairs. She had watched as the breeze blew gently down the tree-lined street and she smelled the honeysuckle trailing along the railing of the porch. She thought again of how peaceful it all seemed and took a moment to take it all in. She let her mind go free for just a moment and wondered if there were people out there who had nothing to worry about but the breeze in the trees and their honey-suckle vines.

The front door opened and Elijah stepped out. He looked at Sydney briefly and then to the porch beneath him.

Sydney stood. "Does Deb need to see me again?"

"No, she said that we were finished and you can call her later if you want," Elijah replied.

"Oh, okay. Come on, sweetie." Sydney put her arm around Elijah and they walked back to the car. Her mind was racing, curious as to what Elijah and Deb had discussed, but she knew her curiosity didn't take precedence over Elijah and his level of security in discussing the matters at hand.

"So, can you tell me what you and Deb discussed?" Sydney asked, as nonintrusive as possible.

Only a moment passed, but Elijah's slight hesitation let Sydney know that he was unsure about sharing that information. It was clear he thought she may not like it, and that let her know that she probably wouldn't.

"Elijah. Listen, sweetie," Sydney said as they got in the car, "I know this is hard. It's very hard. And I know that you know how upset all of this makes me. Maybe that is why you're hesitating. Elijah, you are what is most important, period. Whatever Deb said, and whatever you discussed, is fine with me. I want you to know that you can talk to her about anything and everything, and you can trust her. Because you are my son and you are not an adult, I would like to know what was said. You don't have to tell me details if you are uncomfortable, but please tell me something."

Sydney knew it would be just as easy to get all of the information from Deb with that one phone call, and although she would be following up with Deb after she returned home, she wanted and needed Elijah to know that he could talk to her, even if it may be something that was difficult for her to hear. Her feelings about whatever it was had to be put to the side, for his sake.

She pulled out onto the tree-lined street she had just been savoring, even for a moment, and waited for Elijah to say something. Her reality had set back in one hundred percent.

"Well, we talked about Dad."

"Okay."

"And we talked about what he did."

"Okay."

"She asked me if I remembered her videotaping me with the dolls and I told her no."

"You don't remember that at all?"

"No."

"Okay."

"Anyway, she said she did, and that she and I had spent time together and I had told her everything he did to me when I was little."

Sydney didn't say a word.

"She said that Dad is sick and that he needs help, but that he never got help. She said that people who do the things that Dad has done can't be alone with children. She said that even if I decide to see Dad one day, I can never leave my children alone with him."

Sydney felt like she'd been punched right in the gut. "She said if you ever see your dad again? Did you tell her that you may want to see him?" She sounded as calm as she could. This was her test. This was the defining moment. She had to keep it together and assure Elijah that he could talk to her. "Be objective, Sydney. Be objective," she told herself, as impossible as it seemed.

"She asked me if I ever would and I told her maybe."

"You did? Would you want to see your dad again, Elijah?" Stay calm, Sydney. Stay calm.

"I don't know, Mom. Maybe. She just said that can be normal. She said sometimes children need that closure or something. She said he never admitted to what he did and since he didn't get help, he probably never would admit it. She said he'll probably always lie about it and I need to know that. She said that even if I see him when I'm older, I can't forget what he is or what he did, and I will never be able to leave my children alone with him."

Sydney continued to sound as normal as she possibly could, keeping all emotion in close check. "That's true, Elijah," and in a flash she thought of herself looking at Bear's dad every single day in high school, even though he did those things to her. She thought of hugging the old fuck after she and Bear were married and going right along with the fiasco, as if nothing had ever happened. She thought of Skye still having a relationship with her father and mother even though he did those horrible things to her, and out of self-preservation, her sisters and her mother still sliding it all under the rug. Looking at it objectively, she might need to understand. But then, in another flash, she reminded herself that that behavior, and that reaction to abuse, was wrong. It was wrong then and it was wrong now and the cycle must be broken.

"What's true, Mom?"

"Oh, um, everything she said. He still lies and denies everything, which means he'll continue to lie to you if given half a chance. If you do ever see your dad for closure, Elijah, you can never forget what he did. Never forget. If you do, you'll let your guard down and may trust that he's okay and can be around your children. That's why Deb said that. You can never put your children in that kind of danger or that kind of situation."

There was a long pause. "Do you understand that, Elijah?"

"Yes, ma'am."

"Honestly, if you decide to see your dad as an adult, that is your decision, but knowing all of this, it would be much easier not to."

Sydney changed the subject and Elijah welcomed it. She rolled down the windows and they talked about music, school, and plans for the upcoming weekend all the way home, leaving all of the sadness, best that they could, in Merriweather.

Chapter 49

A full year had gone by when the ugliness reared its head once again. Bear had since remarried a woman named Beth and they had a daughter named Emily. In his effort to portray the family man, he arranged to see Elijah and he would be bringing his bride, Emily, and Cody. Bear was off probation now, but he also knew that Sydney wouldn't allow him to see Elijah alone, so he didn't even bother to ask. He didn't want to poke that hornets' nest and risk Beth finding out more about her dear, devoted husband than he would have wanted. Sydney and Bear agreed to meet for dinner.

Sydney and Elijah were already seated front and center when the little family filed in and sat. Bear immediately started to talk about how Cody lived with them now. Sydney couldn't begin to imagine how that could have happened, but knew that whatever happened, Bear had likely manipulated Annette, and Annette had made a contemptible mistake. Cody sat close to his dad, not uttering a word. Bear let Elijah know that they had a pond and four-wheelers and any time he wanted to come for a visit, maybe in the summer, they'd love to have him. Bear also made sure to mention that Cody would surely like to get to know his big brother. Cody looked at Elijah and smiled. Their baby girl was eight months old and precious. It didn't take but that simple statement from Sydney, and Beth handed her their baby and started snapping pictures. Five were taken before Sydney could pass the baby back to her mom. There wasn't a lot of exchange between Beth and Sydney, but just enough for Sydney to know that Beth was a bitch on wheels. She had an attitude, and no doubt she cracked the whip on Bear. It didn't matter. The wind would be knocked out of her sail soon enough. Bear would eventually poke a hole in it and before she'd know it, she'd have nothing left and wonder where it all went. No, Sydney wasn't falling for any of this shit. She knew from experience and she knew from Annette's experience. It was all just a matter of time and this was nothing more than a fiasco. It didn't matter who they showed those damned pictures to, trying to paint some "we're all okay" picture. It didn't matter. Sydney knew the truth and that's all that mattered.

Sydney and Elijah got into their car and headed home, their conversation short and sweet.

"You know I can't let you go stay with your dad in the summer," Sydney said.

Elijah may have been old enough to make that decision for himself, but he more than understood and he understood why. "I know," he said. And that was that.

It was decided after that night that Sydney and Skye would get a caller ID for their telephone at home. Elijah never wanted to be put on the spot by his dad calling him during the hours after school and before Sydney or Skye got home from work. It served its purpose well and alleviated any stress they may have felt by answering the phone to the unknowns.

Chapter 50

Three more years went by like the wind. The only communication from Bear was the yearly birthday cards signed "Love, Dad."

In 2000, Elijah turned seventeen, and was a senior in high school. He had done wonderfully in high school and he was enrolled in accelerated courses for the gifted. Sydney had kept her eye on him, always being mindful that if another trip was ever needed to see Deb, there they would be. Thankfully, Elijah was happy, healthy, and thriving. He was not just okay, but better than okay, and better than okay was a wonderful place to be.

Elijah walked into Sydney's room, his arm outstretched in front of him as far as he could reach. He was holding the phone and looking at Sydney wide-eyed, but he didn't say a word.

"Elijah, who is it?"

"It's Dad."

Sydney took the phone from Elijah's hand and he immediately left her room.

As she put the phone to her ear, Sydney could hear Bear still talking to Elijah. He was just talking, totally unaware that his son had already ended their conversation.

"Bear. Bear." Sydney tried to interrupt him. "Bear!" She raised her voice over his ramblings.

"Yeah?" He was shocked and confused.

"This is Sydney. Elijah just handed me the phone."

"Oh, okay," Bear said, actually sounding cheerful and as if all was right with the world. Sydney could always tell that someone else was in the room by the tone of Bear's voice. This time, she felt sure it was Beth.

"Did you hear what I said, Bear? Elijah handed me the phone. Why are you calling here?"

"Yeah, uh, we just decided to call and talk to Elijah for a few minutes. He's graduating in a few months and we have an idea for his graduation."

"Bear, I'm sure Beth is sitting there, isn't she?"

"Yeah," he said, still sounding as though he was in a perfectly friendly conversation with his ex-wife. "Like I said, we thought we'd call Elijah to—"

"Listen, Bear, and listen carefully," Sydney interrupted. "Elijah remembers what you did to him."

"He does?"

Bear's instantaneous response was nothing short of inconceivable, but Sydney didn't pause. She kept her stride in the conversation.

"Yes, he remembers, Bear. Do not call here acting like nothing ever happened and expect to have a normal conversation with Elijah."

"Oh, okay. Well, tell Elijah that we said we'd be in touch by his graduation and that we love him." With that, the son of a bitch hung up.

Poor Beth. Poor, poor Beth. She was a bitch, but Sydney couldn't help but feel sorry for her. Bear sat right in front of her face and acted as if he were having a completely different conversation than the one that was actually taking place.

"Elijah, come here, sweetheart," Sydney called out.

Elijah came and stood at the door, not saying anything, but still seemed shaken by the call.

"Come here." Sydney hugged her son. "Listen to me. You know how we've talked about you always looking at caller ID before answering the phone?"

"Yes, but it's been so long. He hasn't called in so long."

"I know, but we got it for this very reason. I know that it gets easy to forget to look at it every time the phone rings, especially since Bear hasn't called in so long. But this is the reason why it's so important to look at it each and every time. I don't want you to ever feel this way." She hugged him again. "Okay?"

"Okay."

⅄

Two weeks had gone by and there were no calls from Bear. It was a daily concern of Sydney's and she reviewed the caller ID every evening after work.

Then, another surprise.

"Mom, I got a letter and it says it's from Beth," Elijah said, coming in with a handful of the day's mail.

"Really, honey? Let me see." Sydney was the master at keeping it together in front of Elijah, but she felt that the façade she had long presented was melting away.

"Hmmmm…I feel something inside." Sydney handed the envelope back to Elijah. "Go ahead and open it."

Elijah opened the envelope and in it was a piece of tissue wrapped tight with tape around it. He opened the tissue and a gold ring with five small diamonds across the top fell out onto the floor.

"Wow! A ring? What the…" Elijah picked it up and brushed it off.

"Yeah, 'what the' is right," Sydney said, taking the ring from his hand. "Why don't you read the letter? Maybe it will say something about it."

Elijah opened the letter and began to read as Sydney walked around the kitchen bar. Elijah turned to her and handed her the letter after just seconds. "It's about you, Mom."

Sydney read the letter. It was to Elijah and handwritten by Beth. It stated that Sydney was a liar and that she was trying to turn Elijah against Bear. It stated that Sydney had planted lies in Elijah's head and all that Bear ever wanted was to love and be close to Elijah. She went on to say that Cody and Emily would love to get to know their brother and they would like for Elijah to come stay with them one summer.

Sydney looked at Elijah. There were no words to describe how Sydney felt at that moment.

Beth, completely immersed in lies and deceit, sent Elijah a letter. This was beyond anything Sydney would have ever expected. The letter attacked Sydney in the worst possible way, but Sydney was convinced it wasn't just to attack Sydney. It was to give Beth some sort of solace, some sort of satisfaction. Maybe by pretending that Sydney was the evil one, she could stand to look at the man she had married. How could she, after all, be married to a man who had been accused not once, but twice, of molesting his two sons and not have even a tinge of doubt regarding his self-proclaimed innocence? Sydney knew this act of Beth's was more complicated than just what was written on paper, but it didn't really matter. What mattered was that the bitch had drastically stepped over the line and that was not okay, not ever.

⅄

The next morning, Sydney didn't waste any time upon entering her office. She closed her door, picked up the phone, and called directory assistance for the sawmill's phone number. She knew that Bear still worked shift work and by the grace of God, the bastard would be on the day shift.

"Yes, I need to speak to Bear Keane, please."

"Okay, ma'am. Do you know what area he's workin' in?" the receptionist asked with a heavy Southern drawl.

"Last I knew he worked on the wood grinders," Sydney answered.

"Okay. One moment, please," and Sydney was transferred.

"Hello!" a burly sounding man hollered over the noise of the machines.

"Yes, I need to speak with Bear Keane, please!" Sydney yelled.

"Who?!"

"Bear Keane!"

"Hold on!"

Sydney was placed on hold and took a deep breath. He was there and about to be confronted one more time.

"Hello!" Bear yelled.

"Bear, this is Sydney!"

"Sydney?!"

"Yes, Bear, and I need to talk to you!"

"Well, I can't hear you right now! No way to have a conversation! Can I call you back?!"

"Yes, you can! And please do! This is important!" She gave Bear her number.

"I'll call you as soon as I get off at four!"

"Okay!"

The two hung up.

Sydney felt that Bear would call back. She knew he would be curious and as long as it was just the two of them talking without his regular audience, he would definitely call back and hopefully listen.

Bear called back at four thirty sharp.

"Sydney, that Bear Keane ass is on the line. For real?" Harlene said.

"Yes, Harlene. Put him through, please."

Sydney felt so odd saying that. The last time Bear called her office, he had threatened to exercise his parental rights and a war was to ensue. That was four years ago. Now, he was returning her call.

"Hi, Bear. Thank you for calling me back."

"No problem. What's up?"

"Can you talk? Is Beth or anyone around?"

"No. I'm out here in my workshop. If Beth or Emily come out here, I'll have to hang up real quick. Beth doesn't know I'm callin' you."

"No problem."

Jesus. Sydney couldn't believe she was making conversation with him, nor that he was actually listening. What Sydney did know was that arguing with Bear or threatening him would most certainly not get her the results she wanted.

"Bear, I need to talk to you about something and I really need you to listen."

"Okay. What is it?"

"Yesterday, Elijah got a letter from Beth with a ring in it."

"He did?"

Sydney wanted to puke. Of course, he knew, but Sydney had to keep the conversation going to get the outcome she needed.

"Yes, he did. And in that letter Beth called me a liar, told Elijah that I had planted ideas in his mind about what you had done to him, and all the two of you wanted was to be a family with Elijah, Cody, and Emily."

Bear was silent. Not a word, nor breath, came out of his mouth.

"Listen to me, Bear. I don't give a shit about what lies you tell Beth to keep your little family together, but when she starts sending my son letters calling me a liar, I do give a shit."

Bear was still silent.

"Are you there, Bear?"

"Yes. Sydney, I didn't know she was going to write that letter or mail it. I was half asleep the other night and she was goin' on about somethin', this that and the other, and I just said 'yeah, whatever,' and went on to sleep."

Once again, Sydney knew Bear was full of shit. More lies, but as long as he knew Sydney wasn't putting up with the shit, she didn't really care.

"Do you remember the other night when I told you that Elijah remembers what you did to him?"

"Yes."

"Well, he does. Elijah remembers, Bear." Sydney paused, waiting for any reaction from Bear, but none came. "So, when Beth sends letters like this, calling me a liar and saying the things she did, it only makes her look like a fool, and it is apparent that you are lying to her and telling her God only knows what."

Bear breathed in deep and loud, but kept his silence.

"And what is the deal with the ring? Where did that come from?"

"That was a ring my mom gave me. She said it had belonged to my biological dad. I thought it would be nice for Elijah to have it."

Sydney closed her eyes and grounded herself the best that she could. She paused for just a moment and continued.

"That's fine, Bear. But just know this. If Beth ever, and I do mean ever, sends another letter to my house or if she ever calls my house... Let me just say this…if Beth ever tries to contact Elijah again, she will be hearing from me and she won't like it. Okay?"

"Yeah. I'll tell her not to pull that shit again."

"Thank you. And by the way, with regard to Elijah's graduation, only very few tickets are handed out. There is a limit on tickets and my family is going."

"Sounds good."

"Well, all right then. That's it."

"Okay. Goodbye, Sydney."

Sydney hung up the phone and couldn't get a handle on how she felt. She hated him. He was the devil. And yet she had a conversation with him. An open conversation with him to remind him that Elijah remembered, to tell him to keep his wife at bay, and to let him know that under no uncertain terms would any more shit be tolerated. And he agreed? No name-calling, no anger. Nothing. That was the best way to describe it. There was nothing. Even though Sydney knew it couldn't possibly be real, it satisfied her for now. But she knew all too well: you can't trust the devil.

Chapter 51

Sydney should have kept a box of Kleenex attached to her hip during Elijah's entire senior year. She couldn't pass his room or a picture of him without crying. Her son was going off to college now. He had graduated with honors and was accepted to UT in Austin. Sydney, Skye, and both of their families couldn't have been more proud of Elijah. Sydney's family attributed Elijah's rise above it all to the love and support Elijah had always received. That was true, but Sydney also gave credit where credit was due, and that was to God. She had made her pact with God all those years ago and she knew without Him watching over Elijah and her, nothing would be as it was now.

Elijah excelled in college. He majored in English with minors in both music and philosophy. He was an artistic talent. His words and music flowed on pages like crystalline waters over white sand. He was truly a shooting star in the midnight sky: beautiful and awesome.

During Elijah's first two years in college, he spread his wings, as all young adults do. He needed to find his way and make decisions on his own. Sydney knew this and understood this, but that didn't make loosening the apron strings any easier. She worried herself sick most of the time, especially when Cody began contacting Elijah in order to forge some sort of relationship with his big brother. Sydney understood Elijah taking the olive branch and opening his heart to Cody. She would have done the exact same thing under the same circumstances. But Sydney wasn't in those circumstances. She was the mom and she could see the big picture. She knew that although Cody wanted to develop his relationship with Elijah, Bear would likely use that bond to forge his own relationship with Elijah, and there wasn't a damn thing she could do about it, but pray.

⨺

Over these years, Sydney had asked Elijah to please always let her know if Bear ever contacted him. Just as surely as she knew the sun would set, she knew that day would eventually come. Elijah assured her that he would always let her know if Bear were to contact him, and Sydney knew that her mind would always have to be open and her heart sensitive to her son's feelings and wishes.

The day did finally come, much to Sydney's dismay. Cody contacted Elijah and asked Elijah to attend a Father's Day function in New Braunfels. He told Elijah that Clara, who Elijah had not seen since he was a small child, would be there, as would Bear's sister, her husband, and some of Elijah's cousins. Certainly, it piqued Elijah's interest and curiosity. He accepted the invitation under the guise that it was important to Cody that he attend. Sydney knew different. That was only the partial truth. This was the single biggest thing she had dreaded all of these years, and it was also the inevitable.

Chapter 52

In the month prior to Father's Day, Sydney felt she was losing her mind. Her heart hurt. Her soul hurt. She was exhausted. She had spent her entire adult life protecting her son from someone, and now she had to retreat. She had told Elijah everything he needed to know and she had reminded him of everything Deb had said all those years ago. Would he take those words to heart? Would he remember everything? Or would he see what he wanted to see, as so many do?

Sydney decided to make an appointment with a wise woman named Meihui Tong. Meihui was Ruby's acupuncturist and she had referred Skye to her as well. But Meihui was more than just an acupuncturist. She was a wise old owl and she could read people without them saying a word. While Meihui was a woman of few words, her messages were profound, and Sydney reached out to her out of absolute desperation.

⋏

"This you first time?" Meihui asked Sydney.

"Yes, it is," Sydney answered.

"Tell me what on you mind," Meihui said.

Before Sydney could open her mouth to do just that, the tears began streaming down her face and Meihui left for a moment to retrieve a box of tissue.

"Here, love. Tell me what matter." She handed Sydney the tissue.

Sydney did tell her. How do you put twenty years in a five-minute conversation? But Sydney managed.

"You feel guilty," Meihui said, and it took Sydney by complete surprise.

"No. No, I don't feel guilty."

"Yes, you do."

"No, I don't," Sydney said, and didn't care how defensive she sounded. "From the moment I knew anything…" She stopped, gathering herself, and wiped away the tears. "From the moment I knew anything, from the moment Elijah told me, I took care of things. I took care of Elijah, and I took care of things immediately."

"You still feel guilty or you not try to fix things all the years, make things better."

"That's my job, Meihui. I am his mother."

"Yes, you his mother. You protect son."

"That's right. That's right."

"Sydney, you son is grown now. He man now."

"I know that. I do." Sydney continued to wipe her tears.

"He have to make own decision. You cannot make for him."

"I know, Meihui." Sydney began to sob.

"Let me tell you story," Meihui started. "There was a man, and his mother do everything for him. She do anything for him. Her son thrown in jail. He call his mother. 'Mother, come to me,' he say. She go to him and say, 'What do you want, son? What can I do for you?' Her son say, 'Give me your breast, Mother. Let me suckle your breast.' The mother give her son her breast and he bite it off."

"I don't understand. Why did he hate her?" Sydney asked, shocked at the outcome of Meihui's story.

"He did not hate his mother. He show her he man and no longer need to suckle her breast. She has to let him be man."

"I see." Sydney had nothing left. She felt empty.

Meihui laid Sydney back on the table and filled the front of her body, head to toes, full of needles. She dimmed the lights and closed the door.

Sydney lay there alone in the dusky room and thought about what Meihui had said. Part of her wanted to yank out every needle and run like hell, but there was a part of her that knew it was the truth. Elijah was a man. He was her son, but he was also a man, and any mistake he would make would be his mistake, and he would be the one to suffer the consequences, as hard as that may be for Sydney to imagine. That was the part Sydney could not get past. This wasn't about normal consequences. This was about life choices that would surely affect his life, and therefore his children's. Sydney had to keep trusting God and trusting Elijah, but she was afraid. She was afraid for Elijah. Elijah didn't know who he was dealing with, but she did.

Meihui came back into the room and it wasn't until that moment that Sydney realized that she had completely relaxed. Meihui removed all of the needles and gave Sydney a much-needed hug before exiting so that she could dress.

Sydney dressed and walked slowly to the reception area to check out. She felt numb. She didn't feel the same torment and anxiety as she had when she arrived, but she still felt detached and incredibly sad.

"What are these?" Sydney asked, touching a stack of cards as she handed the receptionist her check.

"Oh, those are cards that we have for our patients. They have Chinese proverbs and inspirational messages on them. Take one." The receptionist smiled at Sydney and kept her attention on her as Sydney chose a card from the middle of the stack.

The card had a beautiful, colorful design on it with the word "Opal" in the center: opal, long known to represent hope, innocence, and purity. Sydney turned the card over and read. *"Your children on Earth and in Heaven are happy and well cared for by God and the angels."*

Sydney took a breath, holding the card with her right hand and grasping the counter with her left.

"Are you okay, Ms. Keane?" the receptionist asked.

Sydney knew this was a message from God. No one could take away this message God had given to her. Elijah was in the palm of God's hand and surrounded by angels, and truly always had been. And for the first time in a very, very long time, she thought of her baby that was never born all those many,

many years ago. She knew that God was letting her know that this child too was safe, with Him, and surrounded by His angels. She had felt empty, totally empty. Now, her cup was being filled once again.

"Yes, I am fine. Thank you so much." Sydney smiled as she placed the card in her purse. It would be a reminder for always of the promise He would never break.

Sydney was walking out the door when Meihui came to her and placed a card firmly in her hand and closed Sydney's hand over it.

"You come to me for acupuncture and healing. This my nephew. He teacher and healer too. Call him. Good for you."

"Thank you, Meihui." Sydney walked out the door and waited to reach her car before looking at the card.

The card read "Junjie Tong" and had his phone number printed under it. Sydney had no idea what this was about, but she knew it could only lead to somewhere better than she had been, mentally and emotionally, and she trusted that Meihui knew that also. She also knew that this was yet another message from God.

⋏

Sydney poured herself and Skye a cup of tea. She showed Skye the Opal card she had drawn at Meihui's office. There was no doubt the message was meant for Sydney, and Skye knew it too. It brought a great sense of peace to them both. Sydney then told Skye of the card Meihui gave her as she was leaving.

"So, Junjie Tong, huh?" Skye asked.

"Yes," Sydney said, looking back at the card Meihui had given to her.

"I wonder why Meihui didn't tell me about Junjie. I think I might be jealous," Skye said, winking at Sydney.

"Very funny. Maybe if you were losing your mind, you too would get Junjie's number." Sydney smiled.

"So are you going to call him?"

"Of course."

"Well, what are you waiting for?"

Sydney looked at Skye, knowing she had hit the nail on the head. What was she waiting for? She picked up the phone and dialed.

"Hello, Sydney," the voice on the other end said.

"Excuse me?" Sydney said, not grasping how this man knew it was her.

"I said 'Hello, Sydney,' but don't be alarmed. I joined the rest of civilization and have caller ID."

"Ah! Very good!" Sydney said, laughing.

Junjie sounded much younger than she expected and he sounded very Americanized.

"You are Meihui's nephew?" she said, not really knowing how to begin the conversation.

"Yes, I am. Aunt Meihui. She's a force to be reckoned with."

"Yes, she is." Sydney laughed again, instantly feeling comfortable.

"She told me about you, Sydney. Aunt Meihui can help you, but so can I."

Sydney had no idea what to say next, but simply asked, "How?"

"Well, I teach a skill called Kung fu."

"I'm sorry, Junjie, and I don't mean to be dismissive or disrespectful in any way, but I am not really interested in Kung fu."

"Please listen, Sydney. Kung fu is not necessarily what you think. Many people immediately think of martial arts. That certainly can be part of it, but Kung fu actually refers to any skill achieved through practice and hard work. It refers to study and learning, and requires patience and energy."

Hearing these words instantly made Sydney feel impatient and tired. She was too wired, too high-strung for anything such as this.

"Junjie, I don't know. I really don't."

"Please come meet with me, Sydney. If you don't like what I have to say or what I have to show you, no problem. But I think you will."

Sydney let out an exasperated breath and looked at Skye.

Skye threw her hands in the air. "What do you have to lose?" she mouthed to Sydney.

"Okay, Junjie. Okay. I'm trusting you here, but no pressure if it's not for me. Okay?"

"Agreed." He let out a deep breath as well, but one of thanks. He gave Sydney his address and she was set for eight o'clock the next morning.

⚔

Sydney walked into the martial arts studio. Everyone was dressed in their martial arts garb and Sydney felt awkward in her peasant skirt and t-shirt. All eyes were on what appeared to be "little girl lost."

"Sydney!" From across the room came a handsome young man who was full of light.

"I thought you said this wasn't about martial arts." Sydney smiled as she glanced over at a class already in session.

"No, that isn't what I said." Junjie smiled back. "I said martial arts can be a part of Kung fu, but the actual practice of Kung fu can encompass many things. It refers to the study and learning of a particular thing or things and it requires patience and energy."

"Mmm-hmm." Sydney looked at Junjie and then at the class. "Well, what will I be studying and learning?"

"You tell me. What interests you?"

"Junjie, I really don't know." Sydney looked out the door she'd just come through and wondered whether she should hop right back in her car and drive home.

"Hey, hey. I'm over here, so don't get any ideas of leaving me before I even have a chance to talk to you," Junjie said, instantly reading Sydney mind.

She looked back at him and decided to relax and listen. "Tell you what, Junjie. You tell me. I'm sure that Meihui gave you at least a little bit of information about me, so you tell me how you can help me."

"Okay. Before you say anything, Sydney, start by opening your mind to new ideas and possibilities. Start by being open to change and doing things you hadn't necessarily thought of before."

"Where are you going with this, Junjie? Tread lightly because I'm a girl who doesn't like a lot of change. I've had my share of it and my preference is to not."

"Remember, open your mind. Don't have any preconceived notions and let's start fresh and new. Open yourself to change and possibilities and most importantly, trust me."

"Trust me, he says." Sydney rolled her eyes and looked back out the door.

Junjie put his hands on her shoulders and turned her to directly face him, and looked her in her eyes. "Yes, trust me."

⅄

Skye met Sydney at the door when she pulled into the garage. "Well…"

"Look at you, Ms. Eager," Sydney said, laughing.

"Well, what happened? Did you like Junjie? What did he say?"

"I have officially lost my ever-lovin' mind, that's what happened."

"What do you mean?" Skye asked, as Sydney walked out to their patio to enjoy the Sunday sun.

"I have officially signed up for Kung fu, and yes, that would be referring to martial arts."

Sydney gave her best martial arts pose and the two laughed.

"Well, that's interesting, and unexpected," Skye said.

"You're tellin' me. But you know what, I've got to do something, Skye, and what he said did make some sense."

"Give it to me."

"He said that he feels an energy from me, physically and emotionally, and it would be beneficial for me to put that energy somewhere. He said I have a great deal of stress because I don't put my energy somewhere, at least not in the right places. He feels by me applying the Kung fu principles to martial arts training, I'll get the cleansing and focus I need to be healthy: physically, mentally, and emotionally. It's either that or I lose my shit, and the little men in white coats come haul me away." Sydney chuckled, but she was only half joking. She was spent, and at the very end of a very long road.

Skye brought Sydney to her and hugged her close. "Honey, you're going to be fine. We're going to be fine, Elijah is going to be fine, and everything you worry about is going to be fine."

Sydney stayed wrapped in Skye's arms. "Keep saying that, Skye, and keep believing it. Without a crystal ball, that's all we can do. Believe."

"When do you start your classes?"

"Tomorrow after work. I'll be going three times a week, so let's pray now that this provides the relief I need."

And they did just that.

CHAPTER 53

Father's Day arrived and Sydney couldn't recall a day she had dreaded more. For Elijah to be seeing his father was her very worst nightmare and for him to be seeing his father on Father's Day was like pouring acid in an open wound. She worked double time to keep herself in check, and she told herself over and over that she was not losing her mind. Each time Father's Day entered her mind, she stopped, she prayed to God above, and she immediately put into practice the Kung fu techniques she had only recently learned. She then let out the physical and emotional energy Junjie so often referred to on a punching bag Skye had purchased for her and installed in the garage. The martial arts classes were much more beneficial than Sydney had expected and she was stronger now, physically. She felt as though she was hanging on by a thread in other areas, but she at least had that and it felt like more than she'd had just weeks before. Yes, Father's Day required a great deal. It required constant prayer, meditation, beating the hell out of her punching bag, and the bottle of wine she would have that night. Sleep would not come for Sydney.

⟁

Sydney rolled over and looked at the clock. It was seven o'clock in the morning. She would have normally been sitting in traffic at this moment, but she had taken the day off from work and Skye had followed suit. Sydney hadn't slept, but at the same time, she was in no hurry to leave her place of comfort and thought, remaining safe from the world for a moment. Her thoughts were staying centered in her faith and she recalled times long past when as a young child she had called the evening's televangelist to ask for prayer for herself and her family, prayer requests she made specific to whomever and whatever was going on at the time. She knew as a young girl that God had heard her prayers and watched over them all, protecting them from further hurt and harm. And she recalled the Christmas Eve when she was just fourteen years old. Her mother, Hayden, and Memaw were downstairs laughing and carrying on after she had gone to bed. Sydney felt blessed that special evening—blessed to have her family—and she thought about all of those who she loved so dearly. In doing so, she began to sob, wondering what she would ever do if she ever lost her family—if she ever lost her mother, her Memaw, her Mama Scurlock and others. She cried uncontrollably and in an instant, she felt something move right through her, taking her breath with it and she could not cry. She could not shed another tear. Yes, she was only fourteen, but she knew that something significant had just happened and never once doubted that it was the spirit of God letting her know that she would always be taken care of.

Sydney's faith remained intact and her armor on, shielding them the very best she could from the evil that had been thrown their way. She prayed again that Elijah was sitting perfectly in the palm of God's hand, protected, and that she would be hearing from him soon.

The phone rang and her prayers were answered.

"Hey, Mom! It's Elijah!"

Her son knew her all too well. It was the day after Father's Day, and no doubt, he knew his mom had been on pins and needles, to say the very least.

"Elijah! Hi, honey! You okay? It sounds really noisy where you are!"

Skye rolled over and smiled at Sydney. The only person who could possibly be happier than Sydney that Elijah had called was Skye. They could breathe now.

"Yeah, I'm on my way home and the windows are down! Let me roll them up!"

"On his way home?" she thought, but didn't say a word.

"Okay. Is this better? Can you hear me now?" he asked.

"Yes, much better. So, you are on your way home? From where?"

"Oh, I went ahead and stayed the night at the campground with everybody."

Sydney steadied herself, mentally and emotionally.

"Oh? Tell me what all you did yesterday." Sydney had no idea how she was able to sound so calm. There was no viable reason that came to mind. It was nothing short of God and the fact that she loved Elijah so much.

"Well, yesterday morning, I met Dad, his new girlfriend, Grandma, Cody, Emily, Abigail, her husband and their kids for breakfast."

"That's a lot of people you met for breakfast, Elijah. You say your dad's new girlfriend was there also? What about Beth?"

"He and Beth are divorced now. Cody thought he'd told me, but he hadn't."

"How was your visit with everyone?"

"It was fine. It was kind of weird, but it was fine."

"So tell me. You know your ol' mom. Give me details ad nauseum."

"Yeah, I know my ol' mom." Elijah laughed. He sounded good and relaxed, and Sydney didn't quite know what to make of it.

Elijah continued. "We all met for breakfast and then we all drove down to where they were all camping. We just rode the rapids and hung out and stuff. Dad and Beth sold their property in Merriweather when they divorced and now he has an RV, so we had that and tents to sleep in."

"An RV?"

"Yeah, he's traveling to different mills and working long-changes, so he has his RV since he's pretty much all over the place now."

Sydney's mind took flight and there was no stopping it. "All over the place now," she thought. He's all over the place. In and out before anyone would know what just happened. In that millisecond, she wondered if he had a girlfriend in every town and if they had children.

"Mom, you there?" Elijah asked.

"Yes, I'm here, Elijah. So, your dad is working in different towns, you say?"

"Yes. He still has a home base in East Texas in some little town, but I can't remember where. Everyone was joking around about how he keeps a PO Box because you never know where he's going to be, or when."

"Hmm." That's all Sydney could say. Her mind was still working double time knowing that there was a reason for Bear's movement.

"Mom."

"Yes?"

"Everything was fine. It really was. Nothing bad happened."

Sydney didn't say anything. What was there to say?

Elijah continued. "I got some pictures while I was there. Want me to email them to you when I get home?"

"Yes. That would be great, sweetie. I'd like to see what everyone looks like now. Curiosity, I suppose."

"I'll be home soon and I'll send them right away."

"Sounds good. I'll be looking forward to getting them and you be safe driving home."

"Will do. Love you, Mom."

"I love you too, Elijah." The two hung up.

"Come here." Skye motioned for Sydney to lie on her shoulder. "Talk to me."

Sydney nestled in, staring at the ceiling fan. "You know, I really know that it is not easy for Elijah to tell me that he hears from Cody or that he's going to see his dad, and on Father's Day, no less. I know that he knows no matter how I sound, it kills me, but he does it because he said he would and he honors that. God bless him." Sydney took a deep breath. "I know this isn't easy for him at all. And I'll tell you, it's the hardest thing I've ever had to do, just listening to it. Listening to it and knowing it's a bunch of Bear's manipulative shit, but not saying a word."

"That's it, Sydney. You basically just said it. Elijah tells you these things, even though it's hard, because he loves you and he respects you. You put your feelings aside about all of this when talking to him because you love him and respect him. I don't know what to say about all of this, but I do know one thing: Elijah is smart. He's a very smart young man."

"Elijah is a very smart young man, absolutely. But regardless of how smart someone is, we're talking emotions here. We're talking emotions that are stirred up from childhood. What does every child want most, Skye? The love of their parents. That's it. That's what they want. When a child doesn't get that, they want to know why and many times they internalize that and question themselves or even blame themselves. Couple that with the fact that no child wants to ever think a parent would hurt them intentionally—that's the double whammy. It's only natural to venture into uncharted territory if you think you may get answers."

"Listen to yourself. You're answering all of the questions right now, Sydney. You're lying here, saying exactly why Elijah is likely doing this. "

"Yes, that I am. It's easy to look at this objectively when I'm talking about an overall situation, when I'm making a blanket comment about a group of people. It's easy to say. But when I bring it back home and it pertains specifically to my son, who yes, is a man, it's vastly different. It's personal. I know who we're talking about here when we're talking about Bear and I know the end result. So, I stand by and watch while everyone learns on their own? No. I can't and I won't." Sydney flung the covers back and grabbed her robe.

"Where are you going?" Skye yelled out, Sydney already halfway down the hall.

"I'm making coffee and waiting on pictures," Sydney yelled back.

"This is all just a matter of time," Sydney said under her breath, pulling the coffee grounds from the freezer. "Just a matter of time and, God, please show me the way."

⅄

Sydney kept watch over her computer all morning. She worked in the yard, back to the computer, baked a cake, back to the computer, bathed the dogs, back to the computer. No pictures.

"What the hell?!" Sydney yelled from the study. Still no email from Elijah.

"Sydney, it's eleven o'clock in the morning. Give him some time. He just got home two hours ago and I'm sure he needs to unpack and maybe he got distracted with something."

Sydney hit Send/Receive once more before she left her computer yet again, and there it was. "Hallelujah!" she yelled, seeing Elijah's name pop up in her email and seeing the paperclip that indicated an attachment.

"Yes, hallelujah and praise God!" Skye yelled back, knowing Sydney's obsession with not yet having the pictures would now transfer to who was in them.

Sydney sat down and prepared herself the very best that she could. She thought of all of the Kung fu techniques she should have practiced before receiving the email, but quickly dismissed that notion and knew her punching bag would come in much more handy afterwards.

"Here you go. Love you!" was the note in Elijah's email to her, and there were a mere five pictures attached. Sydney opened each attachment. Three of them were group photos, all from a distance. One showed a group of people, all on the side of a hill right over the water rapids below. The photo was taken far enough away that Sydney couldn't tell who was who. The other two group photos showed Bear's mother, sister, her two grown children, and a woman Sydney didn't recognize, likely Bear's girlfriend.

Then, there were the final two pictures.

"God in heaven," Sydney thought as she opened each one. The first one was a picture of Elijah, Cody, and Bear, all sitting in lawn chairs in a circle; each held a beer and smiled for the camera. Sydney looked long and hard at Elijah. He looked different to her. He did not look like himself at all. She opened the next photo attachment and knew she was looking at pure evil and pure evil was most certainly, with full intention, looking right back at her. It was a picture of Bear, between both Elijah and Cody, his arms around each, and all were smiling. Bear's smile was a half-cocked, sarcastic, "ha-ha, gotcha" smile and he was eye to eye with the camera. It was as if he were looking deep inside it. His arm, which was draped over Elijah's shoulder, was outstretched, index finger pointing directly to the camera as if to show a child where to look so their picture could be taken. "Look at the camera, Elijah, and smile." Sydney could hear the words coming from his mouth. It was the undeniable "fuck you" that Bear had waited oh so long to say to Sydney, and Sydney knew it.

Skye put her hands on Sydney's shoulders, startling Sydney.

"I'm sorry. I thought you heard me come in. What world were you in just now?" Skye asked.

"This one." Sydney pointed to the picture of Elijah, Bear, and Cody.

"Oh." Skye leaned over Sydney's shoulder and gazed at the picture on the screen.

"Do you see what I see?" Sydney asked.

"How could I not? Unbelievable," Skye said.

Sydney knew what she saw, but she was glad that Skye did too. There was no mistaking this.

"I want to talk to Elijah, but what do I say?"

"Sydney, you're going to have to..." Skye raised her head from the picture on the computer screen and headed toward the door.

"Have to what?" She looked at Skye, stone-faced. "Tell me. Have to what?"

"Just forget it." Skye stormed out of the study, down the hall, and slammed the back door behind her.

Sydney didn't blame her. She herself was so tired of all of this. How could she blame Skye for being tired too? Sydney closed her eyes and thought how best to handle the situation, how best to approach this with Elijah. She didn't want to shoot herself in the foot and make Elijah wish he'd never said a word, or wish he hadn't sent the pictures. But Sydney was no head-in-the-sand type of woman or mother, so her carefully addressing a concern with Elijah certainly wasn't foreign to him. What she did need to do was wait. This day was definitely not the time. She had her mind set on the upcoming weekend to talk to Elijah, and she would if all felt right.

⅄

Friday rolled around and not soon enough. It was a daunting week at work for both Sydney and Skye. Skye was inundated with new employee orientations and Sydney couldn't keep her mind on her work responsibilities for thinking about the pictures and the conversation she would be having with Elijah.

Skye pulled up in front of Sydney's building, smiling like a little girl going on vacation. Sydney slid in for the ride home.

"You're all grins," Sydney said, looking at Skye and stroking her cheek.

"I am."

"And why, may I ask?"

"Because I'm looking forward to a nice, relaxing weekend with my honey." Skye smiled and placed her hand on Sydney's leg.

Sydney looked out her side window, knowing full well that Skye certainly deserved a nice relaxing weekend.

"I know you're having your talk with Elijah and that's fine, but after that, Sydney—"

"Stop right there. I hear you and you're right," Sydney said.

"Say what?" Skye stopped in her tracks after being fully prepared to plead her case for a weekend without Bear Keane's name being mentioned.

"That's right. I'm in total agreement. I am going to talk to Elijah and then Bear's name will not be mentioned for the rest of the entire weekend."

Skye looked at Sydney.

"And I promise," Sydney said.

"And she promises! Thank you, Lord!"

Sydney rolled back the sunroof and envisioned all of the anger, hurt, and worry she had felt all week flying out into oblivion. Her focus was kept on Elijah, and she would not allow any of what she had just shucked off to creep back in. Besides, Sydney had gone over the conversation she would be having with Elijah, and all of the possible scenarios, a million times. And she had prayed long and hard enough about it that she had to keep her faith it would all be okay.

⅄

Sydney wasted no time upon arriving home. There was no time like the present. She called Elijah.

"And hello, Momma," Elijah said, sounding as if he was having a very good day thus far.

"And hello, Elijah," Sydney said. "You sound like you've had a good day, sweetie."

"I have."

"And how so?"

"It's just been a really good day and I'm glad it's the weekend. TGIF."

"I hear ya, sweetie."

Sydney paused. She didn't want to ruin Elijah's day, evening, or weekend, but would there ever be a good time to bring up Father's Day weekend? She knew there wouldn't be, and now would have to do.

"You have a sec?" Sydney asked, angry once again that any of this ever had to be a thought. It infuriated her.

"Sure. What's up?"

"Well, I have just a couple of questions about last weekend, Elijah."

"Oh."

"It's all okay, Elijah. It's just a couple of questions, that's all. No big deal."

"Oh, okay. What is it?"

"Okay," Sydney started, and quickly placed herself on autopilot. It was the best way to approach what had her so concerned. Just forge ahead, Sydney, and trust God to give you the words. Forge ahead. "Did you feel different that day that you were with your dad?"

"What do you mean? Did I feel different?" Elijah sounded somewhat confused.

"Elijah, I am going to say this and please just hear me out. In the pictures of you, your dad, and Cody, you look different. You don't look like yourself to me in these pictures. Did you feel different that day?"

Elijah took a long pause and Sydney let him. "Yeah, I did."

"You did feel different? How so?"

"I don't know how to explain it. I just did."

Sydney gave a sigh of relief. She knew what she saw and she was grateful that Elijah trusted her enough to admit it.

"You know, Elijah. I understand that. I truly do." Sydney settled in for an open and honest conversation with her son. "I remember when I was a child and sometimes I would act differently based on who I was around."

Sydney had, and remembered those times. It was self-preservation, she supposed. It was also the fact that Sydney was of such a sensitive nature, in her own quest for approval and love, she could easily conform to the expectations of whatever adult she was around. Sydney was always herself in her heart, but she understood the need to please. What made Elijah any different from her? He was her son, and the apple had not fallen far from the tree.

"What do you mean?" he asked.

"Just what I said. I think when we're looking for approval, and certainly from a parent, it's easy to open ourselves up to what their expectations are and maybe try to adhere to that."

"I didn't realize I felt different while I was there," he said.

"I know. But now, looking back, you see that you were?"

"Yes."

"I don't necessarily think it's always a conscious thing that we do. I do believe that many times it's subconscious and it stems from our desire to be accepted. I felt it from your pictures. It just wasn't you."

Elijah didn't say a word and Sydney hoped she had not said too much, but she continued. She had to.

"I want you to be okay, Elijah. I want you to have a happy life. We can't choose our parents, sweetie. We are born to them. Sometimes things can be wonderful, beautiful. Other times, bad things can happen, and we can't be expected to keep tight the tie that binds. The fact is, the tie doesn't bind. We can make the decision for our own health and well-being to move on. Don't sacrifice yourself in an effort to get an answer that you may feel you want or need. Many times, the answers aren't the ones we're seeking anyway."

Sydney had almost felt as if someone else was speaking. The words flowed from her and they were true: the truest of words, and those that represented so many, and that included her.

"Thanks, Mom."

"What are you thanking me for?"

"Just thank you. I don't want to be around him ever again. I'm writing him a letter and asking him to never contact me again. And I'm going to tell Cody not to ever invite me to anything or expect me to go if Dad is there. No more. I don't want that ever again."

"Are you saying that because of what I said, or is that how you feel? This needs to be how you feel, Elijah, over and above anything else."

"Yes, it is how I feel. I don't want anyone or anything dragging me down and that's how I felt after I got back home. I had a good time while I was there, but I didn't like anything about it after I got home."

"I understand, Elijah. You keep your head up and your feet planted firmly beneath you. There is a path already laid out before you, Elijah. Remember the story I told you about when I was seven months pregnant?"

"Yes, Mom, and you gave me back to God to protect me, guide me, and all that."

Sydney let out a small chuckle. She was thankful and happy that Elijah remembered the story and the older he got, he would have no doubts of the truth it held. He would know it even more when he had children of his own.

"Yes, that's it. God is there, always there, to protect you, guide you, and I've told you as long as I can remember that fantastic things are in store for you, Elijah. I've always known it. You're going to have a beautiful, happy, and healthy life. Keep looking upward and onward and stay on the path that you know in your heart is yours to take. It's all good. I love you so much." Sydney could feel her emotions rising: relief—pure relief.

"I love you too, Mom, and don't cry."

"I'm not. I'm fine. Okay. Well, I don't know what to say after all of that, so how about I say again that I love you very much and you have a fantastic weekend. On with your Friday. Big plans?"

"I think I'm going to call Daniel and go shoot some pool and then I'm going to take care of the other thing we discussed tomorrow."

"That sounds like a plan to me. Have a wonderful evening, sweetheart, and give that Daniel a hug from us."

"Will do and love you."

"Love you, sweetie." Sydney blew a kiss over the phone, and the two hung up.

"Thank you, Jesus. Thank you, Jesus. Thank you, Jesus!" Sydney said, rounding the corner into the living room.

"I take it that all went well?" Skye handed Sydney her first glass of wine for the evening.

"It did. I love him so much, Skye." Sydney couldn't hold back the tears. "He is so precious and thank you, God, for watching over him and guiding him where he needs to be. Thank you, God."

"Yes, thank you, God," Skye said.

Elijah did write the letter to Bear the following day. He called Sydney and read it to her before he mailed it. It was heartbreaking to hear his words and the emotions they held. Sydney wasn't listening to the words of the boy she had so long tried to protect, but rather was listening to the words of the man that boy had become. It was done. For now. Again. It was done.

Chapter 54

"Hey, darlin'. You busy?" Maeve asked.

"I was about to hop in the shower. Can I buzz you back?"

"Can you put on a robe? This won't take but a second."

"Okay. Is everything okay, Momma?"

"I'll let you be the judge, but I would say no. No, everything isn't okay."

"What's the matter?"

"I just hung up with Denton and guess who he saw the other day."

"God, Momma. I thought someone was sick or died or somethin'. Who did Uncle Denton see?"

"Bear."

It had been a mere one week since Elijah had written the letter to Bear, and Sydney had hoped upon hope that bad news wouldn't come so soon.

"What?! He saw Bear? Where?"

"Well, it seems that Bear has moved back to Merriweather."

Sydney grabbed her robe and sat on the bed. "That can't be right, Momma. Bear would never move back to Merriweather. Everyone there knows what he did to Elijah. It may have been all those years ago, but people haven't forgotten. And look at what he did at the mill. Remember Uncle Denton telling us he stole some equipment from the mill some years back and he was charged with theft? Anyway, everyone at the mill knows that too. There's just too much. He would never move back."

"Sydney, the mill has been closed for years now and if you'll remember correctly, there are, and were, people who know what Bear did to Elijah. But there were a whole slew that he had convinced he didn't do it."

Sydney didn't say a word. It was true. He could move back if he wanted, whether she could imagine him doing it or not.

"Anyway, Denton was at the El Chico's there on the loop and when he was leaving, he saw Bear come out of a building next to El Chico's. Bear didn't see Denton." Maeve paused, but Sydney sat silent. "Sydney, are you listening?"

"Yes, I'm listening. Just tell me." Sydney felt the familiar feeling of her heart sinking and at the same time, her resilience taking over.

"Well, Denton waited until Bear left and he went on over there and it's some appraisal company. He went in and told the girl at the front desk that he saw Bear leave...well, he said he saw Bear Keane leave and he made it sound very professional... And said that he knew him, hadn't seen him in years and asked if he worked there. The girl said yes. So, he's back in Merriweather, Sydney, and apparently the son of a bitch has a job at that appraisal company."

"Jesus, God. How? First off, Elijah told me that he is working shift work and long-changes at different sawmills." Sydney couldn't get her thoughts together. None of this made sense.

"Sydney," Maeve started.

"No, Momma. Wait," she continued, trying to make any kind of sense of it as she spoke it out loud. "Regardless of where Bear is working, why would he ever want to move back to Merriweather? There is a reason, I'm telling you, Mother. There is definitely a reason. And why in God's name would a company hire his fucking ass? All they have to do is run a background check and it shows that he's a thief. If they check further into it, they'll see that it was a previous employer that he stole from. Stupid fricking people!"

"I guess you forgot that he got deferred adjudication on that theft charge, or did you just block that out? And I still think about how unfair it was that Bear got that deal where once he completed his probation, his record would be clear of child molestation. Free and clear and the son of a bitch didn't even have to register as a sex offender."

The system was clearly broken and Sydney couldn't bear to hear another word. "Mother, don't go there. I'm serious, don't go there."

"I'm not goin' there, darlin'. I'm just sayin'."

"Mmm-hmmm. You're just sayin'. Well, drop it. Where is Bear living?"

"Sydney, I don't know," Maeve answered, irritated. She didn't like Sydney talking to her like that whether she'd said too much or not, and she knew she had. "Denton didn't get a mailing address for him, for goodness' sake."

"I'm not saying that, Mother! I just thought I'd ask. That's fine. Can I shower now?"

"Go shower and I'll talk to you later."

The two hung up and Sydney was shaking. Without question, Bear was in Merriweather for a reason. Sydney felt as if it was him snubbing his nose at her, the law, and anyone else who believed he did such horrible deeds back then. What better way to say "screw you" than to crawl right back into the lion's den and show them all that he wasn't afraid? He was a free man and there wasn't a damn thing anyone could do about it. Sydney immediately thought of the pictures of Bear with Elijah and Cody. He was saying "fuck you" then, and he was saying "fuck you" now.

Sydney stepped under the hot water and tried to make sense of any of it, to no avail.

"Sydney, Elijah's on the phone!" Skye yelled from the hallway. "You almost done?"

"Elijah's on the phone? Give me two seconds. I'm getting out." Sydney never postponed a conversation with Elijah, and certainly not now. "I'm drying off," Sydney yelled.

"Hello," she said, grabbing the bedroom phone. She wouldn't be telling Elijah about the conversation she'd just had with her mother. She wouldn't be telling him that Bear was in Merriweather until she knew why he was there.

"I'll talk to you later, sweetie. I love you," Skye said.

"Love you too," Elijah replied and Skye hung up the phone.

"Hey, sweetheart. How are you?" Sydney said, excited to be hearing from Elijah, and still reeling from what Maeve had just told her.

"I'm doin' good. I'm doin' good."

"What's the matter?" Sydney knew her son and this didn't sound like the normal "checking in" phone call.

"Oh, nothing. I was just talking to Cody a few minutes ago and he said something interesting."

Sydney took in a deep breath and readied herself. "Really? What did Cody have to say?"

"Well, he brought up that stuff about Dad again."

"What stuff?"

"You know. Just the same stuff. He said he knows what I think Dad did to me, and he went through all that again about how you said it because you're gay and didn't want to be with Dad any more, blah, blah, blah. Once again, I told him to stop talking about things he doesn't know anything about. I told him to just shut up about it and if he wants us to have any kind of a relationship, he's got to stop bringing it up. I told him that he doesn't know the whole story, again."

"I'm sorry you have to keep hearing that from him, Elijah. He just doesn't want to believe it, that's all."

"And get this. Before we hung up, he said that he thought the same thing happened to him at one time and so did his mom, but come to find out it was a teacher."

"He said 'come to find out it was a teacher'?" Sydney repeated. It all came rushing back.

"Yeah. Isn't that what Dad said to you when you confronted him about me?"

"Yes. That's exactly what he said. He tried to blame it on someone at your daycare."

"Well, that's what Cody said. He said that he thought Dad did that to him too, but that it was a teacher."

"Elijah, Annette filed charges on Bear, and he was investigated and everything. Remember, I told you that? Cody was too young to give a solid testimony and Annette didn't continue to pursue things. The court gave Bear mandatory supervised visitation with Cody that would last through the remainder of time that he had supervised visitation with you. Basically, it would last through the remainder of his probation period. So they apparently believed it, but Annette never stuck to it."

"Yeah, well, she wound up agreeing that it was a teacher, apparently."

"What?! No, no, no! She knew better than that!" Sydney shouted, remembering clearly the conversation she and Annette had all those years ago.

"Mom! I thought you would be interested in knowing what Cody said, but I didn't mean to upset you."

"Elijah, I am upset! Bear is a liar and a manipulator, and I can't believe how everyone just goes along with it! Don't you see, Elijah? Cody wants so desperately to believe his father didn't do that to him, he tries to convince himself, and you, that none of this ever happened. For him to admit that it happened to you would be acknowledging that it probably did happen to him also, which then leads to all the other lies and cover up, and Cody's world, well…"

"I know."

"I think in that deepest part of Cody, he really believes that Bear hurt you, and I think he knows what Bear did to him. I think he just makes himself go along with the fact that a teacher did it because it makes things easy and it goes along with what everyone else has said, including his mother. And would you like to know why she supported that lie?"

"Why?"

"Because she got on drugs so badly that she started letting Cody stay with Bear and Beth, and the next thing you know, she let Cody live with them. I'm sure once she let Cody stay there without supervision, Bear had her in his grip. Regardless, because of drugs, she allowed it, knowing what Bear had done to Cody. If she didn't go along with the fact that a teacher did it, she'd have to admit that she placed her son directly in Bear's hands knowing what she knew. No way would she ever admit to that. Hell, she's covering it up even now."

Elijah didn't say a word.

"Interesting," Sydney said. "Did they ever investigate a teacher? Did anyone ever go to the school and question the teachers?"

"No. Cody said nothing ever came of it."

"Exactly. If you thought a teacher had molested your child, wouldn't you stop at nothing to find out who did it?"

"Absolutely."

"Okay then. They didn't investigate because they all knew the truth. And here's a little tidbit for you. Did I ever tell you that Annette lost custody of her second child, another little boy, for that very reason?"

"Cody has another brother?" Elijah asked, completely taken aback.

"Yes. He's never mentioned him?"

"No."

"Well, isn't that interesting. Yes, he has another brother."

"How did you know?" Elijah asked.

"Let's just say it was through the grapevine called Merriweather, Texas. Nothing stays a secret for long in Merriweather and definitely not that. Annette lost custody of her son to her second husband. He fought Annette for custody and won because in court he pointed out that Annette had let Cody go stay with, and later live with, Bear, the man she had accused of molesting Cody. If she would use that kind of judgment with her own son, he didn't feel their son would be cared for and protected. The judge agreed. I guess Cody won't ever mention him because that would be admitting his mother wasn't 'mother of the year' after all."

"Wow. I can't believe all that. He's never said a word."

"And he likely won't. Are you going to ask him about it?"

"No. I'm leaving it alone."

"Well, I've had it. I have absolutely had it. I'm so tired of the lies. I'm tired of it all. It all started with Bear's mother covering up what Bear's stepdad did—"

She had slipped. She had never told Elijah what Bear's stepfather had done to her. Of course not.

"What did Dad's stepdad do?" Elijah asked.

"Never mind that." Sydney hoped Elijah would move on with the conversation as quickly as she was. She had said the words and now instantly realized that she herself had just shoved it under the rug. No matter. That had to do with her, not Elijah. This was about Elijah and any other children being harmed by Bear, prior or today.

She continued, "Then Bear's lies, then Annette's lies and all the while everyone is just protecting themselves...keeping things status quo...and no one is protecting their children, or anybody else's. Everyone may turn their heads or bury them in the sand, but I won't. I won't do it."

"I hear you, Mom. I didn't mean to upset you."

"You didn't upset me, Elijah. They upset me, but I'm not letting them upset me anymore."

Elijah and Sydney said their I love yous and goodbyes. Sydney sat motionless on the edge of her bed, feeling uncontrollable fury. It all was so much; so very, very much.

Her entire life had been filled with so much happiness: some that she had accepted as a gift from above and some that she had created for herself. And at the same time, her life had been filled with so much dirtiness and nastiness. And why? Why? Why does one person have the ability to cause so much hurt and sadness and it just rocks on and on and on and on? They move from one child to the next and inflict so much pain on the child and everyone who loves that child. In Sydney's mind, she had stayed right on top of things when it pertained to Elijah and Bear Keane. She handled each and every issue the moment it presented itself. She wasn't afraid and she made sure to stay at the helm, ready for the storm that would surely come again. And it always did. This was Elijah's life to live and one to be lived happy and healthy and whole.

She, too, had a life and had hoped for the same things for herself. She thought about what might have come of her life had she not been abused. She knew that statistically, sexually abused children would typically turn to alcohol, drugs, and promiscuity, just to name a few. She also knew she was that statistic as a teenager and didn't even realize it at the time. So, back to the question. What if she had never been abused? Would she have been an honor student? Would she have been class president? Would she have taken up a musical instrument? Would she have gained full scholarship to the college of her choice? Would she have been an actress, an astronaut, a television reporter, a congresswoman, or a great novelist? Would she have been a leader of many or a Pulitzer Prize winner?

Sydney looked at herself in the mirror. Those were questions that would never be answered. They could never be answered. But she looked herself in the eyes and as they filled with tears, she saw love and acceptance and knew that who she was today was not because of what had happened to her. It was in spite of what had happened to her. She was wonderful, magnificent, and beautiful just as she was at this very moment, and so was her precious son. Indeed, he was those very things himself. Yes, life and happiness awaited them both, and she and God would surely see to that.

A

"What did Elijah have to say?" Skye asked, looking up from her latest art project as Sydney entered the room.

"We just talked about Cody and some other things."

"Cody? What about Cody?"

"I'll tell you about that in a minute, but the main thing we need to talk about is the call I got from Mother right before that."

"What did she have to say? Is everything okay?"

"Can you put that down for a second? I really need to talk to you about this."

"What's going on?"

"Bear has moved back to Merriweather."

"What?! Why would he move back to Merriweather?"

"I don't know, but I'm going to find out."

"Wait a minute." Skye wanted answers and Sydney's "going to find out" got her attention. "What do you mean you're going to find out?"

"Skye, he's living there and working there. Uncle Denton saw him and knows he's working for some appraisal company. There's a reason Bear is there, and I need to know what it is."

Skye looked headlong at Sydney. She was looking for any sign of this making sense and nothing came.

"And what exactly do you think you're going to do? He's there and you think you're going to stroll up in there, asking questions, and they're all going to be answered? Come on, Sydney, what are you thinking?"

Sydney was furious. She knew she didn't have good reason to be angry with Skye and that it was understandable that Skye would question her intentions and even doubt her. But right now, Sydney didn't want to hear it.

"Listen to me!" Sydney yelled.

"Calm down, Sydney! What is the matter with you?!"

"I'll tell you what's the matter with me! I'm tired of this shit! I'm tired of every bit of it!" Sydney put her fist to her gut. She was crying now and it was a flood of what hadn't come in so long.

Skye took Sydney in her arms and led her to the sofa. "Shh...shhh. What's the matter, Sydney? Why do you continue to let this affect you and hurt you so much?"

"Because it kills me. It doesn't hurt me; it kills me." Sydney paused and looked up at Skye. "And guess what? Cody told Elijah that he remembers things being done to him, but he said 'come to find out, it was a teacher.' That's what Cody said to Elijah today."

"What?"

"Yes. Cody was trying to tell Elijah that it didn't happen. He was trying to convince him that Bear didn't do it. But in the process, he admits to Elijah that he thought something happened to him, but that it was a teacher."

No words needed to be spoken then. It was the same lie. The same ugly lie.

"Skye, I'm being led there. I feel right here," she said, putting her fist back to her gut, "that I have to go and I'm going."

"What do you think you're going to accomplish by going? Do you honestly think any good will come of you going to Merriweather? Seriously, Sydney. Think."

"I'm tired of thinking. I know what I know, I know how I feel, and I'm going. I'm not ignoring this. I've stepped back and prayed for so long that things would get better and maybe I, too, have a responsibility to see to it that it is. I know God is in control, Skye. But I found out that Bear is in Merriweather and I found out for a reason. It's a sign, maybe even from above, and I'm going."

CHAPTER 55

Sydney's preparation for her trip was swift. She called Uncle Denton and Aunt Iris, letting them know she was coming for an overnight stay—just an overnight visit to the farm. She purchased a wig and a pair of sunglasses. Then, she got in her car and she went. She was steadfast and unafraid. Sydney wasn't concerned about being seen in Merriweather. She had enough family members who lived in Merriweather that her or her car being seen there wouldn't have meant a hill of beans. The wig and sunglasses were just an added touch, specifically for Bear. The drive was easy and nothing was interfering with her plan.

Sydney waited in the El Chico parking lot. She had pulled her black wig tight to her head. It was so black it was almost blue and aged Sydney by about fifteen years. With her wig and nondescript sunglasses, Bear wouldn't give her a second look. It was five o'clock, so he should be getting off work just any time.

Right then, Bear wheeled in to the company parking lot. He had apparently been out on an appraisal and it startled Sydney. Bear climbed out of his truck and went into the building for just a moment. He immediately walked back out with a woman. There he was: tight jeans, sleeveless t-shirt, and a new girlfriend on his arm with her bouffant blonde hair hanging to her waist. The two climbed into his truck and Sydney couldn't help but think the poor soul didn't know she was hooked up with a monster any more than Sydney, Annette, or Beth did. But whoever she was, Bear had managed to get with

Miss Texas personified. Sydney immediately wondered whether she had any children of her own.

The two slowly pulled out of the parking lot. Sydney gave them time to make it up the road and pulled out five cars behind them. It was easy to follow them off Highway 59 North. They would turn right on the loop, Sydney suspected, and she was right. They had just turned right and made a quick turn in to Olive Garden.

"Fucking lovely." Sydney pulled in behind them, but kept her distance. She knew she'd be here a while. It was a Friday and she was sure cocktails would likely be flowing. She nestled into her seat and didn't take her eyes off the door for three hours.

Eight o'clock sharp: Bear, his woman, and two more couples walked out. They had apparently either met friends there or had run into them.

"Please, God, don't let them be going somewhere else. Please," Sydney said under her breath.

They all waved goodnight and each couple went to their trucks. It looked as though the evening had ended for this group gathering. At least Sydney hoped so.

Bear and Miss Texas pulled back out onto the loop and away they went, Sydney pulling up the rear. She was nervous, paranoid almost, that he would know she was behind them—that somehow, some way he would know, but she snapped herself back into reality. He hadn't seen Sydney in almost ten years aside from a picture or two he may have seen on Elijah's Facebook page. He likely wouldn't give her a second glance if she pulled right up beside them. But Sydney wasn't about to be that careless. She would bide her time.

"Good things come to those who wait," she thought, and years of torment was about to have one hell of a payday.

They continued on Loop 750 to Highway 5157 and turned right.

"My God, where are they going?" she wondered. It made Sydney uncomfortable to think that they were headed anywhere near the turnoff to her family's property, but she didn't let herself get overcome with those feelings. She needed to stay sharp and alert. She needed to keep her emotions in check.

They passed the sawmill and continued on. Where had Bear set up house? Or where did this woman live? There wasn't much between where they were and Elnet, Texas, unless you turned down a dirt road off the main highway, like where Sydney's family's homestead was.

There were only two cars between them now and Sydney saw the truck's left blinker come on.

"What the hell?" Sydney said out loud. "Where are you two going?"

And with that, Bear and his woman turned left down a blacktop road.

"Damnit!" Sydney yelled. Neither of the two cars between them turned left, so she had to keep going. Had she turned down that road also, they would have made it a point to see who had turned in behind them. Not because they suspected they were being followed, but because that's just what country folks on lone back roads do. They look in the rearview mirror, or they look dead-on to who is coming toward them in the event they know them, and they usually do.

Sydney was pissed. "Okay, you fuckers. Where the hell are you going?" Sydney tried to visualize in her mind where they might be headed as she eased to the shoulder.

The blacktop road they had turned down was the road immediately before the turnoff to Sydney's family's farm. The only thing Sydney knew about this road was that it was the back way to the farm, but no one ever went that way. It took longer than the way she'd always known. "Where could you two be going?" she thought.

Sydney turned the car around and headed back the way she had come. She realized it had been about a minute since they had turned down that blacktop road, so she would be fine to head down that way now. Sydney turned right on the road and saw the red dust from the connecting dirt road billowing up. "Yes!" Sydney shouted. Sydney knew no one else had turned in behind them, so they had definitely gone down the dirt road and hadn't stayed on the blacktop. "Please God, be with me," she then whispered, knowing that their flying dirt was better than a breadcrumb trail and she was headed to wherever they were going.

⋏

Sydney knew that Bear could be going to his girlfriend's house as easily as he could be going to his own. She had prayed that it was his RV where they were leading her, but to know that he had made his hideaway within such close proximity to her family made her hair stand on end. It made sense, however. Bear would want to be where it was familiar, where he felt comfortable. Bear would want to be where he felt he wouldn't have any surprises and it would be easy to get out if need be. But Bear also got pleasure out of considering everyone else a fool. It would make his day, give him a good laugh, to be setting up shop right up their asses and no one would even know. What an idiot he was. He should know well enough that if Sydney's Uncle Denton ever caught him near their farm, he'd blow his head off. All of it was just another part of Bear's delusional bullshit. He still thought he was smarter than everyone else.

They continued down the road; Sydney could see their brake lights far in the distance. They had stopped for a moment and then turned right. This would be the back way to Sydney's family's farm.

"Where the hell are you going, you piece of shit?" Sydney said aloud.

She hung back, knowing she had them trailed. There was no need to rush and risk everything. Sydney idled down the road until she reached the dead end where they had turned. There were no taillights in sight, so Sydney turned right. She followed the haze of dust and traveled slowly, not sure where she was going. She reached a crossroad that went to the right and she stopped. There was no cloud of dirt directly in front of her, but there was to the right. If memory served her correctly, Sydney knew this was the final turn that headed the back way to the farm. She turned right and drove a little faster now. She had to know where Bear was going. She had to know for certain. Up ahead, she saw the taillights again. They shone for a time and disappeared in the brush to the right. There was nothing for Sydney to do now, but to pass the drive they'd turned in to. There was nowhere else to go. There were plenty of houses past their turn, but none before it. She prayed. She didn't want to pass them in the event they got wise and she would become the hunted and they would become the hunters. Sydney didn't change her speed. She stayed focused and made sure not to divert her eyes to·them as she passed. Good thing. They had stopped a few yards into the brush and waited for her to pass. The night was already dusky. With the sun almost fully set, the thick brush and the billowing dirt lining the drive, they wouldn't be able to tell it was Sydney, especially with her wig, but she'd been risky enough and she needed to get to the farm fast. As she passed, Sydney watched in her rearview mirror and saw their headlights going farther into the woods. If they had suspected anything at all, they hadn't let it bother them enough to interfere with their evening plans.

Sydney pulled into the farm's drive and her adrenaline was still kicked into high gear. She pulled her wig off as she made her way up the drive.

"God, I look like shit." She peered at herself in the rearview mirror. She hung her head out the window and tousled her hair.

The dogs greeted her, barking as usual, and as usual, there were Uncle Denton and Aunt Iris rocking on the porch: Aunt Iris with her martini and Uncle Denton with Scotch in hand. Happy hour had ensued once again.

"Hey there!" Sydney called out as she stepped out of the car.

"Hey there, doll! What can I get you?" Aunt Iris asked, as she rose out of her chair.

"I'll have whatever you're having, only double," Sydney answered as she smiled and tousled her hair again.

"That's my girl." Aunt Iris laughed. "I'll be right back."

"Hey, Uncle Denton," Sydney said, leaning over to hug his neck.

"Hello there, Sydney," he said, giving her a hug. He leaned back in his chair and looked at her. "You doin' all right? You look a little…well—" He stopped and stared a second longer at her.

Sydney looked at her Uncle Denton and laughed. He laughed, too, realizing he had just told her she looked like shit. She already knew it. No need to explain.

"I've got a question for you, Uncle Denton." Sydney took her Aunt Iris's seat next to him.

"Shoot." He always had the answers. He always had for Sydney, anyway.

Sydney leaned over, putting her arms across her knees. "Okay," she said, "if you pass the Hodges' place up the road, what is right past that? Does someone live down there now? As crazy as it sounds, I've never gone down there unless it's huntin' season."

"Well, it just so happens that's what's down there. The deer lease. See, our property shoots back off that-a-way." He pointed out across the pasture in front of them. "Then, it goes all the way back yonder across the creek bed, scoots right around back of the Hodges' place and comes out on the other side. Remember, that's where Iris's kinfolk had their trailer for a while, but ever since they moved out a few years ago, that's one of the places we hunt. It's a ways back down in there, of course. Why?"

"Holy shit!" Sydney thought. He was on her family's property. Bear was on their property.

Chapter 56

"**Sydney, are you** okay? You look like you've seen a ghost, girl." Uncle Denton reached over and touched Sydney's arm. Her mind shot back to real time and Uncle Denton was close in her face. "Sydney."

"Oh, Uncle Denton." Sydney swallowed hard. "Yes, I'm fine. I...I...I'm just tired, I guess, and I haven't eaten all day. That must be it. I'm sorry."

Aunt Iris came back with Sydney's drink. "Did I hear you say you haven't eaten, sweetie? I've got plenty and we're eatin' after this drink."

Sydney quickly shot back the double. "That sounds great."

"Well, somebody is hungry *and* thirsty!" Aunt Iris said with a laugh.

Words were coming from Uncle Denton and Aunt Iris, random conversation, but Sydney was immersed in the fact that Bear Keane was one half mile up the road, on her family's property, and no one knew it. By the grace of God, she hadn't blurted out, "Bear is here! He is here!" That would have ruined everything. There was a reason she didn't speak those words. It just wasn't time. She wrapped up her conversation quickly over dinner and headed into Memaw's place for a hot shower. All Sydney wanted was to be alone. She needed to think. She needed a plan.

Sydney stripped off her clothes and stepped into the hot shower. The water poured down her face. She stood motionless. She let go of every thought and fantasy she'd ever had before about Bear and what she'd like to do to him. This was real. This didn't call for thought or fantasy. She quickly cleaned up and crawled into her Memaw's bed, and eyes wide and facing the white ceiling above her, she began her plan.

CHAPTER 57

"**G**ood mornin', y'all!" Sydney yelled from the upstairs window.

"Mornin'?" Uncle Denton retorted. "Girl, it's almost lunch now."

"I know. I must have needed the rest."

"I was about to make me and Denton a sandwich. You want one?" Aunt Iris asked.

"Sure. I'll be right over."

Sydney got dressed and headed over to the main house. All was in motion.

"Oh, that looks delicious, Aunt Iris. You are the sandwich queen, I must say. Everything but the kitchen sink is piled on here, it looks like."

"You know your Uncle Denton. Gotta fill that man up or he gets like an ol' bear."

"I hear you." Sydney needed to take a deep breath and sound as relaxed as possible. Aunt Iris was no dummy and Sydney wasn't a good liar. "Hey, do you mind if I stay another night? I've been so swamped at work and being here is always so…well, good for me."

"Honey, don't you ever feel like you have to ask to stay here! This is just as much your home as it is anyone's and we love you to come as often as you'd like. Does that mean you'll be here for happy hour and dinner?" Aunt Iris smiled and handed Sydney her sandwich.

"That's what it means. If it's okay, I'll hang with you guys this evening and I'll head on out in the morning."

"Perfect. Get that tummy of yours full and we'll see you on the porch at five o'clock. How's that?"

"Sounds like a date," Sydney replied. "Same order as last night, bartender."

Sydney finished her sandwich and went back to Memaw's, passing Uncle Denton as he headed in for lunch.

"It's hotter than a tin roof out here," he said. "Don't stay out long without gettin' ya some water."

"I'm not stayin' out here, Uncle Denton. I'm heading on in. Maybe read a book, or after that sandwich, rest my eyes," she said, smiling.

He laughed. "Yeah, I'm thinkin' about doin' the same thing; restin' my eyes, I mean," he said with a wink.

"All right. See you at five o'clock."

Sydney walked into Memaw's house and watched through the window as Uncle Denton's screen door slammed shut, and the wood door right behind it. He would be inside for a time and the closed wood door was a sure sign.

Sydney waited ten minutes to be sure all was quiet on the farm. She eased the door open on the side of the house and walked out onto the porch, treading lightly. She shut the door quietly behind her, and tried not to look too obvious in case Aunt Iris was watching out the kitchen window. Then, Sydney realized she didn't need to look as though she was sneaking out for a walk. It was a beautiful day for one, so she walked down the steps and rounded the back of the house. She waited for a moment just in case Aunt Iris had seen her and would question where she was going. Nothing. So, Sydney kept walking to the back of the property line, past the old shed, past the barn and the compost pile. In her adult life, Sydney hadn't walked this far back on the property. This was all new to her. She took in the beauty, but kept her mind on the prize.

Sydney reached the back fence line and bore right, following a path that seemed to naturally be there. Woods were to her right and the fence and more thick brush to her left. There was a thick pallet of pine needles under her feet that covered an open area that was six feet wide. It could have made Sydney feel a bit uncomfortable having a path already laid out, but it seemed that

Mother Nature had done her job in laying out the clearing for Sydney. The pine needles were thick and Sydney's footsteps didn't make a sound.

She knew she would have to pass the Hodges' place before she got to where Bear and his girlfriend had set up house. The property was past the Hodges', but how far? Sydney didn't know exactly. The driveway was a bit down the road, but if the drive cut back at an angle, they could be closer than she would have guessed.

Sydney heard kids hollering in the distance, so she knew she was getting close to the Hodges' property.

"Sarah Beth! Sarah Beth!" a lady called out.

Sydney stopped in her tracks.

"Nanaw, I'm here!" a young girl answered back.

The girl startled Sydney. She wasn't as far away as the other children playing. She was in the woods, not far from Sydney.

"Where are you, Sarah Beth?!" the lady called out again. It was Mrs. Hodge.

Sydney heard sticks and leaves rustling and crunching. The girl couldn't have been more than a few yards from Sydney, but the woods were dense and neither could see the other.

"I'm here, Nanaw! I'm comin'!"

"You get your tail back to this house, young lady! I've told you 'bout runnin' off!"

"Comin'!"

Sydney let out a sigh of relief, whispered a thank-you to above, and kept walking. She passed the Hodges' just as Mrs. Hodge had rustled all the kids up and filed them in through the screen door.

Sydney didn't think she had too much farther to go, but it could be even less than she was anticipating, so she walked slowly and kept her ears open.

She hadn't walked far when she heard a truck start in the distance. It was far enough away that Sydney knew she needed to pick up the pace. She started running now, but looked around her taking in the full peripheral view. She couldn't risk being seen, but she had to know who was in that truck.

There they were. She could see the tan truck through the woods. There was the blonde-haired Miss Texas in a bright red shirt, sitting in the driver's seat.

Sydney squatted down behind a tree, peeking out only enough to keep the truck in her view.

"Baby, come on! I'm gonna miss my bus! There's only one goin' to Tinney today!" the blonde yelled.

"I'm comin'. I'm comin', damnit. Hold your horses." Bear walked to the driver's side. "Move over. I'm drivin'."

"Are you mad at me?" she asked Bear, doing as she was told and scooting to the passenger seat.

"I'm not mad at you. I don't know why you think you have to be gone so long, but I ain't mad."

"Baby, I'll only be gone 'til Wednesday and I'll be right back here with you." She leaned over to kiss Bear. "Besides, I told you Momma and Daddy would love to see you."

"Nah. I ain't goin' to your folks. I need to work, anyway, and I need to catch up on some things around here."

"Jesus," Sydney whispered. She was sickened to even hear such shit. There was no telling what the bastard wanted to catch up on.

Bear closed his truck door and they drove off.

Sydney had hoped to know where Bear was keeping his RV at the very least, where he was living. That was her only goal this day, but the fact that he and his girlfriend had left was a blessing. Sydney couldn't let the opportunity slip by. She waited ten minutes. They were long gone. She was sure of it. It would take them that long to get off of these dirt roads and back to the highway. She had time, but not much.

Sydney walked out into the open. She was wired, but it was more adrenaline than nerves. There was no one around in sight. Nothing but trees and brush blowing in the breeze and the air was loud with locusts. She walked over to the RV, up the stairs, which were pushed under the front door, and reached for the doorknob.

"God, Sydney. Use your brain," she said to herself and picked up a yellow bandana from the stoop.

She unfolded the filthy bandana and turned the doorknob. It was unlocked. Sydney expected as much because no one locked their doors this far out in the country, but it still put a satisfied smile on her face. She walked in and stood on the brown and rust colored shag carpet. The furniture was old and dishes were piled next to the sink. Roaches scurried when the sunlight hit the kitchen counter. Sydney pulled the door closed behind her. She looked around and she could clearly envision Bear living here. She knew him. Not the real Bear; not the sick Bear. But she had been married to him and knew his daily habits, except for those involving abusing children. She pictured him sitting in the leather chair, watching his television. She pictured him eating breakfast at the small dinette table and sitting in the rickety kitchen chair.

Sydney walked back to the tiny bedroom and pictured Bear and his woman crawling into bed and being sandwiched by the walls closing in on them. There couldn't have been more than six inches on either side of the bed and there was a small dresser pushed up against the wall adjacent to the door.

Sydney focused back on why she was there. She was there because she knew that Bear couldn't do what he did and have no "prized possessions" for his viewing pleasure. She knew that he was likely a collector of child pornography. How else would he get his entertainment when there were no actual children around?

Sydney walked back into the living room and looked around, taking it all in. Bear's computer was turned off. She entertained the idea of hacking into his computer for only a moment. There was no time for that. She was sure he had a login and password that were so encrypted, the average person wouldn't be able to figure it out. Next to his computer was a picture of Elijah and Cody. It was one taken on Father's Day, but not one from the group of pictures Elijah had sent to her. Maybe it was one that Bear had taken with his own camera that day, and one that he would keep for himself. Sydney could imagine Bear's wicked smile every time he looked at it, knowing that he had conquered once again, if only for that one day. She wanted to pick it up and bash it into a million pieces.

"Pictures. That's what he likes. Pictures," she thought.

Sydney remembered Bear hiding things under the bed and at the top of their pantry in the past. At the end of their marriage, when he began to lose his hair, he had secretly ordered a packet from the Hair Club for Men, and Sydney found it tucked away after he had already moved out.

She opened the kitchen pantry and saw two medium-sized boxes on the top shelf. She grabbed the rickety chair and carefully balanced herself on it. She pulled down the two boxes and they crashed to the floor. Nails and screws scattered across the small kitchen space. Sydney rushed to collect them all, put them back in their boxes and placed them back on the shelf. She looked at her watch; she had already been in the RV for ten minutes. She didn't have much time.

She walked back to the bedroom and got on her knees at the foot of the bed. She put her palms on the gritty floor and peered into the dark space underneath the bed. Once her eyes adjusted, she thought she saw a shadow of something pushed to the back wall under the headboard. Sydney rose up and grabbed a book of matches on the dresser. She lit a match and saw a box pressed tightly to the far wall. Large, dead tree roaches riddled the floor between Sydney and the box. The bed was too close to the ground for her to crawl under it even if she wanted to. She ran to the kitchen and grabbed the broom from the pantry. She fell back to the floor and used the broom handle to slide the box away from the wall. She turned the broom around and used the straw end to navigate the box to her waiting hands.

Sydney knew the box was hidden out of sight for a reason and she knew what the reason likely was. She pulled the lid back and therein lay what were easily over one hundred pictures of naked children. Their ages ranged from infancy to adolescence. Some were pictures of the children alone, some were close-up pictures of their genitals, and some were pictures of children performing lewd acts on an unidentified man.

Sydney threw her hand over her mouth. She couldn't breathe. Of anything she would have imagined or even felt certain she would find, nothing prepared her for this.

She wiped over the top layer of pictures with the bandana, put the lid back on the box, wiped it down and shoved it to the back wall. She stuffed the matches in her pocket, took the broom back to the kitchen pantry and wiped everything down she had touched. She couldn't get out of this hellhole fast enough.

Sydney closed the door with the bandana, leapt from the top step to the ground and ran to the woods. She stopped about twenty yards in, no longer able to hold the vomit. She was sick. She felt sickened at the loss of so much innocence. How do these children get their lives back? "They don't," she thought. She vomited more.

Her anger wasn't going away. Sydney knew she'd be back and she knew what she had to do. She bit into the edge of the bandana, making a small tear. She ripped a strip off and tied it to a small limb. Sydney's mind was racing on her way back to the farm, but she couldn't allow herself to think about the box. Every time it entered her mind, she felt a welling inside that she wouldn't be able to hide and she had to hide it. For now, she had to hide it.

⋏

"Well, don't you smell good?!" Aunt Iris rounded the corner with two double martinis, olives stacked high in the glass. "I can smell you clear over here."

"Well, thank you, ma'am. That's what soap and water does for a gal." Sydney smiled, and took her martini in hand. It wasn't too hard to smile. She was glad to be back in safe and sane territory. Back with her family and the grounding it gave her. But she couldn't get the box out of her head.

"You okay, pumpkin?" Aunt Iris asked.

"Oh, yeah. I'm more than okay." Sydney took a long swig of her gin martini. "Whew!" she cried out. "Nothing diluting this bad boy!"

Aunt Iris laughed out loud, which was a rarity. "Well, girl, you don't like 'em dirty, right?"

"Right." With that, Sydney took a second swig and braced herself.

"Honey, I can add some ice."

"No, this is much needed and I love it. I just have to—" Sydney started before her face twisted up again from the alcohol.

They both laughed. As they'd always said, "After a few swallows, it all goes down easy."

"Sweetie, you okay? You know I don't want to meddle, but you seem like…well…something is wrong. Is everything okay with you and Skye?"

"Oh, yes ma'am! We're great. I'm sorry if I seem preoccupied. This is a much-needed break from work and I guess it just takes a day or two to decompress. Unfortunately, then it's time to head home."

"Well, you tell that Skye next time she'd better come too. It's been a month of Sundays since we've seen her."

"I'll tell her."

Aunt Iris loved Skye, as did Sydney's entire family. It warmed her heart every time she heard it. She was fortunate and blessed in that way and she knew it.

Uncle Denton joined them for another round of drinks and conversation. Dinner soon followed, as did nightfall and sleep. But sleep was for the weary. Sydney went back to Memaw's bed where she lay, still, waiting to head home at light, knowing she would be back.

Chapter 58

"Hey, babe! I'm headed home!"

"I can barely hear you!" Skye answered back.

"I know! Sunroof back! Beautiful day!"

"Everything okay?!"

"More than! We'll talk when I get home! Love you!"

"I love you!"

All the niceties didn't fool Skye. Sydney's upbeat demeanor was just a curtain to mask what was really going on. That conversation would have to wait until she got home and Skye would be waiting.

"Hey there." Sydney climbed from the car and grabbed her bag.

"Hey there, back. Well?"

"Well. There's a lot. Can you grab this and let's come on in?"

Skye grabbed the bag and followed Sydney into the house. "Don't beat around the bush, Sydney. I've been worried sick all weekend. You called me twice the entire time."

Sydney whirled around and sat on the sofa, trying to look as nonchalant as she could. "Honey, come sit down. You knew I was taking care of things and I really didn't have a lot of time to talk."

Skye sat next to her.

"I called you to let you know I was there safe and sound and that I was staying another night. You knew that much."

"Yes, and last night you left the message on the home number. I didn't even think to check it until late last night when I was already expecting you. Why didn't you call my cell?"

"You know what," Sydney leaned into Skye, "I'm sorry. I should have and I'm sorry. I just had so much going on and, well, I just—" She shrugged her shoulders. She knew she had no good excuse and wouldn't have liked it either.

"Just tell me. Did you find out anything? Did you get any answers?"

"Did I get any answers? You won't believe all the answers I got."

Sydney told Skye everything. She told her about following Bear and his girlfriend from the appraisal company. She told her how he was staying on her family's property and no one even knew it. She told how she followed a path to where they'd set up house, how his girlfriend left town for a few days and what she'd found in the RV.

"You did what?!" Skye bolted up from the sofa. "Sydney, are you fucking crazy?!"

Skye backed up into the living room, looking at her with a look that made Sydney feel as though she possibly was.

"You followed that crazy son of a bitch to where he's staying—he's there on Uncle Denton's property, which really shows how crazy he is—and you just decide to traipse back over there the next day?! Oh! And let's not leave out the fact that you actually went in?! What are you thinking?!"

"I know how it sounds, Skye. I really do, but you have to understand. I knew from the moment Mother told me that Bear was back in Merriweather that I had to go. I felt it. There was no question. And the next morning when I went to find a back way to the property, there was a trail following the fence line. It led me straight to where they're staying."

Skye stood motionless as she listened to Sydney plead her argument.

"And seriously, do you honestly think it was some accident that Bear and that chick were leaving right then and I heard from her mouth that she was leaving town until Wednesday? And then what I found…"

Skye never moved or changed her expression.

"Say something!" Sydney yelled.

"Okay." Skye picked up the phone. "I'm calling the cops."

"Goddamnit, give me the fucking phone!" Sydney yelled, knocking over pictures and books as she hurdled the coffee table.

"What is the matter with you, Sydney?! Look at you!"

"Yeah, look at me! Look the fuck at me!" Sydney stood with the phone receiver in her hand. She hung it up and she started to cry, but this wasn't sadness. It was fury.

"Go ahead! Look at me! Here." She stopped at the mirror in the foyer. "I'll look at me! You know what I see? Someone sick and fucking tired. Tired of shit…just shit!!! I can't say it enough!"

"God, Sydney. I don't know what to do any more."

"I'll tell you what to do. Support me, damnit! I love you. You know that. I would die for you. But if you pick up that phone and call the police, or do one thing against my wishes regarding this situation…" Sydney shook her head. "I don't know, Skye. I just don't know."

"Are you serious? After all this? You would be that angry with me?"

"Yes, especially after all this. You're my partner. You know me, and you have to trust me. I have to do this, Skye. It's time and I'm not waiting anymore."

"What then? What are you going to do?" Skye sat on the floor beneath her. "God help us," she whispered as she put her face in her hands.

Skye knew that she had to retreat. She knew that Sydney was in this place because of so much. It was all so, so much and had been for a very long time. Skye didn't like it. She didn't like it at all. But to keep Sydney, she had to let her go.

Sydney told Skye of her plan. There was no time to wait and she would be leaving the next afternoon. She called Ruby and asked for a ride for the following day, and they were set.

Chapter 59

Ruby pulled into the driveway and honked.

"I love you." Sydney draped her arms over Skye's shoulders. "You know that, don't you?"

"Yes, I know that. I love you too. Sydney—" Skye started.

Sydney put her finger to Skye's mouth. "We've talked about all of this. I'll be fine."

"But how do I know that when I can't talk to you? This is crazy."

"Skye, you know I can't take my cell. We've already talked about that. Please. I'll be fine. Everything is going to be okay." Sydney pulled Skye closer. "I'll see you at Sam's by noon. Deal?"

"And remind me why I'm not driving you to Sam's?" Skye asked, hoping for Sydney's last-minute approval.

"Honey. We've talked about it. You know why. I need you here. Remember? It's just better that way. So, again, I'll see you at Sam's by noon. Deal?"

"Deal. I love you."

The two kissed goodbye. Sydney grabbed her purse and bag and ran to Ruby's car.

"Hey there!" Sydney said with her best "everything is okay" impression as she opened the car door.

"Sydney, are you sure about this? I'm worried about you and that's an understatement," Ruby said.

Ruby. Again, the voice of reason. Sydney understood her concern and the fact that she was truly worried about her.

"Please don't worry, Ruby, seriously."

Ruby shot her a look of "as if" and kept driving.

"I know. I do. I would be worried too if the shoe was on the other foot."

"Well, thank you for validating my feelings, Sydney," Ruby said, with a hint of sarcasm.

"Hey. What's the matter? I wasn't trying to validate you. I'm saying I understand."

"I'm sorry. I'm just worried. Skye is worried. You're keeping this whole thing some big secret from me and in all honesty, it scares me."

"Look, I hear you. But I'll tell you like I told Skye. You have to trust me. I know what I'm doing and I need to do this."

"Trust me, she says." Ruby smiled and put her hand on Sydney's. "Okay, tell me where the hell I'm going."

Sydney clutched her best friend's hand and gave her directions to FM 7137.

"Okay, turn left here."

"Here? Where are we going exactly, Sydney?"

"Just turn left here and I'll show you."

"Can you fill me in prior to us actually getting there?"

"There's an old man. He sells vegetables on the side of the road about two miles out of town. Skye and I ran across him one day while we were on our way to Garden's Gate."

"This is the old man you've told me about. You and Skye get your garden goods from him, right?"

"Yes, that's him. Sam. He's wonderful. He told us about how his grand-father was a slave and how his family persevered and, well, they made it. His grandfather made a good life as best he could, and provided for Sam's father and then Sam's father did the same for him and his brothers and sisters." Just another reminder that those who are strong can most certainly persevere and Sydney remained mindful of that.

"Okay, and…" Ruby knew she only had part of the story and she wanted all of it. "Stop dancing around the subject, Sydney. Why are we going to meet Sam?"

"Sam has an old pickup truck that he's looking to sell. He's had a For Sale sign on it for as long as I remember and he doesn't want but three hundred dollars for it. He brings it filled with gas every day, hoping to sell it. Said his son will come pick him up when he finally does."

"And you're buying this truck for…oh, Sydney. You're not."

"No, I'm not buying it. But I'm—"

Ruby knew enough from all that had happened recently that this likely had to do with Bear, but what exactly, she didn't know. "You have lost it, Sydney! You're going to Merriweather to deal with some Bear thing, and I know for a fact you're not telling me everything. And you're taking a clunker of a truck that this man can't even sell for three hundred bucks? Give me a break!"

"Okay, here he is. Slow down so we don't kick up too much dirt. Pull off the side of the road right here."

Ruby did as Sydney instructed without a word. It was clear that she loved her best friend and wanted to be there for her, but she wasn't offering her approval, not for a minute.

"There he is and there's the truck," Sydney said, with a smile on her face and staring intently at her soon-to-be new ride. She had hoped and prayed that nothing would have changed since she had seen him just a few weeks before, and thankfully, it had not. The car had barely come to a stop when Sydney opened the door.

"I'll be right back and I won't be more than just a second."

Ruby gave Sydney a half smile and didn't say a word.

Sydney closed the door behind her and the hot summer air seemed to take her in with it.

"Hey there, Sam!" Sydney hollered.

"Well, hello there, young lady. You're just in time for my homegrown watermelons and peaches," Sam said with a grin that would make anyone's day.

"You know that's my favorite, Sam," Sydney said, giving him a smile and a pat on his shoulder.

Sam was a kind man, Southern in every way, and beautiful inside and out. Sydney had never asked his age, but she knew he was at least in his eighties. His soft Southern drawl was music to Sydney's ears. His skin was as dark as molasses and he had kind, gentle eyes. One eye was a light brown, the color of golden amber, and the other was ocean blue. As every other day Sydney had seen him, he was dressed in his overalls, handkerchief draped over the bib, and dirt stains on both side pockets from where he'd pull fresh cherry tomatoes as a snack.

"What can I get you, Miss Sydney? I've got some of your favorite black-berries and new potatoes too."

"And they all look delicious, Sam. But I'm here about something else today."

"Oh. What can I get ya?"

"Well, you still have that truck for sale, I see."

"Now, Miss Sydney. Don't tell me you want that ol' truck."

"I don't want to buy it, Sam, but I'll pay you double what you're asking just to borrow it for a day."

"What you mean, Miss Sydney? If you need the truck, just take it. I'll get my boy to come get me."

"I won't borrow your truck without compensating you, Sam. I want to pay you for it."

"Miss Sydney, you and Miss Skye are good to me. I appreciate you young ladies and if I can help you with somethin', I'd be much obliged to do it. You need my truck, here are the keys. I'll call my son to come fetch me this evenin'."

"Sam, please—" Sydney started.

"Now, Miss Sydney," Sam looked at her intently, "I already said no. I won't hear of it." He placed his keys in the palm of Sydney's hand. "The tank is full and ready to go."

"One thing, Sam. This has to stay between us. Please. No one can know."

"Don't you worry. I don't know nothin'." He winked and squeezed Sydney's hand over the truck keys. "You get on outta here and I'll see you tomorrow?"

"Yes, Sam. You'll see me tomorrow." She hugged him for the first time and it felt like hugging an old friend. Sydney savored every moment.

She walked back to Ruby's car and motioned for her to roll down her window.

"What's going on, Sydney? You're not getting in? Please," Ruby said, fully aware now that Sydney was determined in her cause.

"No. I'm heading out from here. Would you hand me my purse and bag and please stop by the house and tell Skye that the truck was here and I'm heading on out? I'll be home by lunch tomorrow."

Ruby handed Sydney her purse and bag, and it was apparent that she was worried sick.

Sydney leaned in the window. "Listen. Trust me, remember? I know what I'm doing. Skye knew I would be leaving from here if the truck was still here. Just go to my house, let her know, and I'll be in touch. I love you." She hugged Ruby goodbye and walked to the truck, not looking back.

Sydney heard the gravel under Ruby's tires as she turned around and headed back the way they'd come. Sydney couldn't have felt more alone at that moment. This was it. This was really happening, but she shook that feeling of "alone" as quickly as it came over her. This was the day.

Sydney checked her purse. She had her wallet with her driver's license, proof of insurance, American Express, and cash. She prayed the only thing she'd have to use, if anything, was the cash, but she had to be prepared just in case. She then checked her bag. Sydney had her wig, her tiny flashlight, gloves, the bandana, and the rope. She shoved the bag deep under the seat directly behind her legs and then checked her pocket for the flash drive. She was set. She put the truck in first gear and readied the steering wheel to make the U-turn. Sam was standing about ten feet behind the truck. Sydney rolled down the window and leaned her head out.

"Sam, I can't thank you enough."

"You take care of yourself, Miss Sydney. I'll be seein' you tomorrow."

"Yes, you will."

Sydney gave Sam a nod and waved as she made the U-turn back. Sam never moved from his spot, except to turn and watch Sydney as she drove away. He never moved for as long as Sydney had sight of him in the rearview mirror.

It was strange to her, but Sydney wasn't afraid. Not a bit. Maybe Mr. Sam was her guardian angel.

Sydney took the back roads to Highway 59 North.

Chapter 60

Sydney drove down the main dirt road that led to the farm and hoped to kick up as much dirt as possible before she hit her final destination. She needed all the help she could get in being unnoticed and that dirt road provided the perfect smoke screen to hide the truck. Red dirt billowed from the back of her truck as Sydney pulled into the drive at Aunt Ruth's and stopped. Aunt Ruth was Mama Scurlock's sister. She had long passed away and her family home, just one mile before the farm on this old dirt road, had long been abandoned and was now used as the hay house. Sydney turned off the truck lights and coasted up the dirt drive.

"Jesus, it's dark," Sydney said, half spooked. It was dead silent except for the rumble of the truck's engine and if it weren't for the clear night and the full moon, Sydney wouldn't have been able to see a thing. She coasted around to the back of the hay house. Sydney sat in the truck and let her eyes adjust to the darkness. She had her flashlight ready, but the use of it would be minimal and she would have to be very careful in using it. A flashlight shining through the dark woods might as well be a spotlight saying, "Here I am." Tonight had to be perfect, just as planned. There was no room for fear or mistakes.

Sydney stepped out of the truck, grabbed the wig, the rope, and the bandana from under her seat and slowly eased the door shut. As silent as it was around her, this place screamed of life. Sydney tried not to think of the creatures that had made their home here. She was in their space now and just wanted out with no battle scars. There was nothing to do but pray and start walking. Sydney pulled the wig tight to her head, put on her gloves, and tied the bandana to her belt loop, tucking the hanging ends into the front of her jeans. She draped the rope over her right shoulder and put the flashlight under her shirt to filter the light. She turned it on. It was perfect. It illuminated the area in front of her just enough that she could maneuver through the brush and cross the road.

Sydney crossed the road and just past the ditch, she reached the property line. A barbed-wire fence surrounded the property. She was very careful as she maneuvered her way between the ties. There wasn't a sound to be heard except for Sydney's feet crunching the leaves beneath them. It was terrifying and at the same time, a relief. The last thing Sydney wanted was a passing car or a barking dog.

She cut through the brush heading north, northeast to her family's farm. She would run into the creek bed before she reached their property line and there was no going around it. She had to go through it and felt thankful it had been a dry season. Just as Sydney approached the creek bed, the lights of a truck shone in the distance, headed her way. Sydney hurried to the creek and eased herself down the embankment by the bridge. This bridge was built by her great-grandfather almost one hundred years ago and had never been rebuilt, but just secured a few times over the years. It was a one-lane bridge that everyone had to cross getting to and from on this dirt road. It had stayed steady and strong for this long. "God, be with me," Sydney whispered as she crawled under it and stayed on the slanted embankment below. She turned off her flashlight and prayed that God's creatures around her would know she was friend, not foe.

The truck passed over her on the bridge. Sydney watched a beer can fall into the creek bed beside her.

"Yeah, they're all at that party in Callings," a young man said.

"Let's head there, man," his friend replied and they hit the gas hard once they were on solid ground.

That told Sydney that was one less truck she'd be seeing, for the next little while, anyway.

She waited until it was dark again, knowing they had passed the bend ahead, and she turned on her flashlight. Sydney stepped carefully on the creek stones beneath her feet, grabbed a tree root shooting from the embankment on the other side, and pulled herself up.

There it was: her family's farm. The porch light was on and it looked as welcoming as ever. Sydney didn't let that thought linger long. She walked through the brush to the left, to the farthest back point of the property line, and stepped through the wooden fence. Here she was. She walked carefully, taking the steps to the path that had been laid out for her.

Sydney followed her path through the woods. She had the rope secured across her torso now and the bandana tied to her belt loop hung loose. She held her flashlight tight in her hand and pointed it at the ground in front of her. If she looked into the dark woods around her, she knew she'd turn around and run from the monsters, lurking. She stayed focused and strong. She was going to get one of the monsters now.

Sydney made her way through the woods, past the back side of the farm, and there was her first landmark. She could see the Hodges' back porch light to her right. She was getting close. "Fifty yards, Sydney, fifty yards," she thought to herself. She stayed focused and kept walking. There wasn't a sound in the hot summer air except the sound of her breathing. Her head pounded as she walked, but she didn't think about anything except seeing Bear. She kept her head down following the path to freedom for Elijah, for herself, and for everyone Bear had hurt.

She heard a dog bark. "Shit!" Sydney whispered to herself. She stopped and stood motionless. "God in heaven, please," she thought. She hadn't come this far for a damn dog to ruin—

"Godammit, shutup!" she heard a man holler. "Get your black ass in here!" And with that, a yelp of a dog and a slamming door.

"Son of a bitch," Sydney said under her breath.

She kept moving. She saw her second sign. There was the yellow bandana strip tied to the bush. "Hallelujah," she thought. "Twenty more yards." She untied the bandana strip, shoved it in her pocket, and kept moving.

Sydney counted her steps. She didn't want to underestimate how far she'd come and end up in the clearing before she realized it. There could be no mistakes. She counted.

"Thirty-five, thirty-six, thirty-seven," Sydney whispered and she stopped. She could hear a thousand crickets around her. God, it all sounded so peaceful. These were the sounds that always made Sydney feel peaceful. "Peaceful" would soon come. But right now, in this place, it was anything but.

Sydney turned off her flashlight and tucked it in the front of her jeans. The only hint of light came from the light over the kitchen sink to the side of the RV. Flashes of blue came through the curtains; Sydney could hear the television, and the people on the television were laughing. "How ironic," she thought. She took a deep breath, signed her heart with the cross, and made her way.

She pulled the rope from her torso, untied the bandana from her belt loop and eased through the final edge of brush. She ran across the drive past Bear's truck and dropped the rope and bandana by the tree, never missing her stride. She headed straight toward the RV. For a split second, she thought she could have very possibly lost her mind. It didn't last long. Sydney was firm in her resolve and it was too late to second-guess herself now. She crouched down as she made her way under the kitchen window. Bear had the folding windowpanes opened and Sydney could hear him laughing along with the television show.

Sydney reached down and grabbed a long, thin tree limb off the ground. She reached up and ran the stick down the slats of the windowpanes above the kitchen sink. It made the sound of dominos falling.

Silence. Bear muted the television and there wasn't a sound. Sydney didn't move. Bear didn't move. Thirty seconds passed like minutes. Bear turned the television volume back up. Sydney reached up and ran the stick down the slats again, but louder this time. Bear muted the television again.

"What the hell?!" he said, and Sydney heard him stand up. "There better not be some mother fucker messin' with me," he said, and she heard him walk across the floor.

Sydney moved from under the kitchen window to the edge of the RV and watched the front door. She waited by the edge for Bear, praying he would come down the porch steps.

The door flew open. "Who the hell is there?" Bear asked.

He stood in the doorway and Sydney could see his shadow on the steps. His shadow looked much bigger than the little man standing in its shoes. His voice sounded different to Sydney.

"I said, who the hell is there? Don't fuck with me."

He sounded pathetic.

Sydney eased from around the corner and took three steps into the open. The moon's reflection illuminated Sydney, baring little to the details.

"Who the fuck are you?!" Bear asked, and walked deliberately down the stairs.

He didn't bother grabbing his gun, nothing. Sydney was sure it was because of her small stature. He wasn't afraid, but he should have been.

Sydney stood still and straight, feet one with the ground.

"I said, who the fuck are you, asshole?!" He came straight for Sydney.

She waited until Bear was within four feet of her. She leaned back, and just like she'd learned in class, she kicked high and aimed for his head.

Bear lay flat on the ground, addled. He looked up at Sydney. It was clear, through his glassy-eyed gaze, that he was trying to compute what was actually happening. He gained focus.

"Sydney?" And with that, she gave him one blow to his face, breaking his nose and knocking him out.

᛭

Sydney undressed Bear completely. It would have sickened her any other time, but this was different. This was justice. She dragged him to the tree. She grabbed the rope and tied him up, binding his hands behind him and his feet together. She sat him up and bound his body to the tree. She then tied the bandana tight around his mouth, making sure to jimmy it between his teeth. She made sure Bear was tucked in for the night and then made her way back under the kitchen window. She squatted down under it, positioned herself, not taking her eyes off Bear, and waited for dawn.

A

Sydney watched the sun rise that morning. She hadn't slept all night, but her adrenaline kept her in check.

The birds sang and the morning sun flickered off the dew that had settled here and there.

And then there was Bear. He groaned and shook his head slowly back and forth. Sydney watched him and imagined that he surely thought he was dreaming. His eyes were still closed and he looked as though he was trying to rid himself of the cottonmouth from the night before. No such luck.

His eyes flew open and he flailed his head back and forth, searching for a sign that this wasn't anything more than a bad, bad dream.

"Good morning." Sydney's voice was so calm it sounded haunting.

Bear stopped. He looked at Sydney, widened his eyes, and took in a deep breath, as if he were going to scream.

"Sssssssshhh." Sydney pressed her finger to her lips. "Don't bother, Bear. No one can hear you."

Bear didn't make a sound. He didn't scream. He didn't even attempt it. He looked down at himself, his genitals exposed, and then back at Sydney. He just stared at her, his eyes wide, and his nightmare and the terror of it all was sinking in.

She raised herself off the ground and walked toward him. "Yes, you're naked, Bear. I find it very fitting. It's time that you are exposed, in every sense of the word."

She looked him in the eye, raised her leg, and thrust her boot hard in his groin. Bear heaved and gagged in pain. It mattered not to Sydney.

She lifted her foot off Bear and walked toward the steps to his RV. She looked back at him. He was still in pain, head down; saliva oozed through the bandana.

"Hey, piece of shit!" Sydney called out. "Look at me. I don't want you to miss any of this."

Bear looked up at her, eyes filled with tears. It took him a minute to gain his composure, but once he saw Sydney at the steps of his humble abode, he was no doubt thinking about the things he had inside—all of his sick secrets.

"What's the matter, Bear?" she said. "Something wrong?" Sydney took each step slowly, one by one, to the front door.

Bear began writhing, trying to escape what was happening to him. He couldn't let Sydney in his space: so much darkness and so much to keep hidden away.

Sydney ran down the stairs and over to Bear. She grabbed his face hard with her hands.

"Listen to me, you mother fucker. If you do one thing, if you breathe wrong, I'll blow your fucking head off."

Sydney didn't have a gun, but Bear didn't know that. All he knew was that she was crazy enough to do it and that was enough. He went limp, dropping his head, knowing what was coming.

She took her hands off his face and kicked his leg hard on her way back to the steps. She climbed each step again and opened the door. She went in and there it all was. Not a thing had been moved from its place. Pictures were shuffled around, undoubtedly from Bear scouring over his prized possessions, but that was it. His computer was on, ready for action.

Sydney scoured the RV, top to bottom, finding even more places Bear had chosen to hide his filthy secrets. It was amazing how much he had hidden in such a small space. And it was just as amazing that Miss Texas hadn't dared to look in any of Bear's boxes. Or had she?

Sydney gathered every picture and every box, and placed them all outside at the tree and surrounding Bear. She carefully saved everything that Bear had opened on his computer to her flash drive.

"Jesus, God Almighty," Sydney said, as she went through the process. It was unfathomable to her that anyone could hurt a child. It was even more unfathomable that anyone could abuse a child in such a vile, horrific way.

With every box and group of pictures Sydney carried out, Bear raised his head as if to see if she was done, just to lower it again when she made her way back into the RV. It sounded as though he was crying. It made Sydney ill. Far too little, and way too late.

Sydney stepped inside for the last and final picture. It was the framed picture of Elijah and Cody: Bear's two most prized possessions. The good father he was, by all accounts. That was his trick. That was his story, his manipulation. Seeing Elijah and Cody in the picture made Sydney feel as sad as she'd ever felt. She placed the picture in her shirt. It would be one that he could never call his own again.

She put the flash drive back in her pocket, unplugged the computer, and carried it and the monitor outside. She laid the computer next to Bear and placed the monitor directly in front of him, facing him.

Bear raised his head, his face wet with tears and sweat. His face was distorted and twisted.

"Please, please," he cried out, pushing the words as clearly as he could through the bandana.

"Please, please?" Sydney repeated. "Are you serious?" She let out a gasp of disgust. "I wonder how many times you've heard those words, Bear. Please, please." She pulled the picture from her shirt and grabbed his face again, hard, and made him look at it. "Did Elijah say those words to you? Yes! Did Cody say those words? I'm sure he did! Look!" Sydney shoved the back of his head against the tree; pieces of bark knocked to the ground. She put the picture back in her shirt and looked at him with contempt. Tears streamed from his eyes. She walked away, keeping her back to him, and stopped.

"You know what, Bear?" She turned to look at him. He looked at her and for the first time, she saw him. She saw him: she saw the raw, stripped down version of a pedophile.

"I hate you," Sydney said. There was no remorse, no caring. He had hurt her baby, her child. "I hate you for every terrible thing you've done. Every single terrible thing that has happened is because of you, and why?"

There was no answer and Sydney knew that. Had there been, she still wouldn't care. There wasn't an answer good enough for all the pain he had caused.

Sydney turned her back to him and walked away.

"Wait, wait!" Bear screamed through the cloth. "Don't leave me here!"

He was broken. His time had finally come.

Sydney paused and looked back at him for the last time. "Yes, I'm leaving you here, Bear. But don't worry. You won't be alone for long. Before your visitors get here, think. Think about what you've done. If you have one shred of decency left inside, think about that."

Sydney turned and walked back through the brush that she'd come through just hours before. She was sure and steadfast. It was done.

She could hear the faint cries of Bear. It wouldn't be the last time he cried, and Sydney got satisfaction from that.

Hurt is something that can carry throughout lives and even generations. Shedding tears for his transgressions was something Bear should do sooner or later, and God was seeing to that.

Chapter 61

Sydney was making excellent time. It was only ten thirty in the morning and she was in the home stretch.

"Home," she thought. Home to her safe haven. It would be safe now.

She followed the same back roads that had gotten her there, and relished in the pure peace she now felt.

She turned onto FM 7137 and took a deep breath, feeling more like herself than she had in years and feeling blessed that she was home. Sydney was close to Sam's place and could see a dot in the distance. Tears filled her eyes. She kept driving. Was it her? Yes. There they were: Skye and Sam sitting knee to knee talking, laughing, and Sam was whittling something for Skye, as he'd done so many times before. They both looked up as Sydney eased to the side of the road and parked the truck exactly where she'd borrowed it from, not twenty-four hours before. Sam stood, smiling as bright as the sun. Skye ran to Sydney.

"My God. Thank you, God." Skye picked her up the moment she stepped from the truck.

"I told you I'd be fine." Sydney smiled at Skye. "I told you."

"Yes, you did." Skye smiled back at her and eased her to the ground.

"I thought I said I'd see you by noon," Sydney said.

"I couldn't sleep," Skye said, with a half-smile and tears softly falling down her cheeks.

"Let's go tell Sam goodbye and let me thank him again. And then let's go home," Sydney said, finally feeling free.

Chapter 62

The phone rang. Sydney saw that it was Heath Bridges from the caller ID. She took a deep breath.

"Hello," Sydney said.

"Sydney, this is Heath Bridges. How are you?"

"What a nice surprise! How the heck are you, stranger?" Sydney replied, sounding as normal as she could.

"Well, I'm doin' real good, Sydney. I've got some news for ya."

"Oh, and what's that? Good news, I hope," Sydney replied.

"Yeah, it's real good news, actually. At least I think you'll like it."

"Go on," Sydney said, and waited.

"It seems that someone had all they could take of Mr. Bear Keane and beat the hell out of him. We got an anonymous call yesterday that Bear had been dealing in child pornography and we could find everything at his RV. And get this. He was right up the road on your family's property, where the deer lease is. My men are talkin' to your uncle now. I know he's havin' a fit."

"You've got to be kidding me!" Sydney said. "That son of a bitch has been on my family's property?! For how long?"

"Well, we don't really know. All I know is that he was beat to hell, tied to a damn tree naked, and hundreds of child pornography photos were scattered around him, along with his computer. It's the damnedest thing I've ever seen."

"My God," Sydney said. "I can't believe this."

"Yeah, well, I couldn't either. But I gotta tell ya, if anyone deserves what happened to him, I can honestly say it happened to the right person. It's been a long time comin' and he's goin' away for a long, long time."

"Thank God! Thank you, God!" Sydney started to cry. She kept her wits about her, but there was a flood of emotion that there was no containing.

"You okay, Sydney?" Heath asked.

"Yes, I'm okay. I'm just so thankful that he was caught. He's done horrible things and he will finally pay for it."

"One more thing, Sydney. Bear kept saying that it was you who did this to him."

Sydney knew this was coming. There was nothing to do but deny it. It was her word against his—a sick, perverted scum.

"He said what?!" Sydney shot back. "That it was me? Please, Heath."

"Yeah, I know better than that. But we still have to dust the entire place for fingerprints. You know the drill."

"Yes, I know."

"Hell, I think he's just sayin' it to try to get back at you. That sorry son of a bitch would probably say anything. I told my team I was sure we could verify where you were yesterday. We can, can't we?"

"Of course you can."

"I may need to check just for the record. And get this…there was no weapon used whatsoever. No gun, no knife, nothin'. Even Bear said that. There was no sign of forced entry. Whoever it was just beat his ass and strowed those pictures around him. And let's face it, it could have been anyone with as many kids' pictures as he had, and some were of kids here in Merriweather. Looks to me like whoever did it did everyone a favor."

"I couldn't agree more," Sydney said, easing into relief.

"So, what's in store for you now, Sydney? I know Bear finally gettin' caught has probably lifted a huge weight off you. Any plans for the future?"

Sydney wasn't sure where this question was coming from, but Heath was her friend and she knew that much.

"You know, I've been giving it some thought. This whole process with Bear, from the beginning to even now, with what seems to be the finish…

well, it's changed me, and I feel a really strong need, and desire really, to help people in these types of situations. I've been thinking about going into detective work myself, or maybe as a private investigator. I'm really not sure."

"I'll be damned," Heath said, with a chuckle. "I can't think of anything better than you goin' after the bad guys. They'd have a bulldog on their trail, I'll tell you that."

Sydney laughed and was happy to hear the approval from one of the good guys. "Well, thank you for the vote of confidence, Heath. I'll keep you posted."

"You do that, little lady, and if you ever decide to make it back to the Piney Woods, you holler. We'd find a place for you here, I can guarantee."

"Well, thank you for the invitation, sir, but these feet of mine are staying firmly planted in Houston, Texas."

"Alright, but if you change your mind—"

"I hear you, and thanks again, Heath. Thank you for everything."

"Go get 'em, girl."

"I will. Don't you worry. I will."

And she and God would surely see to that.

About the Author

Born in Texas, Laryl Dixon has lived most of her life in Houston, where she is a successful business owner.

Her passion for writing began as a young girl with a particular interest in mysteries and thrillers.

Life experiences have brought about a passion for Dixon in seeking changes in laws pertaining to sexual predators.

Dixon lives with her partner and is the mother of an adult son.

Author's Message

This story is not about one child, one perpetrator, or one family. This story is about thousands of children, thousands of perpetrators, and thousands of families. They are outside your front door. They are down the street and around the corner. They are all over the world.

To say that childhood sexual abuse and the exploitation of children are prevalent in today's society is a gross understatement. Disturbing? Yes. We are appalled when hearing of it or speaking of it. Why then have such horrific crimes against children remained so commonplace? It must STOP.

We all have a voice, and together we have one enormous voice to speak the same words and seek the same justice for our children and ourselves.

It takes one voice to sing a beautiful song, one stroke to create a masterpiece. Let us do our part in creating a world that is safe for all children.

Resources

The US Department of Justice NSOPW is the only US government website that links public state, territorial, and tribal sex offender registries from one national search site. Parents, employers, and other concerned residents can utilize the website's search tool to identify location information on sex offenders residing, working, and attending school not only in their own neighborhoods, but in other nearby states and communities. In addition, the website provides visitors with information about sexual abuse and how to protect themselves and loved ones from potential victimization.

www.nsopw.gov
http://www.nsopw.gov/en/Education/FactsStatistics
http://www.nsopw.gov/en/Education/ResourcesMaterials
*Website and information shared from www.nsopw.gov

SMART | Office of Sex Offender Sentencing, Monitoring, Apprehending, Registering, and Tracking
The SMART Office was authorized in the Adam Walsh Child Protection and Safety Act of 2006, which was signed into law on July 27, 2006. The responsibilities of the SMART Office include providing jurisdictions with guidance regarding the implementation of the Adam Walsh Act, and providing technical assistance to the states, territories, Indian tribes, local governments, and to public and private organizations. The SMART Office also

tracks important legislative and legal developments related to sex offenders and administers grant programs related to the registration, notification, and management of sex offenders.

http://www.smart.gov

AskSMART@usdoj.gov

202-514-4689

*Website and information shared from http://www.smart.gov

SOL-Reform.com ™

Reform the Statute of Limitations on Child Sex Abuse to Identify Hidden Predators and Increase Access to Justice

Professor Marci A. Hamilton

© 2015 Marci A. Hamilton

www.sol-reform.com

http://sol-reform.com/justice-denied/

*Website and information shared from www.sol-reform.com

NCSL | National Conference of State Legislatures is a bipartisan organization providing states support, ideas, connections and a strong voice on Capitol Hill. www.ncsl.org

Review your state's civil statute of limitations in child sexual abuse cases.

http://www.ncsl.org/research/human-services/state-civil-statutes-of-limitations-in-child-sexua.aspx

Contact your local legislator. http://openstates.org/

*Website and information shared from www.ncsl.org

RAINN | Rape, Abuse & Incest National Network is the nation's largest anti-sexual assault organization.

www.rainn.org

1-800-656-HOPE (4673)

- National Sexual Assault Hotlines are secure, anonymous, confidential crisis support for victims of sexual assault and their friends and families. Both hotlines are free and available 24 hours a day, 7 days a week.

Visit online.rainn.org to chat one-on-one with a trained RAINN support specialist, any time 24/7. https://rainn.org/get-help/national-sexual-assault-online-hotline
- Search for a specific crisis center in your area. http://www.centers.rainn.org/

*Website and information shared from www.rainn.org

Darkness to Light (D2L) is a nonprofit organization with the mission of reducing the incidence of child sexual abuse through public awareness and education. The D2L programs raise awareness of the prevalence and consequences of child sexual abuse by educating adults about the steps they can take to prevent, recognize, and react responsibly to the reality of child sexual abuse.
www.d2l.org
1-866-FOR-LIGHT (866-367-5444)
- Toll-free Helpline—(866) FOR-LIGHT [(866) 367-5444]—for individuals living in the United States who need local information and resources about sexual abuse.

*Website and information shared from www.d21.org

Enough Is Enough® (EIE) is a nonprofit organization focusing its efforts on confronting online pornography, child pornography, child stalking, sexual predation, and other forms of online victimization. By leveraging its expertise, growing national partnership network, and positive reputation among the public, the media, law enforcement, and the Internet industry, EIE continues to advance innovative initiatives and effective communication strategies to protect children online.
www.enough.org
- Internet Safety 101® multimedia program. www.internetsafety101.org

*Website and information shared from www.enough.org

National Center for Missing & Exploited Children (NCMEC) is an organization that serves as the nation's resource leader on the issues of missing and sexually exploited children. The information and resources provided are for law enforcement, parents, children, and victims.

www.missingkids.org

1-800-THE-LOST (800-843-5678)

- CyberTipline is a resource that allows anyone to report incidents of child sexual exploitation, including the possession, manufacture, and/or distribution of child pornography; online enticement; child prostitution; child sex tourism; extra-familial child sexual molestation; unsolicited obscene material sent to a child; and misleading domain names, words, or digital images.
  - ° Make a report at http://www.missingkids.com/CybertipLine or by calling 1-800-THE-LOST if you have information that will help in the fight against child sexual exploitation. The CyberTipline is staffed 24 hours a day, 7 days a week.
- NCMEC Child Safety Publications offer easy-to-use safety resources to help address prevention education topics. It is most beneficial to help build children's confidence and teach them to respond to a potentially dangerous situation, rather than teaching them to look out for a particular type of person. http://www.missingkids.com/Publications

*Website and information shared from www.missingkids.org

YOU HAVE A VOICE